Sempre Avanti:
Always Forward

The Tenth Mountain Division in World War II

Kris Tualla
with Thomas Duhs

Published in the United States of America.

ISBN-13: 978-1977956064
ISBN-10: 1977956068

*This book is dedicated to the young men
who braved harsh high-altitude conditions
to surprise and defeat the German Army
in the Alps in the dead of winter 1945.*

*This book is also dedicated to Jimmy Hanks
whose belief in the story of the
10th Mountain Division
and their contribution to the Second World War
made this project possible.*

*And to the readers who might be discovering this bit
of American history for the first time:
while the two main characters are composites of real people
all the historical events in this story did happen
~ but not everything that happened
is in this book.*

*Photos and a map of Italy
are located at the back of this book.*

Chapter One

"Come sit over here, Papa Jack." Seventeen-year old Taylor grinned as his hands rested on the back of Jack's favorite leather recliner. "Just get comfortable and tell me a story. That's all."

All?

Jack Franklin squinted at his earnest and smiling great-grandson. The boy obviously had no idea what he was asking Jack to do.

Like most veterans he didn't like talking about his wartime experiences, except maybe to other vets. Even then the conversation only went as far as *where were you*, *who were you with*, or *when were you there*. Veterans kept their wartime experiences to themselves for a reason.

Jack's reason was based in bitter disappointment.

Though the Tenth Mountain Division successfully completed one of the most difficult maneuvers in American military history, when the soldiers returned from Italy no one in the states had any idea about what transpired.

And when Jack tried to tell people about their exploits they seemed unable to grasp the significance of the Tenth's efforts. So he stopped talking about it and locked those memories—and his personal pride—deep inside.

But the senior project in Taylor's Advanced Placement American History class was to prepare a report based on an interview with someone who lived through an historic event. And because he deeply loved his great-grandson, Jack agreed to talk about his experiences in front of a camera.

Besides, Taylor was a good kid and Jack was proud of his upcoming full-ride academic scholarship as a freshman at Texas A&M University.

"Let me help you, Grandpa." Taylor's dad Bill took Jack's elbow. "I don't want you to trip over the cords."

Bill never did anything by halves, so the living room was strewn with cables, multiple cameras on tripods, a microphone dangling over the leather chair, and two big square photography lights covered in white cloth.

"It's like a German mine field in here," Jack grumbled. "Is all of this really necessary?"

"Yes." Bill let go of Jack's elbow and Jack lowered himself into his familiar seat. "You're ninety-seven years old, Grandpa, and I don't want to miss a single word of what you say."

Damn that "Band of Brothers" series.

Jack shifted his gaze to the daughter he lived with. "And you agreed to all this mess?"

Linda's eyes moved anxiously around the usually pristine and perfectly ordered living room. "I did... But this is a bit more than I imagined."

"It'll be fine, Mom. I'll clean it all up." Bill grinned at Linda. "You won't regret this. I promise."

Taylor pulled a wooden chair from the dining room and set it beside one of the cameras facing Jack at eye level. "I'm going to sit here, off camera, and ask you questions. You just tell me what you remember."

What I remember?

"I might be old, son." Jack tapped his temple with one arthritis-sculpted finger. "But there are some things that get burned so deep into your mind they never fade away."

"Good." Taylor's smile dimmed and he gazed at his great-grandfather. "I really, *really* appreciate this, Papa Jack. I'm so glad you agreed to be my project."

Jack chuckled a little and waved a casual hand toward his

daughter and her son. "Well, I like you better than the rest of these scoundrels."

Taylor's smile brightened again. "I knew I was your favorite." He lifted a pad of paper. "The teacher gave us some questions he wants us to ask, so I'll ask them, but I really just want you to talk. Say whatever you want to about the war."

"Even if you don't think it's important, Grandpa," Bill said as he adjusted one of the big square lights. "It's those crazy little details that are usually so fascinating."

Linda opened a bottle of water and set it on the TV tray next to Jack's recliner. "Let me know if you get tired, Dad. We can stop and start again tomorrow if we need to."

She gave Bill a warning look. "Right?"

Bill put up his hands in surrender. "Right. Taylor's high school is on spring break so we have the whole week."

Jack's lips twisted in a grin. His very particular daughter's house in this chaotic disarray for an entire week might give her a heart attack.

"Don't worry, Linda," he told her. "I don't have that much to say."

"Ready, Dad?" Taylor asked Bill.

He nodded and sat on a tall stool behind the main camera. "Yep. All set."

Taylor looked at Jack. "Ready, Papa Jack?"

Jack heaved a sigh. "As ready as I'll ever be, I guess."

"Okay." Taylor looked at his notepad. "We're supposed to start by you telling us your whole name."

"My name is John Edward Franklin the second. But I've been called Jack my whole life."

Taylor looked up from his notes. "When and where were you born?"

"I was born on January third, nineteen-twenty in Oakland, California."

"When did you get into the war?"

Jack shook his head. "Can't start there. I need to tell you what happened before that. I need to tell you about the skiing."

Taylor's brow furrowed. "Skiing? In California?"

"Kids." Jack laughed and wagged his head. "Anyway, I was in the Tenth Mountain Division, and we were skiers and mountain climbers."

Taylor looked at his dad. "Did you know that?"

Bill nodded. "But that's all I know."

Taylor returned his attention back to Jack. "Okay. Where do *you* want to start?"

"Let's start with Sugar Bowl in Norden, California. It was a ski resort opened by John Wiley and an Austrian immigrant by the name of Hannes Schroll." Jack shrugged. "It's still there."

Taylor was writing on his pad. "Is that close to Oakland?"

"Couple hundred miles. On Donner Pass."

"Go on, Papa Jack." Taylor looked up from his notes. "I'm listening."

Jack closed his eyes and let the far-away recollections wash over him. They came to him slowly like old friends—some warm and welcomed, some rough and painful. Time seemed to have sanded away their harshest edges though, and the worst memories were just about tolerable now.

Jack opened his eyes and focused on Taylor. "I was nineteen, almost twenty, when I started helping around Sugar Bowl with ski lessons for kids…"

Chapter
Two

December 22, 1939

Jack Franklin stepped down from the Southern Pacific Railroad car onto the platform next to the Norden, California telegraph office and wondered why he had bothered to make this trip.

"What do you think, Harry?" he asked his brother.

"I think there's no snow and we just wasted our money," Harry grumbled, squinting and shading his eyes against the bright winter sun.

"Yeah." Jack sighed his disappointment at the sight of brown, snowless mountains and hefted his homemade skis onto his shoulder. "Might as well take a look around. Since we're here."

The brothers followed a small line of people—a mere fraction of the six-hundred that the train was built to carry—through unneeded snow sheds so new that they still smelled of pine sap and sawdust. They climbed into a tractor-drawn wagon for the wind chilled mile-and-a-quarter ride to the Sugar Bowl Ski Resort.

When they reached the resort they saw a makeshift ice rink the size of a tennis court had been set up in front of the four-story slope-roofed lodge. A dozen people were skating on this sunny though cold day and a small crowd watched them with indifferent expressions.

Guess we weren't the only ones disappointed.

Once inside the lodge, Jack paid for their room. The five dollars for the train ticket, plus the three dollars per night for the lodge was digging a deep hole in Jack's hopes for the weekend.

"At least we packed food." Jack looked at Harry. "You didn't leave it on the train, did you?"

"No, it's right here." Harry turned so Jack could see the pack on his back. "Relax, will ya?"

The brothers climbed the stairs and trudged down the hall to their room, a neat space with Alpine décor and two twin beds. Jack claimed the bed closest to the window and tossed his suitcase onto it before leaning his skis in a corner.

He looked at Harry. "Let's go check out the famous chair lift."

Harry's face brightened. "Let's see if we can ride it. See the view."

The brand-new chairlift was the first one built in California and was clearly going to be the most exciting thing about being here this weekend. Jack and Harry waited in a long line to pay their twenty-five cents to ride the six-and-a-half minutes to the top.

Harry elbowed Jack and pointed at the sign. "It's two dollars a day if you're skiing. How many runs do you think we'd do in a day?"

Jack wagged his head. "Won't know until we try. But it wouldn't be worth coming this far for just a couple."

Jack let Harry go first and he sat on the next moving seat that swung around the base's wide wooden tower. As he rode to the top, his legs dangling five yards over the side of Mount Disney, his pulse surged in anticipation. This run—once there was snow—was going to be utterly amazing.

"Woo-HOO!" Jack hollered at his brother. "Will ya look at that?"

"We'll have to come back!" Harry shouted over his shoulder. "We've never skied anything like this before!"

Jack grinned.

Even if I have to keep working the docks with Pops, it'll be worth it to return to this mountain as often as I can.

*****

After finishing a supper of sausage and cheese sandwiches in their room, Jack and Harry went down to the lobby to have a beer by the fire and talk to the other thwarted skiers. Jack noticed a tall, smiling man in an Austrian-style sweater moving through the scattered chairs and introducing himself to the small and unhappy crowd.

Eventually he dropped into an empty seat facing Jack and Harry. "Hello, boys," he said in thickly accented English. "I'm Hannes Schroll. I own this resort. Welcome."

Jack stuck out his hand. "I'm Jack Franklin, this is my brother Harry."

"Pleased to meet you, Mister Schroll." Harry shook Hannes' hand next, his eyes twinkling. "When are you bringing in the snow?"

Hannes laughed, seeming unfazed by the question. "I ordered it for delivery ten days ago. I guess the truck broke down."

Jack chuckled—their effusive host demonstrated a decent sense of humor in the face of possible financial disaster.

"We rode the chair lift anyway so we could see the course," he said. "We'll definitely be coming back."

"Good." Hannes' evaluative gaze moved over them. "Where did you boys learn to ski?"

"Sierra Club," Harry answered. "Our dad made our skis."

"Hmm." The Austrian rose to his feet. "I'll be watching for you, Jack and Harry. I hope to see you again soon."

As he walked away, Harry leaned closer to Jack. "He thinks we're amateur hicks from the poor side of town."

Jack huffed into his beer. "We *are* amateur hicks from the poor side of town."

"But we don't ski like we are."

Jack faced his younger brother with a crooked grin. "No. We sure don't."

February 3, 1940

On January fourth a blizzard moved through northern California and delivered Hannes Schroll's order of snow in generous abundance. Jack and Harry boarded the Friday night train to Norden two days later and made the overnight ride to Sugar Bowl with two of their buddies in tow.

The skiing was spectacular. So spectacular that they made the increasingly crowded train trip the following three weekends, and brought friends along with them every time. They even let some of them sleep on the floor of their room at the lodge to save money.

Even so, the cost of the weekends hit Jack's pocket hard. Four dollars for lifts, plus five for the train, plus the room, some food, and their evening beers by the fire took a decent chunk out of his twenty-seven dollar and fifty-cent weekly paycheck from the loading docks. He tried to squeeze in six or seven runs each day to justify the expense before he and Harry boarded the train home on Sunday afternoon.

At the end of the day, though, the cost didn't matter. The thrill of flying down the mountain again and again as fast as he could go was worth every penny. The frigid wind stinging his cheeks. The pristine snow glittering away in crystallized arcs with every sharp turn. The scents of the pine trees and the wax on his skis.

Nothing else in Jack's uneventful work-a-day life made him feel so alive.

As the weeks went by Jack realized with surprise that the regular skiers considered him a local expert. While he demonstrated various skiing techniques for his friends, other novice skiers gathered around to watch and ask questions.

Apparently, Hannes Schroll noticed.

On this, the fifth consecutive weekend that Jack and Harry had appeared at his resort, Hannes skied over to them as they waited in line for the lift.

"Hello, boys." He pinned Jack with a piercing blue gaze. "I see you brought more of your friends."

Jack grinned. "Yes sir, Mister Schroll. The more the merrier, right?"

Jack's attention was diverted by one of his friend's attempt to descend the slope. "Hey, Mike! Point your toes together and press your heels out," he shouted. "Yeah. Like that!"

Hannes watched Mike's progress for a moment then turned back to Jack. "You know you're taking business away from my ski school, don't you?"

Jack felt a rush of blood to his cheeks. He had a lot of respect for the big, gregarious Austrian and didn't want to anger him. Or worse, be banned from skiing at Sugar Bowl.

He straightened his shoulders and hit the situation head-on. "That's because they can't afford your ski lessons, sir."

Hannes grunted. His eyes moved to the slopes before he faced Jack again, his expression pensive. "You're wasting an opportunity, you know."

That surprised Jack. "What opportunity?"

"You could work for me as a ski instructor." Hannes' head tilted and his eyes narrowed. "How old are you?"

Jack was stunned into silence.

Hannes Scholl wants me to teach skiing? An amateur hick from the poor side of town?

That was like having President Roosevelt ask if he wanted to give any advice on the German situation.

Hannes repeated the question.

"Oh!" Jack blinked. "I—I just turned twenty last month."

"Do you have a job?"

Jack nodded. "I work at the shipping yards in Oakland. With my father."

Hannes paused, clearly considering his options. "Well, I guess I really only need you on weekends."

"I can come every weekend." Jack's excitement fizzed in his chest at the exciting and unexpected opportunity suddenly set in front of him.

"I'll have to watch you for a while. See if more than just your friends like you and learn from you before I put you on the payroll."

That was disappointing but it made sense. And Jack really wanted the job, even if he wasn't getting paid.

Yet.

"Let's try it for the rest of February and see how it goes." Hannes' smiled a little. "Of course, you'll be able to ride the chairlift for free as an instructor."

"Thank you, sir!" Jack blew a relieved sigh. That savings was almost like getting paid.

Not that Pops would agree.

"What about his room?" Harry interjected. "Can he get his Saturday nights for free, too?"

Hannes chuckled at that. "Yes. If he promises not to fill the floor with your friends any more."

He addressed Jack while he pointed at Harry. "Only your

brother from now on. No one else. Are we clear?"

Jack felt his face flush again. He had no idea Hannes knew about the extra guys piled into their room. "Yes, Mister Schroll."

Hannes shook hands. "If you're going to work for me, you better call me Hannes."

Jack straightened. "Thank you again, Mister—I mean Hannes."

Hannes saluted them and skied off, yodeling at the top of his lungs as he went.

*****

That night while Jack and Harry enjoyed their regular beers with their buddies, Hannes Schroll introduced them to a pair of Austrian brothers named Wilhelm and Frederick Klein.

"Bill and Fred run the ski school at Sugar Bowl." Hannes looked at Wilhelm and pointed at Jack. "Jack here will be working with you starting next weekend."

Bill looked to be a couple years older than Jack, and Fred a couple years older than Bill. The startling realization that the three men in front of him had fled their homeland out of necessity suddenly hit Jack hard.

America wasn't at war, but news of Hitler's bullying chaos played on the radio every night. Jack couldn't imagine having to leave California, much less his country, and not knowing if it would ever be safe to return.

He held out his hand, his respect for these men abruptly magnified. "I'm pleased to meet you."

Bill had a strong, firm grip. "Same here. Come by the school tomorrow and we'll show you the ropes. You'll start with the beginners, of course,"

Of course.

Jack tried not to look disappointed.

Fred shook Jack's hand as well. "That means assisting them with their equipment and getting them acquainted with the resort. You okay with that?"

Jack nodded. He had to be if he wanted the job. "Sure."

"If you stay on with us, you'll need to learn first aid." Bill shrugged resignedly. "Skiers always injure their knees and ankles.

They break bones. They ski into things."

True.

"That makes sense."

Fred pointed at Harry. "And you two might want to consider joining the National Ski Patrol."

"What's that?" Harry asked.

"It's a new organization that was created to train skiers on how to evacuate injured skiers." Fred tilted his head toward the mountain. "You never know when that might come in handy."

April 13, 1940

Much to his relief, Jack was hired on as a paid ski school instructor beginning the first weekend in March. Though Pops continued to grumble about their expensive weekend excursions, he couldn't stop Jack and Harry as long as they paid for them from their own pockets.

Three weeks later, as the end of Sugar Bowl's first ski season loomed, Hannes Schroll announced that he decided to hold a skiing competition to bring attention to his resort.

"I'm calling it the Silver Belt race," he told the ski school staff that Saturday night. "It will be a giant slalom starting at the top of Mount Lincoln at eighty-three-hundred feet, and descending down thirteen-hundred vertical feet of the steepest terrain at Sugar Bowl."

Jack blew a low whistle.

Impressive.

"The course will be designed to draw world-class skiers," Hannes continued. "We all lost our Winter Olympics thanks to that idiot madman marching stiff-armed around Europe, and so we're all looking for high-stakes competitions." Hannes grinned. "I intend to give them the most challenging race to be found anywhere."

Today, just three weeks after the announcement, there were thousands of eager spectators crowded into bleachers at the base of the mountain, all gathered to watch what they could see of the race.

Jack rode up the chairlift along with the Klein brothers to take their places as judges at the slalom poles. As employees of Sugar Bowl Ski Resort they weren't eligible to compete for the Silver Belt. Instead, it was their job to report if any of the skiers missed a gate, thereby disqualifying their run.

The cold day was bright but the sun was diffused by a layer of gauzy clouds. There was no wind, making conditions perfect for fast times.

Three dozen male and female skiers were competing that day, so Jack settled in for the duration. His gate was an easy one to judge—it required a wide swing so it would be obvious if a competitor simply skipped it.

After eight skiers, or maybe it was nine, swooped around the poles in front of him and headed down the hill Jack stopped trying to count. He'd know he was done when the triple shots of the starter pistol echoed from the top. Then he could ski down to the bottom behind the last competitor and get warm again.

And then it happened—a skier skied straight past him without attempting to circle the poles.

Jack squinted at the number on the skier's departing back, pulled his mittens off with his teeth, and wrote the number down on his notepad. Then he tucked his hands back into their cozy sanctuary and continued to wait, curious about who the disqualified skier might be.

*****

"Aston Hollinghurst." The head judge for the competition stated before he looked up from his list. "You say he didn't go around pole number twelve?"

The name sent a jolt of shock through Jack's core. He shook his head to clear it as much as to answer the question. "Yes, sir. He skipped the gate and skied straight past me. Didn't even go near it."

"Hmm." The judge walked to the leader display board and moved *A. Hollinghurst* to the bottom, adding *DQ* where his time would normally be posted.

That disqualification took the offending skier out of the seventh place slot—a rank he wouldn't have achieved without shaving three seconds off his time by skipping the widely placed gate.

"Disqualified?"

An enraged young man stormed up to the judge. "What do you mean, disqualified?"

The judge pointed at Jack. "He says you skipped gate twelve."

"What?" Aston glared at Jack, a myriad of angry emotions working across his handsome face. "Hey. I know you."

"Yes." Jack straightened his six-foot-one frame, refusing to be intimidated. "I work in your father's shipping yards next to the Oakland docks."

Aston faced the judge again, his cleanly-shaven chin jutting forward and his expression thunderous. "Obviously he's biased against me, then. I did *not* skip any of the gates."

"Yes," Jack said sternly. "You did."

Aston rounded on him and jabbed a finger in his face. "I did *NOT!*"

"Gentlemen, please!" the judge barked. "It's irrelevant, Mister Hollinghurst, because you would not have placed in the top six anyway, and no one below you moves into an awards position."

"It's *not* irrelevant!" Aston jabbed a thumb in Jack's direction. "This little pisser is calling me a *cheat*."

Jack's jaw clenched.

Yes. Because you cheated.

"That's enough, sir," the judge growled. "I don't want to have you forcibly removed."

"No need for that." Aston flipped a furiously wild hand in the air. "I'm leaving this lousy joke of a race on my own."

*****

In the end the Women's Downhill Slalom was won by Gretchen Fraser, the American-born daughter of German and Norwegian immigrant parents. The Men's Downhill Slalom winner was an engaging young man with a toothy smile by the name of Friedl Pfeifer. Yet another Austrian skier.

"He left Austria in thirty-eight because of Hitler's invasion," Bill Klein told Jack. "He became an American citizen right away."

Jack watched Pfeifer and Schroll chat like they were old friends.

Maybe they are.

"Is he living off his winnings?" Jack wondered aloud.

"Nah, he's just like the rest of us." Bill shot Jack a knowing look. "He's the director of the ski school up at Sun Valley in Idaho."

"Speaking of which." Fred Klein stepped up behind them. Curious, Jack turned to face him. "Bill and I are organizing the California Ski Instructors Association. Want to be our first official member?"

Chapter Three

1941
Oakland, California

Jack had spent the last two summers counting the days until November and the first hope for snow. Sugar Bowl Ski Resort's first year was wild, opening with no snow and finishing the season with the Silver Belt competition.

During those long, monotonous weekdays spent working under his father's supervisory position and with Harry by his side, Jack loaded and unloaded railroad cars. It was hard work and kept both brothers in solid physical condition.

But it was mindless work. While he labored, Jack constantly thought about Sugar Bowl. Talking with Harry about skiing and the resort kept Jack from going crazy from impatience and boredom.

Jack initially worried that Aston Hollinghurst might make trouble for him after he called Aston out for cheating, but thankfully the shipyard owner's son hadn't appeared in the yard.

Harry laughed when Jack mentioned the possibility. "Probably too busy chasing the ladies. Have you taken a good look at him?"

Jack sneered. "He's still an asshole."

"Yeah. A *rich* asshole." Harry shrugged. "Be glad he's forgotten about you."

Harry was old enough to become a ski instructor along with Jack for the second season at the Sugar Bowl Ski Resort, but both brothers were intentionally vague when their father asked how much they were being paid.

"No point in making Pops mad," Jack said. "We don't want him to tell us we can't do it."

"You're twenty-one now, and I'm twenty," Harry pointed out. "We could get our own place."

Jack nodded. "If he gives us more grief, we should talk about that. But I don't know if we can afford rent *and* skiing."

Harry grinned. "Don't worry, Mom'll be on our side. She'll take her Polish temper out on Pops if he drives her little boys out of her house."

Hannes Schroll ran his second Silver Belt competition in April of nineteen-forty-one, and once again Friedl Pfeiffer won. Thankfully Aston Hollinghurst was nowhere to be seen.

"Jack! Come here." A beaming Hannes waved Jack over. Friedl was standing beside him. "Come meet one of the best skiers in the world—and another Austrian, of course!"

Jack approached and held out his hand. "It's an honor, Mister Pfeiffer."

Hannes clapped Jack's shoulder. "Friedl, this is Jack Franklin, the best ski instructor at Sugar Bowl."

Hannes Schroll's praise floored Jack—he had no idea Hannes thought so highly of him. "My brother's pretty good, too," he deflected in case Harry was nearby.

"Don't be too modest, Jack." Friedl smiled at him. "Champions can't afford that luxury."

"No, sir." Jack struggled with what to say next. "And you should know," was what came out of his mouth.

Friedl chuckled. "Yes. I suppose so."

Hannes turned to Friedl and said something in German. The skier nodded, and the tall pair walked away leaving a slightly star-struck Jack watching them depart.

Harry appeared at his side. "They're only a few years older than we are. And look what they've done."

Jack considered his younger brother. The two young men looked alike in many ways with their same height, brown hair, and blue-gray eyes. But their personalities were not similar at all.

I wonder what the next five years will be like for us.

December 7, 1941

When he turned his last student free, he shouted to Harry, "I'll see you inside."

Harry waved back. Jack figured the pretty blonde twins his brother was instructing might hold his attention for a while longer.

"Don't miss the train!" he warned.

Harry looked at his watch. "I won't! Thanks!"

Harry made it just in time.

"Talk about a ladies' man," Jack teased.

Harry blushed ferociously. "You're just jealous."

"There were two of them," Jack pointed out. "You *could* share with your poor, lonely brother."

"Shut up."

When the train pulled to a stop at the station in Oakland at eleven o'clock that night, John Franklin was waiting on the dimly lit platform. His expression was grim and he kept shifting his weight from foot to foot.

"Pops hasn't ever picked us up before." Foreboding compressed Jack's chest and he couldn't draw a full breath. "I hope Mom's okay," he croaked.

Harry shouldered his skis and bent down to look out the train's windows. "Why is it so dark? Is the power out?"

Jack stepped off the train first, his heart bashing against his ribs. "Hi, Pops. Is everything okay?"

"You haven't heard?" he asked.

"No. We were out on the slopes until three, and then we got right on the train," Harry explained. "What's going on?"

John reached for their skis. "I'll tell you in the car. Let's get home to your mom."

Jack let out the breath he didn't realize he was holding. "Mom's okay?"

John looked startled. "Yes. Mom's fine. Well, as fine as any of us are tonight."

John strapped their skis and poles to the top of the car while Jack and Harry tossed their small, beat-up suitcases into the trunk before climbing inside. It was eerie with all the streetlights out and only slits of indoor light slipping past drawn window shades.

Even the cars on the roads weren't using their headlights, only their dim running lights so that other drivers could see they were there. At least the stoplights were blinking the confused and blessedly sparse traffic into some semblance of order.

"The entire Bay Area is under blackout orders tonight," John told his sons. "Might even be the whole west coast."

Jack looked at Harry, whose eyes were huge. "Why?"

"Japan attacked our navy fleet in Pearl Harbor in Hawaii today. Sunk or destroyed all of our ships."

That didn't make any sense. "But—but why? What'd we do to them?"

"Nothing. That's just it." John sighed. "It was completely unprovoked."

Jack and Harry sat in silence for the rest of the bewildering drive home. Inside the house all of their drapes and curtains were pulled closed and none of the lights were on. They found their mom sitting at the kitchen table listening to the radio by candlelight.

She got up and hugged her boys as soon as she saw them, her tears wetting Jack's cheeks.

"I'm so glad you're home safe," she said thickly; her Polish accent was always heavier when she was upset. "This is a very sad day."

Then Edyta Bankowski Franklin, a trained nurse who met their father in France while he was in hospital during the First World War, did what all mothers do in a crisis no matter the time of day: she started cooking.

Jack and Harry sat at the table to listen to the account of the attack which, according to John, had been repeated nonstop for the last several hours. In spite of the inconceivable and tragic news, the comforting smell of beef and cabbage wrapped Jack in a warm and familiar cocoon. For the moment his world was still safe.

December 8, 1941

"We're officially at war with Japan." John greeted Jack with that confounding statement the next morning at breakfast.

His father was dressed for work and sitting at the table sipping his coffee. The radio continued to blare the shifting world affairs from its corner of the tabletop.

"Are we still working today?" Jack asked.

John scowled at him. "Of course we are. Harder than ever now."

Words like *our West Coast forces are shaken* and *not prepared for battle of this magnitude* continued to escape the radio with terrifying repetition. Edyta sniffled non-stop and wiped her nose on her apron as she wordlessly cooked a pan of scrambled eggs with ham.

"It says Oakland and San Francisco are afraid of being invaded next," Jack argued. "Shouldn't we be doing something?"

"We are," John countered. "We're going to work and keeping this fine country fully functioning in the face of this atrocity."

"But—"

John's fist hit the table. "No *buts!* Until we receive further orders from our Commander in Chief, we'll keep doing what we need to do!"

Harry sidled into the kitchen without looking at his father and silently took his seat at the Formica-topped table. He glanced nervously at Jack.

Jack shrugged. He had nothing more to say.

December 12, 1941

Four days after Japan attacked Pearl Harbor and three days after President Roosevelt declared war on that little nation, Adolf Hitler, in an eighty-eight-minute rambling speech, declared that Germany would join with Japan in the war against the United States.

By this time, Germany had taken control of Europe and was deep into Russia and North Africa. But as was so often stated on the radio after Japan's attack, the United States armed forces weren't prepared to fight simultaneously in *two* major theaters of war.

"I suppose we'll be drafted," Harry said the next day at work.

"Unless we enlist," Jack countered. "That way we get to pick which service we go into."

Harry stopped working and made a face, looking at Jack like he was a raging idiot. "You know Pops will expect us to join the Marines. He's got that nineteen-eighteen citation for 'exceptional gallantry' framed on the living room wall."

For some reason Harry's words irritated Jack. "I meant we'll be drafted into the *Army* unless we enlist and pick."

"Oh." Harry flashed a wry smile. "Marine legacy boys in the Army? Pops would never let that happen, for sure."

"The Marines it is, then." Jack sighed. "When should we enlist?"

*****

"Not before Christmas," Edyta declared when the subject came up at supper. "I absolutely forbid it."

"Edyta, they have to enlist before they are drafted," John said gently. "Because they will be drafted."

"Not yet, they won't." She folded her sturdy arms over her chest and glared defiantly at her husband. "This war has been going on in Europe for three years already. It's not going to end until that filthy little bastard is dead in Germany—and who knows how long in Japan."

"Edyta—"

"No, John! Jack and Harry have time to enjoy Christmas and New Year's before they enlist." Her eyes watered again; their mother had done a lot of crying this week and with good reason. "We don't know when we will be celebrating another Christmas together after that."

"Fine." John looked irritated. "But they'll both be at the Marine recruiting office before the end of January."

He pointed at Jack and Harry. "And that's a direct order."

January 10, 1942

Jack, Harry, and a couple of their friends took the train up to Sugar Bowl to go skiing for what they all figured would be the last time that season. America was going to war in two different hemispheres, and with such an uncertain future hanging over their heads, people would be reluctant to spend their free time and hard cash on the diversion of lessons in an expensive winter sport.

While their friends took the last run on Sunday, Jack and Harry went into Hannes Schroll's office to resign from their positions as instructors. Jack figured it would be easier on the affable Hannes if they quit, and then the Austrian wouldn't have to fire them because his business suddenly bombed.

"Come on in," Hannes said. "I have something to talk to you both about."

Jack and Harry sat facing their boss.

What now?

"I know a man, his name is Charles Minot Dole—"

"He started the National Ski Patrol, right?" Jack interrupted.

Hannes pointed an approving finger in Jack's direction. "Yes, he did."

The big Austrian folded his hands on his desktop and leaned forward, his gaze intense. "Most people don't know this yet—and Bill and I only do because Friedl told us—that two years ago Minnie Dole met with Army Chief of Staff George Marshall to propose the creation of an American counterpart to the German and Italian ski troops."

Jack felt a jolt of adrenaline flood his frame.

Could this be true?

He straightened in his chair. "Do you mean American ski troops?"

"Yes. And Marshall assigned Dole to form this group. It's the First Battalion of the Eighty-Seventh Regiment." Hannes paused. "Bill Klein has already enlisted."

"He's gone?" Jack was sorry he couldn't say goodbye. "Is he skiing?"

Hannes nodded. "He's just started training in Washington state on Mount Rainier."

Jack looked at Harry, barely believing the good news. "We could be skiing soldiers!"

"In the *Army*." Harry wagged his head and shot Jack a warning look. "Pops would be furious!"

Jack looked back at Hannes, asking even though he figured he knew what the answer would be. "Will there be a ski division in the Marines?"

Hannes shook his head. "No. This is Army Infantry only. But I do think you both should consider enlisting in the ski troops. They are looking for men with your experience in skiing and mountaineering."

"Our Pops expects Jack and me to be Marines, just like him," Harry said sternly.

"I have no doubt that both of you are tough enough to be Marines," Hannes said carefully.

"Damn straight," Harry growled.

"But…" Hannes stared at Harry. "Not everyone who is tough is skilled enough to be in the ski troops."

Jack knew that his father would be livid if he chose to do this. But he also knew without any hesitation or doubt that this was the only choice he *could* make.

Jack stood and shook Hannes' hand. "Thank you, Hannes. For everything."

Hannes smiled softly and shook Harry's hand. "Thank you Jack, Harry. And God speed to you both."

Chapter Four

April 1942

Jack and his father were at a fiercely determined stalemate—one that thrilled his mother. The longer Jack delayed his enlistment, waiting for information about the Army's pending ski troops, the longer he and Harry remained at home and in relative safety.

John was beyond furious that his firstborn son and namesake hoped to join the Army instead of his beloved Marines, but Jack stood firm in the face of his father's constant barrage.

"*Ski* troops, Pops," Jack argued again and again. "Skiing in the mountains and fighting the Germans. This is *elite* training—and I already know how to do it! I could probably be an officer and instruct other soldiers."

John shook his head emphatically. "No. The *Marines* are the elite corps, Jack. Not the Army—they'll take anyone!" His hands fisted. "When I got you involved in the Sierra Club and made you boys your first pairs of skis, I never thought it would lead to anything like this."

"Neither did anyone," Jack growled. "Because we all believed there would never be another World War." He drew a steadying breath and unclenched his own fists. "But there *is*. And it's *different* this time, Pops."

John bristled. "Don't presume to tell *me* what war is, Jack. I've been in the thick of it and—"

"And got a citation! I know!" Jack interrupted, pushed by his own undeniable frustration.

He dragged his fingers through his hair and stomped an angry circle in the living room while his shocked father glared at him. The phone rang repeatedly in the hallway, but neither one of them moved to answer it.

Jack faced his scowling father again and struggled to lower his voice. "You're a *hero*, Pops. I know that."

His father's sarcastic tone challenged his words. "Do you?"

"Yes!" Jack pounded a fist against his own chest. "And the ski troops is *my* turn to be one. Why can't you understand that?"

The phone continued to ring.

"God *damn* it." John strode into the hall and grabbed the receiver. "Hello!"

Jack stood in the doorway and tried to calm down. He was so angry he was shaking inside and out.

"Who? Oh. Yes." John turned around to look at Jack. If looks could kill, Jack would be sprawled bleeding and lifeless on the hallway rug right about now.

John dropped the receiver on the little phone table. "It's for you."

While John stormed away in the opposite direction, Jack picked up the hand piece. "Hello?"

"Jack? Fred Klein."

The familiar voice helped calm him. He drew a quick breath and forced his tone to sound casual. "Hi, Fred. It's good to hear from you."

"Same here, Jack. How's Harry?"

"Good. But we both miss Sugar Bowl," Jack admitted. "A lot."

"Well, business has been slow, I'm afraid. The war, you know?"

"Yeah."

"Anyway, Hannes and I are coming to Oakland tomorrow."

Jack's mood brightened. "You are?"

"Yep. We're coming to see a movie called *Ski Patrol*."

Jack frowned. "Never heard of it."

"It's the second film by an Army captain named John Jay. I thought you and Harry might want to come see it with us."

Jack's mood shifted and he smiled. "Yeah. Okay."

"Great! Give me your address. We'll pick you guys up at six-thirty."

*****

Hannes and Fred seemed to completely fill the entryway to the modest Franklin home. The pair arrived right on time, a fact that Jack knew would give his father one less objection to these men.

"We've heard a lot about you," John said as he politely shook the skiers' hands. "I thought you'd be older."

"We feel older at times," Hannes joked.

"Especially when we see how skilled our ski instructors are at Sugar Bowl," Fred added. "Jack, here, was one of the best."

"We better go," Jack said to cut off any retort his father might make. He turned around and shouted up the stairs. "Harry! Now!"

"Coming!" Harry ran down the stars, pushing his hands through the arms of his sweater. "Let's go!"

"You stayed upstairs so you didn't have to be there when they met Pops," Jack accused his brother when they were outside.

"Sure did." Harry laughed. "And it worked."

As soon as the four men were in the car, their conversation went straight to skiing.

"You guys already know that Minnie Dole got the contract with the Army to recruit for the ski troops right after Pearl Harbor," Hannes said.

"Yeah," Jack and Harry said in tandem.

"Dole's a pretty charismatic guy, apparently." Fred turned around in the front seat of the car to face Jack and Harry. "So he was able to convince the Army to let him have this Captain John Jay as his recruiter."

"Because he makes ski films," Hannes finished the explanation.

"That's what we're going to see tonight?" Jack asked. "A film about ski troops?"

"Yep."

Jack was confused. "Are there already ski troops?"

And if there are, why don't I know about it?

"Skiers are enlisting and training in preparation for the actual creation of the Tenth Division," Fred explained. "Jay received his orders to report to the Eighty-Seventh Regiment at Fort Lewis in January as the Second Lieutenant to the ski troops. Then last month he led an eight-man detachment on the first winter ascent of Mount Rainier in Washington."

Hannes looked at Jack in the rearview mirror. "They did very well. Jay won a commendation for his troops' success."

"Can we join the Eighty-Seventh?" Jack asked.

Hannes smiled. "Hopefully, that's what we'll find out tonight."

Harry turned and looked out the window of the car. Jack suddenly became aware that his brother wasn't taking part in the conversation. A sad thought marched up and stood at the forefront of his mind. Harry would join the Marines, no matter what.

And I won't.

*****

The theater darkened and a spotlight shone on the wooden stage in front of the screen. A pretty brunette walked out from the side stage and welcomed the crowd of about two hundred men and women.

"Captain John Jay and I are traveling around the country showing the captain's renowned film *Ski Troops* for your information and enjoyment," she said in a clear lilting voice.

Jack was entranced. He let out a low whistle and whispered to Harry, "She's quite a looker."

Harry chuckled. "Dream on, brother."

"When the film is finished, the captain will take your questions, and I will pass out applications for the Ski Troops to those who are interested." The woman, whose name was never mentioned, smiled a perfect Hollywood starlet smile and waved one arm at the screen. "Now let's get on with the show, shall we?"

Applications to get into an Army unit?

Jack leaned over and whispered to Harry again, "No one has to apply to get into the Army. They're drafting everyone."

Harry gave him an *I don't know* shrug.

Jack was skeptical that this film would be an accurate depiction of skiing, but as soon as the men on the screen made their first downhill run he was cheerfully surprised.

He found himself tensing and breathing along with the skiers on the screen, leaning in his seat when they leaned. Straightening when they skidded to a stop.

As he watched the soldiers training, the longing ache to be a part of what they were doing actually hurt in his chest.

"You can join the Marines after seeing this if you still want to," he told Harry when the credits appeared on the screen. "But I'm joining these guys."

Harry considered him soberly in the reflected light. "Thanks, Jack. Because I *will* be a Marine."

"We'll still be brothers." Jack elbowed Harry to lighten the impact of his stern declaration. "Can't get away from that."

The lights came on in the theater and Captain John Jay strode confidently to the center of the brightly lit stage. "I hope you enjoyed my effort to honor the Ski Troops…"

The crowd applauded as was obviously expected.

"Now, do any of you have any questions?"

Even Jack could see how handsome John Jay was. Charming too. He handled himself with ease, answering every question thrown his way with erudite exactness, but without talking over the heads of the people in the audience.

This guy could run for president.

And win.

"He's wearing a wedding ring," Harry pointed out. "Wanna bet the beauty's his wife?"

Jack shifted his attention to the beauty in question, now standing in front of the stage. She hugged a stack of applications close to her chest and stared adoringly up at the captain.

"Yeah. Looks like it."

Not like I had a shot anyway.

"If there aren't any other questions…" Jay paused and scanned the audience. When no one raised a hand, he continued. "Then I thank you all for coming. My lovely assistant has plenty of applications for those of you who are interested."

Then he left the stage.

Hannes slid forward in his seat and looked past Fred directly at Jack. "What do you think?"

"I'll pack tonight." He was only half kidding.

Hannes' gaze slid to Harry. "And you?"

Harry wagged his head. "I'm going to follow our dad. I'm going to be a Marine."

Fred and Hannes exchanged a glance and Jack felt like one of them had just won a bet.

"Are you going to go up and get an application?" Hannes

prodded.

Jack looked at the crowd surrounding Jay's wife. "I'll let them get out of the way first."

As the crowd thinned, the gal slowly moved up the center aisle of the theater handing out applications, chatting and joking with those men and women who engaged with her.

Not only was she beautiful, but she moved with an easy grace that made Jack wonder if she was a skier as well.

That Jay is one lucky man.

Jack stood when she reached his row near the back of the theater. Harry stood as well and stepped into the aisle.

"Meet you in the lobby," he murmured.

Jack nodded, his eyes fixed on the pale green eyes of the woman who was extending an application in his direction.

She smiled. "Are you interested in joining the Ski Troops?"

Jack blinked, momentarily caught by her exquisite loveliness.

Hannes or Fred poked him from behind.

"Yes! Absolutely." Jack felt himself blushing as he accepted the application. "I was already sold, I think, but your husband did a great job with the film."

Her jaw dropped and she looked like he'd punched her. "My husband?"

Jack pointed at the stage and said, "Aren't you—"

Only then did he notice that she wore no ring.

"Oh, gosh! I'm so sorry! I just assumed…" *Idiot.* "Forgive me, Ma'am. I mean Miss. Is it Miss?"

Jack waved his hand and shook his head. "Never mind. It's none of my business."

Something in her demeanor shifted and she held out her hand, almost defiantly. "Elizabeth-Anne Harkins. Most people call me Betty."

Jack froze and stared into those green eyes. He took her hand without thinking about it.

"John Edward Franklin, the second. People call me Jack."

"Hello, Jack."

He smiled. "Hello, Betty. It's very nice to meet you."

"So." She lifted one haughty brow. "Do you think you have what it takes?"

"For the Ski Troops? You bet I do."

Hannes leaned out from behind him while Fred sat in his seat smothering a laugh. "He's just what you are looking for, young lady."

She tilted her head. "And you are?"

"Hannes Schroll. I own Sugar Bowl Ski Resort." Hannes gripped Jack's shoulder and gave it a shake. "Jack is one of our very best ski instructors."

From the look on her face, Betty was familiar with the property. "He'll still have to prove himself."

She returned her regard to Jack. "Fill out the application and send it in. Someone will look it over and decide if you're Ski Trooper material."

Her speculative gaze swept over Jack from top to toe and back again. When she looked into his eyes, his belly did a back flip. Her lips quirked with amusement.

"But I'd say you'll make the cut. If you're as good as he says you are."

"I'm better." Jack gave her his most charming smile. "Want to get a drink sometime?"

Betty didn't have time to answer the question before Captain Jay came up the aisle behind her.

He rested his hand in the small of her back. "Ready, Betts?"

She smiled over her shoulder. "Just about. I'll meet you in the lobby. This guy had one last question."

"Oh?" Captain Jay moved his expectant gaze to Jack. "What is it?"

Jack opened his mouth to repeat the awkward question when Betty blurted, "Yes. Let me get a pen and write that down."

She faced the captain. "Just give me five minutes. I need to write down the recruiting office's address."

She turned back toward Jack and winked.

*****

After Hannes and Fred said their goodbyes and drove off, Jack took a deep breath and followed Harry into their house. Jack knew he was up against another fight with Pops, but between the application for the Ski Troops in his hand and the date he'd set up with Betty for tomorrow night, Jack felt invincible.

John read the paper in his big leather chair next to the huge Zenith Stratosphere radio while Edyta, in her seat on the other side of the radio, darned a pile of socks. Fibber McGee and Molly were broadcasting between commercial breaks.

John didn't look up when the brothers entered the room. Instead he asked, "How was it?" before he deigned to lift his gaze and regard his sons.

"Fantastic, Pops," Jack said emphatically. "The Ski Troops look exactly like what I hoped for."

He handed his father the application.

John took the form and read over it with obvious, undisguised disdain. "Tell me again, Jack, what's wrong with being a Marine?"

"Nothing, Pops," Jack said honestly, drawing his father's curious gaze away from the paper in his hand. "But with *my* skills, I believe the Ski Troops is where I can do the most good."

"Well you know what I always say. The only thing you can't do is *nothing.*" John narrowed his eyes and grunted. "I guess this is slightly better than nothing."

John turned his attention to Harry. "Do you want to be a soldier on skis too, now?"

Harry shook his head. "No, Pops. I think I can do the most good in the Marines."

John handed the application back to Jack without looking at him. "At least one of my sons has some common sense and loyalty."

Then he turned his attention back to his newspaper. Their conversation was finished.

*****

The next evening Jack and Betty settled into a booth in the dimly lit bar at her hotel. Since Jack didn't have a car, and the city was still under blackout orders, it was the simplest solution to where they should go for their drink together.

Jack jumped right into the subject that was foremost on his mind. If he had a rival for Betty's attention, he wanted to know that up front. No point in spinning his wheels and getting nowhere.

"I'm sorry about the confusion last night," he said after they ordered their drinks. "So who *is* Captain Jay to you, Betty?"

"He's just a longtime family friend from back home. We're from Massachusetts." Betty mindlessly twirled a lock of her shoulder-length brunette hair. "When he got this opportunity to travel the country, and use his film to recruit for the Ski Troops, he asked if I'd come along."

"Why not his wife?" Jack had to ask.

"They just got married."

Jack gave her a knowing look. "All the more reason to be together, if you ask me."

Betty's gaze fell to the polished walnut tabletop while her fingers relentlessly worked the hank of hair. "Lois isn't the type."

Interesting.

"Is it up to the captain whether or not I'm accepted into the Ski Troops?"

Betty shook her head. "No. Minnie Dole has sole authority to approve applications for the Ski Troops."

Jack waited for their drinks to be served before asking his next question. He wanted to know more about the captain who, despite Betty's obvious adoration, chose to marry someone else.

And he also wanted to know what was so damned special about Jay that, even after he did so, Betty was still willing to trail after him, let him rest his hand intimately on her back, and call her by a pet nickname when she had no hope of a permanent relationship.

"*Ski Patrol* is Jay's second ski film," Jack began. "What was the first?"

"*Ski the Americas, North and South.*"

Jack shrugged. "Never heard of it."

"I'm proud to say on John's behalf, that it packed in over fifty-thousand viewers during its tour, and enlightened people to the thrills of traveling the world to ski." Betty looked wistful. "I always wished I could travel like that, but the war got in my way."

"But not his?"

"He's four years older than I am. He had the chance, I didn't."

Jack lifted his beer to his lips. "How old are you, Betty?"

I need to give her a nickname of my own.

If she sticks around.

"I'm almost twenty-four." She considered him over the rim of her wine glass. "And you?"

"Just turned twenty-two." Jack decided to check his hunch from last night. "Do you ski?"

Betty's face lit up so brightly that Jack was afraid she might violate the blackout orders.

"I am actually one of the first certified female ski instructors in the entire United States." Her tone was brimming with pride. "So yes. I most certainly do."

Chapter Five

October 1942

What Jack didn't know when he picked up the application—and Captain Jay didn't bother to mention in his question-and-answer session—was that along with the completed application, all Ski Troop applicants had to provide three letters of recommendation.

And not just any letters. All three letters had to be from people who could attest to the potential soldier's current skills in mountain climbing or skiing.

That wasn't a problem for Jack, of course. He immediately made a phone call to Sugar Bowl to ask Hannes Schroll and Fred Klein to recommend him, and then asked one of his buddies from the Sierra Club to write his third letter.

Unfortunately, with the drop-off in skiing customers, Hannes had apparently decided to close the resort Monday through Friday and only operate during the weekends. No one seemed to be at the resort when it was closed either, because no one answered the phone during the week.

So even though Jack left weekend messages, it took nearly a month for him to get to speak with each of the men and ask for their letters. And while everyone he asked was eager to help him, Jack didn't have all three letters in hand until the middle of June.

Jack bundled everything into a sturdy envelope, added extra postage stamps just in case, and sent his application to New York the next day. If only it had happened the week before that.

On June seventh, Japan sent over ten thousand troops to occupy the islands of Attu and Kiska in the Alaska Territory's Aleutian Islands. Kiska was actually two hundred miles closer to the Alaskan mainland than it was to Japan, sending renewed panic and fear of attack up and down the western coast.

"Jack, you need to drop this ridiculous dream of yours to ski, and go enlist in the Marines," John grumbled when they heard the news. "The Japs are getting closer and you're just sitting on your ass."

Jack had no argument to present that his father would accept. So he said nothing until the next week when he finally mailed his ski troops application.

John Franklin Senior was not impressed.

One surprising thing did lift his spirits after these frustrating six months—a cheerfully chatty letter from Betty. He'd given her his address back in March but by now he'd given up hope that he would ever hear from her.

Jack carried the letter upstairs after work and took the time to wash up before he read it, as if Betty really was sitting there in his room for the conversation. He settled on his bed and leaned against his headboard. Then he carefully opened the envelope.

Hello, Jack,

I meant to write you sooner, but I never seemed to be able to find the time. I hope this letter finds you in good health!

Did you send in your application for the Ski Troops? I hope so. It might take a while for you to hear back if you did, though. That's one of the reasons I wanted to write to you.

John's moods have been all over the place lately. There are plenty of Generals in the Army and the War Department who don't care for special units like the Ski Troops, so he has to constantly fight to keep doing what we're doing.

What really chaps these guys is that the National Ski Patrol's recruiting efforts are actually bringing in the most men! With us going around the country to show the ski movie, pass out applications, and chat up young guys like you, the Ski Troops is getting more applications than you can imagine. Thousands on thousands!

And since Minnie Dole has to look at each one and read the letters of recommendation, it's taking some time to go through it all. But that's a good problem to have, right?

The second reason I wanted to write to you was to finally thank you for the evening we spent together. We each come from very different backgrounds, Jack, but I found your conversation interesting and I hope we can do it again the next time our paths cross.

I would love to hear from you, but the only permanent address I can give you is my parents' home in Massachusetts. And while I do love them, if I start getting letters from a man they don't know they'll give me the third degree.

In the meantime, take care of yourself.

Affectionately, Betty

Jack read the letter three times. A couple things jumped out at him and he wanted to think about them. The first was that Betty called the captain 'John' with such familiarity, and talked about his moods.

"They *are* old family friends," Jack reminded himself. That didn't soothe his irritation, however. He couldn't help but wonder whether Betty pined for him futilely, or if Captain John Jay was taking advantage of the beautiful woman at hand while his wife was elsewhere.

The second thing was her comment about coming from 'very different' backgrounds. He knew Betty went to college and he didn't, and wondered if that was what she meant.

"Doesn't seem like that big of a deal," he muttered.

Jack's father hit the bedroom door with one knuckle and then walked into the room. He tossed an open magazine onto Jack's bed.

"In this magazine are two articles," he said abruptly. "One is about the fight the Marines are engaged in out in the Pacific. The other is about the glorified ski club you want to join which, by the way, will never see combat."

Jack's anger bubbled up at his father's repeated denigration of the Ski Troops. "Pops—"

"That magazine tells it the way it *is*, Jack. And I told you that the only thing you can't do is *nothing.*" He pointed an angry finger at the magazine. "That right there? That's the very definition of doing nothing."

Jack glared at his father, his jaws clenched against what he really wanted to say. Pops never failed to point out the exploits and glories of his beloved Marines. But the Marines were in jungles with snakes and bugs and miserably hot humid climates.

If Jack went that route, aside from being completely miserable he wouldn't be able to ski again for years.

After a minute of tense silence, John turned around and strode out of Jack's room, slamming the door behind him. Jack's determination to follow his own path and prove his father wrong boiled in his veins, solidifying his determination like nothing else could.

By the way, Pops. Did I ever thank you for making *my first pair of skis?*

December 1942

Harry joined the Marines.

"It's been a year since Pearl Harbor, I can't wait any longer," he told Jack. "You're on your own with Pops."

Jack understood. "I just wish I had the ski troops' answer by now. Then maybe I wouldn't look like such a slacker to him."

Harry wagged his head sadly. "You're choosing the Army over the Marines, Jack. In his eyes that *defines* a slacker."

Christmas was a very uncomfortable holiday that year with Edyta's frequent tears over Harry's imminent departure. John's oft-expressed pride in Harry and his corresponding disappointment in Jack set Jack's mood simmering. He left the house whenever he could to keep his anger from boiling over.

Harry was awkward around Jack, but whether he was still uncomfortable about enlisting first, or far more disappointed in Jack's stubborn determination to join the Army than he let on wasn't clear.

Either way, Jack hugged his younger brother before Harry got on the bus for San Diego.

"I love you, Harry. Stay safe, will ya?" Jack pounded Harry's back before he released him. "*Semper Fi*, eh?"

Harry nodded and wiped his eyes. "Kill some Nazis for me."

Jack punched his brother's arm. "That's my plan."

*****

Jack's long-awaited Western Union telegram arrived the next day. He ripped it open as soon as he and Pops got home from work.

DECEMBER 30 1942
YOUR APPLICATION FOR THE MOUNTAIN TROOPS
IS APPROVED. PLEASE REPORT TO THE
RECEPTION CENTER AT PRESIDIO, MONTEREY,
CALIFORNIA WITHIN ONE WEEK.

THE CLASSIFICATION AND ENLISTED
REPLACEMENT BRANCH OF THE ADJUTANT
GENERAL'S OFFICE WILL ORDER YOU ASSIGNED
TO THE MOUNTAIN TRAINING CENTER, CAMP
HALE, PANDO, COLORADO FOR BASIC TRAINING.

DIRECTOR OF PERSONNEL SELECTION
NATIONAL SKI PATROL SYSTEM

Jack held the telegram in the air and whooped so loud that his mother came running from the kitchen, dishtowel in her hands and worry sculpting her face.

"What happened?" she yelped.

"I finally got in!" Jack grabbed her hands whirled her in a little dance. "I'm a Ski Trooper, Mom!"

John Franklin stood in the front doorway, his expression grim. "I guess that's it, then."

Edyta tried to smile, but Jack knew that losing both her boys in such quick succession was extremely hard on her. She had seen the horrors of the First World War up close as a nurse, and held no illusions about the dangers that both he and Harry were walking into.

"When do you leave?" she managed.

"I need to go to the Presidio in Monterey as soon as possible." Jack glanced at John, wondering if his father would drive him the hundred-and-thirty miles from Oakland.

Judging from his expression, the answer was no.

Jack looked back at Edyta. "I'll take the train on Monday."

John grunted. "I assume you're quitting your job as of today."

Jack gave John an apologetic look. "Yes, Pops."

John shifted his attention to his wife. "What's for supper?"

January 4, 1943

Jack got off the train in Monterey and asked directions to the Presidio. Satchel in hand, he walked the mile and got there in under fifteen minutes. He found the Reception Center and joined a line of men checking in.

I wonder if any of them are Ski Troopers.

"Next."

Jack stepped forward and handed the soldier sitting at a long table his birth certificate and the telegram from the Director of Personnel Selection, who he knew was actually Minnie Dole himself.

"John Edward Franklin, the second..." The soldier moved his finger down a typed list. "Here you are."

He looked up at Jack. "Raise your right hand and repeat after me: I, state your name..."

Jack lifted his hand. "I, John Edward Franklin, the second..."

He continued phrase by phrase as the soldier dictated the Oath of Enlistment. "Do solemnly swear that I will support and defend the Constitution of the United States against all enemies, foreign and domestic; that I will bear true faith and allegiance to the same; and that I will obey the orders of the President of the United States and the orders of the officers appointed over me, according to regulations and the Uniform Code of Military Justice. So help me God."

The soldier nodded. "Congratulations, soldier. Follow the white line on the floor to the next station."

Jack was issued his basic Army uniform before he received several vaccinations.

The last station was transportation. "Here's your train ticket, which will get you to Camp Hale. You leave in two days."

Jack nodded and accepted the voucher. "Colorado, right?"

The uniformed soldier nodded and gave Jack the once-over. "You a skier?"

Jack beamed. "Yes, I am!"

Chapter Six

January 8, 1943

Jack's train took him through Salt Lake City in Utah, and then up and over the Continental Divide. During the daylight hours, Jack couldn't keep his eyes away from the majestic scenery. Mountain peak after mountain peak rolled by, all covered in pristine white snow that glared in the sunlight and glowed in the moonlight. Jack felt like he had died and gone to a skier's heaven.

Only the drab green uniform he wore reminded him that his purpose was much more ominous.

When the train chugged into Denver, Jack followed directions to the United Service Organizations' building—USO for short. He planned to wait there until the overnight train to Camp Hale was going to depart, and enjoy coffee and donuts in the meantime.

"Mind if I join you?"

Jack looked up at the source of the voice. The athletically-built man who spoke to him looked to be a couple inches shorter and a couple years younger than Jack.

"Not at all. Have a seat."

The soldier, whose uniform was obviously new as well, dropped into the chair across the little table from Jack and set down his steaming cup. "You going to Camp Hale?"

"Yeah. You?"

"Yup." He extended his hand. "Steve Knowlton."

Jack shook it. "Jack Franklin. Pleased to meet you."

"Same." Steve blew on his coffee. "You're a skier, then."

Jack nodded. "I was an instructor at the Sugar Bowl Ski Resort in California."

"I've heard of it."

"What about you?"

Steve looked a little embarrassed. "I'm a competitive skier. Started in high school doing downhill, slalom, jumping, and cross-country."

"Wow. That's impressive," Jack said sincerely.

"I was on the University of New Hampshire ski team when I heard about the Ski Troops." His cheeks split in a grin. "So I quit school and signed up."

That simple statement made Jack think about Betty. How could he hear from her now that he wasn't in Oakland? His mom might forward any letters if she thought of it.

After I tell her how to reach me, that is.

"I couldn't wait, either. Seemed to take forever." Jack paused, then asked. "How'd your folks take your quitting school?"

"My dad was okay. He's Army from the first war, so he figured I might as well use the skills I have." Steve chuckled. "But I don't think he expects us to see combat, to be honest."

"Well, my dad's a decorated Marine from the first war," Jack replied. "So you can imagine how well my defection to the Army went over."

"Yikes."

Jack flashed a rueful grin. "Exactly." He looked at the clock on the wall. "Better head back to the station."

Both men gulped their coffee and crammed the last bits of donut into their mouths. They exited the cozy USO onto frosty, snow-covered streets and turned toward Union Station.

*****

Jack and Steve sat next to each other on the crowded train. Some of the uniformed men chatted nervously while others tried to catch some shut-eye. Jack closed his eyes, but he was too nervously excited to sleep.

It took all night for the slow train, groaning with the strain and belching black smoke, to climb up the Tennessee Pass. Jack's first glimpse of Camp Hale came at dawn as the train eased back down the steep grade toward Pando Station.

Majestic snow-encased peaks and granite cliffs surrounded a huge, flat-bottomed valley where hundreds of white two-story barracks squatted, row after row, in perfect alignment. The sky above the camp was hazy and thick with smoke.

The train slowed to a halt at the whistle stop optimistically called Pando Station. Jack peered out the window and saw nothing but a few small wooden buildings by the platform.

"There's no station at this station," Steve said over Jack's shoulder.

"Guess it's just for the camp," Jack opined.

The men in their train car slowly came to life, standing, stretching, and yawning. Jack and Steve shouldered their duffel bags and stepped out of the warm car into a blast of freezing wind.

At nine-thousand four-hundred feet elevation the air was thin and clearly overwhelmed by the heavier smoke from the camp's coal-burning facilities. Everything Jack could see was covered with a slick film of soot. The air smelled of coal dust.

Steve loosed a deep, hacking cough. "Gee. I love it here already."

From the station platform, Camp Hale looked like a stark and austere place. But the mountains surrounding the camp were breathtaking in the rising sun.

Jack heard his name called and he joined the group of recruits standing around a sergeant. When Steve's name was called as well, he grinned at his new friend.

"Can't go anywhere without me, Dropout?" he teased.

"Somebody's got to watch your backside, Oakland," Steve retaliated.

They fell in with the other recruits while the sergeant led them to the camp reception center. Jack and Steve were both assigned to the Eighty-Seventh Mountain Regiment, I Company, of the Third Battalion. Then another sergeant came to collect them and took them to their assigned barracks.

"Take any bunk you want that's empty," he told them. "Breakfast's at eight in the mess hall. Don't be late."

After the sergeant left, Jack tossed his duffel onto a bottom bunk. "Here we are, Dropout. Home sweet home."

Steve grabbed the top bunk. "I hope you don't snore, Oakland."

Jack unzipped his bag and gave Steve a sideways look. "I hope you don't wet the bed."

Steve laughed and opened one of the two footlockers at the foot of the bunk. "I make no promises."

*****

Jack and Steve spent their first miserable week at Camp Hale on Kitchen Police—KP—duty. Their assigned Second Lieutenant was on bereavement leave so their temporary platoon leader explained why this was actually very important duty.

"You're working at a high altitude here. Some men get sick from it, and the sooner you acclimatize, the better."

"They just needed some poor suckers to do the grunt work," Steve grumbled. "Who better than the new guys?"

"I wonder how long before we ski?" Jack pulled a rack of plates from the steaming dishwasher then wiped sweat from his brow with his sleeve. "We can't get through basic training by pushing mops, wiping tables, or wrestling garbage cans."

Steve refilled his bucket with hot water and poured in a hefty amount of bleach. He dipped a thick brush into it and started scrubbing the chopping block in the middle of the huge kitchen. "I have to admit, I'm less out of breath than I was at the beginning of the week."

"That's what I hate about you, Dropout." Jack loaded another rack of dirty dishes into the huge stainless steel machine. "Always looking on the bright side."

Week two brought an exercise cheerfully called the Transition Range.

"The object here is to simulate battle conditions," their temporary second lieutenant explained. "You men will be crawling through the snow under barbed wire while machine guns fire over your heads."

He paused and grinned evilly. "And yes, men. The ammunition is live."

It's baptism by literally firing at us.

When Jack's turn came he dropped to his belly and scrambled like a lizard being chased by a hawk. The snow beneath him had been flattened by those who used the course before him and had turned to ice overnight—slick, rough-ridged, and freezing cold.

He couldn't hear anything but the loud and random rat-a-tat of the machine guns behind him. He thought he felt the bullets flying by and hoped that was his imagination.

Certainly they wouldn't risk killing their recruits. Not after asking so much of them to get accepted into the Mountain Troops in the first place.

Would they?

Jack emerged from under the barbed wire and rolled to the side out of the machine guns' fire. He climbed to his feet and brushed away what little snow stuck to his pants.

"Good job, Private," the second lieutenant said. "Yours was the fastest time in your squad."

Jack nodded modestly. "Thank you, sir."

"I'll be sure to let your platoon leader know when he returns."

Jack had to ask, "Do you know when that will be, sir?"

The man looked relieved. "Day after tomorrow."

January 22, 1943

Jack and Steve took their seats in the Field House for their class on *Proper Care of Uniforms and Equipment.* Because the Ski Troops were so unique to the Army, Minnie Dole was allowed to recruit men and send them directly to Camp Hale without benefit of regular basic training.

So when they weren't on KP or getting the crap scared out of them on the Transition Range, the skiers-turned-soldiers had to learn the basic rudiments of military life, including who to salute and when, preventing frostbite, and recognizing and treating altitude sickness.

Jack found the classes interesting, especially when he realized he already knew some of this stuff because of his dad.

"Me, too," Steve said when Jack mentioned it. "My dad had a recording of bugle calls. He thought it was fun to play it when we were on school breaks."

"You too?" Jack groaned on disbelief. "I used to hear reveille, retreat, and taps in my sleep!"

Spread out on the platform in front of the bleachers today were mittens, snow pants, a snow jacket, skis—*finally*—poles, knit cap, helmet, goggles, and snow shoes in two sizes.

And all of the fabric was white.

"Camouflage, gentlemen," the instructor said. "Being a dark target against a white background is signing your own death certificate."

"Makes sense," Jack murmured, and Steve agreed.

"I need a volunteer to put all this on."

Jack leapt from the bleachers before he finished the sentence. "I'll do it, sir!"

The instructor flashed a crooked grin. "All right, Private. Take off your boots."

Layer by layer, the instructor held up each item and asked Jack to put it on.

"The snow pants go over your fatigues." He waited until Jack had them on, then held up the jacket and pulled back the front. "The coat is reversible. White on one side and olive drab on the other. This allows the soldier to wear the coat when mountain climbing in areas where there is no snow."

Jack put the coat on white side out. He was already beginning to sweat from the body heat trapped by the coat and pants.

"Now, to keep the private from overheating, we'll look at your boots next."

Too late.

The instructor lifted Jack's Army-issue boots. "This groove on the back of the heel is for the ski cable."

While Jack balanced on one foot, the instructor fastened a ski to his right foot.

"This is how you loop the cable for cross-country skiing. It allows the heel to lift during the stride."

Jack stood on the ski and the instructor strapped the other ski on his left foot. "And this secures the heel for downhill skiing."

The man straightened. "Any questions?"

Jack wasn't sure if anyone asked a question because his attention was pulled by the second lieutenant entering the Field House to his left.

Jack sucked a quiet gasp of horror.

It can't be.

The sergeant giving the lesson saluted. "Welcome back, Lieutenant Hollinghurst."

Damn.

Maybe he was just observing the class…

"Thank you." Hollinghurst waved a hand toward the assemblage. "I was told this is I Company."

"Yes, sir."

"I don't mean to interrupt, Sergeant. Carry on." Hollinghurst sat in the front row of the bleachers next to the three other second lieutenants who were the platoon leaders for I Company.

Jack turned his head away and twisted his body a little so his back was toward Hollinghurst.

Shit shit shit.

SHIT.

Aston Hollinghurst, Sugar Bowl slalom cheater and consummate asshole, was apparently his platoon leader. The one who was away from camp on bereavement leave.

Hope it wasn't his father and Pops still has a job.

Jack didn't think Hollinghurst noticed him. Of course there was no reason for either of them to expect to see the other here. Even if they were both at Camp Hale, so were eight thousand other men so far.

How should I handle this?

"Private?"

Jack's attention snapped back to the instructor. "Yes, sir?"

The sergeant stood with one of each size of the snow shoes in his hands. "Will you remove the skis?"

Jack bent over to do so, forcing himself to pay attention to how they were attached to his boots.

"This." The instructor held up the larger piece of equipment. "This bear paw is for regular use in situations where skis aren't appropriate."

He handed it to Jack who figured out how to put it on—it was easier than the skis.

"And this." The instructor waggled the smaller one in the air before handing it to Jack. "Is for emergencies."

Jack put the smaller bear paw on his other foot.

The sergeant handed him the knit cap, goggles, helmet, and

mittens while Jack put everything on.

Sweat was now running in constant rivulets down his back.

"Are you warm enough, Private?"

"I believe I'm melting, sir." Jack said without thinking.

"Good." He turned back to the men in the bleachers. "Once you are correctly outfitted, you should remain both warm and nearly invisible to aircraft or lookouts."

Then he turned back to Jack and released him from hell. "You may remove the snow gear, Private."

Jack couldn't get it off fast enough.

*****

Thirty-nine men waited at attention in the snow outside their barracks, some oh them coughing in the smoke-fouled air, and all of them braving a brisk, frigid breeze while Second Lieutenant Aston Hollinghurst conferred with the officer who had stepped into his place and got their platoon of new recruits started once they arrived.

After what felt like an hour, Hollinghurst nodded, shook the officer's hand and thanked him. Then he turned to address the platoon.

"At ease."

Jack sighed his relief and spread his stance. He was standing in the back row, hoping Hollinghurst didn't notice him.

The best he could figure was that the rich kid must have done four years of Reserve Officers' Training Corps when he was at Berkeley and then joined the Ski Troops when he graduated from the university. That would pull him into the Army as an officer.

From his own experience with the man, Jack couldn't see him wanting to take orders from anyone he considered beneath him.

"I've had good reports about your progress so far, and that pleases me. There are three of you I'd like to congratulate personally."

Jack closed his eyes and willed himself not to be one of the three.

"Private Knowlton, please step forward."

Steve did so.

"I understand you were very helpful during the platoon's class on preventing frostbite. Congratulations. And thank you for sharing your expertise."

Steve smiled. "Thank you, sir."

Hollinghurst called out a second name. "Private Winston, please step forward."

A lanky blond moved to the front.

"Your insights on altitude sickness were apparently very helpful." Hollinghurst's gaze swept over the soldier. "Where do you hale from?"

"Brian Head, Utah, sir. Ninety-eight hundred feet."

"Congratulations and thank you for sharing your expertise as well."

Winston smiled as well. "Thank you, sir."

Hollinghurst consulted his notes. "The third soldier who has shown promise during the first two weeks is Private Franklin."

Damn it.

Jack made his way through the assemblage until he stood in front of Aston Hollinghurst and looked him squarely in the eye.

Hollinghurst was obviously surprised, though he recovered fairly quickly. "Well… look who's here."

Chapter Seven

Jack said nothing. He just stared at Hollinghurst, intent and unblinking.

The second lieutenant lifted one corner of his mouth in what could be called a grin, but looked more like a sneer. "It says here that you had the fastest time in the platoon during the Transition Range exercises."

Jack did not smile. "Yes, sir."

Hollinghurst lifted one eyebrow. "I guess we'll have to see how *else* we can make use of you crawling on your belly."

It wasn't a question so Jack didn't reply. He just maintained unwavering eye contact. For wolves, that was a direct challenge. He wondered if Aston knew that.

"You three are dismissed."

Steve, Winston, and Jack saluted before returning to their spots. Steve shot him a *what the hell* look on the way.

"Tomorrow you will all be kitted out with the gear you saw demonstrated today," Hollinghurst said loudly. "After that, we'll start your actual ski training."

Finally, thank God.

Jack couldn't help but smile.

"In the meantime, make sure you know the history of the Eighty-Seventh. There will be a test." Hollinghurst looked over the men as if evaluating their worth. "You are dismissed."

*****

"What was that 'crawling on your belly' crap about with the lieutenant?" Steve asked Jack as they walked to the mess hall for supper. "Do you know him from somewhere?"

"My Pops works for his father. In a shipping yard by the Oakland docks."

Jack felt a zing of inadequacy telling the New Hampshire college dropout about his own unimpressive background. But he might as well go all in—as platoon mates they were now brothers.

"I worked there too." Jack admitted. "I needed a way to make enough money so I could take the train to Sugar Bowl and ski every weekend."

Steve peered at Jack. "That seemed like more than the boss's kid recognizing a worker, though."

"Yeah." Jack struggled with what else to say. He didn't want to undermine their platoon leader—he was a brother too, after all, and honor was honor.

"I was a judge in the first Silver Belt race at Sugar Bowl, and he and I didn't agree on a call that was made." Jack looked at Steve. "Can we leave it at that?"

"Sure." Steve nodded and his brow furrowed in thought. "How far is Sugar Bowl from Oakland?"

"Eight hours by train." Jack was relieved at the shift of their conversation. "My brother Harry and I caught the train at ten on Friday nights, and got home at eleven on Sunday nights."

"I skied twenty minutes from my house." Steve tossed him an apologetic glance. "So I got to ski almost every day."

"We went every weekend that the resort was open." Jack smiled a little. He missed Harry. "We were both instructors."

"Do you want to instruct here?" Steve looked hopeful.

Hell yes.

"Sure. But we'll have to see what the lieutenant says."

*****

The warning about the test didn't faze Jack—during their first weeks at Camp Hale he'd heard plenty of stories about the Eighty-

Seventh Regiment's experiences. He knew it was the first regiment formed in what would be the Tenth Division once the Eighty-Sixth and Eighty-Fifth were added. The plan was to have three full mountain infantry regiments, with three battalions per regiment.

He also knew the Eighty-Seventh was activated at Fort Lewis Washington in November of forty-one, because that was where Bill Klein went right after the attack on Pearl Harbor. And that the first designated 'mountain troops' in the history of the United States Army carried out their initial training at Mount Rainier, sixty miles from Fort Lewis.

I wonder when I'll see Bill again.

Mount Rainier was also where the incomparable Captain John Jay excelled so magnificently and received his stellar commendation.

Someday the filmmaker was expected to rejoin their division. That was a double-edged possibility that Jack would think about at another time.

When Camp Hale opened in November of forty-two the growing Eighty-Seventh relocated here. New recruits were still pouring in three months later.

"Unfortunately our equipment was really heavy and primitive," one guy told Jack and Steve at supper. "Pack it all in the rucksack and it weighed ninety pounds, way too much to carry on skis."

The man laughed, then. "Poor suckers who were carrying the pack and fell down couldn't get out of the straps and get up again. Their buddies had to lift them back onto their skis."

Jack found that scenario hilarious—like beetles on their backs, legs flailing.

"There'll be ten thousand men here eventually," one soldier in the barracks groused as he rinsed and then wrung out his shirt in a latrine sink designed for shaving. "But no place to do my damned laundry except here."

True enough. The camp was technically ready for the soldiers, but in reality the newly constructed facility left a lot to be desired. Construction trash, like scraps of wood and discarded nails, lay hidden under the snow and constantly punctured the tires of trucks and jeeps.

Though construction on additional facilities was started, there were no theaters completed, nor clubs for enlisted men or officers. In fact, there was no entertainment on the post whatsoever.

And there was no entertainment outside the camp, either. The closest town was ten miles to the south—but the old mining town of Leadville was placed off limits for military personnel by camp commander Brigadier General Onslow Rolfe until the prostitution and gambling in the town were cleaned up and under control.

That same night Jack told Steve about seeing Captain John Jay and his movie, and how that sold him on the Ski Troops.

"No one's made a film at Camp Hale yet, have they?" he asked.

Steve huffed. "You mean where the arriving recruits are shocked that things aren't just like they look in the movies?"

Jack laughed at that. "They'd have to call that movie *Camp Hell.*"

Steve winked. "Maybe the decorated and dashing John Jay can make it look glamorous."

When the lights went out and Jack rolled over to try and fall asleep, he regretted mentioning Captain Jay. Because thinking about the captain made him think about Betty.

His date with her was almost a year ago now, but he still thought about her often. Her letter arrived in October, though, proving she hadn't forgotten him either.

He really enjoyed that evening with Betty a lot and hoped he'd have the chance to get to know her better. Most girls he knew had no idea what skiing meant to him, or why he was so eager to join the Army's skiing soldiers. But Betty understood perfectly.

Granted, with a world wide war going on, Betty traveling constantly, and him now actually *in* the Army in Colorado, their prospects didn't look good. But truthfully, she had a better shot at contacting him at Camp Hale than he did of tracking her down.

Find me, Betty. Write me another letter.

I'll be waiting right here.

January 29, 1943

When Brigadier General Rolfe lifted the ban on Camp Hale soldiers going into Leadville the soldiers scrambled like ants to get away from the camp.

Every soldier at Camp Hale got a two-day weekend pass, meaning they could be gone from Friday night until formation on

Monday morning—providing they could either find a place to stay in Leadville or secure transportation to another town.

"Remember," Lieutenant Hollinghurst warned the platoon after they watched a truly terrifying film on venereal diseases and their horrifying consequences. "It's against regulations for Army personnel to contract a venereal disease. So either keep it wrapped or in your pants."

Jack had no problem with that.

That weekend Camp Hale looked like a ghost town. Those soldiers who had connections managed to find ways to get to Aspen to ski. The less fortunate spent their time in Leadville and returned to sleep in the barracks.

While Steve was one of the lucky ones to be able to afford Aspen, Jack opted to take the bus into Leadville on Friday night with a few other guys from their platoon. They joined a hundred or more other men at the Silver Dollar Saloon, one of the two main establishments in Leadville.

While his companions bought drinks for the local girls who were being very free with their companionship, Jack didn't join in. He wasn't a great dancer, so sitting on the sidelines with his beer and watching the show was enough entertainment for him.

Ditto for Saturday night at the Pastime Bar—the other Leadville establishment catering to servicemen. Besides, he saved a lot of money that way. And when he only received fifty-one dollars in private's pay every month, he felt the need to be careful.

I used to spend half of that every weekend going to Sugar Bowl and still had cash to spare.

Now he felt like a pauper.

But a happy one, to be honest. He wouldn't trade his training here for anything.

This past week he was on the slopes every single day. It soon became apparent that even though every soldier in his platoon had to apply and be accepted into the Ski Troops, they didn't all have the same level of skill.

Hollinghurst, to his credit, split the platoon in half. He took the more skilled skiers with him, and left Staff Sergeant Brooks in charge of those who were struggling.

"I'll stay with Brooks," Jack offered. "He'll need another instructor."

Hollinghurst glared at Jack. "You are *not* an instructor, Private

Franklin."

Jack bit back his retort, and instead offered, "I misspoke, Lieutenant. He'll need an assistant."

Hollinghurst looked like he wanted to bite Jack's head off, but Jack had been very careful not to give him a reason.

Watching the second lieutenant grapple with his obvious desire to knock him down a peg at any opportunity, coupled with Jack's determination to be the better man and not give him one, proved surprisingly entertaining for Jack.

"Fine," Hollinghurst growled. "If Sergeant Brooks has no objection?"

Brooks shook his head. "None, sir. I'd welcome the help."

Hollinghurst skied off with his men at that point, leaving Jack in relieved peace.

"Have you taught skiing before?" he asked Brooks.

"No. Have you?"

Jack just smiled.

By the end of this week, every one of the men in Brooks' and Jack's group was skiing with a confidence that sometimes outstripped their actual ability.

"Better that than being scared," Jack told Brooks. "Just wait until next week."

February 1, 1943

Jack woke up on Monday eager to return to their ski training. Steve walked to breakfast with him, babbling on and on about the conditions at Aspen and all the incredible runs he made during his two days there. Even though there was no comparison, Jack was itching to get back up the mountain.

"Private Franklin?" Staff Sergeant Brooks stood next to Jack's table and handed him a slip of paper. "Report to I Company office as soon as you're done."

Steve looked alarmed. "What'd you do?"

Jack scowled. "Nothing!"

"Then why do they want to see you?"

"I don't know." Jack shoveled his scrambled eggs into his mouth and gulped his coffee. "But I'm not going to wait to find out."

As Jack trotted carefully across the snow-and-ice covered camp to I Company's headquarters, he replayed the previous week's activities and interactions in his mind. Try as he might, he couldn't come up with a single reason for Hollinghurst to have him disciplined. Plus he'd behaved like a saint over the weekend, unlike most of the guys.

Guess we'll see.

Jack pulled the door open and stomped inside, loosening snow from his boots. "I'm here to—*Bill?*"

"Technical Sergeant Wilhelm Klein to you, Private." The Austrian approached with a wide, toothy grin splitting his face and grabbed Jack's hand. "It's good to see you."

Jack was so stunned he couldn't begin to follow still-unfamiliar Army protocol. "When did you get here?"

"Before you did, I can tell you that." He beckoned Jack to follow him. "Let's talk in here."

Jack followed Bill into a little office. Bill pointed to one chair and sat in the other. Jack sank into the proffered seat.

"Why haven't I seen you?" Jack asked, feeling a little hurt.

"Because I've been busy." Bill blew a wide-eyed sigh. "I'm Lead Instructor for the Eighty-Seventh and you boys are streaming in here faster than I can get you all settled."

That was impressive. And it made sense. "I had no idea."

"Of course not. And what *else* you don't know..." Bill paused and his eyes twinkled mischievously. "Is that ever since I saw your name on the new arrivals, I've been working to get you on my crew."

Jack had no idea what he meant by that. "Your crew?"

"The instructor cadre, Jack. I want you to *teach* skiing. And mountaineering."

Jack's jaw dropped and his pulse surged with excitement. "How?"

"As soon as you finish basic training, you'll come over to the Mountain Training Center."

"What about I Company?"

"That's your permanent assignment," Bill explained. "But you'll be on loan to the instructor branch at the MTC. The Army calls it Temporary Additional Duty."

Jack's mind was reeling. "Does it come with temporary

additional pay?"

Bill's head fell back and he hooted. "No, Private Franklin," he said between outbursts of amusement. "Unfortunately it does not."

"What about Steve Knowlton?" Jack asked. "Have you looked at him?"

"No. Should I?" Bill retrieved paper and a pen from the desk they were sitting in front of.

"He was on the University of New Hampshire ski team. And he's skilled at a lot of things," Jack lobbied. "Plus he's a solid guy."

"I'll check him out. Thanks." Bill scribbled the name on the paper and tucked it in his pocket. "In the meantime, how the hell have you been? How's Harry?"

*****

When Jack saw Steve later that day he told him about his history with Fred and Bill Klein—Technical Sergeant Wilhelm Klein—and Jack's recommendation that he should look at Steve as instructor material.

"Thanks, Jack!" Steve looked gobsmacked. "I really appreciate you mentioning me. I'd love that opportunity."

"I think you'd do a great job," Jack replied honestly. "And we'd have a blast together."

The best part was that the start of Jack's new duties shouldn't be far off.

Technically the Eighty-Seventh wasn't considered an infantry regiment, so their basic training routine was less rigid than for the infantry units. For example, they didn't have the manual of arms an hour a day or have to stand inspection twice a week. They were too busy skiing.

But there was still the usual toughening-up routine where they ran obstacle courses, did push-ups, and jogged for miles with full equipment. All of that was necessary to be able to function during mountain battles at soaring altitudes above the tree line.

As soon as I can do this without panting, I'll be ready.

He looked at Steve who was jogging next to him. Bill had taken Jack's recommendation and tapped Steve to be an instructor as well.

"Race ya."

Steve took off running. "See you at the MTC!" he shouted over his shoulder.

Jack grinned and bolted after him.

Chapter
Eight

February 2, 1943

While Jack and the rest of his platoon straggled into the barracks, exhausted by a long day of training with full packs, their Platoon Guide swerved off toward I Company headquarters to collect the mail. Some lucky soldiers got letters nearly every day from their families, wives, or sweethearts.

Jack, on the other hand, got weekly letters from his father telling him all about Harry's latest triumph as a Marine in the Pacific. And every last one of them was pointedly signed, *Semper Fi.* Pops didn't miss a single chance to let Jack feel his deep disappointment in his eldest son's actions.

Jack hadn't answered any of them.

He did write to his mother though, telling her all the things he knew she would want to know: he was getting enough to eat, he was warm at night, and he was happy with his decision. He also tried to include at least one amusing anecdote in every letter just to lift her spirits.

Of course his father would read his letters. And his conviction that Jack was still 'doing nothing' would be confirmed.

There was nothing Jack could do about that at this point. Not until they were deployed somewhere and using their unique skills. No one knew when that would be, only that the soldiers were nowhere near ready to go anywhere as yet.

"Franklin!"

Jack grabbed for the envelope tossed in his direction. When he saw the handwriting he sucked a happy gasp. Jack retreated to his bunk and tore open the envelope.

Dear Jack,

I hope this letter reaches you. I asked John to find out if you made it into the Ski Troops and he just told me that you did, and that you are part of the 87th just like he is. Congratulations! Are you an instructor?

We have gone all over the place with his film and are still getting tons of guys taking applications. While that's very encouraging for John as Public Relations Officer, he told me that Camp Hale's commanding officer, Brigadier General Rolfe, has asked Army Ground Forces to stop sending him raw recruits.

But the Army made a deal with Minnie Dole that new recruits would be sent directly to Camp Hale. I guess that means you are receiving Basic Training and Mountain Training at the same time. How is that going?

Because my parents are so old-fashioned, I have made arrangements with a friend of mine back in Boston so that you can write back to me and send the letters to her address. She will forward them to me, wherever I am.

But only if you want to, of course. For all I know, you could be an old married man by now!

But to be honest, of all the guys I've met on this tour, you're the one I can't forget. I can't even explain why.

I hope to hear from you.

Betty

Jack read the letter again, elated that Betty was still thinking about him. She made arrangements for him to write to her—finally. That was about the best news he could imagine.

Jack pulled out a notepad and copied the Boston address on the inside of the cover, in case the letter got waylaid somehow. Then he flipped the cover back and began to write on the first blank sheet.

Dear Betty,

It's really great to hear from you…

February 3, 1943

Something big was happening at Camp Hale.

Rumors were flying through I Company that some sort of test was going on. Because the mountain troops were still not universally accepted, and since Camp Hale was a mountain training center where troops were preparing to fight in the mountains, Army Ground Forces Headquarters was apparently requiring the test of a battalion in the field.

Brigadier General Rolfe selected a combat team comprised of the Headquarters Company of the Second Battalion, supported by a battery of the Ninety-Ninth Field Artillery Battalion. He then attached Medical, Quartermaster, Signal, Antitank-Antiaircraft, and Engineer units and ordered them all out on a two-week field exercise.

The test force would take the field twelve miles from Camp Hale at an elevation of over eleven thousand feet. The tactical requirement entailed holding a defensive position at thirteen thousand feet, just below the peak of Homestake Mountain, and repelling raids by a platoon of enemy ski troops against their bivouac areas and lines of communications.

Tonight, the night before the test was to begin, Rolfe was holding what the Army called a 'dining in'—a banquet for everyone who was participating in the Homestake Maneuvers. The point was to encourage the men and praise their efforts in preparing to live and fight under harsh conditions high in the mountains.

Rolfe's special guests were Minnie Dole and John Morgan, War Department Consultant of the National Ski Patrol.

Even though his Battalion wasn't involved in the maneuvers, Jack wanted to go to the banquet because he really wanted to meet Minnie Dole. He easily convinced Steve to come with him, and the two friends snuck in the back and sat at a table near the door.

When Dole stood up to speak the room grew so quiet that Jack thought he could have heard a pin drop on fresh snow.

Looking over the assemblage of men he recruited and soldiers he assigned, Dole described the fireside conversations that first began the idea of the mountain troops.

"I pointed out to those in charge that the United States Army did not have one *single* Mountain Division for combat—but the Germans have *four*." Dole sighed and shook his head. "Do you have any idea of the endless miles of red tape that John Morgan and I had to navigate just to get our ideas in front of Secretary of War Stimson and General Marshall?"

Dole chuckled. "If you *think* you do, then multiply that by ten."

A wry laugh moved through the crowd.

When Dole sat down again, Rolfe stepped up and addressed the soldiers present. "You men seem to have the idea that you are *ski* troops."

Jack frowned at Steve. "We are. Aren't we?"

"I thought so…"

"I need to correct that right now," Rolfe continued. "You are *mountain* troops."

A low rumble of dissent vibrated around the room.

If Rolfe noticed, he didn't acknowledge it. "And anyone who knows anything about mountain warfare knows that we need mules to carry the equipment and mountain artillery."

"Mules will be useless in six feet of snow," Jack scoffed. "Hell, *three* feet! I don't get what's happening here."

"Some sort of tide has turned," Steve murmured.

Rolfe paused and smiled a little. "Mules won't go anywhere without a bell mare to lead them. We'll soon have a new bell mare here at Camp Hale." Rolfe's smile widened. "I propose to name her Minnie."

"What the fuck?" Jack whispered. Steve shot him a horrified glance.

Minnie Dole accepted the dubious honor graciously. "I'm happy to be associated with the outfit in any way that I can."

Of all people, Camp Hale's commanding officer should know better, but it was obvious to Jack that Rolfe saw the Ski Troops as typical soldiers, not as soldiers having unique skills. Jack figured the upcoming test was going to clear that misconception right up and quickly.

Then Minnie Dole repaid Rolfe's gesture by handing him a gift that symbolized the pride of every man in the room: a pair of skis.

Rolfe's gratitude was clearly strained, as the man himself didn't ski.

And every soldier there knew it.

"Thank God we're Third Battalion," Steve said at breakfast the next morning. "That altitude is going to be killer."

"Look at the weather outside," Jack countered. "They're walking into blizzard conditions with high winds, heavy snow, and temperatures well below zero."

Steve shook his head. "This can't turn out well."

February 5, 1943

True to his word, Bill Klein made the arrangements for Jack and Steve to take the ski test to become instructors at the Mountain Training Center without going through the actual training.

"You guys know this stuff," he said. "I want you teaching as soon as possible."

Jack was thrilled, because it meant he'd move to the MTC and get out from under Hollinghurst's microscope. Ignoring the man's constant needling was getting harder by the day—and it was made worse because his platoon mates noticed. The mood in the platoon was growing tense.

"I really need all the qualified skiers to move up," Bill continued. "The Mountain Division is so popular that recruits are walking into induction centers and signing up—and the Army is sending them here even if they never skied in their lives!"

"What about Minnie Dole checking them first?" Jack clearly saw the problem, even if the Army didn't.

"There are too many applicants so his rules aren't being followed."

Jack looked at Steve. "I'm ready."

Steve grinned. "Me, too."

"Then let's get started."

The course was five miles long. The instructor candidates followed a well-marked path that crossed partially frozen streams full of willows—and crossed them several times.

There was a steep climb through a narrow gap in the rocks, then a rapidly dropping run out. The course led them through a field of boulders which necessitated the skilled placement of their nearly seven-foot-long skis.

They skied through a grove of Aspen, went up a logging road, and then had to negotiate their way across a section of felled trees.

The final stretch was a flat run for three quarters of a mile to the finish line. In order to pass the test, each soldier had to complete the entire run in one hour while carrying a full rucksack and rifle.

Jack's time was forty-nine minutes.

Steve followed across the finish line two minutes later.

The friends pounded each other on the back.

"We did it!" Jack shouted.

Bill Klein was beaming. "I knew you boys wouldn't let me down. Now let's make it official."

February 7, 1943

Two days later Jack and Steve moved into the barracks at Cooper Hill, six miles from Camp Hale up Tennessee Pass, to live with the other Mountain Training Center instructors.

"Hey." Jack pointed across the bunkroom to a man wearing corporal's insignia. "Isn't that Friedl Pfeiffer?"

Steve nodded. "I think so. Should we introduce ourselves?"

Jack was already walking toward the Austrian skier. "Corporal Pfeiffer?"

"Yes?" Friedl turned toward Jack.

"You won't remember me, but I was a ski instructor at Sugar Bowl. I saw you win the first Silver Belt competition there."

Friedl flashed a friendly smile. "You do look familiar... weren't you the judge who disqualified one of the top times?"

Jack glanced at Steve. Understanding washed over his friend's expression, but he held his tongue.

"Uh, yeah. That was me."

"And now you're an instructor here?" The smile broadened. "Welcome to our ranks!"

"Thanks." Jack pointed to Steve. "This is Steve Knowlton. He qualified along with me."

Friedl shook both their hands. "Well done, men."

When Jack and Steve walked back to their bunks, Steve simply said, "Hollinghurst."

"Yes," Jack replied softly.

"Understood."

February 12, 1943

Now that he was an instructor, Jack could see the overall plan for training the soldiers. And it was a good one.

There were four moderate slopes at Camp Hale plus Cooper Hill. While the slopes around the camp made use of common tow ropes, Cooper Hill boasted a T-bar lift, one of the first in the country.

The lift was shaped like an upside-down T and two men at a time sat on the cross piece. The lift pulled skiers a mile-and-a-quarter to the top of the mountain at an impressive seven miles an hour.

The skiers-in-training ran Cooper Hill and the four practice slopes eight hours a day, six days a week. But on Sundays most of the instructors went to Cooper Hill to ski just for the fun of it.

Jack was on the practice hills six days a week, helping the soldiers who transferred in from flatland units to learn to ski.

And he was there when his platoon came to train.

The first time Hollinghurst encountered Jack in his elevated position as an instructor he refused to acknowledge him, barking instructions to the platoon members as if Jack wasn't there.

Jack watched the soldiers that he and Brooks had worked with. They didn't seem to have improved since Jack was loaned to the MTC, so he skied over to Sergeant Brooks.

"Can I give you a hand?"

Brooks nodded. "Sure."

Jack knew Hollinghurst wasn't dismissive of him only because the second lieutenant held a personal grudge against him. When privates were instructing officers there was always an inherent sense of tension. Most Army officers were resistant to taking orders from those ranked beneath them, and they often displayed a dismissive attitude of privilege.

"They don't take kindly to being taught by enlisted men," Friedl offered. "Especially from those among us who are younger and more skilled than they are."

"They'll need to get past that," said an instructor with an accent Jack didn't recognize. "Otherwise we'll never be ready."

Jack turned to Steve. "Do you know him?"

"Huh uh."

Friedl noticed. "Steve, Jack, come meet Torger Tokle. He's a champion ski jumper from Norway."

Jack shook hands with the Norseman. "Pleased to meet you."

"Ski jumper?" Steve's eyes lit up. "I jumped competitively in college."

"Before he dropped out," Jack clarified, always ready to harass his friend.

"How far did you jump?" Torger asked.

"A hundred and seventy feet," Steve said. "You?"

"One ninety-eight." Torger grinned. "Two hundred is teasing me right now."

Steve let out a whistle of respect.

"Hello, everybody—Steve!" A lean, dark-haired man strode toward the group of four. "I didn't know I'd see you here!"

"Pete Seibert, you scoundrel." Steve shook the younger man's hand. "What are you doing here?"

"Same as you, I expect."

Steve turned to Jack. "Pete's from Massachusetts. He was competing as a senior in high school the same year I was a freshman in college."

"Nice to meet you, Pete." Jack shook hands as well. "Jack Franklin from Oakland."

Pete waved a hand around his head. "So, how is it here at the MTC?"

Jack's glance slid to Friedl. He was definitely going to defer that question to the corporal with seniority.

"We are, how should I explain this?" Friedl looked at Steve as if seeking confirmation. "We are left to our own, I would say."

"That's what it seems like, Pete." Steve shrugged. "As long as the soldiers are learning to ski, nobody bothers to ask us what else is going on here."

Jack tried to hold back his grin without success. "Should we tell him about the beer keg in the rafters?"

Friedl frowned and shook his head, though there was a definite twinkle in his eyes. "No. Not for at least a week."

Pete faced Steve. "He's joking, right?"

"Sure he is. We don't have any fun here at the Mountain Training Camp." Steve winked at Jack. "Not one single bit."

Chapter
Nine

February 13, 1943

Jack, Steve, and Pete watched the dejected men trudging back into camp after the drastically shortened Homestake test and immediately knew how lucky they were not to have been with that battalion.

"It's just a damn shame that the test had to include so many men who had no idea what they were doing," Steve muttered. "It wasn't fair to them. None of us are ready for this."

As if to underscore Steve's words, the lines at the camp hospital stretched down the road. Just because the men survived their tortuous ordeal didn't mean the soldiers escaped unscathed. Frostbite claimed some, but the most common ailment was acute mountain sickness. And that was nasty business.

Symptoms included fatigue, headache, loss of appetite, nausea, respiratory distress, and accelerated heart rate. Even though he never succumbed to it himself, Jack had experience with altitude sickness at Sugar Bowl and he had helped plenty of skiers who were afflicted.

Back in the MTC that night, instructors from the Second Battalion looked shell-shocked as they told the others what happened on Homestake Mountain.

"We lost a quarter of the men the *first day* from frostbite, exhaustion, and altitude sickness," one said. "By the end of the week, two hundred and sixty men were casualties."

"Out of nine hundred?" Jack asked. He blew a low whistle. "That's rough."

"Minnie's guys did okay," another clarified. "It was the raw recruits who fell. They had no training in winter camping yet and none of them were conditioned for camping in snow."

"The tactical exercises were immediately cancelled, of course. We spent the rest of the week just learning to live and move under winter conditions."

The first guy nodded. "The test was supposed to evaluate our training, ski clothing and equipment, and re-supply, so we succeeded at that, at least..."

"Who oversaw all of this?" Jack asked.

"Two majors from Army Ground who are mountaineers and skiers. They went through the exercise with the troops."

"Minnie Dole and John Morgan were there, too."

It was clear to Jack after listening to the men who were involved that the breakdown in the field exercise resulted from the combination of severe weather, raw recruits, and the excessive loads they were expected to carry. Overall it was a tragic failure.

If Pops gets wind of this I'll never hear the end of it.

February 16, 1943

Captain John Jay swept into the Mountain Training Center looking like he could tear the building down with his bare teeth.

Jack's first thought was, *is Betty with him?*

His second thought was, *of course she isn't.*

Jay was here in his role as the overseer of the Mountain Training Center. And the devastating debacle of the field test was what pulled him from his movie tour and brought him to the embattled center which fell under his jurisdiction.

Jack decided not to approach the captain. He hadn't actually spoken to Jay that fateful night when he was introduced to both the Ski Troops and Betty Harkins—two things which redirected the course of his life. So while Jack was aware of Jay, to Jay he was just another face in the crowd of instructors who gathered to hear what he had to say.

"Welcome, gentlemen," he began. "First of all, I want to congratulate you on the job you are doing here. From what I've seen, you are dedicated to your task, and competent in your skills."

Jay paused and drew a deep breath. "Unfortunately, through no fault of yours, events of the past weeks have not proven that."

The instructors exchanged resigned glances. None of them could reasonably expect a good report from the Homestake exercises which had gone so very badly.

"Army Ground has reported serious deficiencies in the soldiers' preparations for the ordeal to which they were subjected," Jay quoted. "They stated that the men had not been sufficiently trained in cross-country skiing, snowshoeing, or snow camping."

Jack couldn't argue with any of that, considering the range of men that were sent. New recruits should not have been anywhere near the planned maneuvers and he could not understand why Brigadier General Rolfe chose them to go.

Jay's gaze swept over the assembled instructors. "Major Wood reported that about half of the men had been issued special items of equipment, including the mountain tent, the mountain stove, and in some cases the sleeping bag, for the *first time* the day before the exercise began."

Jack's eyes rounded in shock. But his shock quickly turned to fury. The general was handed a unique opportunity to shine a very complimentary light on the ski troops. But instead, he'd shot them all in their proverbial feet. Rolfe really made a mess of things—and his troops paid the price.

Considering Rolfe's comments at the banquet, Jack had to wonder if that was intentional—even at the expense of the soldiers involved.

Captain Jay's mouth curled in a faint, wry smile. "Though those soldiers had not been adequately trained to use them, their clothing and equipment were found to be satisfactory in their performance."

Jack snorted.

Well, there's that.

"What's going to happen to us now?" he whispered to Steve and Pete.

Both men's expressions reflected the deep concern that was gutting Jack.

"The Army's built—hell, they're *still* building—this camp for fifteen thousand men to train for mountain warfare," Pete said.

"That isn't going to stop."

"But the hammer's going to fall somewhere," Steve opined. "I'd hate to be in Rolfe's boots right now.

*****

While the men of Camp Hale were waiting for the final outcome from the Army Ground's forced field test, they now went about their daily business with a palpable sense of urgency. As poorly executed as the maneuvers had been, they did prove to the Camp Hale soldiers that they all needed to take their mountain training very seriously.

If they didn't, they weren't likely to survive their deployment— and that would have nothing to do with their enemy's efforts.

One factor that complicated their renewed efforts was the extremely poor air quality at Camp Hale.

Throughout February a pall of smoke hung over the flat valley, which was isolated from any cleansing wind by mountains on all sides. Soot particles continuously belched into the subzero air from five hundred smokestacks and infiltrated everything in the camp— including the soldiers' lungs.

Exacerbating their situation was the thin mountain air, which compelled soldiers to take deep breaths. And what little air hovered in the valley was extremely dry.

Many of the troopers developed a rasping cough that they began calling the Pando hack. Violent coughing often left the soldiers weak, watery-eyed, and out of breath. A nasty throat condition often resulted from the sustained coughing, and both afflictions had the camp's medical staff working overtime.

Long ski marches were part of the soldiers' field exercises and even though they were forced to carry heavy packs, rifles, tents, and radio equipment, the conditions in the valley were so bad that the men actually looked forward to marching out of Camp Hale and getting the chance to breathe clean air.

Jack had managed to dodge the condition so far, but it discouraged him to see layers of soot darkening the snow— especially as train after train of heavy freight chugged its way through camp, pulled and pushed by three giant, coal-burning locomotives spewing more smoke and soot into the already fouled air.

February 21, 1943

Captain John Jay was still at Camp Hale when Betty's next letter arrived. Her reply came less than three weeks after he sent his letter to her friend's address—much faster than Jack expected. That simple fact lifted Jack's spirits tremendously during this frustrating time.

After a long and exhausting day on the slopes pushing soldiers to repeat drills until they improved noticeably, he sat on his bunk in the MTC barracks and carefully tore the envelope open.

He smiled when he saw Betty's elegant writing.

> *Dear Jack,*
>
> *I was so happy to receive your reply! I had just arrived in Boston, having left John as he was preparing to head your way, and my mood was brightened by the sight of your letter.*

Jack grunted. The message was clear: leaving Jay's side had made Betty sad. Was he competing with a married man for the pretty brunette's attention?

> *I loved everything that you wrote! Your description of life at Camp Hale is so vivid that I have no trouble imagining your life there.*
>
> *I have to confess, I am so envious of your ability to ski every day. While I'm traveling with John, I get to talk about skiing all the time. But talking and doing are nothing alike, as you know well.*
>
> *I deeply miss rushing down the slopes with the wind and snow in my face, and I hope that during this break in our duties I'll be able to spend some time on my poor, neglected skis ~ before I forget how to use them!*
>
> *I'm smiling as I write this to you. I have tried to tell my*

girlfriends who don't ski how much I love it, but they can't understand my passion. And while my friends who do ski also share my enjoyment of the sport, none of them have any desire to go through the rigors of becoming a certified instructor.

Jack realized that he sent his first letter to Betty before Bill Klein offered him the chance to test into being an instructor here. That was the first thing he'd mention in his letter back to her.

Writing to you, Jack, is a very interesting thing. I'm not afraid to speak my mind and tell you my thoughts. Maybe that's why I tried to stay in touch with you when it wasn't possible for you to write back. Somehow I know you'll understand me.

I do have some exciting news: there are rumors of another ski movie to be made ~ one that will be filmed at Camp Hale. I suppose whether that happens will depend on how things turn out while John is there now.

But if the film actually is made, I'm going to ask John if I can come along as a civilian assistant. I'd be able to see you again, and I would like that very much.

Jack's heartbeat stuttered at the possibility of seeing Betty again. He wondered if Captain Jay would object to them spending time together—clearly Betty didn't think so.

And as a married man, Jay could not monopolize the single woman's time without raising serious questions about his fidelity to his wife.

Anyway, the postman will be here soon so I'm going to close and get this letter in the mail. I look forward to hearing from you again.

Affectionately yours,

Betty

February 23, 1943

Captain Jay called the ski instructors together for one last meeting at the Mountain Training Center the night before he left Camp Hale. Jack wondered if Jay had any idea that one of the men in the audience was corresponding with his beautiful assistant, but he wasn't about to introduce himself to Jay and tell him that.

No reason to rock the boat.

"After all is said and done, Minnie Dole and John Morgan said that Brigadier General Rolfe understood and concurred with the observations made by Army Ground," Jay told the men. "Unfortunately, some of the problems they encountered during the Homestake test were caused by situations out of Rolfe's control."

"What situations?" The question came from Friedl Pfeiffer.

Jay faced the Austrian champion. "The biggest problem comes from who is allowed to join the Mountain Troops."

Jay swung his arm wide in a gesture that encompassed all the instructors present. "You men know all about that. Even though Dole tries to qualify every recruit, the Army continues to assign men to the Mountain Troops who've either never worn skis or set foot on a mountain. Or both."

Heads bobbed in agreement all around the room. But that was no excuse for sending those raw recruits on the dangerous Homestake maneuvers.

"Do they say why they are being assigned?" Jack risked calling out.

Jay looked at him with absolutely no flicker of recognition. "They'll only say that the draft is just too cumbersome to accommodate Dole's request."

Chapter
Ten

March 29, 1943

In the wake of the Homestake debacle most of the men who joined the Tenth through transfers from flatland Army divisions, and did not meet Minnie Dole's requirements, were transferred out. It was obvious by now that they couldn't take the cold climate, the high altitude, or the rugged mountain life that the ski troops' elite training required.

At the same time the intensity of the remaining soldiers' ski training was stepped up several notches.

The new and inexperienced recruits trained on the four slopes around the camp. Ski classes began on the level, followed by sidestepping or herringboning up the hill. Next the soldiers learned to snowplow with a ninety-pound rucksack on their backs. After that came cross-country skiing and downhill skiing along with marksmanship practice.

After completing six weeks of drill, the units were marched the six miles up to Cooper Hill from Camp Hale while packing enough gear to spend a month in training. There the ski instructors tested the men on a course with numerous strategically placed obstacles which created a hazardous run that was intentionally exhausting.

To accommodate the intensified training, a barracks was built at Cooper Hill for the ski instructors. They would take turns living there for three weeks at a time in order to work with the soldiers on advanced skills at the high altitude.

Jack and Pete were in the first group of instructors sent up.

"Lucky," Steve grumbled.

"That remains to be seen," Jack replied. While he looked forward to the challenge, being so far removed from camp would slow down his ability to receive mail on a daily basis.

Three weeks later Jack stood next to Steve and watched his friend's squad as the twelve men tackled the course. "They're doing pretty good, Dropout."

Steve flashed a crooked grin. "Yeah, I got lucky this round."

"I'm looking forward to going back down with you. The training here is challenging, but I'm looking forward to some easier duty for a while." Jack stretched and yawned. "Anything exciting going on down there?"

Steve looked at Jack with a skeptical expression. "Rolfe just arranged for the ski instructors who are regular enlisted men—but college graduates—to go to Officer Candidate School, and then come back to the MTC as second lieutenants."

Jack looked at Steve in disbelief. "I didn't think OCS graduates could be reassigned to the same unit they came from."

"Not normally, no. But Rolfe's still under the gun because of Homestake. So he convinced the Army to let him have his *ski-instructing* officers back once they graduated. I guess he told them that privates instructing captains wasn't going so well."

Jack laughed. "Good point. But that leaves you, me, and Pete out."

"Doesn't bother me. I don't trust any of the Army's promises after what they did to their agreement with Dole." Steve's gaze moved back to the course. "There's always a possibility those guys could be reassigned to a flatland infantry division afterwards, in spite of the handshake agreement."

*****

Jack returned to his bunk in the Mountain Training Center and dropped his rucksack on the mattress, relieved to be back. He already found it easier to breathe at the lower altitude and smiled at the realization that ninety-four-hundred feet was now his normal environment.

"Franklin?"

Jack turned around. The platoon guide from I Company platoon walked up to him. "You have some mail."

Jack rifled through the four envelopes. Two from his mother, one from his dad, and—*hallelujah!*—one from Betty.

He'd save that one for last.

Jack read his mother's letters first. As usual, she didn't have much to report except that she missed him, prayed for him and Harry, and wished he'd write to her more often. Then he took a deep breath and opened the letter from his father.

The words *Homestake Mountain* leapt from the page and glared at him like they were alive.

"Shit!" Jack folded the unread pages and stuffed them back into the envelope, his hands shaking with rage.

He knew there was a chance that the devastating test of the Army's mountain training might go public, and he also knew that if it did his spiteful father would rub his face in it.

But I don't have to make it easy for him.

Jack tore the letter in half with a satisfying rasp. Then he walked to the latrine and unapologetically flushed the pages. He watched his father's unread vitriol spiral down into soggy oblivion with great satisfaction.

He left the latrine and returned to his bunk.

Now for Betty.

Jack dropped onto the thin mattress, laid back, and opened her envelope.

> *Dear Jack,*
>
> *I am so glad you're a ski instructor! I'm so proud of you. I'm sure you're doing great.*
>
> *I also have exciting news: the movie that I wrote you about is going to be made! Warner Brothers Studio is calling the film "Mountain Fighters" ~ and they are filming the skiing scenes at Camp Hale's Cooper Hill!*
>
> *Even better, John says the studio wants to use the ski instructors in the shots. You could be a movie star.*
>
> *John will be there the whole time as Public Relations Officer and the liaison between the film crew and the camp. The best part is that he agreed I can come along and still be his assistant.*

We are going to see each other again!

I don't know how much free time I'll have ~ or how much you'll have ~ but let's do try to have another drink together. We should be arriving at Camp Hale by April 1st so the filming can be done before the snow melts.

I can't wait to see you again.

Affectionately,

Betty

Jack bolted upright in his bunk. April first? In three days Betty would be at Camp Hale! He smiled so widely his cheeks hurt, his father's letter happily forgotten.

April 1, 1943

Pete blew a low whistle. "Who's the looker?"

Jack turned around in time to see Captain John Jay stride through the crowded Mess hall with a small group trailing behind him.

"Wait—" Pete grabbed Jack's arm. "Is *that* your girl?"

Of course Jack's best friends knew about Betty. At least they knew she existed.

Jack's gaze rested on the brunette walking quickly to keep up with the captain. Her gaze flicked from side to side and he knew she was looking for him.

Jack stood up and waited for Betty's gaze to shift back toward him. When it did, he smiled and raised one hand, giving a flick of a wave.

Betty's light green eyes brightened with her smile. She gave him a chest high finger-wiggling wave and kept walking.

Jack figured out she was working at the moment and knew he'd probably get a chance to talk to her at the end of the day. For now it was enough just to know they were once again in the same place at the same time.

He sat back down to his meal and stuck a forkful of meatloaf past his painfully broad grin.

Pete and Steve gaped at him like he was some sort of powerful

Nordic god.

"That's *Betty?*" Steve's tone was filled with awe.

"How'd a scruffy like you nab a girl like that, Oakland?" Pete demanded.

"Charm, boys." Jack stabbed another bite of meatloaf and waved the laden fork in front of his delighted smile. "Pure, lady-killing charm."

*****

By now more buildings were finished in the camp, including the laundry—thank goodness—and the officer and enlisted men's clubs. Jack wondered if he could ask Betty to join him there for a drink, or if she would have to leave the camp at a certain time.

He didn't see her all day, but at dinner she was sitting with Captain Jay and his crew in the mess hall's officers' section. Jack wound his way through the mess with his tray, looking for a spot near her.

"Jack!" Betty motioned him toward her.

Jack stood in front of her, knowing he was grinning like an idiot. "Hello, Betty!"

"Can you sit with us?"

Jack cut his gaze to Captain Jay, who stared back at him like he had two heads. Obviously Betty had never mentioned *him* to the captain.

"No, I'm not an officer. Sorry." Jack motioned with his head. "I'll be right over here when you're done."

Betty picked up her tray. "Then I'll join you."

Jack didn't look at Jay again, afraid of what he might see in the captain's expression. He just led Betty to a table that had room for both of them. He set his tray down and Betty took the seat across the table from him.

Once they were settled, a wave of shyness seemed to envelope them both. This was only their second face-to-face conversation after all, even though their frequent letters were frank and friendly.

"It's great to see you, Betty," Jack began the conversation as he attacked his food. "You look wonderful."

"You too, Jack." Her cheeks pinkened adorably. "I have to say, you look very manly in your uniform."

"I feel like I've aged years since I met you, to be honest." Jack shook his head. "Being up here is completely different from skiing at Sugar Bowl."

"I'll bet it is." Betty bravely dug into her chipped beef on toast. "I'm excited to watch the film being made."

Jack chuckled. "And if I'm in it, you'll be dating a movie star."

Betty's eyes jumped to his. "Are we dating, Jack?"

Jack wanted to jam his big fat Army boots into his mouth and leave them there. Talk about too much too soon.

"Um, well…" All of his words seemed to have marched right out of his head leaving a silent, empty void.

Betty's gaze fell back to her supper. "Because I'd like to think so. Only if you do, that is."

The heavens opened up and the mess hall disappeared from Jack's awareness. All he saw were Betty's beautiful green eyes. "I'd love that, Betty."

"Good." She smiled at him again. "Then it's settled."

Jack beamed at his *girlfriend*. "Where are you staying?"

"In Leadville with the film crew. John found me an adorable bed and breakfast inn run by a sweet older couple."

"Tomorrow's Friday. I can get a weekend pass and come see you," Jack offered. "Take you out for drinks or dinner both nights?"

Betty's expression turned impish. "I'll happily accept under one condition."

Jack was intrigued. "And that is?"

Betty leaned forward and those green eyes pinned his. "You let me buy *your* dinner one of those nights."

Jack shook his held emphatically. "No. Absolutely not. I'm a gentleman. I can't let you do that."

"Jack, you're a private. I know how much you get paid." Her eyes narrowed with determination. "If you don't let me buy your dinner one night, then I won't go out with you on either one."

Jack didn't feel right about that at all. "Betty—"

"Jack," she cut him off. "I have money. Let me show you *my* appreciation for your choice to serve in the Army instead of the Marines."

As stubborn as Jack could be, he realized Betty was going to give him a definite run for his money in that department. And if that was the only way he could go out with her twice…"Okay, fine. It's not polite to argue with a lady."

Betty laughed at that. Her eyes pinched at the corners and sparkled happily. "Wonderful."

Then she sighed and her expression softened. "It really *is* great to see you again, Jack."

April 2, 1943

The filming began the next morning. Jack and the four dozen other ski instructors who were asked to be part of the film gathered in one of the newly-completed theaters at the camp to receive their instructions.

"What the hell is *he* doing here?" Jack growled to Steve when Second Lieutenant Aston Hollinghurst walked up on stage to converse with Captain Jay. "He's not an instructor."

"I heard from the guys in the platoon that he's going to take the test soon," Steve admitted. "Maybe that's why."

Jack watched the handsome and suave John Jay chat animatedly with the handsome and suave Aston Hollinghurst—with Betty smiling in between them. The conversation involved lots of nodding and laughing and gesturing and it made Jack uncomfortably sick to his stomach.

How can I compete with any of that?

He mumbled something to that effect to Steve.

"Hey, Oakland. Don't get me wrong when I say this, okay?" Steve leaned a little closer and lowered his voice. "You're a good-looking guy. You're what, six feet tall?"

"Six one."

"And you've got that dark hair and blue eyes combination that girls love." Steve grinned. "And all of you have the standard issue body parts, so don't sweat it."

Jack had to laugh at that. "Thanks, buddy."

"No problem."

Hollinghurst had apparently gotten what he wanted—*didn't guys like him always?*—and after shaking Jay's hand he descended the steps to the stage and took a seat in the front row.

Betty smiled up at Captain Jay, said something Jack couldn't hear, and then followed Hollinghurst to the front row. Jay stepped up to the microphone.

"All right, let's get started. First of all, as Public Relations Officer for Camp Hale, I am very excited about this project, and grateful to Warner Brothers Studios for their participation." Jay started the applause.

When it died down, he continued. "Now I'll bring the director of the film onstage, Mr. B. Reeves Eason, and he's going to explain the process to us and give us our assignments."

A middle-aged man ambled on stage from the wings and stood in front of the microphone. He carried a clipboard and wore reading glasses perched halfway down his nose.

"Gentlemen, thank you for your willingness to be part of our project, *Mountain Fighters*. We'll be filming in Technicolor, with multiple cameras at each location, and the finished documentary will be approximately twenty minutes long."

Eason looked down at his notes. "Let me introduce the actors so you'll know who they are."

Five men walked onto the stage and turned to face the assembled soldiers.

"John Ridgely will be playing Lieutenant Evers, Peter Whitney is Sergeant Blake, Warren Douglas is Private Kramer, Frank Wilcox is the Camp Commander, and Henry Rowland will be a volunteer instructor from Norway."

As Eason called each actor's name, the man stepped forward, waved, and stepped back into the line. Every one of them looked like they'd been stamped from the mold of a Nordic god.

Jack had to wonder how Betty wasn't smitten with every single one of them.

Or maybe she was.

Her adoration of Captain John Jay was as clear as it was the first time he met her, and once again the idea surfaced that maybe more than a work relationship passed between her and her long-time family friend.

I'll ask her tonight, he decided.

It was far better to be disappointed now, than be surprised later.

"I'm going to split you men into four groups of twelve, and each group will demonstrate a different skill on different parts of Cooper Hill. This way, we can get you back to your training as soon as possible."

Steve groaned. "No. Take your time," he whispered.

Jack smothered a chuckle.

"There are four buses outside to take you to the sets, and your name will be on one of the lists so you know which bus to get on." Eason reached up and removed his glasses. "The crews are already setting up. Go grab your skis and let's get going."

*****

Jack waited for the signal that would send him down the hill. His group was demonstrating the slalom, so of course Hollinghurst was there as well. Jack avoided his platoon leader as much as possible, until Hollinghurst jostled him sharply from behind and nearly knocked him to the ground.

"Hey!" Jack barked not daring to say more to his commanding officer.

"Watch where you're standing, Private," Hollinghurst sneered. "You're getting in the way."

Jack glared at the lieutenant from behind his green goggles, his jaw clamped shut. But he didn't move.

The signal came and Hollinghurst skied off with two other men to begin their swerving descent.

Asshole.

Now it was Jack's turn. "Want to make it interesting?" he asked the two men waiting with him.

"How?" one of them asked.

"Let's see who can make the most slalom turns." Jack shrugged. "Count your own and go on the honor system. What d'ya say?"

"Sure."

"I'm in."

The horn blasted from below, and Jack pushed off first, skiing left, then right, then left, and right again. Jack zigged and zagged his way down the slope, weaving in and out between his mates while they laughed and shouted good natured insults along the way.

He hadn't had this much fun in ages.

They passed camera after camera on the mile-long run and Jack grinned broadly at every one of them. By the time he reached the bottom his thighs were quivering with exhaustion.

"Fifty three," one of his companions said. "You?"

"Fifty nine."

"Sixty two." Jack chuckled. "And now if you'll excuse me, I'm going to sit down before my legs give out on their own."

When the skiers were bused back to the camp at the end of the day they found nearly every soldier remaining in Camp Hale dressed in their snow camouflage and marching in formation through the camp streets past more cameras.

"That'll be impressive for sure," Steve said once the friends found each other. "Thousands of Ski Troopers all dressed in white is something America's never seen before."

Jack agreed. "I wonder if my father will see this. When did they say it'll be released?"

"He didn't. Why don't you ask Betty tonight?"

Jack nodded. "I will."

Among other things.

Chapter Eleven

Jack rode the camp bus into Leadville that evening to have dinner with Betty. He walked from the drop-off point to the little inn where she was staying and waited for the proprietor to call her down from her room.

Betty appeared at the top of the stairs wearing a yellow dress which was Jack's favorite color—the color of Aspen leaves in the fall.

And it set off her green eyes beautifully.

Jack helped Betty don her coat and scarf, and then offered her his arm. "Where should we eat?"

"There's a little Italian place around the corner," she offered. "Do you like Italian food?"

Jack grinned. "Who doesn't?"

The restaurant was three blocks from the inn. Jack held Betty's arm so she wouldn't slip on the icy sidewalks. Striated clouds looked like gauzy ribbons overhead and a crystal ring circled the moon. While they walked, Jack told Betty about his day of filming.

"My legs are so stiff right now," he admitted with a rueful smile. "But maybe we'll make it into the final film. We were skiing like madmen."

"I think the director will let John see what scenes he's shot," Betty offered. "I might be able to go with him. Then I could let you know if he likes the one you're in."

"That'd be great." Jack opened the door to the restaurant and a gust of cold air from behind them preceded their entry. "Do you know when the film will be released?"

Betty stepped inside and answered over her shoulder. "John says August is the target. Before school starts."

Jack waited until he and Betty had placed their orders and a carafe of Chianti was set on their table before he broached the subject that weighed so heavily on his mind. "Can I ask you about John?"

"Sure," she said while Jack poured her a glass of the red wine.

"I know he's a family friend and that he got married over a year ago," Jack said carefully. He filled his own glass before asking, "But why didn't he marry you?"

Betty began to twirl a lock of her shoulder-length brunette hair. She looked like she was trying very hard not to react to the question's impact on her emotions.

"What an odd question, Jack." She sipped her wine and didn't meet his eyes.

"It's not odd, Betty." *Still need a nickname for her.* "Because it's obvious to me that you're in love with him."

The hair-twirling momentarily stilled and her widened eyes cut to his. "What?"

"Maybe love's too strong a word," Jack back-pedaled. "But if I was to guess, I'd say you've had a crush on him since you were younger."

Betty's gaze flicked away from him and then back. The hair twirling resumed.

"I was still eleven when it started. He just turned sixteen."

"But you got older…" Jack let the comment dangle.

Betty shook her head. "I was fourteen when he went away to college. He never gave me a single thought."

"But he didn't get married until he was twenty-seven," Jack pushed. "You were twenty-three and out of college by then."

Betty's eyes filled with angry tears. "What do you want from me, Jack?"

Jack reached for her hand but she pulled it out of the way. "I just want to know if I have competition for your heart."

"Competition?" she yelped. "He's a married man!"

"Does he act like one?"

Betty's jaw fell open and her dark brows plunged dangerously. "Exactly what are you suggesting, Jack?"

"Nothing on your part," Jack said quickly. "Cross my heart!"

Betty glared across the table at him. "John Jay is an absolute pillar of integrity."

"As are you, Betty. I know that." Jack shrugged helplessly and gave her an apologetic look. "But he's—he's—"

"He's what, Jack?"

At the risk of sounding unmanly, Jack spoke the truth. "He's handsome. And charming. And persuasive."

Betty's expression shifted and she stared at him, horrified. "Do people think we're having an affair?"

"I don't think—I don't know." That was the truth.

"But *you* wondered."

Jack sighed. "We can't always help who we fall for, can we?"

Betty took another drink of the Chianti and dabbed her eyes with her napkin before she answered. "No. We can't. But nothing inappropriate—not one *single* thing—has ever happened between us."

"I believe you, Betty." This time she didn't pull her hand out of his reach. "I just needed to clear the air. I mean, you're so beautiful that men flock to you. Handsome and rich men, especially."

She huffed. "Having valuable things doesn't make anyone a valuable person."

Jack flashed a sly grin. "Score a point for the guy from Oakland, then."

Their dinner was served, halting their conversation for a moment. That silence seemed to help dispel some of the intensity of their uncomfortable discussion.

When the waiter left Betty didn't pick up her fork. Instead she sat with her hands in her lap and gazed intently at Jack. "That took guts."

"What?" He figured he knew but asked anyway.

"To ask me about John. Considering everything you were thinking."

Jack set his fork down. "I care for you, Betty. But I need to know if there's a chance for us before I keep writing to you."

Betty's eyes moved to her fork. She picked it up. "That's fair."

Jack tipped his head to the side. "Is there? A chance for us?"

Her green eyes were still watery but her regard was steady. Her cheeks dimpled though she wasn't fully smiling. "I'm buying you dinner tomorrow night, aren't I?"

April 11, 1943

Eason and his film crew were leaving Camp Hale after nine days of filming and re-shooting a variety of scenes. Jack had been able to go out with Betty on Friday and Saturday of both weekends that she and Jay were at the camp. And when he asked her to, Betty wore the yellow dress again.

Last night when he escorted her back to the inn he finally got up the nerve to kiss her.

Jack leaned forward and tentatively placed his lips on hers. Betty reached up and looped her arms around his neck, encouraging him to take the kiss deeper, to add more urgency.

He did.

They stood in front of the inn for at least a quarter of an hour, holding each other close and exploring their physical connection. For Jack, Betty's kisses were like no other he'd ever experienced. He lost track of time and place, focusing on the taste of her in his mouth and the feel of her body pressed tightly against his.

"Wow…" he breathed when he pulled away from her at last.

"That was nice, Jack," Betty whispered.

Jack wrapped his arms around her and rested his chin on top of her head. "I wish I knew when I'll see you again."

"Just keep writing to me, Jack. Whenever you can. And I'll do the same," she promised. After a moment she added, "And please, always be honest with me. Just like tonight."

Jack knew better than to try and kiss Betty goodbye before she climbed into the bus with the actors and film crew. It brought enough unwanted attention that he was there to see her off.

Hollinghurst sidled up next to him. "She's out of your league, Franklin."

Fuck you.

"I know."

"She asked me to write to her."

His platoon leader's words cut a jagged slash through Jack's gut, but he couldn't let the lieutenant see that. Had she really—or was he lying just to get under Jack's skin?

If she did, Jack figured her request was just a ploy to make Hollinghurst leave her alone.

After all, letters don't have to be answered.

"Good for you." Jack turned around to walk away.

"You know the snow's melting, right?" Hollinghurst called after him.

Jack turned back around. "So?"

"So when it does, all the ski instructors return to their units." Hollinghurst sneered. "I'll be waiting, Franklin."

"You forgot the other option, sir."

"What? Be assigned as a rock climbing instructor?" Hollinghurst made a face. "You should be so lucky."

Jack smiled grimly. "I agree. Sir."

Then he saluted and walked away.

May 6, 1943

The changeover from ski instructor to climbing instructor had to be done in such a way that ensured the mountain climbing was taught with as much skill and competency as the skiing had been.

"Falling on your skis can break a leg," Jack pointed out to Pete and Steve. "But falling off a cliff can break your head."

"You going for climbing instructor, too?" Pete asked.

"I've been climbing with the Sierra Club since I was a kid," Jack said. "Don't see why not."

"It'll keep you away from A.H.," Steve snickered.

Pete frowned. "A.H.?"

Jack looked around before he answered quietly. "Aston Hollinghurst."

"Or ass hole," Steve added. "Either one works."

Steve hadn't had any trouble with the second lieutenant, but obviously he noticed how Hollinghurst treated Jack. Whenever the opportunity arose, Hollinghurst baited Jack, trying to push him to the point of insubordination.

So far Jack had held strong. After all, he had some high level training in that skill by dealing with his own father.

But he hadn't told Steve or Pete about Hollinghurst's claim that Betty asked him to write to her. And he hadn't asked Betty if it was true. After his last confrontational conversation with her, Jack figured he should take it easy for a while.

He's probably lying anyway.

June 3, 1943

A week ago Jack saw something walking into the camp that he never imagined he'd see: women. Wearing uniforms. Uniforms that were a lot like his.

Steve showed him the article on the front page of the Camp Hale newspaper, the *Ski-Zette*. "On the fourteenth of May last year, Congress approved the creation of a Women's Army Auxiliary Corps. WAACs for short."

"Are they part of the Army?" Jack scanned the article.

"No..." Steve said slowly like Jack was simple. "They're *auxiliary*."

"This is an advance detail from Fort Des Moines, Iowa. It says a hundred and forty more are coming next week." Jack looked at Steve. "So what are they doing here?"

"They'll replace soldiers in non-combat-related stuff, like administration and nursing." Steve took the newspaper back from Jack. "It remains to be seen if they can handle the altitude, though."

Now Jack watched the newly arrived group of a hundred and fifty-odd women as a sergeant showed them around the mess hall. They were all trim and attractive in their drab green uniforms, as if decent looks was a requirement for enlistment.

"Having women around won't be bad," he mused. "And if they're looking for husbands, they'll have plenty to choose from."

Steve punched Jack's arm. "Should Betty worry, Oakland?"

Jack punched him back. "Shut up, Dropout. Let's go see if they posted the instructors who made it into the climbing group yet."

Jack and Steve crossed the camp to the Mountain Training Center. Both of them—plus Pete Seibert—had applied and been asked to show basic skills like harnessing and knot tying. Jack actually ended up showing some of the candidates when they wound the ropes the wrong way, so he was pretty confident of his place.

He wasn't around when Steve and Pete had their evaluations, but he hoped his friends made it, too. The three men enjoyed a relaxed camaraderie that offset the physical strain of their tough training, and Jack looked forward to continuing to work with them.

"Franklin... Knowlton..." Jack's finger skimmed down the list. "And Seibert!"

He grinned at Steve. "The three musketeers are still together."

"Don't you mean the three *mountaineers?*" Steve joked.

"Hey—they gave us those forty-year-old bolt-action Enfield rifles to practice with," Jack countered. "*Musket*-teers isn't that far off!"

June 7, 1943

Indoctrination began early the next morning for the troops who would be going through the climbing instruction.

The initial training area for rock climbing was right in Camp Hale, as opposed to Cooper Hill which was six miles away. Troops could make the short march to the instruction area and watch their introduction to climbing relatively easily.

Now, less than a week into their summer season training, Jack and the other instructors were in gear and on the rocks when Brigadier General Rolfe came to announce that Lieutenant General Leslie McNair—the officer in charge of Army Ground Forces—was coming to at Camp Hale for an inspection.

"McNair's never been in favor of the idea of special troops," Rolfe told the instructors.

I thought you felt the same…

"He's also the type of guy who has to see things for himself in order to make a decision. So we're going to put on a show for him."

"What sort of show, General?" one brave soldier asked.

Rolfe squinted up at the man who was hanging on the rock face about twenty feet above Jack. "We're gonna spruce this place up so it shines like a new penny. And you men—" Rolfe waved a finger in their general direction. "You're going to put on a demonstration that'll impress him."

We are?

Jack was confused until he remembered Rolfe's contention that they were *mountain* troops, not ski troops. With that limited mindset, showing off the rock climbing made sense. He wondered what their demonstration would entail exactly, but he didn't ask. He was afraid that the brigadier general might actually make some suggestions.

"Yes, sir!" he called down instead. "Do we know when?"

Rolfe shifted his gaze to Jack. "You've got three days."

June 10, 1943

Rolfe made good on his promise. He had every soldier who wasn't climbing the rock faces assigned to sweeping, trimming, hosing off, and shoveling until the grounds looked better than new. By the time McNair arrived, there wasn't a single cigarette butt or spent casing to be found anywhere.

Jack and the other instructors worked out a demonstration of mountain climbing techniques between them and did not allow recruits to take part. Harsh memories of the Homestake debacle still stung, and the men wanted to ensure a seamless presentation this time.

"Rolfe told McNair that the reason Homestake was such a disaster was because there was a lack of physical fitness in the troops," Friedl Pfeiffer told the ski instructors at the time. "He said that the Army's sending raw recruits who had no skills was the main problem here."

The climbing instructors couldn't let a mess like that happen again. And they didn't.

"Thank you, gentlemen," Lieutenant General McNair said when the two-hour-long demonstration ended. "I'm very impressed."

Jack sighed his relief and wiped his sweating brow. "Thank you, General."

"Morale at Camp Hale seems high." McNair's statement was obviously a question.

"Yes, sir," several instructors chorused.

He nodded and considered the assembled instructors and curious spectators thoughtfully. "The men I've observed today are energetic, well organized, practical, and in excellent physical condition."

Several instructors nodded. "Thank you, sir."

Once McNair started heading toward camp headquarters, Jack heaved a huge sigh of relief.

We did it.

Chapter
Twelve

June 11, 1943

Word reached Camp Hale the next day that the Eighty-Seventh Mountain Infantry Regiment was going to be deployed for a combat assignment. Apparently Army planners concluded the soldiers at Camp Hale should be given the opportunity to demonstrate their unique capabilities.

At least Pops would be happy to hear about that.

For Jack it meant he was no longer a climbing instructor. His temporary additional duty was abruptly ended and he would return to his platoon immediately—and fall back under Hollinghurst's authority as an infantry soldier in I Company.

Jack and Steve attended a briefing in one of the camp theaters that same afternoon, waiting impatiently to hear what they were going to be doing.

A captain Jack didn't know stepped up to the microphone and gazed at the assembled division. "Welcome, gentlemen. Let's get started. You all know that back on June seventh of last year the Japs occupied Attu and Kiska, landing ten thousand troops. And on May eleventh of *this* year, the Army invaded Attu in order to take that island back from the Japanese."

"Did you know about this?" Jack asked Steve.

Steve shook his head.

The captain paused. His expression held a decent amount of disgust. "Unfortunately, the invasion force that went to Attu was neither well led nor properly equipped for Arctic conditions."

"Why didn't they send us?" Jack whispered.

"Bet they are now," Steve whispered back.

"Their combat boots were totally inadequate. Trench foot was rampant. Frostbite was common. In short, it was miserable for everyone." The captain sighed. "On the battle front, the Japanese took positions on the high ground, forcing our crippled soldiers to attack uphill."

He looked up from his notes and gave a little shrug. "In the end the enemy staged a banzai charge but, in spite of the ragged condition of our soldiers, we prevailed triumphantly and took Attu."

The captain closed his folder. "I'm sure you can see now where this briefing is headed. Once General Marshall heard the after-action reports and the steep toll on our men, he asked if the Army had any troops that *were* adequately prepared to fight in Arctic conditions."

A startled rumble rippled through the assemblage.

The captain smiled and nodded. "Now it's your turn to show the Army what our *very* special troops can do. Go pack your gear. You leave on Sunday."

A spontaneous and deafening cheer shook the theater.

*****

Once his gear was ready and before lights out, Jack tucked into his bunk and wrote Betty a letter. He'd just written her the day before, but now his situation had drastically changed.

Dear Betty,

We got big news today. Tomorrow we are being sent to Fort Ord in California for amphibious training (don't ask me what that is) and then we'll be deployed for combat against the Japs.

All this time we've been thinking we were going to fight Nazis in Europe, but now we'll be fighting Japs in an

American Territory. And, we won't even need to take our skis.

How's that for a kick in the pants?

Anyway, I won't be able to get any of your letters while we're gone but I want you to keep writing to me. When we get back to Camp Hale after this is over, I'll want to sit down and catch up with you.

Because I will come back.

Jack stopped writing. One thing weighed heavily on his mind and he debated with himself whether he should say anything to Betty about it. But if he didn't say it to her, there wasn't anyone else he could say it to without feeling embarrassed.

Jack pulled a deep breath and resumed writing.

I am scared about one thing though. I'm going to be honest with you like we promised and tell you what that is.

I've never killed anyone before, obviously. So I'm afraid of how shooting men dead might affect me.

How will I go back to a normal life after killing Japs or Nazis? Or seeing my friends die? Will the memories of the dead haunt me the rest of my life?

I don't want to end up so rigid like my father. He was a good dad, don't get me wrong, but he went through some rough stuff during the first war and it had to have changed him.

It will change me as well, I suppose. That can't be avoided. I only hope I can remain the sort of man who deserves a woman like you.

Anyway, that's it. I hope you don't think I'm weak for writing this, because I fully intend to fight with all my might. I joined the Army to use my skills to win this war and that's exactly what I plan to do.

I really miss you a lot, Betty. Maybe we'll get a chance to see each other when I get back, though I don't know how long that will be. In the meantime, keep me in your thoughts and prayers, and in your heart, because you are always in mine.

Yours,

Jack

June 13, 1943

Five months after the three battalions of the Eighty-Seventh Regiment had arrived at Camp Hale, the soldiers boarded the train at Pando Station and headed for Fort Ord on Monterey Bay in California—about two hours south of Oakland.

"You're so close to home," Steve said as he gazed at the Pacific Ocean. "So this is what your world looks like."

"Yep." Jack felt good to be back in his home territory. "What do you think? Mountains or the ocean?"

Steve pulled at the front of his damp uniform. "On a hot day like this, that water looks mighty inviting, I have to admit."

The Eighty-Seventh soldiers were initially put through training in standard infantry tactics, which frustrated Jack and pretty much every other soldier that came with him.

"We know this stuff," Steve grumbled. "Why are they wasting our time?"

"At least the classes on Japanese weapons and tactics are interesting," Jack replied. "But judo? What do they expect us to do? Drop our rifles, run up to 'em, throw 'em on the ground, and they'll just surrender?"

Unfortunately, Second Lieutenant Hollinghurst overheard Jack's rant. "Do as you're told, Private. Any more complaints out of you and I'll send you back to Hale to repeat your basic training there."

Jack's jaw clenched and his hands curled into fists. "Yes, sir."

Relief arrived that afternoon in the form of an old Marine troop ship sailing into Monterey Bay. Apparently the amphibious part of their training was finally going to begin.

Jack and the rest of the Eighty-Seventh were trucked to the dock and taken to the ship via amphibious landing craft called Higgins Boats. While fitted out with full combat gear, the soldiers had to climb up landing nets to board the ship as both rocked in the ocean's waves.

After everyone in the Eighty-Seventh was onboard the ship, the bellowing Marine sergeants in charge of the Army soldiers' training ordered them to climb back down the nets and reboard the landing craft. Jack shook his head.

Pops would have a field day with this.

July 2, 1943

And the ammunition seemed to just keep piling up on his dad's side. Today's newspaper headlines proclaimed that yesterday afternoon President Franklin D. Roosevelt signed a bill appointing women to the Army of the United States.

In ninety days from today, the Women's Army Auxiliary Corps (WAAC) will be discontinued and replaced by the Women's Army Corps (WAC). All enlisted women will receive full military status and the benefits thereof.

Jack figured his father would have a stroke when he heard about this. Imagine—his oldest son was serving in the Army alongside a bunch of women.

Jack sighed, wondering how soon this scathing letter would arrive at Camp Hale and if he should just flush it again instead of reading it.

It could easily be worse. If Pops had any inkling that Jack was training so close to home, he just might just make a trip down here to talk to the seasoned Marines leading their training about the sad state of the Army, and about the son he was so disappointed in.

If only the Marines had started this.

July 26, 1943

The Eighty-Seventh soldiers endured endless judo classes, and the repeated boarding and disembarking routine for weeks, through blistering sunshine, sharp wind, and dense morning fog. The only break in the monotony came on July fifteenth.

"As of today, the troops at Camp Hale will no longer be call Ski Troops or Mountain Troops," their commanding officer informed the assembled Eighty-Seventh when their day was finished. "From this point on, we'll be known as the Tenth Light Division—Alpine, under the Eleventh Corps of the Second Army."

Steve looked at Jack. "We really sound official now."

Jack agreed. "I just hope that hurries up the end of training and gets us into the war."

Eleven days later, the Marine sergeants finally released the Eighty-Seventh soldiers and sent the division south for testing at Camp Pendleton, the Marine base near San Diego.

Jack was very glad to put distance between himself and any possibility that his father might catch wind of what he had been doing for the last six weeks so close to Oakland. But being surrounded by Marines did make him wonder how his brother Harry was doing.

Camp Pendleton was Harry's base, though Harry was somewhere in the Pacific. Letters from their mother relayed to Jack as much as Harry was able to tell her, but the letters were sparse. There were no post offices in the middle of the ocean.

At Camp Pendleton another set of Marine sergeants tested the men to be certain they could actually disembark the troopship, climb down the nets, enter the Higgins Boats, proceed to the shore, wade ashore, attack inland, and engage a non-existent enemy.

And of course, they could.

"They act like we're stupid," Jack grumbled.

"Marines think everyone who isn't a Marine is stupid," Steve observed. "Now I understand what you've told me about your dad."

After the test, the Marines sailed them back up the coast to San Francisco Harbor. There they were loaded into a larger troop ship, the *USS Grant*, which would finally take the Eighty-Seventh Mountain Regiment north toward their objective: the Japanese-held island of Kiska.

August 10, 1943

After fourteen days of sailing north, Jack decided that the next time he had to sail anywhere he would try to find a way to stay on deck for all of his waking hours, no matter the weather or the task. The constant motion of the waves made him queasy and the difficulty of sleeping in an enclosed bunk that was an inch shorter than he was meant he couldn't ever get comfortable.

One of the Army's requirements for soldiers being sent into battle was that they write a letter to those who would survive them. Jack sat at a table, pen in hand, and wondered what the hell he was going to say to his father.

Gee, I guess I'm dead, Pops wasn't going to cut muster.

Because he couldn't get the picture of his father's disappointed sneer out of his head, Jack decided to write the letter with his mother in mind and just address it to both of them. His mother would be devastated if Jack died, and he truly believed his father would be, too.

But Mom won't put the blame on me.

The *USS Grant* stopped for three days at the island of Adak—about two hundred miles east of Kiska—and the Eighty-Seventh was briefed on the battle plan. That's where they found out they were part of a larger force than Jack ever imagined.

The three thousand men of the Eighty-Seventh Mountain Infantry joined three other Army infantry regiments, along with the Thirteenth Canadian Infantry Brigade and additional artillery, communications, and associated supporting units. Thirty thousand men in all.

"We're all part of Operation Cottage," Hollinghurst told their platoon as he passed out circular Long Knife shoulder patches for their uniforms. "Our orders are simple: just go and get 'em."

August 15, 1943

When they reached Kiska two days later, the Eighty-Seventh's job was to go ashore first and take the high ground, with the three other Army regiments following right behind them. Jack's battalion—the Third—was assigned to attack the southwestern leg of the island.

Before they left the ship, Hollinghurst gave the platoon the operation's challenge and password. "If you don't know who you're facing, shout *long limb*," the second lieutenant instructed. "The password response is *that thing*. Got it?"

Steve smothered a laugh with the palm of his hand. "I know Headquarters assumes the Japs can't say those words right, so now all I can think of is *rong rimb* and *dat ding*."

The soldiers crowded against each other on the deck of the swaying Higgins boat, shoulder to shoulder and lined up to take the beach. The frost-laden wind beat against them without mercy and the boat rocked in the shallow water like a drunken sailor.

Jack followed the man in front of him and launched himself into the surf.

Though still liquid, the salt water was freezing—literally thirty-two degrees—and Jack's calves immediately cramped. He splashed through the roiling seawater and onto solid ground, then tried to trot up the rocky beach's incline on unsteady legs which had gone numb in the frigid water.

The fog that morning was so thick that even Jack, who hailed from the San Francisco Bay Area, had never experienced such low visibility. And this envelope of cloying wet mist was nothing like their night maneuvers because it couldn't be pierced with a flashlight.

The wind screeched over the small, mountainous island with a breath-stealing force that Jack had never felt before. Even though he could make out the forms of the soldiers flanking him ten feet on either side, he couldn't hear anything they might be saying. The roaring wind blew away their words as if they hadn't been spoken.

Just do what we've been told to do.

The fog made their maps useless because the reference points were completely obscured. Jack's platoon knew they were assigned to take the high ground, so they just kept moving uphill in the stinging mist and tried to keep each other in sight.

The summer's ground on the thawed tundra was soggy and muddy, and pulled at their boots with every step. Jack began to pant with the exertion of fighting the grasping ground just to take another step up the steep incline.

His heart beat so hard in his ears that even without the bitter wind he'd have trouble hearing Hollinghurst's passed message: "Stay alert—the enemy's close."

The three I Company platoons took positions on a hill above Gertrude Cove, one of the landing beaches, though they had to trust their compasses for their location as visibility was still zero.

Jack couldn't help but wonder why the Japs weren't defending the beaches. Was it because of the fog? Maybe they didn't know the forces had landed.

But we weren't silent.

And we're on the move from several directions.

He, and probably Hollinghurst, expected there would be radio reports of enemy engagements by now. The Japs were known to be a vicious, tenacious enemy, and the Army expected to encounter ten thousand Japanese troops on Kiska.

But the radio remained silent.

Jack heard a lot of random rifle fire, though. Every time he thought he saw a helmet pop up through the thankfully thinning fog somebody started shooting at it.

The Third Battalion Headquarters was supposed to be set up in a sheltered area on the island, and after a distant burst of machine gun fire, the radio finally crackled to life.

"Reg HQ—this is Third Blue. We are surrounded. Request immediate reinforcement."

When the machine guns started firing again, the soldiers all around his platoon started firing as well.

Jack aimed his rifle at anything that moved. Thankfully their antiquated bolt-action Enfields from training had been replaced with Garand eight-shots. With the Garand he could shoot in rapid succession.

The problem was, he couldn't tell if he was aiming at a Jap or an American. Were those figures in the fog the Japs surrounding his battalion's headquarters? Or were they the reinforcement troops coming to the rescue?

Jack felt a tug that pulled his left hand from his rifle and a searing sting set his arm on fire

I've been shot.

He looked at his sleeve, alarmed. Several inches below his shoulder the fabric of his field jacket was ripped away. Jack flexed his arm trying to assess the wound, causing blood to soak the edges of the torn sleeve. He had full range of motion though, even if it hurt like hell.

I'll live.

He resettled his grip on his rifle and ignored the pain for now, even as warm blood ran down the inside of his sleeve.

Through the gradually dissipating fog, Jack saw two second lieutenants lead their platoons downward, presumably in search of Battalion Headquarters. With an explosion of rifle fire from several directions, both of the officers and three of the soldiers went down.

Jack heard a multitude of shouted orders to *cease fire* and calls for the medics passing up and down the line. Because the fog, wind, and mist had soaked his clothes and rifle, he took that opportunity to change the clip just in case, and returned to ready position.

Though blood still trickled down to his elbow, Jack's wound wasn't life threatening and he'd deal with it when the battle ended. There was no point in calling the medics away from the men in sprawled front of him who might actually be dying.

When no order to resume fire came their way after half an hour, Jack and the rest of the platoon in his sight dug their foxholes and waited.

The hours passed agonizingly slowly, with the cease fire order remaining in effect well into the dusk of the pale northern summer's night.

Jack shivered in his mist-dampened clothes and flexed his fingers to keep them from going numb inside his gloves. Water dripped from the edges of his helmet and he watched the drops roll down the sleeves of his field jacket.

A medic made his way along the slanted hillside asking, "Anyone hurt?"

"Here." Jack waved his rifle.

Steve had dug in a couple yards to Jack's right and now looked at him in shock. "You are?"

Jack twisted his torso to show Steve his torn sleeve. "Just my arm."

The medic helped Jack pull his arm out of the jacket, which hurt a hell of a lot more than he let on, and then rolled up his sleeve. "Went clean through. That's good."

He cleaned the wound and sprinkled it with sulfa powder before wrapping it in gauze first, and an Ace bandage after that. "Might have nicked the bone. Can't really tell. How's the pain?"

Jack shrugged with his right shoulder. "Not bad. I've been hurt worse."

The medic unrolled Jack's sleeve, put his arm in a sling, and helped him back into his jacket. "Keep it immobilized and wrapped for a week if you can, then come get it redressed. But if you start to run a fever, come to the hospital tent immediately."

"Got it." Jack's arm throbbed after being disinfected, but the dressing and sling were comforting.

"You qualify for a Purple Heart for being wounded in battle. I'll add you to the list…" He looked at the dog tags hanging against Jack's chest. "Private J. Franklin."

"Thanks."

"Well, well, Oakland," Steve teased when the medic had moved down the line. "Maybe your Pops will be proud of you now."

Jack snorted. "He'll probably just blame me for getting in the bullet's way."

August 17, 1943

It took the Army officers a couple of cold, windy, wet, muddy, and miserable days to sort everything out, and when they did the answers were more than disturbing.

There were no Japanese soldiers on the island. None. Only one Japanese body was found, hidden in a cave.

The Japs had evacuated Kiska at some point, spiriting all ten-thousand of their troops away right under the noses of the American Navy.

And the Marines.

Jack wondered if his dad would realize that if he ever heard about the snafu which was Operation Cottage. The price paid by the Eighty-Seventh for the desolate and deserted island was steep: fifty men were wounded, including Jack. Twenty-four men were shot dead, and four more were killed by Japanese land mines and booby traps.

The twenty-eight casualties were carried to a makeshift morgue near the beach, where their bodies were tightly wrapped with blankets and laid out on litters. The name of each deceased soldier was printed on a casualty card and tied to the bindings.

Jack, Steve, and the other soldiers from I Company went to pay their respects. Even Hollinghurst looked shaken by what happened. He kept wagging his head in scowling denial and rubbed his face with visibly trembling hands.

Jack thanked God that he never shot blindly into the fog, or he might have killed one of these men. Knowing it wasn't his fault they were dead was small comfort against the rage and grief that they all died needlessly.

The I Company Commander was the last to pass through the line. He paused by the two lieutenants and spoke to each of the bodies. "I sure am sorry boys. It should not have happened this way."

Jack stared at the line of bodies. "I was watching them when they died," he told Steve.

"Me, too," Steve said softly. "I don't think I can ever forget that."

Jack gingerly rubbed his wounded arm. He was lucky.

It could have been me.

Chapter Thirteen

August 31, 1943

It took less than a week for Jack and the Third Battalion to find out that they weren't leaving Kiska any time soon.

"All those ships that brought us to Kiska have moved on to other tasks," Hollinghurst told the platoon. "Shipping schedules are made up months in advance, as I well know from personal experience."

Jack grunted.

Hollinghurst couldn't resist pointing that *out.*

"Now, unfortunately, we're a low priority."

"Are you saying we have to stay here because we don't have a ride home? Sir?" Steve's disbelieving expression defined what the men were all probably thinking.

Hollinghurst looked uncomfortable. "Yes. That's exactly what we were told."

"So we're stuck out here at the end of the world?" Jack blurted.

The second lieutenant was clearly so unhappy himself, that this time he didn't bother to chastise Jack for his angry reaction. "We just have to make the best of it."

Since there was absolutely nothing the soldiers could do to change their situation, there was every reason to do what they could to make their indefinite habitat livable.

The stranded soldiers immediately dispersed around the island, scavenging for materials to build shelters. They stripped metal from abandoned Japanese buildings, and carried back anything else they could use to protect themselves against the constant force of the Arctic Ocean winds and the ever-present misting rain.

They even used Jap sandbags to build walls around their pyramid tents, which were dug into the hillsides for protection against the battering wet and windy weather.

When they found out they weren't leaving the island, Jack and Steve volunteered to help build caskets using scavenged planks from the Japanese shacks.

"No man deserves the indignity of rotting in a blanket on this God-forsaken rock," Jack growled as he kneeled on a plank and sawed with his uninjured right arm.

Steve agreed. "And their families should be protected. They shouldn't see this."

Jack's gut clenched when the wind shifted and he smelled the decay. He coughed and spat the stench out of his mouth.

War literally stinks.

Jack grabbed another plank. "Poor bastards."

"Give me a hand, guys?" another soldier asked.

Jack held his breath against the sickly odor as he and Steve helped the man lift a dead soldier into a completed coffin. Long past rigor mortis, the body slumped and rolled and made the task difficult.

Steve straightened once the corpse was in the box and wiped his brow with his sleeve. "Killed by friendly fire. Worst thing to have to tell the families, in my opinion."

"That…" Jack settled the next plank to be cut. "And that they were killed while fighting an enemy that wasn't even there."

September 15, 1943

Jack's arm was healing and he only required one shot of penicillin when the wound started to fester. His main source of discomfort was that his clothes were constantly damp, and that made it hard to stay warm. He and Steve started leading other men in the platoon on runs around the island just to keep their body temperatures up.

As they ran, they explored the island. This particular afternoon Jack and Steve stumbled upon several cases of canned beef that the Japanese left behind.

"Beats the shit out of K-rations," Steve said as they dragged the boxes back to their campsite on a makeshift sled of branches. "I'm tired of cold canned pork."

Jack grinned. "What about the C-rations—candy, chocolate, and crackers for dessert. Yum."

"Don't forget the four cigarettes." Steve rolled his eyes. "Like we don't get enough smoke in our lungs at Hale."

"At least there's plenty of salmon up here." Jack switched hands and kept pulling.

Steve did the same. "Yep. And an endless supply of grenades to kill them with."

*****

Not very sporting I know, Jack wrote to Betty about how they killed the salmon. *But it sure improves our diet.*

Of course he had no way to mail the letters yet. But someday he would, and for now spilling his emotions onto the pages was a temporary distraction from their overall dreadful situation.

> *There are tons of caves and tunnels all over the island and we explore them when we find them. To be honest, the guys are searching for Jap souvenirs to bring home, but I don't see the point. We do have to be careful of booby traps, though, and leftover Japanese ordnance. But so far we've been lucky.*
>
> *Every company in the regiment has hiked to the north end of the island and climbed the volcano here on Kiska. It's the highest point on the island, and on those rare clear days we can see it from where we are camped.*
>
> *Speaking of clear days, there aren't many of them. There's always wind and mist here. We're cold and wet all the time and we can never get dry. And the blasted wind blows the tents down all the time.*

I guess we're actually supposed to be testing the equipment here so things can be better if we ever go to Europe. Besides our tents blowing down, we also found out that they leak. Lucky us!

And our boots don't prevent trench foot at all. That's a really big problem. Guys are seeing the medics all the time for it. I've escaped it so far, but I do change my socks every day and dry them over a fire.

To pass the endless time we play a lot of cards and craps, using rocks to bet with. Sometimes we even read the Bibles a few guys packed along. Some of those battles in the Old Testament are pretty epic.

Other than that, we don't have anything to do. We're all so tired of being bored and wet. It's made a few of the guys edgy, and some of them act like they're about to crack.

One afternoon our platoon's second lieutenant said he was going to look for the ships and he wandered off. After a couple hours Steve and I went looking for him. We found him on a hill, insisting he could see the Navy battleship approaching.

We had to convince him to come back and radio the ship before he'd return to camp. By the time we got back his mind had cleared. He said, "Sorry, guys, There wasn't a ship. Just clouds that played tricks on my eyes."

I was glad because I sure didn't want to have to report him.

As you can imagine, none of us has been paid since we left Camp Hale, but even if we had been there's no place to buy anything. We're stuck on a damned miserable island stranded in the middle of absolutely nowhere.

October 15, 1943

The wretched autumn weather on Kiska never changed, but the daylight grew shorter and the darkness longer with each passing day. That depressing shift just added to the soldiers' overall melancholy.

The regiment was returning home in drips and drabs as ships with available space swung by Kiska to gather whomever they could. They retrieved the dead first, of course, and the wounded and sick went with them. The better a soldier's health, the longer he was doomed to stay in this hellhole.

And Jack, unfortunately, had the constitution of an ox.

He did have one thing to be happy about—the senior sergeants of the Third Battalion unexpectedly promoted both him and Steve to corporal.

They said we deserved it, he wrote to Betty the day their promotions were announced. *Because we both kept our heads when so many were losing theirs. And they also said they could depend on me to get things done.*

Jack smiled. He knew his girl would be proud of him when she was finally able to read this.

Hollinghurst burst into the mess tent at lunch, beaming uncharacteristically. "We're next!"

"Next for what?" Steve asked.

"A ship!" Hollinghurst was practically dancing. "Day after tomorrow we'll be on our way back to San Francisco!"

"Hope it's a real ship this time," Jack muttered once Hollinghurst departed.

Steve choked and spit his coffee.

November 1, 1943

Jack survived the sailing back to San Francisco better than he had the trip up to Kiska because, even with the constant nauseating motion, conditions on the ship were so much better than those on the island. For starters, he was dry. And he was warm. The food was hot. He slept in a bunk. There were showers.

And, he could finally get out of the wind.

Once they docked on the first of November, the soldiers returning from Kiska were given furloughs with orders to report back to Camp Hale by November fifteenth. Jack was so close to his parents' house, he figured he'd get a good ten days of his mother's home cooking before he had to board the train back to Colorado.

There was a time in his life when he couldn't imagine leaving

California. Now he thought of Colorado as home. He smiled to himself.

Must be the draw of skiing those endless mountains.

He decided not to bring up anything about their disastrous deployment when he arrived and to wait and see what his father already knew.

And then he'd only admit what he had to.

"Jack!" Edyta threw her hands around him and started bawling when he walked into the house. That was exactly what he expected her to do.

"You're so skinny," she scolded when she finally let go of him. "What do you want to eat?"

"Anything, Mom," he answered truthfully. "If it doesn't come in a can that I have to open with my bayonet, I'll love it."

When his father got home from work, Jack noticed a little softening in his Pops' attitude toward him. Edyta told him that John was following the news of the war from the newspapers and radio, hoping to hear anything he could about where his sons were.

"So you've seen action now?" John asked. "In Alaska?"

"Yes, sir," Jack answered the question in the way he'd become accustomed to. "And while we were in Kiska I was promoted to corporal."

John's brow lifted. "Really?"

"Yep." Jack shoved a forkful of stuffed cabbage into his mouth before he offered an explanation. "I was recognized as a good and dependable soldier. I kept my head in battle."

John looked at Jack and Jack swore he saw the first glimmer of respect in his father's expression. "Good for you, son."

Jack smiled a little. Harry hadn't been promoted, last he heard. "Oh—and I'm getting a Purple Heart."

"What?" The question exploded from a wide-eyed Edyta who whirled away from the stove. "Were you shot?"

"The bullet just hit my arm, Mom," Jack hurried to assure her. "I'm fine now."

"Damn Japs," John muttered.

Jack felt an undeniable stab of guilt. He realized that he was going to have to tell his father the truth eventually. Pops was bound to find out at some point anyway from one of his Marine buddies— or even from Harry.

"It was actually friendly fire, Pops."

John's expression shifted to concern. "How did that happen?"

Jack glanced at his obviously worried mother, and then faced his father again. "I'll tell you after supper."

*****

After pie and coffee, Jack sat in the living room with his father and told him everything that happened during his three-month deployment in Kiska, including the lack of correct military intelligence that precipitated the whole mess in the first place.

"They snuck off the island and the Navy guys didn't even notice," Jack said carefully, wondering if Pops would make the connection.

He did. "The Marines missed them too, then."

"Yes, sir. They certainly did."

Pops' expression was grim. "How bad was it?"

Jack drew a deep breath. "Twenty-four Eighty-Seventh men were killed by our own soldiers because of the damned fog, and because we believed there actually *were* ten thousand Japs on that island shooting back at us."

An unsmiling John listened intently, asking a dozen or more questions about the Third Battalion, the officers, and the noncommissioned officers. Jack answered as best he could. "Did you shoot your weapon, son?"

Jack shook his head. "No, sir."

"Why not?" his father pressed. "Were you scared?"

Jack hesitated, thinking about how to answer. "I wasn't scared of shooting my rifle. But I was concerned about taking a life."

"That's your job," John grumbled.

"I know." Jack scowled at his father. "And I'll do it when the time comes."

"How will you know?"

"I'll be able to *see* my enemy, Pops!" Jack almost shouted. "Not shoot my own men!"

John seemed satisfied with that answer because he changed the subject. "This guy Steve, he was promoted too?"

His battle-experienced father was clearly trying to understand the quality of men that Jack was serving with, but the sudden shift in the conversation was unsettling.

Jack leaned back in his chair and tried to relax after his angry outburst. "Yes, sir."

"Where's he from?"

"He went to college in New Hampshire."

"So he's one of those rich Eastern college boys, eh?" Pops' tone shouted his disdain.

Jack anger began to surface again. "*Most* of the officers in the Eighty-Seventh come from northeastern states. They went to some of the best colleges and several are pretty wealthy."

"How well did those blue blood guys fight?" John pressed.

"They did a damned fine job. Sir."

"They held up under the conditions?"

"Better than you'd expect." Aston Hollinghurst's moment of weakness flashed through Jack's mind. "For the most part."

John sighed and he got a distant look in his eyes. "In nineteen-eighteen in France we lived in the wet and mud for months. I know what that's like." His gaze refocused on Jack's. "Did you get trench foot?"

Jack shook his head. "No, sir. I dried my socks over the fire every night."

John nodded. "Good. That's good."

November 2, 1943

Jack went to the post office the next day to mail twelve letters to Betty. He thought to number them on the back of the envelopes so she'd read them in order. He also added a post script to the last one, saying that he wouldn't get any letters she wrote him until he returned to Camp Hale on November fifteenth, but he'd write again after he did.

On the walk back home he passed a movie theater and stopped to see what was playing.

Bullets and Saddles starring Ray "Crash" Corrigan.

Whoever that is.

"I guess the old wild west is as far from the Army as it can be," he told the pretty girl selling tickets. "I'll give it a try."

She frowned a little. "Do I know you? You look familiar."

Jack shrugged. "I've lived in this neighborhood all my life."

"But I haven't." She handed him his ticket, still frowning. "I'm staying with my aunt while my husband is on a Navy ship."

Jack took the ticket. "Sorry. I don't recognize you."

"Hm. Well, enjoy the show."

Jack bought some popcorn and a soda pop and sat in the center of the theater. The seats were less than a quarter filled on this Tuesday afternoon, so obviously "Crash" wasn't drawing a crowd.

Jack munched on the salty, buttery treat, not realizing how much he'd missed it until now. The theater darkened. Three coming attractions for three new war movies played.

Hollywood doesn't miss a beat.

The newsreels were next. Jack found them mildly interesting. He finished the popcorn and took a big swig of the soda.

The next thing that appeared on the screen nearly made him spit the soda all over the seat in front of him.

The words *Mountain Fighters* spilled across the screen over images of white-clad Camp Hale skiers in bright and beautiful Technicolor.

"Well, I'll be…" Jack stared at the short film, transfixed, as he watched his buddies ski across the screen.

And then, there *he* was. A close-up of him smiling as he got ready to put his goggles on. And then he winked at the camera.

Jack had forgotten all about doing that.

The cameraman told him to pretend the camera was a pretty lady, and Jack winked just for the hell of it. He never expected that would be part of the film.

Jack started to laugh. He actually *was* a movie star.

*****

"Yes, I saw it." Edyta pulled a casserole from the oven, straightened, and beamed at Jack. "I don't know how many people have talked to me about it."

"Why didn't you tell *me?*" Jack asked, surprisingly annoyed. "When did it come out?"

Edyta set the heavy pottery on top of the stove. "I saw it in the middle of August, I think."

"Oh. Okay. We were already deployed by then."

"That's right." Edyta pulled off her oven mitts and considered her son while she spoke in her accented English. "Yesterday I was so excited to see you, and so worried about you getting shot, that I didn't think about it."

"Has Pops seen it?"

"Sure. I think he went once a week for a while."

That was interesting. "Did he have anything to say about it?"

Edyta pressed her lips together and shook her head.

Figures.

Jack forced a smile. "So what's for supper? It smells great."

November 7, 1943

Jack's ten days at home began to drag. Here he was, a twenty-three-year-old corporal with some war experience, sleeping in his childhood room. Meanwhile Pops went to work at Hollinghurst's rail yard every day and Mom had her regular household chores to do besides doing his laundry and ironing.

Most of Jack's friends had either been drafted or were working full time. He did meet up with one friend who hadn't enlisted yet, and he asked Jack a lot of questions about being in the Army in general, and the ski troops specifically. As a result, Jack's thoughts kept returning to Camp Hale.

Jack wondered if the camp would be different because of the Eighty-Seventh's absence and the subsequent staggered return of the three battalions. The summer climbing season was long past and snow would cover the mountains now. As a new corporal, would he still be able to teach soldiers to ski? He hoped so.

"One thing I learned," he told his friend, "was that fighting is no joke. Scared men with loaded guns are dangerous. We've mostly been training men to ski and climb—fighting and killing have been an afterthought."

That was the sad truth. He would never admit it to Pops, but Camp Hale felt like a big ski club. The seriousness of being in the Army while their country was at war had suddenly become very real to the soldiers at Kiska.

November 14, 1943

When it was time to leave, Jack felt like he'd done little more than eat and sleep the whole time he was in Oakland.

Probably needed both.

The rationing of sugar and meat was in full effect for civilians, so he felt a little embarrassed that Camp Hale wasn't subjected to the same limitations imposed on his parents. At least the requirements for blackouts had lifted.

His mom didn't want to go to the train station so Jack said goodbye to her at the house.

"I pray for you every day, Jack," she said while wiping persistent tears. "My church ladies pray for you every day, too."

"I appreciate that, Mom." Jack hugged her tightly. "It sure can't hurt to have assistance from above."

Pops drove Jack to the same train station he used so often to travel to Sugar Bowl. On the platform, he gave Jack a brief hug and handshake.

"Stay lucky, Jack."

Pops believed that in war, luck was a real commodity; one that everyone hoped to have in sufficient quantity.

"Yes, sir."

Jack shouldered his rucksack and climbed the steps into the passenger car. Once he found a seat, he stowed the pack overhead and dropped onto the bench, sliding close to the window. He waved at his father, who waved back.

John Franklin remained on the platform, somber and with his arms folded over his chest, until the train pulled away.

Chapter Fourteen

November 15, 1943

Camp Hale was swarming with soldiers.

"Looks like the Eighty-Sixth and Eighty-Fifth are filling up with recruits," Jack said to Steve while he unpacked in the I Company barracks.

"Thanks to you and that wink!" Steve teased. "Never pictured you as a flirt, Oakland."

Jack felt his face grow hot. "You saw the film?"

"Oh, yes." Steve beamed at him. "I certainly did."

"I was just goofing off. I didn't think they'd use it." Jack stowed the last of his gear and deftly changed the subject. "I'm going to see if I can find the platoon guide and get my mail."

Steve hopped down from the upper bunk. "I'll come with you."

As they walked through the camp Jack noticed men wearing unfamiliar patches. "Who are those guys?"

"The Ninetieth Regiment." Steve's tone displayed his disgust. "The Army brought them in to replace us after the Eighty-Seventh was annihilated on Kiska."

"Are you fucking *kidding* me?" Jack growled. "They expected us to fail?"

"Yeah." Steve sniffed and spat on the frozen ground. "Or die trying—literally."

Jack gave him a sharp look. "You coughing?"

"Nah. Caught a cold at home." Steve shrugged and flashed a reassuring grin. "I think it was being inside with the heaters blasting after all that fresh island air we enjoyed in Alaska."

Jack gave a wry laugh, shaded his eyes, and squinted at the soldiers. "So what's the Army going to do with them now?"

"Beats me."

Steve opened the door to I Company's headquarters. Jack walked inside and Steve followed him.

The soldier on duty looked up from the desk. "Can I help you?"

"I'm looking for our platoon guide. Seeing if I have mail that's backed up since we deployed."

"I can check. Name?"

"Corporal John Franklin."

The soldier got up from the desk and walked through the door behind it.

"Did you get your mail already?" Jack asked Steve.

Steve nodded. "I got back yesterday."

"What about our back pay?" None of them had been paid since they left California.

"Should be tomorrow, I'd guess," Steve said slowly. "Since we were all required to report to camp by today."

The duty soldier reappeared through the door with a bundle of letters which he handed to Jack. "Here you go."

"Thanks." Jack tried not to grin like a fool at all the letters from Betty. "You know when we'll get our back pay?"

The soldier consulted a calendar on the desk. "Wednesday."

Two days. Jack could manage that. "Thanks."

Jack and Steve left the building and Jack tried not to bolt back to the I Company barracks. He imagined the bundle in his arms was warm and beating against his heart as if he held Betty herself close to his chest.

Even so, walking as quickly as he was made him pant for breath. After spending the last five months at sea level it seemed he'd lost his altitude tolerance.

"Man, I'm out of breath," he grumbled. "It's like starting over again."

"I skied while I was home," Steve said. "So I got a little of it back in the mountains in New Hampshire. But I feel it, too."

Damn.

"Hey." Steve nudged Jack's arm. "Look."

Striding toward them was a group of five women dressed in the female version of an Army uniform complete with trousers. They smiled as they passed Jack and Steve, and Steve smiled back.

"I like having the WACs here," he admitted. "Makes everything feel a little more normal, you know?"

"Yeah." Jack tightened his grip on Betty's letters. "You going to ask one of them out?"

"I'm sure thinking about it."

Jack climbed the steps to the barrack's door and drew a deep lungful of the thin air. "You got your eye on anyone in particular?"

Steve wagged his head. "Not yet. But there are about two-hundred-and-fifty to choose from."

"And what—twelve thousand men doing the choosing?" Jack clapped his free hand onto Steve's shoulder. "Don't wait too long, or there won't be any left!"

*****

Jack spent the next hour in his bunk reading and re-reading Betty's letters. Mostly she chatted about her life and her travels around the country with Captain Jay, but there were a couple of things that stood out like they were written in flashing neon.

The first was that Betty enclosed a picture of herself in one of the letters—and she looked stunning. On the back of the photo she wrote: *To Jack ~ You hold my heart in your hands.*

Jack could hardly believe that this amazing woman was his girl. He wasn't sure he could hang on to her, but he sure was going to try his best to be worthy of her, no matter what that took.

The second thing was that she kept mentioning how much she appreciated that she could be completely honest with him, because Jack didn't have any expectations of her.

You don't know what my life in Massachusetts is like, Jack, because you've only seen me in my role as John's assistant ~ a job which my father isn't very happy about, to tell you the truth.

He thinks I should stay home and do more appropriate things like my mother, who volunteers in the Mayor of

Boston's Office of Civilian Defense and is involved with the Garden Club of Boston. He expects me to spend my time running and attending various charity events, and to help my mother as hostess for his company parties.

And all the while I'm supposed to be on the lookout for a suitable husband, of course.

But I didn't go to college to just be a mannequin smiling prettily next to the buffet. I'm a grown adult and in charge of my own life, and those things are not what I choose to do.

I want to teach skiing and be of actual help in the war effort. To have my days count for something. To be needed.

Most of all, I'm so tired of having the same conversations again and again with the same clueless people who don't seem to understand any of that.

And what my parents think is suitable, and what I think is suitable, are not the same thing. Not even close.

The man I choose as my husband will respect me for who I am as a person, not for what I have.

Jack's heart thumped hard against his sternum. What she has? What did Betty mean by that?

Jack pulled out all the letters he saved and combed through them to see if there was something he had missed.

And there was. He hadn't put the pieces together until now.

My father, Laurence Harkins, graduated from Williams College in 1914…

My mother, Victoria Perthstone, attended Smith Women's College in Northampton…

But I was a rebel and went to the Geneva College for Women instead…

My father works in shipping in Boston…

Works in shipping?

More like he *owns* a shipping company.

Jack slumped in his bunk, stunned to his core. He'd been completely blind all this time. Betty—Miss Elizabeth-Anne Jane Harkins—was wealthy. Rich. She was part of the same Eastern Seaboard, private college, upper-crust socialite society that so many of his Mountain Training Center cohorts were. The same class of person that his father despised as being privileged and useless.

And thereby proving Betty's point.

What the hell was she doing with the son of an immigrant mother and a dock worker who hadn't been educated beyond high school?

Jack laid back on his bunk and rubbed his eyes hard, pondering this unsettling revelation.

How was their story going to end? Was there any hope for him and Betty in the future?

The man I choose as my husband will respect me for who I am as a person...

If Betty's words could be trusted, then the very things that attracted her to him were the differences between them. He lifted the letter in his hand and considered Betty's neat, feminine handwriting that contrasted sharply with the strong emotions scribbled across her personalized stationery.

And there's another clue he missed. Personalized and embossed stationery.

Jack sighed and rubbed his forehead. He really had no reason to mistrust Betty's words, and every reason to believe her heartfelt letters were sincere. He trusted her as much as she seemed to trust him.

What would Pops say if he knew?

Jack decided that there was no reason to say anything to his parents about his relationship with Betty or her social status at this point. Wartime romances often ended when the war did—or before—and his mother had told him plenty of stories to back that up. The fact that she and his father actually did get married was highly unusual.

Jack looked at Betty's photo again and his heart ached with missing her. Was he falling in love with her?

Possibly.

You hold my heart in your hands.

Was she falling in love with him?

Maybe.

He made his decision right then. He was going to court Betty as he would any girl he was enamored with. Either she'd fall in love with him or she wouldn't. But he needed to be as honest with her as she was with him.

Jack tucked Betty's picture into the bunk frame above his head so he could see it. Then he sat up and reached for pen and paper.

Dear Betty,

What a happy surprise it was to finally get back to Camp Hale after so many months and receive a stack of your letters! I missed you a lot and thought of you constantly while we were stuck on Kiska for so long.

Yes, I did see "Mountain Fighters" while I was on furlough in Oakland last week. A funny thing happened when I did! The girl who sold me the ticket thought I looked familiar, but I'd never seen her before. Then I saw my face on the screen and realized that's where she'd seen me.

So after the movie was over, I went back to talk to her.

I said, I know where you saw me. Then I smiled and winked at her like in the film. Well, she got so excited she squealed and asked for my autograph.

So it's official, Betty. Your boyfriend is a movie star.

*****

That night at supper, Jack received another shock: Brigadier General Lloyd Jones had taken over the command of the Tenth Light Division at Camp Hale back in July while the Third Battalion was deployed.

Jack shot a startled gaze at Steve. "What?"

"Yep." Steve pointed at Jack with a fork loaded with mashed potatoes and gravy. "After we left, McNair moved Brigadier General Rolfe to the Seventy-First Light Division at Camp Carson as their Assistant Commander for the Jungle Training Center."

Jungle training?

In Colorado Springs?

Jack was stunned by the news. He figured Rolfe must have been moved and demoted because the Homestake Maneuvers were such a complete and utter snafu. Even their impressive rock climbing demonstration for McNair couldn't save him.

"Brigadier General Jones comes from Alaska," Steve said with his mouth full. "I expect he understands cold conditions pretty well. Better than Rolfe, anyway."

"But he's the one who assumed we'd die on Kiska and brought in the Ninetieth?"

Steve shrugged. "Guess so."

"Huh. I wonder what he'll do, now that we're all coming back." Jack shoveled a scoop of the potatoes into his mouth. "Guess we'll see soon enough."

November 17, 1943

It didn't take long to find out.

Jack and Steve waited in the pay line at the I Company office to receive their compensation for July, August, September, October, and November. With his raise for being promoted to Corporal at the end of August added in, Jack wondered how much he was going to collect.

"Corporal John Franklin."

He was handed a stack of bills after Lieutenant Hollinghurst counted the money—twice.

Jack counted it out again in front of his platoon's commanding officer a bit stunned. "Two hundred and ninety dollars. My pay is correct, sir."

He signed the ledger, pocketed his fortune, and turned to go when Hollinghurst stopped him.

"Read this, uh, Corporal." Jack's promotion still seemed to bother the second lieutenant. He held out a typed sheet of paper. "New regulations since we deployed."

"Yes, sir."

Jack waited for Steve to collect his pay and the two of them headed toward the mess hall for lunch, reading aloud as they walked.

"Fraternization between officers and enlisted men is frowned upon?" Jack gave a derisive laugh. "That's not going to work at the Mountain Training Center. The instructors all have different ranks."

"Which Jones is now calling the Mountain Training *Group*, by the way. The MT*G*."

"Why?"

Steve shrugged. "Who knows. Anyway, what about all those guys who went to Officer Candidate School at Fort Benning and came back as lieutenants? They're not supposed to drink beer with their buddies anymore? The service clubs are for enlisted men *and* officers."

"Look at this one." Jack shook his head. "No one will be allowed to go to the hospital without justification. 'Pando Hack' is not an acceptable reason to be excused from field training."

Steve huffed. "Thanks go to those guys who faked being sick so they could go to the hospital and talk to the WAC nurses."

"Sons of bitches screwed it up for all of us," Jack muttered.

"What are you going to do with your money?" Steve asked. "Buy something for Betty?"

It came to Jack in a flash.

Beth. I'm going to call her Beth.

That seemed like a more respectable name considering what Jack had just figured out about her social class. But he'd only use the nickname in their private or written conversations. That would make it their own personal code.

And unlike the slang-sounding 'Betts' that Captain Jay so casually tossed around in public.

"I don't know, maybe." That depended on when he'd see her again. "For now I'm going to hold on to it all."

*****

The remaining batch of rescued soldiers from the Eighty-Seventh's Third Battalion returned from their furloughs a week after Jack and Steve did. Once all of them settled in, and the gear they used in Kiska was cleaned, repaired, and again stowed in the supply sheds, it was time to resume their training.

"Since the First and Second Battalions aren't all back to Camp Hale yet," the ski instructors were informed, "we have time to focus on battalion training at the small unit level. This is important because the Army has given the Tenth Light two missions…"

"Here we go," Steve murmured. "What now?"

"First, they want us to test our clothing and equipment for actual mountain work." The officer's lips twitched. "Not 'sitting on an island in the rain' work."

The men in the battalion chuckled and nodded at that.

"The second mission is for our soldiers to be trained to operate *primarily* in mountains and primitive terrain, where roads are poor or nonexistent, and under extreme weather conditions."

Jack snorted inwardly.

Sounds like fun.

It also sounded like Jones from Alaska understood that their training here at Camp Hale actually was unique. That they weren't run-of-the-mill Army infantry soldiers. They were on their way to becoming an elite specialized force with specific skills for deployment in a certain type of terrain.

That's encouraging, at least.

"While we'll be pushing the limits of the Weasel," the officer continued, referring to the Army vehicles which were jeeps on the top and tanks on the bottom. "We'll also be making use of the mules."

Jack rolled his eyes.

Was the Army actually planning on shipping mules to Europe? If so, in how many situations would the animals actually be able to pull heavy weaponry up the side of a mountain? He imagined writing to Betty, *I'm a muleskinner now*, and her laughing at the news.

Of course, Pops would have an entirely different response: *There are no mules in the Marines.*

December 6, 1943

The three platoons of I Company and their ranking officers, a hundred and forty-eight men altogether, marched out of Camp Hale toward the back country of the Colorado Rockies for a week of maneuvers and training.

It was cold, sure, but surprisingly there wasn't much snow yet. And the air was clean and clear.

This was the first time any of them were out in the field since their extended and fruitless ordeal at Kiska. Jack couldn't help but compare the two experiences—as he was certain his comrades were doing, judging by their comments.

"At least it's not foggy."

"And it's too cold to rain."

"Hope our tents hold up better if the wind picks up."

"There's no mud!"

Throughout the week, Jack's company commander worked the men mainly on defensive positions and night patrolling, which involved orienteering skills.

"I did this all the time with the Sierra Club," Jack told Steve as he compared his compass with the stars overhead. "Stick with me and you won't get lost."

Their platoon was divided into four groups of ten for an orienteering challenge.

"To make it interesting," the captain said as he handed out written instructions. "Each group is assigned to reach an object and carry it back. First group back gets an extra day of Christmas furlough."

Steve was in Jack's group. So was Hollinghurst.

"I'll take that." The second lieutenant grabbed the instructions from Jack. "Follow me, men."

As the soldiers traipsed after Hollinghurst, Jack gripped Steve's arm and the pair held back. "He's going the wrong way."

"He is?" Steve's gaze followed the departing soldiers. "What should we do?"

Jack resumed hiking behind the group. "There's nothing we can do, is there? I can't call him out on it."

Steve fell in step beside him and sighed his disappointment. "Sure would have liked that extra day."

One of the other soldiers held back until he was alongside Jack and Steve, still trailing behind the rest of the men. "Did I hear you say you were with the Sierra Club?"

Jack nodded. "Yep."

The private looked uncomfortable. "So—I might be rusty—but are we going the right way?"

Jack shook his head. "Nope."

"You gonna tell him?"

Jack shook his head again. "I'm not. But you can."

He bounced a nod and trotted forward. "Lieutenant?"

Hollinghurst stopped and turned around. "What?"

"I don't think we're going the right way, sir."

Hollinghurst smiled into the light of their flashlights. "I assure you, Private. We are."

"But this direction feels wrong to me, sir," Herbert pressed. "And I asked Corporal Franklin. He agrees."

Shit.

Chapter Fifteen

December 24, 1943

Hollinghurst's group came in dead last that night after circling around and accidentally finding the bucket that they were assigned to retrieve.

Hollinghurst was livid at Jack's ultimately correct suggestion that they were lost and took his anger out on Jack for the rest of their week-long training.

Several of the platoon members who witnessed the challenge stepped in to help Jack if he stumbled from exhaustion on yet another assigned repetition of an exercise. They knew Jack was right, the second lieutenant was wrong, and saw that Jack was being unfairly punished as a result.

At least Jack regained his altitude tolerance quickly as a result of the extra physical activity.

There's one good thing.

And because of the continued lack of snow, their daily routine now consisted of climbing the cliffs around Camp Hale, rappelling down their sheer faces, hiking uphill carrying heavy rucksacks, and setting up bivouacs out in the training areas.

All in all, the equipment was holding up pretty well.

Better than in Kiska, that's for damn sure.

As the holidays approached, Jack volunteered to forgo a Christmas pass in favor of a New Year's one. He also volunteered to take his twenty-four-hour duty in the company headquarters from seven in the morning on Christmas Day through seven in the morning on the day after.

Jack had a very good reason for that.

He wrote to Betty as soon as the duty roster was officially posted and gave her the phone number of I Company headquarters.

I'll be there for twenty-four hours, Beth, he wrote. *If you can call this number, I'm the one who will answer.*

Turned out, Betty loved his nickname for her. *And I'll call you Jeff, for John Edward Franklin*, she wrote back. *If that's okay with you, of course.*

Jack thought it was just great.

Thousands of Christmas furloughs had been approved, so every day this week several hundred soldiers from the Tenth Light and the still-in-limbo Ninetieth regiment boarded the train from tiny Pando Station into Denver to head to their hometowns for the holidays. The normal bustle of bodies at Camp Hale quieted dramatically as the number of soldiers and WACs decreased with the festive exodus.

On Christmas Eve the mess hall was decorated with a Christmas tree, and the kitchen staff served a surprisingly delicious turkey dinner. The soldiers remaining in camp sang carols along with their more boisterous regimental tunes.

Four of the WAC nurses sang Bing Crosby's new hit *I'll Be Home for Christmas* in a harmonious quartet that left most of the men surreptitiously wiping their eyes on their sleeves.

After dinner Jack headed straight to his bunk for some shut-eye before his upcoming twenty-four-hour duty. A beautiful Christmas Eve snowfall left six inches on the ground during supper and continued in big, wet flakes that danced on the intermittent wind.

Jack had a surprisingly good time this evening, considering where he was and what horrors were going on in the world. Walking across the quiet camp with the snow falling and the sound of a few last carols still wafting from the mess hall suffused him with a pleasant sense of hope and peace.

For the moment, he was content.

Merry Christmas, Beth.

December 25, 1943

On Christmas morning Jack reported for duty promptly at seven to relieve the yawning soldier who had been there for the past twenty-four hours. He brought a book to read, figuring that with so many soldiers gone from the camp that there wouldn't be much going on in the company office.

He was right.

The hours passed excruciatingly slowly, and his isolation was only relieved when a WAC brought him his lunch, and later his supper.

He convinced her to stay and talk for a little while when she brought his lunch, but she said she had a date and couldn't stay while he ate his evening meal.

The phone rang exactly seven times on Christmas Day. Each time Jack answered, hoping to hear a woman on the other end, but he was disappointed every time.

As the evening crawled into the late hours, Jack added two hours to the time on his clock and knew Betty wouldn't be calling him now. It was far too late—or early, rather—in Massachusetts. At some point he put his head on the desk and closed his eyes, depressed and deeply disappointed that she hadn't called him.

But *why* hadn't she called?

Maybe she didn't get the letter.

Or maybe she was too busy with friends and family to give him a thought.

Or friends *of* the family.

Stop it.

The jarring, jangling ring of the phone next to his head woke Jack so suddenly that he jumped to his feet and nearly fell over backwards before grabbing the metal edges of the desk for support.

The second ring cleared his head and he looked at the clock.

It was four in the morning.

Six o'clock in Massachusetts.

He seized the heavy black receiver and put it to his head with so much force that he winced in pain when it hit his ear.

"I Company. Corporal Franklin speaking."

"Jeff? It's me. Beth."

Jack's bones dissolved and he melted back into the chair. "I was beginning to give up hope."

"I'm so sorry. But I needed to call in secret."

Jack wondered how long he'd need to remain her secret. "How long can you talk?"

"As long as I want to. I'm using Daddy's home office phone. The company will pay for the call and he'll never know."

Yep.

Rich.

"Merry Christmas, Beth."

"Merry Christmas, Jeff. Was it bearable for you?"

"Only because I hoped to talk to you," he answered truthfully. "How was yours?"

"The usual." Her tone was non-committal. "John and his family came over on Christmas Eve. Daddy drank too much champagne and berated John for not marrying *me* in front of his wife, Lois. Mother introduced me to someone's cousin who is quote, very well connected, unquote."

Betty giggled. "What was *not* connected were the flaps of his ears to his head. I'm afraid that in a stiff breeze he might catch wind and be thrown on his back."

A hearty and relieved laugh burst from Jack and filled the stark little office with incongruent gaiety. "So then he didn't win your heart, I guess."

Betty paused. "My heart is already won, Jeff."

Jack felt like his chest swelled to twice its size. "As is mine, Beth."

"Really?" She sounded happy.

"I would never lie to you." Jack hesitated. "But we do have some things we need to talk about."

"Like what?" Now she sounded scared.

"Like your family. And my family. And why…" Jack cleared his throat. "Why neither one of our families knows about us."

"Oh…" The word came out like a whoosh of breath. "You haven't told your family either?"

"No. I mean, not since our first date in Oakland. Obviously they know about that."

"Yes," she said slowly. "I suppose we do have things to talk about."

"Things that can wait until we see each other again," Jack offered. "They'll be a lot easier to discuss when we're face to face."

"Oh, Jack! That reminds me!" she practically squealed.

"What?"

"There's going to be *another* movie at Camp Hale, a full length feature called *I Love a Soldier.* Paramount's doing it this time with real movie stars, camera crews, equipment, and all that stuff." Betty's words came out in a rush. "Paulette Goddard and Sonny Tufts are the stars!"

Jack's jaw dropped. "What? When?"

"Early February. John told me last night."

"Are you coming to Hale for the filming?"

"I think so. I know John is. I'll ask him to be sure and I'll write you to confirm."

"Gosh, Beth. I hope you do come."

"So do I, Jeff. Don't worry, though. I'm pretty sure I can convince John to let me tag along."

Jack and Betty continued talking until Jack noticed that they had been on the phone for three-quarters of an hour. At three dollars a minute, the cost of this phone call would eat up half of the back pay from his deployment.

"Are you sure it's okay for you to talk this long?"

"Actually I should hang up and sneak back to my room before my parents get up." Betty sighed. "This was great. Can I call you again sometime?"

"Sure! I'll send you the phone number for the Servicemen's Center. We can arrange to talk at a certain time on a certain day and I'll be there to answer."

"Okay."

"Yeah."

Silence.

"I don't want to say goodbye, Jeff."

Jack smiled sadly. "Neither do I. But I'll see you in just six weeks."

"Yes. You will." Betty sounded resolute. "Six weeks. That's not too long."

"No it's not. And I'll write you today with that phone number and the hours I can take a call."

"Please do."

"I promise." Jack sighed. "Take care, Beth."

"*You* take care, Jeff. Don't fall off a mountain or anything."

"I won't... Bye."

Jack heard Betty sniff wetly before the line went dead.

December 31, 1943

Jack was pleasantly surprised when he got a three-day pass for New Year's. That meant he could go to Denver with Steve—who had a car—and they didn't have to be back until January third.

"That's great!" Steve grinned when Jack told him. "I have a reservation at the Brown Palace. You can bunk with me if there aren't any more rooms left when we get there."

That was fine with Jack. "I can pay for my own room if I can get one. I still have plenty of my back pay."

Steve saluted him. "Then let's ring in nineteen-forty-four with a bang!"

The pair got to Denver that afternoon and checked into Steve's room on the top floor. The place was crawling with soldiers and accommodations were tight.

Jack held up his dress uniform. "Nothing but class tonight."

"Girls love a man in uniform." Steve winked and nodded. "And I love girls. So that works out."

The bar off the lobby in the Brown Palace was already hopping with servicemen. Guys from Camp Hale clumped side-by-side with Army Air Corps guys from nearby Lowry Field.

"Watch yourself, Oakland," Steve warned softly. "Some of these Air Corps guys resent our coming to the hotel because they consider this place their private reserve."

"It's still a free country, thanks to us too," Jack grumbled. "All I want is to have a few drinks, eat, and relax."

"Don't forget we have to find some girls to kiss at midnight," Steve added. "Or are you too tied to your girl to do that?"

Jack realized with a shock that he actually was. But he didn't want to admit that to Steve just yet, or to anyone for that matter. Not until he spent time with Beth in February and could find out if she felt the same.

Jack shrugged noncommittally. "We'll see. You never know."

Jack and Steve ordered beers and snaked through the crowded bar to a tiny recently abandoned table by the wall. Along the way a couple of the Air Corps guys bumped into him hard enough to slosh his beer over his wrist.

"Hey!" Jack barked. He turned to confront the men just as two Military Police soldiers entered the hotel.

Calm down.

Jack turned away from the pair of clearly inebriated fliers and followed Steve.

"Scared of us, ski boy?" one of them slurred. "Why don't ya go build a snowman or somethin' and get outta our way."

Jack tried to ignore the taunt but his temper wouldn't let him.

"Why don't you shut up," he tossed over his shoulder.

The Air Corps guy pushed Jack from behind. "Wanna make me?"

Jack set his beer on the tiny table and spun around. He crouched with his bladed hands in front of him. "Leave me alone. I know judo."

The guy scowled at him. "What are you, a Jap sympathizer?" He unbuttoned his jacket. "I hate Japs."

The meaty hand of one of the MPs clamped down on the Air Corps soldier's shoulder. "There'll be no fighting in here."

Jack straightened and looked at the MP. "I was only going to defend myself if I needed to."

"These guys started it," Steve stated from behind Jack.

Their harassers tried to play innocent, but their unsteady stances and slurred objections made it clear that Steve and Jack were telling the truth.

The MP glared at the Air Corps guys. "Get out of here now and don't come back tonight. If you do I'll lock you up faster than you can say *above the best*. Understood?"

Jack bit his lips to keep from laughing at the Air Corps guys' impotent alcohol-fueled rage. He turned his back on them as a final insult.

"Their slogan might be *above the best*," he said to Steve as they claimed their seats. "But they need planes to get there. All we need is a rope and some crampons."

"True..." Steve looked impish. "And we have rope..."

"What are you thinking?" Jack asked.

Steve grinned. "Tell you later."

After they bought another round of drinks, a pair of pretty girls made their way toward them.

Jack watched Steve straighten and adjust his tie. "Hello, ladies. Can we buy you a drink?"

"Sure, handsome." The girls stopped at their table. "What's your name?"

"I'm Steve." He hooked a thumb in Jack's direction. "This is my buddy Jack."

"What are you drinking?" Jack asked. "I'll get it."

"Champagne if they have it," the shorter of the two answered. "I'm Stella, by the way."

"And I'm Sally." Sally dimpled adorably. "Thank you, Jack."

Jack slowly zigged and zagged through the crowd to the bar. He figured that since he wasn't interested in engaging with the girls he'd let Steve claim the one he wanted first, and Jack would chat up the other one just to be polite.

When he returned with the glasses of champagne he found the trio discussing skiing.

No surprise there.

"Here you go." Jack set the glasses on the table. "So you ladies are skiers?"

*****

Jack and Steve danced with Stella and Sally—who were co-eds from the University of Denver—and took turns buying the drinks. Loosened by the beer, feminine company, and general gaiety surrounding them, Steve pulled Jack aside.

"I have a great idea for midnight," he said. "Are you in?"

Jack laughed his delight as Steve outlined his plan. "It's perfect!"

When half an hour remained before the stroke of midnight, Jack and Steve asked the girls to follow them, and then stay put and wait.

Jack grinned. "We've cooked up a little treat for you."

"Something memorable, that's for sure," Steve promised. He slipped an arm around Stella's waist. "You'll want to see this."

Stella giggled. "Sure! Why not?"

Steve and Jack led the girls out of the crowded bar and claimed one of the overflow tables in the towering lobby.

"Isn't that Ralph Bromaghin at the piano?" Jack asked.

"Who's Ralph Bromaghin?" Sally asked.

"He's one of the ski instructors," Jack said. "But he's also a talented musician."

The lobby was filled with music as Ralph took requests and played the songs from memory. Stella and Sally seemed to be having a great time, but Jack wasn't sure which one Steve would kiss at midnight, and which one would expect the same from him.

"I have no idea," Steve admitted as they rode the elevator to the top floor. "Maybe both."

"Please do." Jack wasn't joking. That would take him off the hook.

Jack and Steve tied the ropes they'd retrieved from Steve's parked car to the decorative but solid metal banister outside their room on the top floor. As the countdown to midnight began, Jack turned to Steve.

"Ready?"

"Yep." Steve bellowed, "*Geronimo!*"

Both men launched themselves over the railing and began their eight-story rappel from the top of the Brown Palace lobby atrium. Roaring *Happy New Year* on the way down, Jack and Steve were greeted with hoots and hollers from the crowd below, even from the Air Corps guys. They landed on the floor right at the stroke of midnight.

The hotel staff, however, was not in the least bit amused.

"What the hell do you think you're doing?" the manager shouted when the men reached the lobby. "You could have killed somebody!"

Jack and Steve both pretended to be contrite. They apologized profusely and promised they'd never, *ever* do anything like that again.

"Get those ropes down. Now!"

The truth was that Jack hadn't had that much fun in a very long time. The only thing that kept him from laughing in the manager's presence was his fear that the purple-faced man was so angry he might have a stroke.

"Yes, sir."

Jack grabbed Steve's arm and pulled him toward the elevator. Once inside the enclosed space the friends whooped and guffawed.

"That was utterly amazing," Steve effused. "We'll be famous from now on as the first men to rappel down the Brown Palace atrium!"

"And the last, judging by our reception," Jack countered.

Jack and Steve stowed the ropes in their room and returned to the lobby where they were enthusiastically hailed by well-lubricated Army and Air Corps men alike. Then they each got an unsolicited

New Year's kiss from both Stella and Sally.

"That was incredible," Sally said. "Weren't you scared?"

"Nah." Steve tried to look modest but failed. "We do lots more dangerous stuff than that all the time."

Bromaghin was still at the piano and he played a rousing rendition of one of the songs he'd written for the regiment, *Eighty-Seventh, Best by Far*.

While the Air Corps guys sat relatively quietly, the Camp Hale soldiers sang along, raucously loud and gleeful. Jack thought this was one of the best New Year's celebrations he'd ever had.

Only one thing was missing.

I sure wish Beth was here.

Chapter
Sixteen

January 17, 1944

Jack and Steve returned to Camp Hale on January third—Jack's twenty-fourth birthday. Betty surprised him by calling him at the Serviceman's Center that night to wish him a happy birthday. Once Jack was summoned and actually on the phone, they only had about five minutes to talk.

"Happy birthday, Jeff." Betty's softly musical voice soothed like a tropical wave washing over him.

"Thanks, Beth." Jack smiled into the receiver. "Did you have a nice New Year's?"

"I did. But there was one thing missing."

"Same here." Jack fiddled with the telephone cord. "Looks like I owe you a kiss."

She laughed a little. "Looks like I owe you the same."

Jack sighed. "Five more weeks."

On January second, the First and Second Battalion soldiers who were stranded on Kiska finally returned from their furloughs and resettled at Camp Hale, completing the Eighty-Seventh Regiment. Their planned replacements in the Ninetieth Regiment were moved to Camp Gruber in Oklahoma, but a few of the Ninetieth enlisted men wanted to remain in the Tenth.

They were subsequently assigned to the Eighty-Fifth and

Eighty-Sixth regiments. As a result the Division Regiments were out of balance and the soldiers needed to be shifted around. The goal was to have equal numbers of officers, non-commissioned officers, competent skiers and climbers, and support personnel in each regiment.

On the one hand, Jack looked forward to the possibility of getting away from Hollinghurst's constant disdain.

On the other hand he didn't want to be split from Steve Knowlton. Steve had become his best friend since they met on the train a year ago and the two men trusted and relied on each other—important qualities when they faced deployment into battle.

The company commander looked at his clipboard. "Corporal Franklin, we're moving you to the Eighty-Sixth Regiment, Second Battalion, F Company."

He lifted his gaze to Jack's. "Any questions?"

Jack couldn't ask the questions he really wanted to, but time would answer them in any case. "No, sir."

"All right. Get your stuff and report to their Command Post." The commander's eyes dropped back to the clipboard. "You're dismissed."

Jack went to his barracks and packed up, remembering to take the photo of Betty from the bottom of Steve's bunk above him. He was almost done when Steve walked in. His friend didn't look happy.

Jack straightened. "Are they moving you?"

"Yep." Steve opened his footlocker. "You?"

Jack nodded. "Eighty-Sixth Regiment, Second Battalion, F Company."

Steve stared at him. "Are you kidding?"

Jack frowned. "No. Why?"

"I'm going there too!"

"No shit?"

"No shit!"

"What are you jerks going on about?" Second Lieutenant Hollinghurst called out as he walked into the bunk room.

"Nothing, sir." Jack smiled. "Just packing to move."

"Well I'm moving, too." Hollinghurst's tone didn't reveal whether he thought that was good news or bad. "I'm being transferred to the Eighty-Sixth Regiment, Second Battalion, F Company."

February 7, 1944

Jack waited at Pando Station in the chill of the morning for the first of several trains carrying the Paramount Pictures' movie stars, Paulette Goddard and Sonny Tufts, plus their camera crews, film equipment, and all the gear required to make a feature-length movie.

While the idea of meeting the film stars was interesting, Jack was way more excited to see Betty. He didn't know if she was arriving today, but he vowed to meet every single train until he found her.

Captain John Jay was the first person Jack recognized as the train's passengers stepped out of the car and into the bright but freezing winter's day.

Beth can't be far behind.

She wasn't.

As Jay slid a possessive hand around Betty's waist Jack decided that the captain and commander of the Mountain Training Group needed to know exactly who it was that claimed Beth's affection.

So Jack walked right up to her and kissed her.

It wasn't a long kiss, or a passionate kiss, but it was a hell of a lot more than a brotherly peck.

Beth's eyes widened when she saw him and thankfully she didn't fight the kiss, even though her cheeks turned far redder than the frigid weather would account for.

Jack smiled. "Hello, Beth."

She smiled happily. "Hi, Jeff. It's good to see you again."

Jack didn't look at the captain, but he noticed that Jay's hand fell away from Betty's waist even though he still stood close to her. "It's great to see you, too. And I have something to ask you."

Her brows pulled together. "What?"

Jack reached for her hands and gazed into her beautiful green eyes. "There's a Valentine's dance at the field house this Saturday. Will you be my date?"

She laughed and squeezed his mitten-clad hands with hers. "Of course!"

Surprise and confusion played over Captain Jay's face as he interrupted their conversation. "Come on, Betts. The staff car's waiting."

"I'm coming." Beth replied, though she still faced Jack. "I have to go. We're coordinating the filming schedule with the Paramount people."

"Understood." Jack let go of her hands after another quick squeeze and stepped back. "We can talk later."

Captain Jay considered Jack intently. "Corporal, you're an instructor aren't you?"

"Corporal Franklin," Jack reminded the captain. "And yes I am, sir."

Jack could practically see the wheels turning in Jay's head. "I wonder if you could help with some of the skiing scenes."

Jack nodded sharply. "Yes, sir. Of course. I'd love to help in any way I can."

Jack had no idea if his new company would allow him to participate in the filming of the movie, but he wasn't going to mention that now. Besides, he figured Captain Jay had enough pull to make it happen either way.

He watched Beth walk away, his mood as high as he thought was possible. When she looked back at him over her shoulder before climbing into the car his heartbeat surged to double-time. He grinned like an idiot and lifted his hand to wave.

My God, my girl's gorgeous.

Jack spun on his heel and headed back to the F Company barracks, where he was immediately summoned by the First Sergeant. "Corporal Franklin, you're being assigned temporary duty with the Mountain Training Group again this winter."

That was great news in general, but even better news considering Captain Jay's request. Because the captain was still the MTG director, Jack should be able to work on the film without a hitch.

"Thank you sir. I'll move my gear over there now."

After Jack arrived at the MTG barracks and stowed his gear he searched out Pete Seibert.

Pete grinned when he saw Jack. "Are you back with us again?"

Jack nodded. "I sure am. And it's good to be back. I've really missed skiing!"

"Great!" Pete grabbed Jack's shoulder and gave it a shake. "We missed you while you were in Kiska."

"You don't know the half of it," Jack grumbled. "Is Tech Sergeant Klein around?"

"He's down in the ski warehouse," Pete told him. "The senior

NCOs are deciding on the instructor assignments for the winter."

Jack went down to the warehouse and waited for the meeting to adjourn, his thoughts running in circles and his knees bouncing impatiently. When the men left the room and he found Bill Klein, his old boss lit up like a comet.

"Hey, kid! Glad to see you're back."

"I'm glad to be back. Kiska was a shit hole."

Bill made a face. "Yeah. That's what we heard."

Jack told Bill about the conversation he'd just had with Captain Jay. "Is it possible for me to be assigned to work with Jay while they do the ski scenes?"

Bill's face split into a wide grin. "Only if you promise to wink into the camera again."

Jack rolled his eyes. "You saw it, too."

"Three times."

"Damn."

"Seriously though, let me see what I can do." Bill clapped Jack's shoulder. "You do have experience in front of a camera, so that's a huge point in your favor."

Jack blew a grateful sigh. "Thanks, Bill. I appreciate it."

February 11, 1944

As it turned out, there was a lot less skiing in this film than there had been in *Mountain Fighters*, but that actually made sense. Last year's short film spotlighted the ski troops and was used to recruit soldiers.

I Love a Soldier was a full-length movie focusing on the romantic plot, not the Tenth Light Division.

Bill Klein worked whatever magic he owned to secure Jack one of the coveted assignments in the ski sequences filmed at Cooper Hill. Though Jack and Betty were working near each other, Betty and Jay were so busy helping the Paramount film crew coordinate the skiing shots there wasn't much time for conversation.

We have Saturday night, Jack reminded himself over and over. *And I'll use that time wisely.*

There was one aspect of the filming that Jack never expected— Betty was the stunt double for Paulette Goddard in all of the skiing scenes. Apparently Paulette had never skied in her life and there was no time for her to learn how now.

So Betty dressed in the same clothes as Paulette, and skied down Cooper Hill innumerable times while she was filmed from a variety of angles. Though Jack knew Betty was a certified ski instructor, he'd never seen her ski before.

She was magnificent.

Jack was mesmerized watching her lithe, athletic form as she glided over the snow with ease. If he thought she was the perfect woman before, this sealed that deal.

Jack rode the T-bar to the top of Cooper Hill for the last run of the day. He and the other members of the Mountain Training Group were wearing their snow-white camouflage gear for the ski-action scenes, which actually caused a problem with the cameras.

White clothing against white snow did what it was supposed to do: hide the soldiers. Cameras had to be low to the ground, so the pine trees lining the slopes provided a dark background, or shooting from behind so the valley below the skiers contrasted with their all-white gear.

When they reached the valley at the bottom of Cooper Hill for the final time, the instructors from the MTG were thanked for the part they played.

"Today is the last day we'll be filming with you men," director Mark Sandrich told them. "Each and every one of you is an inspiration and I'm proud to have worked with you."

Jack made a point of finding Betty before heading back to camp. "We're still on for tomorrow night, right?"

"Of course we are. I can't wait." She tucked a stray hank of hair into the hood of her parka. "What time should I meet you at the field house?"

"The dance starts at seven," Jack said. "But I'd like to take you out to dinner before that if I could."

Betty smiled. "I would love that."

"Then I'll come into Leadville and pick you up at six."

Jack leaned in for a kiss and Betty met him halfway. She tasted like the lipstick she wore on camera.

"We have a lot to talk about," she whispered when the kiss ended. Then she touched his cheek before she turned around and walked away.

February 12, 1944

Jack and Betty had a quiet dinner at a steak place in Leadville before heading to the Camp Hale Field House and the Valentine's Day Dance.

Jack decided to hold off on their deepest conversation until later in the evening and began with, "Gosh, Beth, every time I see you you're prettier than the time before."

Betty smiled shyly. "I'd say the same about you, Jeff. You seem to keep getting bigger."

Jack laughed. "Well I can't say I'm still growing at the ripe old age of twenty-four, but as physically hard as we work even I can see a difference in my arms and legs over time."

"So what's new with you?" Betty asked after the waiter took their order. It was apparent that she also wanted to save the harder topics for later.

Jack told her about the reorganizing of the regiments to even out the officers, skills, and jobs. "The good news is Steve and I are still together. The bad news is that Hollinghurst is still my platoon leader."

"Oh, don't worry too much about that. I know plenty of guys like him. More talk than action." Betty took a sip of the fragrant red wine Jack ordered to go with their steaks. "This is delicious. Good choice."

"Thanks." Jack tasted the wine and agreed. "So what's new with you?"

Betty's expression shifted. "Lately I've been feeling like I'm not doing enough for the war effort..."

Jack snapped to attention. "What do you mean, Beth? Are you going to join the WACs?"

Betty began to twirl a chunk of her dark hair—a nervous habit Jack noticed early in their relationship. "Lord, no. My parents would disown me if I did anything like that."

Both relief and disappointment flushed through Jack's body. "So what are you going to do?"

Betty's earnest gaze bore into Jack's. "Well, you know that as a certified ski instructor we had to get a lot of first aid training..."

"Yeah."

"So I asked Minnie for a letter of recommendation and I applied to the Red Cross. To go overseas."

Jack fell back in his chair. "You did?"

"I did." Betty's hair-twirling intensified. "I'm hoping to go to England first, and then be transferred to wherever I'm needed from there."

"Wow." Jack was stunned by the unexpected news. "When will you know?"

"That's a good question. I have no idea." Betty's fingers twisted a different lock now. "But while I'm waiting I'll keep working with John, showing his films everywhere and recruiting skiers for the Tenth."

Jack considered the woman across the table from him.

Beth wants my approval.

Shaken by that sudden realization, Jack knew that whatever he said to her next was going to set the tone for the rest of their relationship. He also knew he needed to continue to be completely upfront with her.

"Well, to be honest, I'd be pretty sad if you were so far away," he began. Then he leaned forward and reached for her hand.

Betty let go of her hair and laid her hand in his. Her green eyes were wide and her expression sober.

"And please excuse my language," Jack continued. "But the truth is that I'm pretty damn proud of my girl right now."

Betty let go of the breath she was holding. "Really, Jeff?" Her eyes filled with tears. "You aren't angry?"

Jack wondered what in her life would make her expect that reaction. "Of course not. Why would I be angry?"

"Because I'm hoping to go into battle—so to speak." Betty dabbed her eyes with her napkin. "It's far away and it could be—will be—dangerous."

"Are you scared?"

"A little," she admitted. "But we'll never win the war if we all aren't brave."

Jack blurted out the words that filled his head and his heart. "Gosh, I love you."

Betty froze. "You love me?"

Stupid stupid stupid.

It was too late to pull the words back now.

We all have to be brave.

"Yeah, Beth." Jack flashed a crooked smile. "It seems that I do."

Now she was crying in earnest, muffling her sobs with her dinner napkin.

Jack began to panic. "I'm sorry, Beth. I don't expect you to feel the same way. This doesn't have to change our friendship."

Betty shook her head. "No, Jeff. I do."

"You do what?"

"Feel the same way."

Jack stared at the beautiful, intelligent, and talented woman across the snow-white linen expanse of their table. He didn't trust what he thought he heard.

"What did you say?"

Betty started to laugh through her tears and the dinner napkin, her green eyes glittering wetly. "I said I feel the same way. I love you too, Jeff."

*****

The field house was crowded with soldiers, WACs, and most of the Paramount Pictures film crew. In addition, single women from Alamosa, Buena Vista, Leadville, and Red Cliff were offered bus rides to the camp for the dance in order to provide the overabundance of male soldiers with dance partners.

Jack and Betty rode the bus from Leadville to the camp after their dinner. They held hands when they entered the field house—Jack's way of saying *she's mine* to any soldiers who might want to take a turn dancing with her.

The effort proved futile.

Both enlisted men and officers who were involved with either of the two films made at Camp Hale descended on the pretty brunette.

"Hey, remember me? I was the guy who fell down."

"Sure is nice to see you again, Miss."

"I saw *Mountain Fighters* when I was on furlough."

"Can you jitterbug?"

"Want to dance?"

Jack resigned himself to sharing Betty only because he didn't want to start a brawl. But it really didn't matter tonight. Not after they declared their love for each other.

None of these guys could change that.

Betty danced several dances with other soldiers, but she saved the slow songs for Jack. She felt so good in his arms. She was such a good dancer that he was better when he danced with her.

"Let me know when you want to leave," Jack said into her ear while she was tucked in his swaying embrace. "We still have some things to talk about."

Betty tilted her head back and looked up at him. "Especially now."

He nodded. "Yep. Especially now."

Chapter Seventeen

Finding a place to speak privately at the camp was proving impossible. Due to a heavy snowfall that started sometime after Jack and Beth arrived at the Valentine's Dance, talking outside wasn't an option. And inside the field house every single alcove and corner was already filled with couples in various stages of spooning.

"Let's take the bus back to Leadville," Jack suggested. "We can talk at your place."

Beth nodded. "I think that's the best plan."

They waited inside the field house for half an hour for the next bus, and then waited onboard for another quarter hour before it left the camp.

Once in Leadville, they walked together through the strengthening blizzard with Jack holding Beth's arm tightly until they reached the little inn where Beth had stayed the last time she was in town.

"I can't have you up to my room," she said as they stomped their feet in the entry way, shook the snow off their coats, and unwound their scarves. "But we can have coffee in the parlor. I don't think we'll be disturbed there."

Jack waited in the parlor for Beth to speak with the sweet older lady who ran the little bed and breakfast establishment. When she returned, Beth sat on the sofa next to Jack, kicked off her shoes, and tucked her knees under her.

"Where do we begin?" Jack asked.

Beth heaved a resigned sigh. "I'm wealthy."

"I know."

That seemed to surprise her. "How do you know?"

"You said your father graduated from Williams College and your mother attended Smith Women's College, but you were a rebel and went to the Geneva College for Women instead..." Jack chuckled. "It's not brain surgery."

"When did you figure it out?"

"The phone call on Christmas."

Her forehead wrinkled. "How?"

"The call you made from your father's home office—that his company would pay for—would have cost me two-and-a-half month's pay."

Beth considered him thoughtfully. "How wealthy do you think I am?"

"You said your father works in shipping in Boston." Jack lifted one brow. "It's more like he owns a shipping company. Am I right?"

Her cheeks pinkened. "Yes."

"Well *my* father actually does work in shipping in Oakland." Jack gave Beth a wry grin. "He supervises crews that load and unload rail cars for Southern Pacific Railroad in the yards next to the Oakland docks."

"Did he go to college?"

Jack snorted. "No."

"What about your mother?"

"My mother trained as a nurse in Poland and worked in a hospital in France during the First World War. That's where she met my dad." Jack smiled at the thought of his mother. "She's a very sweet woman, with a very pronounced Polish accent."

Beth was quiet while their coffee cups were set on the table in front of the sofa. "I'll leave the pot on in the kitchen if you want more."

"Thank you, Mrs. Swanson," Beth said graciously. "Good night."

Beth lifted one of the cups. "Is your mother still a nurse?"

"No. She takes care of the house and volunteers at church." Jack reached for the other cup. "Pops would never hear of her working. He's too proud."

Beth sipped her coffee before she spoke again. "Why haven't you told them about me?"

Jack chuckled. "Two words: Aston Hollinghurst."

Beth frowned. "What does he have to do with me?"

"Aston's father owns the shipping business that my father works for." Jack spooned a little sugar into his black coffee. "He is the epitome of what my father hates about what he calls the private college, upper-crust, socialite society."

"Oh dear." Beth looked crestfallen. "He'd hate me."

"He'd hate the *idea* of you, true." Jack smiled reassuringly. "But if he ever gets to meet you, he'll fall for you. Just like I did."

Beth looked doubtful. "That's a sweet thing to say."

Jack shrugged. "So. Why haven't you told your family about me? As if I have to ask."

"There are expectations for someone of my social status." Beth was blushing furiously and started twirling her hair again. "I'm supposed to 'marry well'…"

Jack steeled himself for what might come. "So knowing that, what is Miss Elizabeth-Anne Harkins doing with the son of an immigrant mother and a dock worker who hasn't gone beyond high school?"

Her eyes met his in desperation. "Falling in love."

Jack took the last gulp of black coffee before he asked, "Is that enough?"

"It is for me." Beth reached over and gripped his arm. "You don't understand what it's like for me."

Jack set his empty cup on the table. "Then tell me."

She pinned his gaze with hers. "You never judge me, or judge the things I do."

Jack was confused. "Tell me more."

"I was supposed to go to college and find a suitable husband. But I actually went to learn about things that interested me."

"So when you were still single at graduation your parents hoped you'd marry John Jay?"

Beth nodded and sighed heavily. "I hoped so, too. At the time. But now I know we wouldn't have been a good match."

"Why not?"

"Because I met you."

Jack shook his head. "I still don't understand."

Beth shifted on the sofa so she was sitting on her knees. "My mother never tells anyone that I was one of the first women to be certified as a ski instructor. She's mortified that I would do such a thing."

"Really?" Jack found that hard to believe. "But that's quite an accomplishment! She should be proud!"

Beth waved her hand at him. "Right there. That's why."

"What about traveling with Captain Jay?" Jack pressed.

"When he didn't marry me, my parents hoped he'd introduce me to someone in his circle who would."

"And applying to the Red Cross?"

Beth winced. "I didn't tell them."

"Oh, Beth…"

Beth recoiled. "Don't turn on me, Jeff. You are the first man I've ever met who sees me for who I really am—and likes me because of it."

Jack stared hard at her. "I doubt I'll ever be rich."

Beth huffed. "I don't care. I already have a trust fund."

Jack startled at that. "Do you expect to support your husband?"

"No, I expect him to work hard!" Beth blurted. "But I also expect him to be willing to accept the fact that our lives will be easier because of my money."

"Because he respects you for who you are, not what you have," Jack quoted Beth's letter.

Her jaw dropped and her eyes widened. "Yes."

"And who you are means you're smart, and capable, and independent." Jack's lips twisted in a knowing smile. "And while you *want* a husband, you don't *need* one. Not if he diminishes who you are."

"Yes." Beth looked like the weight of the universe was lifted from her shoulders. "Now do you understand?"

Jack pulled her into his arms and answered her with a long, deep kiss.

*****

What a startling night.

Jack lay in his bunk and knew that someday—if he wasn't

killed in battle—he would ask Beth to marry him. In a matter of hours the course of his life had changed and solidified.

Beth seemed to sense it, too. They both agreed not to talk to their families yet, since both her job with the Red Cross and his eventual deployment were still no more than future possibilities. And ones with uncertain outcomes.

When the job and deployment became real, and if he and Beth were still sure of their feelings when they did, that would be the time to let their families know that they were serious about each other.

He told Steve, though. When he disappeared from the dance early and reappeared so late to his bunk, Steve pressed Jack for information until Jack caved.

"We said we love each other," Jack admitted. "And we talked a lot about how we grew up and what our families are like."

"Congratulations, Oakland," Steve effused. "You're moving up in the world."

"No congratulations needed," Jack deferred. "We aren't engaged or anything like that."

"Not yet." Steve wagged a finger at Jack. "If she knows you like I do, she won't let you get away."

"Speaking of getting away—how'd you do tonight?"

Steve grinned broadly. "I have a date for next Friday *and* next Saturday."

March 24, 1944

Two days after the Valentine's Day dance the Paramount studio people packed up and departed Camp Hale from Pando Station. Jack and Beth grabbed as many brief opportunities as they could to be alone in the meantime. By the time the crews left, Jack and Beth were closer than Jack had ever been to anyone—including his family.

Jack resumed his ski instructor's role with the Mountain Training Group and his piece of the world returned to its military purpose. A purpose which included preparing for a required readiness test ordered by Lieutenant General McNair, Commander of Army Ground Forces.

McNair called it the Division Series Test—D-Series for short—
to assess all aspects of an Infantry Division as they would be
employed in combat. And though most Army Infantry Divisions
were equipped and employed differently than the Mountain
Division, the criteria for the evaluation were apparently going to be
the same.

"What the hell does that mean?" Jack grumbled when the
soldiers were briefed. "We'll be at the top of a frozen mountain, not
hiking through easy hay fields on a spring day!"

Steve shook his head. "This could be Homestake all over
again."

"I bet that's the bee in Jones' bonnet," Jack opined. "He'll want
us to pass the Division Series test with flying colors so people
forget about that disaster."

"I just hope the guys sent to evaluate us this time have enough
brains in their heads to see the difference between us and a regular
infantry division." Steve blew a sigh. "They'll be out there with us,
so they'll know it's no Sunday picnic in the countryside."

Jack and Steve had to rejoin F Company of the Eighty-Sixth for
the test, so they were back under Second Lieutenant Hollinghurst's
command.

"Welcome back boys," Hollinghurst sneered. "Hope your
playtime with Hollywood didn't make you two soft."

"No sir," Steve answered before Jack could mouth off and get
himself in trouble. "We actually had to do twice as many runs as
when we're training, until the director was satisfied with his shots."

Jack couldn't help himself; Hollinghurst's smug and unearned
superiority made his blood boil. "This'll be a walk in the park by
comparison. Sir."

The Division had been split into two units for the series. The
red force would play the part of the enemy troops, preparing
defensive positions and remaining alert and ready to engage an
allied attack.

The blue force was the Allied attacking force, which would
conduct reconnaissance patrols to find the locations of the red
forces and capture them.

There could be no fires during the test since they were easily
observable at night, and smoke could give away the soldiers'
positions during daylight hours.

F Company filed out of their barracks on a cold and heavily-snowing Friday morning and trudged up the road with their skis tied to their fully-packed rucksacks. Two abreast, they hiked the familiar six miles to the Tennessee Pass.

At eleven-thousand feet the blizzard howled around them like a living thing. Snow stung Jack's eyes and the wind made it even harder to breathe at that altitude. The alpine temperatures during the series were expected to fall to twenty or thirty degrees below zero at night and all twelve thousand soldiers from the Mountain Division would be living outside during the entire three-week test.

"Hope you had enough hot coffee at breakfast to last you a while," Jack said to Steve as they fought through the snow. "With no fires allowed we won't have a meal that isn't frozen for three long weeks."

"Hopefully we can get snow to melt inside our tents," Steve replied. "Otherwise we'll be chewing our liquids."

March 26, 1944

For the first part of the exercise F Company was assigned the offense, so Jack and Steve wore the blue armbands that designated their attack objective.

The umpire for the test directed the company to a predetermined location near Tennessee Pass at the tree line—the startlingly clear altitude line where trees could no longer grow. The men set up a company command post just below the tree line in order to stay out of sight.

After sunset every night, each of the three platoons took turns making three-hour ski patrols to find the red forces. Tonight Jack's platoon was assigned the second three-hour patrol which began at midnight.

The temperature was well below zero and the snow was windblown but they made good progress over the icy conditions on their heavily-waxed skis. The wind had finally stopped howling and the night was clear with a quarter moon lighting the snow through and beyond the trees.

The platoon of forty men, led by Second Lieutenant Hollinghurst, climbed to the top of a vertical ridge so they could see in all directions.

"I'm splitting you guys up," Hollinghurst said. "I want half of you to go down the ridge on the left and the other half to go down on the right."

As the men split themselves into two groups, Hollinghurst continued, "As you descend, be sure to come to a complete stop every five minutes and listen carefully for any man-made sounds nearby. Understood?"

The soldiers mumbled a general sound of approval.

"We'll convene at the bottom of the ridge to report what we've found, and take it from there." Hollinghurst adjusted the grip on his ski poles. "Let's go."

*****

Jack didn't care which direction he went, only that he was not in Hollinghurst's group. When the lieutenant headed to the right, Jack and Steve went left.

The twenty men in that half of the platoon pushed off and skied slowly down the ridge. After five minutes the staff sergeant, acting as squad leader, slid to a stop and the rest of the men did the same.

Jack closed his eyes, opened his mouth, and listened for any whisper, any rattle, any sound at all that would expose the presence of men. He slowed his breathing so he couldn't hear it and waited.

Nothing.

He opened his eyes and stared into the trees. The complex black and pale gray pattern of tree shadow and moonlight on snow revealed nothing. There was no movement, only still silence.

The sergeant murmured, "Let's go." The men slid forward on their skis making almost no sound of their own.

The stopping, watching, and listening in the cold night air of the forest was exhausting. When he skied down a mountain, the exertion kept Jack's body warm. But he wasn't exerting himself on this patrol. The bitter cold of the mountain at night was creeping into his bones. He shivered a little.

Hopefully when we reach the bottom we can warm up on the way back to company headquarters.

When the patrol reached the end of their run, their squad leader led them to the rendezvous point. They reassembled the platoon at the designated point and at the appointed time.

"Anything?" Hollinghurst asked after he did a head count to confirm everyone was back.

"No, sir. Not a peep," the sergeant answered.

"Damn." Hollinghurst checked his watch.

He wanted to shine.

On the one hand, Jack was glad the second lieutenant wasn't getting any glory tonight. But on the other hand, neither was F Company. Seemed like Jack would have to bury his personal war with Hollinghurst and continue to work for the good of the unit— and never let his dislike for the man to hold him back.

After checking his watch again, Hollinghurst gave the hand signal to move out. The platoon of forty men skied back into the trees, finding the tracks in the snow they made when they started the night's maneuvers.

Though Jack still listened for sounds of their camp stirring, he heard nothing.

"If it wasn't for the tracks and the moon, I'd wonder if we were heading the right way," he said quietly to Steve.

"Yeah, it's eerie," Steve agreed. "Wonder what's going on?"

When the platoon skied into the command post after their three-hour maneuvers the answer was obvious. Everyone in the company command post was asleep, from the company radio operator who had the radio next to him, to the umpire who was supposed to be judging their performance.

"God damn it," Hollinghurst growled. "The guards better be awake."

They were. And the next platoon to go on patrol was just getting up out of their sleeping bags.

No one spoke as the returning skiers took off their skis and stowed them next to their tents while the next platoon strapped into their skis and headed out.

Jack and Steve crawled into their two-man tent to get ready to go back to bed. Jack took off his boots and put on dry socks before he zipped and tied himself back into his sleeping bag. He curled on his side, resting back-to-back with Steve to conserve both of their bodies' heat.

Their tent protected them from wind. Not from cold. And it was damned cold up here.

Jack's teeth chattered while he waited for his body heat to

warm his cold, aching legs. He tucked his hands under his armpits. He pressed his back against Steve's.

Jack knew they had done well tonight. Even if they hadn't flushed out any of the defensive enemy units, they had done exactly what they were supposed to do.

And Hollinghurst did a decent job of leading them. Despite his deeply held grudge against Jack, he was proving himself to be a generally good leader otherwise.

Because they completed their objective, the lack of results being irrelevant, there was a good chance that F Company would be moved to another location after they awakened at dawn. From their new location Jack assumed they would continue to search out, and hopefully engage, the red enemy force.

His last waking thought was what he would write about the D-Series test in his next letter to Beth.

Chapter Eighteen

March 30, 1944

F Company Commander Captain Percy Rideout did receive orders to move the company. They were headed toward the town of Minturn, twenty miles north of Tennessee Pass and fourteen miles beyond Camp Hale.

After their breakfast of cold rations from cans, Jack, Steve, and Pete Seibert, who was part of a different platoon in F Company, packed up the company's gear and prepared to take the one-hundred-and-twenty-five soldiers on the march.

That many soldiers stretched out in a long ski march would be easily spotted by enemy forces both here and in actual war, so Captain Rideout ordered the soldiers to march under the cover of the tree line as they traversed northward. Their route would take them west of Red Cliff, and they would need to cross the Eagle River at some point.

Because the evaluators for the D-Series came from the Sixteenth Corps Headquarters in Fort Riley, Kansas none of them skied, nor were they acclimatized to either the frigid mountain weather or the high altitude. For those reasons they followed the ski-marching soldiers in the relative comfort of the Army Weasels.

The irony that their judges could not do what the soldiers of the Tenth Light Division were all expected to do was not lost on a single man.

"Fucking flatlanders," Pete groused when he paused, panting in the thin air. "We better pass with flying colors."

Jack agreed. He looked over his shoulder at the Weasel following F Company and sneered his disgust from behind his scarf.

This was complete bullshit.

*****

The weather remained bitterly cold. The ever-present dry wind sucked the moisture from the men's bodies as they breathed heavily with the constant exertion. Jack had to refill his canteen with snow over and over again, tucking it inside his jacket so the snow would partially melt and he could drink it.

As F Company marched northward they continued to look for signs of any enemy forces while remaining careful not to expose themselves. Captain Rideout sent regular scouting parties ahead of the company to do reconnaissance. Today was Jack's and Steve's turn.

The friends skied forward in the windy and glaringly sunny day, looking for any evidence of human presence. They couldn't talk to each other and risk giving themselves away, so they communicated with hand signals.

For two hours the pair skied, stopped, listened, and skied again without seeing or hearing anything beyond the rustle of the wind through the hardy pine trees living at this upper limit of viability. Hawks and eagles occasionally circled above them, but at this altitude even wildlife was scarce.

Steve slid to a stop and waved his arms at Jack. When Jack turned to face him, Steve motioned him closer and pointed at the ground about five yards below them.

Ski tracks.

Jack looked at the angles and placement of the poles and the direction the snow was thrown and determined that the skiers were headed the same way F Company was.

They are ahead of us, going the same way, Jack mouthed and gestured.

Ambush? Steve mouthed back

Jack nodded and tilted his head back in the direction of F Company.

Let's go.

The men turned around and followed their own tracks back toward their company.

*****

It took an hour to rejoin their slower-moving comrades, and when they reached them Jack and Steve skied straight to Rideout.

"We found ski tracks, sir," Steve began the report while they were still moving

"And they're heading north in the same direction we are," Jack added.

Captain Rideout halted the company. "At ease, men. Take ten."

As the command passed down the line, the soldiers grabbed their snow-filled canteens and sat on their packs to rest. Rideout pulled the map from a pocket of his rucksack, turned his back to the wind, and unfolded the chart.

"How far?" he asked.

"An hour in front of us." Jack leaned closer and examined the map. With his orienteering skills it didn't take long to find the spot. "Here."

Captain Rideout studied the map. "Based on the terrain, the enemy force will be west of our route…"

Jack nodded. He agreed, though he wasn't asked.

"If there *is* a red group there, we'll have to climb up out of the tree line here to outflank them." Rideout traced his plan on the map with his forefinger. "We'll have to ski up on the ridge from here, then proceed north to here, and take a position behind the ambush force here."

"Yes, sir." It was clear to Jack that Captain Rideout knew exactly what he was doing.

"Call the platoon leaders," he instructed his radio man. "We have to get moving again."

*****

Captain Rideout sent a squad of twelve men ahead as a decoy in case the red forces were lying in wait for F Company to appear. Those soldiers were instructed to straggle in a stretched-out line as if they were exhausted and the rest of the company was struggling along behind them.

"If you're shot at, shoot back," Rideout instructed. "We'll hear it and get there as fast as we can."

The remaining two-and-a-half platoons reversed their course. They skied half-a-mile back to a v-shaped gorge in the mountain that continued up to the top of the ridge. Not only was that route protected from the worst of the wind, but the soldiers were hidden from sight by the walls on either side of them.

As silently as possible, the hundred-plus members of F Company climbed the treeless valley on their skis. It took two hours for them all to reach the position above the location where Captain Rideout believed the ambush force was waiting for them.

Below them the sounds of battle cracked into the thin mountain air.

"They took the bait!" Rideout shouted. "Onward!"

The rest of F Company raced down the mountainside toward the ambushing soldiers, taking their enemy completely by surprise. Shooting blanks and throwing dummy grenades, the blue-banded F Company soldiers quickly subdued the stunned red company.

More quickly than in real combat, Jack wrote to Beth later, *because our enemy had to play dead if they were even close to shots and dummy grenades. And we had excellent aim!*

The umpires credited F Company with the win that day. After receiving the official news, Captain Rideout reassembled the men and told them how well they'd done. Jack, Steve, Pete and the others heartily congratulated each other before the company resumed their northward ski march toward Minturn.

In spite of the long and tiring day, F Company's morale was high as the mountain peaks soaring around them.

"We really needed this," Jack said to Steve. "Looks like Homestake will be put to rest at last."

"Your mouth to God's ears," Steve replied, chuckling. "But I'd settle for a warm meal and a good sleep right about now."

The company's trek continued north until the winter sun dropped behind the ridge, throwing the men into a sudden blue-shadowed dusk. Rideout led the company back down into the tree line to establish bivouac for the night.

"Men, I believe that we're safe enough after today's maneuvers that you can use your squad stoves tonight," Rideout told them. "Enjoy a hot meal for a change, and then get some rest. You deserve both."

Jack punched Steve's arm. "Looks like your words *did* go to God's ears, Dropout," he joked.

Jack dug a snow pit for the little stove to hide any chance of the enemy seeing the flames while Steve opened the frozen cans of food with his bayonet and filled a pot with snow to melt. Within half-an-hour the men were sitting inside their tent and enjoying their first hot meal in a very long week, and topping it off with hot cocoa.

When they finished eating and drank a second cup of hot cocoa, Jack turned to Steve. "I am utterly content right now."

Though he expected his friend to look at him like he was off his rocker, Steve just smiled softly.

"We're skiing everyday with good men. We just beat the crap out of our enemy. And we've eaten our fill of a hot meal before tucking in for the night," he said. "What could be better?"

Jack touched his tin cup to Steve's in toast and laughed. "How about the love of a good woman?"

Steve rolled his eyes and shook his head. "Show off."

"Your day will come." Jack pointed a finger at his friend. "But you have to date one woman at a time to find her."

"Oh. Well then, never mind." Steve grinned and downed the remainder of his cocoa.

April 2, 1944

F Company spent two days and nights ski-marching north to reach Cross Creek. Once they found a crossing point where the ice was strong enough to walk on, they waited until after dark to make the crossing before settling in for the night.

The next morning the company awoke to a thick, cloud-covered world. Captain Rideout assigned Jack's platoon to take the lead, and Jack and Hollinghurst were assigned as the scouts for the company.

The scouts' job was to advance a couple hundred yards ahead of the company, one above the tree line and one below, and look for enemy encampments along the way to their next position. They had radios to talk to each other and to F Company—when the mountains allowed a signal to get through—and used both maps and compasses to guide the company.

Jack figured he was given the task because Rideout knew he had navigational skills that the fog wouldn't deter. Why he was paired with Hollinghurst was a mystery. Jack smothered a smile when the answer occurred to him.

Maybe to learn from me.

"Expect to encounter an enemy encampment at some point," Rideout told them. "I know they're somewhere nearby, but I don't have confirmation of the exact location."

"Yes, sir." Jack turned to Hollinghurst. "Which route should I take?"

"You go above the tree line," his platoon commander instructed. "I'll stay in the trees."

Jack was fairly certain Hollinghurst's plan was to expose him to danger while keeping himself safe. "Yes, sir."

The pair set off in their individual directions.

Jack moved along the open ridges of the mountain, keeping his eye on the compass and not the bright spot in the clouds that moved overhead. With the foggy and cloudy conditions it would be easy to get lost if he tried to follow the sun.

Hollinghurst's in the trees and won't be affected by the sun.

Jack stopped every fifteen minutes and used his binoculars to peer through the patchy fog, watching and listening for signs of a camp.

Nothing.

He lifted the radio from his pack and depressed the send button. "Oakland to Shipyard. Checking in—do you copy?"

There was no response, only static.

"Shipyard—this is Oakland. Do you copy?"

Nothing but more static.

Jack changed his direction. "Base—this is Oakland. Do you copy?"

Hissing and an occasional crackle.

Shit.

Jack looked at his watch. He'd been scouting for over three hours without finding anything, and now was more than an hour ahead of where F Company should be.

Should I go back?

Did Hollinghurst go back? Maybe that's why he didn't answer. It would be just like the guy to strand Jack out here alone, and then claim he tried to contact the corporal without success.

Jack stowed his useless radio and made a studied evaluation of the lowering clouds, and the smell and feel of the thin frozen air. Snow seemed inevitable, so he decided he needed to go back. He didn't want to be left exposed when it started to fall. This high up he could be buried faster than he could ski out.

If I ski fast, I'll meet up with them in forty-five minutes.

*****

Jack beat the beginning of the blizzard by a quarter of an hour. His radio signal popped to life when he was about a mile from the company.

"Oakland returning. Hunker down. Blizzard coming. Copy?"

"Copy that, Oakland. Where is Shipyard?"

Jack's pulse jumped. Hollinghurst hadn't gone back?

"I had no signal. I don't know. Copy?"

"Copy."

Shit shit shit.

Had the second lieutenant gotten lost?

Jack pressed the button on the radio and ordered, "Tell the captain to send Dropout and Boston to follow his tracks. Copy?"

"Copy."

Jack skidded to a halt when he reached F Company at the spot where they stopped their march. They were tucked inside the shelter of the trees and quickly setting up camp.

He could see Steve and Pete talking to Rideout several yards away and skied straight to them.

"When did you lose contact with Hollinghurst?" the captain asked.

Jack shook his head in frustration. "After we left camp we talked once an hour. But when I tried to tell him I was turning back because of the weather, I didn't have a signal anymore. It didn't pick up until I was a mile from here."

"With respect, sir, all three of us were members of the ski patrol before we enlisted," Pete offered. "Let us go look for him before the snow covers his tracks."

Rideout nodded. "All right. Take emergency supplies and maintain radio contact as best you can."

"Yes, sir," the trio chorused.

*****

Finding Hollinghurst's tracks out of camp was easy because of the direction he headed. But it didn't take too long for Jack to realize that the second lieutenant's compass readings were off.

"He's veering east." Jack showed the map to Steve and Pete once they were a mile from the bivouac. "See here? He's missed the compass reading by a few degrees."

Pete's concern was obvious. "If he's been traveling for three hours now, who knows where he is."

Jack tried to reach the F Company, but the transmission kept breaking up. "Base this is Oakland. Do you copy?"

"Oak—ase—copy?"

Jack shook his head with frustration. "Shipyard went off course."

"Say again? Over."

"Ship. Yard." Jack over-exaggerated his words. "Off. Course."

"—lost?"

"Yes."

He had no idea what the radio tech said next. He looked at Steve and Pete for help, but their expressions were as blank as his.

Jack stuffed the radio back in his pack and folded the map. "Let's keep following his tracks before they're covered. I'll try the radio every quarter hour and see if we can reach him."

The trio skied single file in Hollinghurst's tracks for two hours as the snow fell increasingly heavier through the trees.

When they stopped to catch their breath in the thin air and check their position on the map, Jack tried the radio yet again. "Shipyard, this is Oakland. Do you copy?"

"O—"

Jack gasped. "Where are you?" he shouted into the mouthpiece. Silence.

"God damn it!" Jack jammed the radio back in his rucksack. "Let's keep going while we still have some semblance of tracks to follow."

Thank God Hollinghurst stayed in the trees. If he'd been out in the open where Jack was, his tracks would have been obliterated hours ago. In spite of the cold there was a trickle of sweat running down Jack's spine, the product of exertion and alarm combined.

A quarter hour passed and the radio crackled to life. "Oakland, this is Shipyard. Copy?"

Jack retrieved the radio from the side pocket in his pack but the men didn't slow down. "Copy! Where are you?"

"By water. And a footbridge."

The other two stopped and Jack tossed the radio to Steve. He pulled out the map and Pete shined a flashlight on it as deepening dusk made it hard to see.

"There." Jack pointed. "Should be just a mile ahead."

"Shipyard, this is Dropout," Steve said into the radio. "Stay put. We're coming."

*****

Hollinghurst had skied forward to meet them.

So much for staying put.

"God damned radios are useless!" he bellowed.

"You're *welcome*. Sir." Pete's sarcasm couldn't be mistaken— but he wasn't in their platoon. If he chose to say anything else to Hollinghurst there wouldn't be the same sort of repercussions that Jack or Steve might suffer if they did.

"What? Oh." Hollinghurst looked more irritated than grateful. "Let's head back before we have to stay here all night."

Rather than risk losing his temper and saying anything that might get him court-martialed and booted from the Tenth, Jack turned his skis around and wordlessly retraced their tracks.

Steve still had Jack's radio, so he tried contacting F Company. "Base, this is Dropout. We have Shipyard. Copy?"

Static that sounded like words and not just noise replied.

"We are on our way back," Steve offered.

"—opy."

Steve tucked radio into his pack. The four men skied in single file for the next hour without speaking another word.

Chapter Nineteen

April 3, 1944

The search and rescue patrol didn't ski into F Company's camp until the next morning, after spending the night in the forest hunkered down in the raging blizzard. The four men huddled together between an outcropping of rock that broke the wind, and the snowdrift that formed in front of them as a result.

Protected by their sheltered spot and the blizzard itself, they used their individual stoves to heat the K-rations that Jack, Steve and Pete brought with them and they melted snow for water. At the first gray light of the cloudy dawn, when they could finally see where they were going, Jack led the quartet back to the company.

Throughout the night, Hollinghurst remained sullen and quiet. Jack wondered what the man was really thinking.

Was he wondering how to explain how he ended up where he did? Was he pissed that it was Jack who came to his rescue? Did he even realize that he *needed* to be rescued?

Their report to Captain Rideout was going to be interesting.

"What happened, Lieutenant?" Rideout asked after the four of them gathered in front of the captain's tent.

"My compass must have been defective, sir. It sent me the wrong direction," Hollinghurst stated.

Rideout held out his hand. "Let me see it."

Hollinghurst pulled the compass from his pocket and laid it in the captain's palm. Rideout compared the readings to his own compass.

"Seems fine now," he said.

"It's the iron ore in the mountains." Hollinghurst waved a hand in no particular direction. "Sometimes a vein can screw with the magnet."

Jack wanted to laugh but he coughed against his arm instead. He didn't dare look at Steve or Pete or he'd lose his fragile composure. Hollinghurst's claim was asinine.

Rideout turned to Jack. "Can you show me where you found the lieutenant?"

Jack nodded and unfolded his map. He pointed to the spot where Hollinghurst said he was.

"Second Lieutenant Hollinghurst said he was by water and a footbridge, which would be here." Jack slid his finger a little. "We headed that way and met up with him here."

"None of us experienced any problems with our compasses, sir," Pete offered. He leaned forward and pointed to the map. "This is the point where the lieutenant's tracks started to veer east."

Jack risked a glance at his platoon leader. If looks could kill, poor Pete would be cold and dead as the granite around them.

Captain Rideout shifted his attention to Jack. "Show me the route you took on patrol."

Jack complied. "I went up above the trees here, continued north and a little west through here, and stopped to turn back here." He looked at Rideout. "The storm was coming and I didn't want to be stranded without shelter."

The captain nodded. "And did you experience any problem with your compass?"

Jack shook his head. "No, sir."

"With respect, sir," Hollinghurst growled. "Corporal Franklin only had to look to his right to see the tree line. He didn't need to rely on his compass."

That comment, while partly true, didn't seem to sit well with the captain. "That's not the question at hand, Lieutenant."

Hollinghurst clamped his mouth shut. His eyes narrowed and the muscles in his cheeks flexed repeatedly.

Rideout stared at the map for a few tense moments. "I'm going to write up a commendation for Corporals Franklin, Knowlton, and

Seibert for their search and rescue efforts—"

"Rescue?" Hollinghurst yelped.

Rideout glared at him. "Yes. Rescue."

"But I was on my way back—sir."

"And with a 'defective' compass in a blizzard which obliterated your tracks, would you have made it?" the captain challenged.

That shut the man up.

Rideout pointed at Jack and his buddies. "You three are dismissed."

The trio stood, saluted, and left Hollinghurst alone with Rideout.

*****

F Company was on the move again later that same morning. The clouds above them didn't hold snow so Rideout gave the orders to pack up and go.

"Wanna bet there's a headquarters located in Minturn?" Pete said as they skied north.

"Regimental?" Steve asked. "Or Divisional."

Pete shrugged. "Either one."

That made sense to Jack. "I'm betting they want to check on how we're doing. I mean, all we have as a witness is our umpire and his radio's no better than ours."

The company followed a high ridge that looked down onto the highway that ran toward Minturn and parallel to the Eagle River. Jack could see the traffic clearly from their vantage point. Cars and trucks moved north and south, their drivers unaware that a war of sorts was playing out around them.

"Look how many Army vehicles there are," Pete pointed out. "A headquarters for sure. Just don't know whose."

"Which side of the river, can you tell?" Jack squinted. "I hope we don't have to cross it."

"It's probably frozen." Steve looked hopeful. "Don't you think?"

"Maybe we could use one of the bridges."

Apparently Captain Rideout was thinking the same thing. He halted F Company and sent their umpire down the mountain to find out who was using Minturn as a headquarters location.

"Eighty-Sixth Regiment," the umpire radioed back. "Come on down."

It was friendly territory—no red armbands. Captain Rideout instructed the platoon guides from the three platoons to take two men each down to Minturn with him while the remainder of the company remained hidden in the trees above the town.

Steve and Pete were selected to go but Jack remained with the company, glad for the respite. When the ten men returned, they brought more field rations and batteries for the semi-useful radios.

"Rideout met with the Regimental operations guys." Steve handed Jack a doughnut he had wrapped in a paper napkin and carried back in his coat pocket. "I couldn't hear everything, but they didn't sound happy."

*****

From the report that Captain Rideout gave F Company later that afternoon, the bitterly cold weather was having a deleterious effect on all operations for both sides of the D-Series test—and more importantly, for their evaluators.

"Apparently it's been an utterly confusing demonstration of the readiness of the Tenth Light Division." The captain didn't seem to believe his own words. "They're saying it's no different from the Homestake Maneuvers last year."

"*What?*" Jack looked around F Company and every man there appeared as shocked and confused as he was. "How can that be?"

Rideout shook his head slowly. "I don't know. They're saying that the umpires and the evaluators are confused. So are the Regimental and Battalion commanders."

"I don't get it," Pete said. "The only battle we've been in went great. Well, for us anyway."

"Some of the officers are reporting in to headquarters claiming that because radio communications are so bad in the mountains, no one really knows the exact location of their companies or platoons. And if headquarters doesn't know where their men are, they can't send supplies." Rideout made an unpleasant face. "Apparently whole battalions were out of communications and assumed to be lost."

"But that's the equipment's fault," Jack protested. "Not the soldiers!"

"And shouldn't we assume this might happen in actual war?" Steve pressed. "If those battalions complete their objectives, will their evaluations be bad because their damned *radios* don't work?"

Rideout put up his hands. "Believe me men, you're making exactly the same objections that I did."

"If you ask me, this D-Series test is going to prove how much hardship a ski trooper can take and still come out fighting." Pete's tone held an unmistakable tone of pride. "None of us in F Company have frostbite, altitude sickness, or even a God damned cold."

Captain Rideout smiled a little. "Well, they haven't pulled the plug on the test yet. We have our orders and our objective. We head out tomorrow."

April 4, 1944

F Company spent the night tucked safely in the trees above Minturn. Jack was glad for the cold by now, because none of the men had showered in nearly two weeks. They couldn't do more than wash their faces and brush their teeth, and only when they could melt enough snow. Shaving was out of the question.

At least their facial hair helped trap the warmth of their breath behind their scarves.

Now rested and fed for a night, the men resumed their trek northward. Once they reached Second Battalion Headquarters they were told to link up with E and G Companies to reform the battalion.

That battalion was then ordered to climb and hold Ptarmigan Peak at over thirteen thousand feet elevation. Second Battalion would set up a defensive position to hold the peak, and they were told to expect an attack sometime around Easter—five days from today.

But first, they had to find a place to cross Eagle River.

At night.

Once F Company found a bridge that seemed suitable for the crossing they hid in the trees, observing vehicles traveling up and down the highway and waiting for a break in the traffic.

Captain Rideout gave the signal to cross the bridge and all three platoons sprinted across, one after the other. They quickly reformed in the woods on the far side.

Jack and Steve grinned at each other.

"We made it!" Jack whispered.

The umpire's radio crackled to life. "F Company—halt in place."

"Damn it." Captain Rideout spat on the ground.

"What's that mean?" Jack asked Steve.

"Don't know," he replied. "But it ain't gonna be good."

A jeep pulled up and a major, one of the senior evaluators, got out. The umpire and Captain Rideout went to the side of the road to talk to him.

Judging by the way Rideout was standing, he was pissed. He saluted the major and stomped back to the company.

"Apparently we were seen crossing the bridge," Rideout said without preamble. "The enemy forward observers called an artillery strike on our position. We were assessed as having several casualties."

"How many casualties?" Hollinghurst asked.

"Seven killed in action and twelve wounded."

Shit.

"That's a lot," Jack murmured.

Just from crossing a bridge.

"What now?" another platoon leader asked.

"We can't move until enough time passes for replacements to be obtained." The captain rested his hands on his hips and spat again. "Make camp."

April 9, 1944

F Company had to remain in place for thirty-six hours until their theoretical replacements could arrive. During that time they coordinated their casualty evacuation with Second Battalion Headquarters.

"I suppose it's good practice," Jack admitted. "I mean, none of us wants to think about getting shot and all, but this part of the test does bring up that possibility."

"It does..." Steve looked a little shaken. "Someday we'll be rappelling down a cliff under enemy fire, not just a hotel lobby with a pissed off manager."

After the prescribed thirty-six hours, F Company got back on their skis and headed for Ptarmigan Peak.

They ski-marched for two long days, enduring the relentless cold and wind, and surviving on the frozen K-rations that they re-supplied with at Minturn. When they arrived at their assigned location and joined E and G Companies, they were exhausted, cold, dehydrated, and hungry.

Jack, Steve, Pete, and the rest of F Company dug into the snow and made themselves as comfortable as was possible in such high altitude and frigid conditions. Thankfully, because of their delayed arrival, the E and G Companies had already formed a defensive perimeter and were ready for the attack that was supposed to be coming.

Jack and the others hoped for a chance to rest, but a storm blew through that same night and dumped an additional six inches of snow on the beleaguered F Company.

"Tomorrow is Easter Sunday," Captain Rideout reminded his soldiers. "The whole D-Series exercise will be suspended at sundown tonight for religious services, and then resume at dawn on Monday."

On that sunny Easter Sunday morning, one of the division chaplains hiked up the mountain on snowshoes, arriving at Ptarmigan Peak in the middle of the day.

Seven thousand soldiers gathered together to literally hear a sermon on the—*pristine snow-covered*—mount, and under a canopy of startling blue skies. The well-known story of Christ's resurrection seemed to give every one of them renewed hope.

It sure did for Jack.

After more than two weeks living outside in the harsh high-altitude conditions, eating frozen food from a can pried open with a bayonet, swallowing snow when he couldn't light his stove to melt it, and skiing without stopping for long grueling hours at a time, he was done in.

And from what he could see around him, the other soldiers of F Company were as done in as he was.

Now the collective sound of seven thousand men singing

Amazing Grace in such a spectacularly beautiful setting actually brought tears to Jack's eyes. Glancing around, he saw he wasn't the only man wiping his eyes by far. Many of the guys sang impromptu harmonies and the result was glorious.

I'm never going to forget this.

April 17, 1944

The D-Series test was called to an abrupt and early halt on April fifteenth.

After the Division, Regimental, and Battalion Headquarters finally located and established communications with all of the units spread across the countryside from Leadville to Minturn, they discovered that many of the troops were starving because re-supplies of rations had been so unreliable.

Radio communications were also sporadic. Some units had not been heard from during the entire three weeks. In addition, both altitude sickness and cold weather casualties from frostbite had reached unacceptable levels.

"I can't say whether the end of the D-Series is good news or bad," Captain Rideout told them with a sly grin. "Because while we *are* returning to the comforts of Camp Hale, we have to ski to get there."

Jack looked at Steve. "I'm just going to think about a hot shower the whole way. That'll motivate me to keep going."

Steve winked. "And I'll think of the WACS who will be waiting for me *after* I get that hot shower."

*****

When F Company reached the camp two days later, they were met with the news that, as the last shudder of winter was about to disappear, Ralph Bromaghin had organized what he called the First Annual Military Ski Championships at Camp Hale.

"Annual?" Steve turned a disbelieving face to Jack while the information was handed out to the returning soldiers. "Will we still be here in a year?"

"Jeez, I hope not." Pops would never let him forget it if he spent the entire war training and never got into battle. He reached for a flyer. "When is it?"

"Saturday. April twenty-second."

Jack scanned the information. "I'll do it. It'll give me a chance to show you high-society dropouts what a real western man can do."

Steve laughed and punched his arm.

When Jack got back to the F Company barracks, he was able to take that hot shower he'd dreamt of, shave, and finally change into clean clothes after three weeks of living rough and cold.

Refreshed and clean, he sat on his bunk and wrote a letter to Beth, even before he went to check if he had mail from her waiting in the company office. His experience was so fresh and raw he wanted to get the words on paper before they faded away.

Dearest Beth ~

I've just come through the most difficult, challenging, and physically draining ordeal of my whole life.

It's hard to find words to describe the continuous wind and cold, the strain of carrying our ninety-pound rucksacks at such high altitudes, the lack of sleep in our tents pitched on top of deep snow, eating nothing but cold or frozen K-rations, and swallowing snow when we didn't have a way to melt it.

Added to that was the responsibility of being a leader in a squad and infantry platoon. I felt like the weight was crushing me at times.

But when things were the toughest, I'd think of you, Beth. I want to make you proud. I want to be the man who's worthy of your love, no matter where our families come from. Because nothing in my life is more important to me than that.

Every time I thought of you, my strength came back. My mood always lifted, and I knew I could do whatever was being asked of me, no matter what it was.

In the end the D-Series turned out to be the biggest

morale booster our division has undertaken. Because we made it, Beth. We did it.

Through those hardships we all grew stronger, and that strength defines every one of our mountain soldiers. Those of us who went through this now have a solid confidence that we could not have gained any other way.

Character can only be grown through adversity. We went through adversity in spades these last three weeks. And we proved we were up to the task.

When it was over, the evaluators declared us fit, tough, and ready for war.

April 21, 1944

Brigadier General Jones addressed the soldiers a few days after they returned to Camp Hale. His unfortunate comments, however, castigated those whose injuries forced them to leave the exercise and return to hospitals and barracks.

He underplayed the effects of the weather and said that those who *completed* the test proved their mettle and were deserving of praise. His choice of words, however, made it sound like those who did not successfully endure all the privations were somehow unworthy.

Steve snorted. "So much for understanding cold weather combat."

"Fucking asshole," Jack muttered. "Where was he through it all? I'll tell you! He was riding around in a Weasel, eating three meals a day in a heated building, and sleeping on a thick mattress."

Steve was clearly gobsmacked. "How does he have the nerve to stand in front of us and throw that bullshit at us?"

Jack grunted. "We can't catch a fucking break. First, the Homestake Maneuvers made us look like a bunch of inept and unprepared boys who wandered into the snow without warning."

"And then the Navy snafu that landed us all on Kiska," Steve pointed out. "We sat in that cold and wet hell for months with nothing to do—except backslide in our training and altitude tolerance."

"Now this. Claiming that it's our own fault that some guys fell after spending weeks in sub-zero weather without supplies or support, when the truth is their God damn Army radios didn't work!"

Jack was so angry at the Army for the way they consistently mishandled the mountain troops that for the first time he wondered if he had made a mistake. Sure, he was skiing and serving with an exemplary group of men, but the powers that be didn't seem to have the slightest clue.

If they can't manage us stateside, how will they do it when we deploy?

Jack sat in miserable silence until the soldiers were dismissed.

Maybe Pops was right.

*****

Two days later, Steve dropped a copy of the *Ski-Zette* in front of Jack at supper. "Looks like someone heard your complaints."

Jack looked at the headline. "Minnie Dole was there?"

"Apparently he was an observer to the D-Series, just like last year at the Homestake Maneuvers."

Jack looked up at Steve. "Did he hear Jones' address when we got back?"

Steve grinned. "He sure as hell did." He pointed at the newspaper. "Read what he says."

I watched officers from the Division staff ride after the soldiers in Weasels. From their lofty perches they berated the enlisted men, demanding that they speed up the march.

I saw officers make many unreasonable demands of these enlisted men, who were living in sub-zero conditions, from the comfort of their own warm tents.

I observed the Division staff enjoying hot meals throughout the D-Series test, which were carried to their location by Weasels, while I ate the same frozen K-rations the soldiers had.

I saw officers criticize young men who labored under their heavy rucksacks and who trudged upward without complaint onto ridgelines at twelve or thirteen thousand feet in elevation. I watched those brave men carry on even when they were exhausted.

Now I'm on my way to Washington, DC to meet with General Marshall. I'll explain to him the extreme lack of knowledge and complete lack of sympathy in the higher echelon at Camp Hale, both of which lead to wasted effort, unsatisfactory results, and poor morale.

And I'll reiterate my demand for a competent, practical-minded general to lead the 10th Light Division into combat. One that the fine, capable troops here can finally believe in.

"Oh, shit." Jack looked up at Steve. "This is worse than Rolfe."

Steve retrieved the newspaper. "Wouldn't you like to be a fly on *that* wall?"

Chapter Twenty

April 22, 1944

The next day the mood in the camp was substantially higher. Ralph Bromaghin's just-for-fun competition among the ski troops was exactly what the soldiers needed after the harrowing stress of the D-series trial and Brigadier General Jones' demoralizing speech.

"Brings back my excitement about being here," Jack admitted. "Reminds me why I love skiing so much."

"What'd you sign up for?" Steve asked as they hiked to Cooper Hill where the competition was being held.

"Slalom and downhill. You?"

"Same." Steve turned to Pete. "What about you?"

"Just the downhill." Pete grinned. "One trophy's enough for me. I'm not greedy."

Jack's pulse pounded with eager anticipation as he rode the T-bar to the top of Cooper Hill for his turn at the downhill run. The time to beat at this point, with two-thirds of the competitors having finished the mile-and-a-quarter run, was one minute and forty-seven seconds.

He closed his eyes and focused on this morning's downhill race right in front of him, and refused to allow his thoughts to drift to the slalom this afternoon. The slalom where he'd be competing against Aston Hollinghurst, known cheater.

Jack considered telling the judges to keep an eye on the man, but with Hollinghurst being his platoon leader he figured his motives would be suspect. There was no way for him to come off looking innocent if he said anything.

Jack sighed and opened his eyes.

I'll ski clean. What he does is up to him.

Jack slid off the T-bar at the top of Cooper Hill and circled around. He took his place at the end of the short line of skiers who were being sent one at a time down the mountain in pretty quick succession.

When his turn came up Jack crouched at the ready, poles planted and muscles primed, and waited for the horn to signal the beginning of his race.

Beeeep!

Jack pushed off. He skated forward several dozen yards before tucking his poles under his arms and hunching down on his skis. He let his knees absorb the bumps of the ridges in the heavily-skied course and used his weight and his thighs to narrow the broad turns on the downhill run. Snow flew in wide, flaring arcs with every turn he made.

The icy wind burned his cheeks and stole his breath as he raced over the blinding snow, muscles flexing and his green-goggled eyes fixed far ahead toward the prize.

This was what made him feel most alive.

Flying.

When Jack crossed the finish line he skied in a wide semi-circle and nearly collided with the spectator fence before he could slow down. He trembled from head to toe with the adrenaline that surged through his veins. He felt glorious. Unbeatable.

Jack lifted his goggles and watched the scoreboard. Waiting for his time seemed to take forever.

One minute. Forty-two seconds.

Jack whooped and punched the air.

*****

It was no surprise that the Austrian champion Friedl Pfeiffer ultimately won the race, placing first with a time of one minute, thirty one seconds. Jack placed a very respectable seventh, ahead of Steve and one spot behind Pete—who received a ribbon for sixth place.

"Not bad for a California guy," Pete teased and added, "In all seriousness, that time would earn you a spot on any eastern college team. Well done, Oakland."

What would Pops say if he heard that?

Jack's cheeks heated and he smiled awkwardly. "Thanks."

During their quick lunch served from the back of a truck, the slalom gates were put in place. Because this whole event was thrown together so hastily, there was no time for the hundred-plus skiers to take a practice run down the course. Each of them would have to take the gates as they appeared.

"This will be interesting," Steve said with his mouth stuffed with a ham and cheese sandwich. "The times will be slower because we don't know where the gates are."

"And if you miss one," *or skip it*, "then you're disqualified." Jack rubbed his wind-burned cheeks. "Better to ski skillfully and hit every gate, I think."

Steve nodded. "Agreed."

For the slalom competition, Jack was skiing in the first third of the competitors. He didn't like that—he felt he'd do better if he knew how his opponents had done before he took his turn.

"You just have to give it all you've got," Steve said. "Ski like the devil is on your tail and don't let up for a moment."

Right. Ski like Hollinghurst was on his tail.

Because he will be.

Once again Jack stood at the top of the mountain waiting his turn. The view was truly spectacular, but he seldom took time to enjoy it.

Breathe, he told himself.

Focus on the race, not the asshole.

Jack gripped his poles and waited, concentrating on taking in what oxygen the air held, and leaned into the hill.

Beeeep!

He was off.

Jack knew there were twenty gates on the course and he counted as he swerved through each one. His thighs burned with the quick and frequent turns. Snow was tossed in glittering sprays away from his skis as their metal edges cut into the course. Nothing existed for Jack but the next gate.

Get there fast.

Make the tight turn as low to the snow as possible.

Speed to the next one.

After he counted twenty gates, he tucked in and skied to the finish line, shaped like a missile and with every muscle straining for speed.

He crossed the finish line with so much momentum that this time he did slide sideways into the spectator fence. Hands reached out and grabbed him to keep him from falling.

Jack struggled to stay upright, jamming his poles into the snow.

"Did you make all the gates?"

That was Steve's voice. Jack straightened, once again steady on his skis, and lifted his goggles. When he saw Steve he nodded.

"All twenty. I counted."

Jack turned to look at the scoreboard, waiting for his time.

Three minutes, thirty-nine seconds.

Steve pounded Jack's back from the other side of the fence. "Not bad, Oakland. Not bad at all!" His voice was thick with respect. "Now I know what time I have to beat!"

*****

Jack didn't place in the slalom, which wasn't really a surprise considering all the championship skiers he was competing against. It was one thing to be fast going straight down, but another thing entirely to be fast in a zigzag course he'd never practiced on.

Thirteen men were disqualified for missing at least one gate. Hollinghurst was not one of the thirteen.

"Guess he skied clean this time. And at least I beat his time." Jack lifted his beer and took a sip. He grinned at Steve and Pete. "Two seconds is two seconds."

"Did he say anything to you afterwards?" Pete asked.

Jack shook his head and set his beer glass down. "Nope."

The camp's new enlisted men's club was packed tonight and conversations all around the trio of friends replayed the day's competitions. Several WACs were there, and each gal was surrounded by a cluster of enthusiastic men waving their arms and mimicking their runs.

Jack sighed.

I miss Beth.

He took another swallow of beer and returned his attention to his friends. "So. Either of you guys found a girl yet?"

April 24, 1944

Brigadier General Jones had allowed the competition, but he ordered the Tenth Light Division to get back to work immediately afterwards. Officers were again being shuffled around, and the spring and summer training schedules were being developed.

The First Sergeant of F Company knew that Jack was rejoining the Mountain Training Group after the D-Series test was completed.

"No reason to wait," he said. "I'll put in the morning report that you're back to temporary duty at the MTG."

The Mountain Training Group now had their own barracks at Camp Hale, not like the facility at Cooper Hill for the ski instructor cadre. Aside from getting away from Hollinghurst, Jack was especially glad to find out that Tech Sergeant Bill Klein had gotten Jack assigned to his team again.

Training would begin immediately after all the ski gear was accounted for, cleaned, and stowed away. So when Jack arrived at the warehouse every instructor in the MTG was working on the many thousands of pairs of skis and ski poles that were turned in by the three regiments in the camp.

All the reconciliation and accounting of equipment had to be logged and documented—and these tasks were assigned to the ski instructor cadre. All of their skis, poles, bindings, and snowshoes had been used hard or broken during the difficult and harsh D-Series test. Someone needed to decide if they were repairable or too far gone to fix.

Bill Klein pulled Jack aside. "I want you to sort and stack all the skis that're no longer serviceable. I trust you to know what to look for."

Jack smiled. "Yes sir."

It's a good day to be at Camp Hale.

*****

Beth's last letter said she still hadn't heard back from the Red Cross yet, and Jack counted that as lucky for him. As long as they were in the same country that meant another chance to see her might materialize somehow.

After spending the day working in camaraderie and conversation with the other skiers, Jack was in a pensive mood. He considered the hundreds of men working and joking with each other, all from different economic backgrounds—even different countries—and thought about how his experiences both at Kiska and during the D-Series test had shaped not only him, but those he was working with.

Some men rose to the top, while others floundered.

Some gave orders well, while others took orders well.

And in the end, judgments were inevitably made concerning the officers and enlisted men who engaged in those endeavors. It came down to who could be trusted and who could not.

He decided to write his thoughts down to make them more clear, and if they made any sense at all he'd mail them to either Beth or his dad.

Letters from his parents had been sporadic but Jack didn't blame them. His own life turned on the whim of the Army and he knew his dad understood military life, even if it wasn't his precious Marine Corps.

He'd heard from his brother Harry now and again. Harry received a few promotions himself and was now a corporal as well. Jack had to wonder if their dad bragged to Harry about Jack as much as he bragged to Jack about Harry.

He doubted it.

Maybe he'd send this letter to Harry. Jack wondered if his brother's experiences were anything like his own. He missed their brotherly conversations and thinking about Harry made him homesick.

There was no sense at all in going down that road. He pulled out paper and pen and started writing

My opinions of the soldiers that I served with on Kiska were established during the months of our deployment, even though the reputation of the 87th took a hit because so many officers were inexperienced at that point.

Then the D-Series test, which was rough on all of us,

showed the strengths of every soldier here, both the officers and the enlisted men. But the pompous attitudes of some of the higher up officers earned them such bad reputations they'll probably never shake them.

Overall I'm very glad to say that the mountain troops are outstanding men and first-rate soldiers.

Do you remember the man I've spoken to you about before? AH?

Jack chuckled and stared at the question on the paper. Obviously in his mind this letter was meant for Beth. He might as well continue it that way.

He proved himself unreliable once again. He got himself lost during the test because he can't orient himself to save his own life, much less anyone else's. Steve, Pete, and I had to go out and find him and ended up spending the night outside on the mountain during a blizzard.

Did he say thank you? No, Beth, he did not. He had the nerve to say his compass malfunctioned and he was on his way back to the company when we reached him. He said he didn't need any rescuing.

Luckily, it didn't seem like Captain Rideout believed his story. So AH's true *reputation has been established with others now, not just with me.*

And as sweet icing on the revenge cake, the three of us got commendations, while it looked to us that AH got a severe dressing down.

Jack turned the paper over and continued with, *I miss you so much, my love...*

In the end he wrote out two copies of the first part of the letter and sent one to his parents and one to Harry.

But Beth's envelope was the thickest by far.

May 1, 1944

Summer was definitely coming to the Rockies. April's snow

turned into May's waterfalls and rushing streams. New schedules were worked out, training areas were assigned to the three battalions by the week, and the entire camp was preparing for the summer mountaineering training.

The summer cadre of instructors—the guys who were skilled rock and ice climbers—wasn't the same group as the ski instructors. Sure, some of the guys stayed on and did both, but an entirely different set of skills, tools and equipment was necessary for summer rock climbing instruction, and not all the skiers were qualified.

Because Jack had those skills, he was once again assigned as a climbing instructor and settled into the Mountain Training Group along with Steve and Pete.

While the ski instructors finished with the ski inventory, the climbing instructors worked on the climbing equipment, which also needed to be counted, cleaned, inventoried and separated for the individual teams of instructors.

"This isn't the most glamorous work," Jack said to Steve as he hoisted a neat coil of rope over one shoulder. "But it sure beats running with a full rucksack any day."

"Yep." Steve hefted a coil as well. "I have to admit, I do wonder what sort of hell Hollinghurst is putting the guys through."

"Don't know. And don't care." Jack turned to carry the rope to a pile of equipment designated for one of the F-Company platoons. He flashed a mischievous grin. "I just hope his compass works."

The next day, Tech Sergeant Klein took his group of instructors to the area where they would be doing the rock-climbing instruction.

"Here's where the battalions will bivouac," he said pointing to a flat wooded area. "The climbing routes will be up this face here."

Jack shaded his eyes and looked up at the craggy granite wall, looking for hand and foot holds.

This will do.

Then he turned to Pete and Steve. "This is gonna be fun."

"All right men." Klein grinned at the assembled instructors. "Scramble. Get to know the rocks."

While he usually climbed with ropes and equipment, Jack loved this kind of climbing best: scrambling up the side of a mountain with only his bare hands and his experience to get him to the top.

"Last man up buys the beer tonight," he challenged.

"You're on, Oakland!" Pete hollered as he started climbing.

Steve laughed and pulled himself up on the granite. "Working up a thirst already!"

Chapter Twenty-One

May 10, 1944

Jack stared at Bill Klein. "Is this a joke?"

The tech sergeant made a disgusted face. "Sadly, it's not."

Jack looked at the other men in Klein's group. Judging from their expressions, they were as stunned and confused as he was.

"But we've been doing climbing training for less than three weeks!" Jack objected, knowing it was futile but needing to express his shocked frustration anyway. "What the *hell* does Army Ground Forces expect the Tenth Light Division to do in *Texas?*"

"Climb a rise?" one man scoffed.

"Ski down a sand dune?" another said derisively and then snorted. "What's the altitude at Camp Swift?"

Klein shrugged. "It's... flat."

"Do we *have* to go?" Jack was grasping at straws that he realized didn't actually exist. "What about our acclimation to high altitudes? After just those few months in Kiska we all lost it and had to readjust!"

"Not to mention," a man drawled, "it's a bit warm in Texas."

"Hot as hell and ten times as humid." The first man punched his own thigh. "Damn the Army."

Bill Klein stood in front of his men with his hands on his hips. "Apparently there's some big traditional exercise every fall that's been conducted in Louisiana for years—"

"*Louisiana?*" Steve hollered. He threw his hands in the air. "Oh, hell. This just *keeps* getting better!"

"—and we're supposed to adjust to the heat and humidity before we're involved. That's why we're going to Texas." The fact that Klein didn't chastise the men under his command for their verbal insubordination proved, in Jack's estimation anyway, that the tech sergeant agreed with their objections. "The good news—"

"Wait!" Jack blurted. "*Is* there good news?"

Klein shrugged. "I think so."

"What is it?" Steve snapped.

"All the other Army divisions have been through these maneuvers and then been immediately deployed to Europe, Africa, or the Pacific."

That shut Jack up. He slumped in his seat and let that realization sink in for a moment.

These Louisiana maneuvers were apparently the precursor to deployment. Once the Tenth Light Division completed them, they'd all be on their way to war.

He lifted his gaze to Bill Klein's. "We'll be sent to Europe after the maneuvers, then. In the fall."

Klein nodded somberly. "That's what I assume. And it's what we've been training for, isn't it? Fighting in the mountains? There aren't any mountains in Africa or the Pacific. I'm guessing the Alps will be our destination."

The mood in the room shifted from frustrated anger to sober consideration.

"The problem is…" Steve began slowly. "We aren't *like* any other division. Nothing we do in Texas or Louisiana can help us be better at what we do."

"It'll only keep us *away* from the training that we require," Pete added.

Jack's temper surged again. "So just like always? The mountain troops are being treated like we're nothing special and *anyone* can do what we do?" he shouted. "But when they run us through some damned test at the top of the world, and even the fucking *officers* can't keep up, they still can't see it!"

A rumble of agreement surrounded Jack, who was shockingly close to frustrated tears. "Is everything we've done here for nothing? The frostbite, or the altitude sickness, or even the damned Pando hack?"

Jack scrambled to his feet and pointed a stiff arm in the general direction of camp headquarters. "What about those guys who *died* in Kiska? What's the Army going to tell *their* families?" His tone switched to sarcasm. "Gee, sorry. Guess none of that was necessary."

Bill stared at Jack, his face a blank mask and his voice calm. "You're dismissed, Corporal."

Jack recoiled, realizing he was way, *way* out of line. He straightened and saluted his mentor, friend, and commanding officer with a shaking hand before stumbling over the other men to get out of the building.

*****

When Steve found Jack an hour later he was at the top of the deserted training wall, flat on his back, and wearing the green sunglasses that hid his now-dried tears. Steve stretched out next to him. He stared wordlessly at the heavy-bottomed rain clouds overhead, gathering to fill the sky, until Jack finally spoke.

"Guess I made a scene."

Steve heaved a sigh. "You only said what the rest of us were thinking."

"Is Bill mad?"

"Nah."

Jack slid his fingers under the glasses—unnecessary in the early twilight—and rubbed his eyes. "What am I going to tell my father?"

"About what?"

"About spending twenty-eight months training in a ski troop only to have it all go to hell?" Jack felt his tamped-down anger rising yet again. "I can't believe that Army Ground Forces is so consistently *stupid*."

"Wish you'd joined the Marines instead?"

Jack's hands dropped on his chest and he turned to look at Steve. "Are *you* kidding me now?"

Steve's lips twitched. "It's a legitimate question."

"No!" Jack sat up and stared down at his prostrate friend. "*Hell* no!"

"Good." Steve sat up as well. "After you left, Klein said we're all going to keep training until the day we actually get on the train."

Jack was glad to hear that at least. "How long will that be?"

"The best guess is some time in June."

A month.

"Maybe they'll change their minds before we have to go," Jack said hopefully.

"I can't see Brigadier General Jones standing up for us to stay here, not after his speech following the D-Series," Steve grumbled. "Can you?"

"No." This was apparently going to happen, then. "I need a beer."

"Or two."

Jack smiled a little. "Or five."

Steve rose to his feet and peered at the darkening sky. "Guess we better climb down, Oakland. Not only is it about to pour on us, but that's a big beer goal. We need to get started on it if we hope to meet it."

*****

Dear Beth ~

You're not going to believe this. I hate to even write it down because that will make it real, not just words hanging in the air. But I guess it's going to happen.

Army Ground Forces is sending the 10th Light Division ~ twelve thousand men who have been training at high altitudes and in frigid snowy conditions in anticipation of fighting in the Alpine mountains of Europe ~ to Camp Swift near Austin, Texas.

Texas.

Flat ~~fucking~~ (SORRY!) Texas.

We're being sent there so we can adjust to the heat and humidity, before moving on to maneuvers in Louisiana.

Louisiana!

Sea level, swampy Louisiana!

And for how long, you might ask? Months, Beth. Until we deploy, apparently. So, long enough for us to forget our training, lose our high altitude tolerance, and grow fat and weak sitting on our posteriors passing the time.

I can't even think about how I'll explain this to my father and brother. There is no justification for the Army's stupidity and their constant assumption that the Mountain troops are just like every other infantry soldier. They could even send us to Africa or the Pacific at this point.

Who knows?

For the first time since the war started, I am regretting enlisting in the Army. I better stop writing before I decide to go AWOL.

Have you heard from the Red Cross yet?

All my love from your...
I don't even know how to call myself now.

Jeff

June 21, 1944

Weeks before the trains arrived at Pando Station on a windy Wednesday morning to begin transporting twelve thousand disgruntled soldiers of Tenth Light Division to Camp Swift in Texas, Brigadier General Jones commanded every company in the division to have its photograph taken.

All dressed and pressed, the companies filed in front of the photographer who took four or five shots each of the assembled groups of soldiers. Jack ordered three copies of F Company—one for Beth, one for his parents, and one for himself, which he also mailed to his parents for safekeeping.

At least there would be some record that these men had trained and served together toward the common goal of mountain warfare, even if that never came to fruition.

Now, as the men waited in seemingly endless lines to file onto one of the waiting trains, Jack wondered what their collective future held.

According to the war reports in the *Ski-Zette*, on June fifth a Lieutenant General Mark Clark and the Fifth Army had taken

Rome: *It's expected that Clark and the Fifth will continue north and push the Nazis out of Italy.*

That meant fighting in Italy was successful so it was doubtful at this point that the Tenth would be sent there.

The news from June sixth, however, was staggering to a man.

More than one hundred and sixty thousand Allied troops landed along a fifty-mile stretch of the heavily-fortified French coastline to engage Nazi Germany on the beaches of Normandy, France.

Over five thousand ships and thirteen thousand aircraft supported the invasion, and by day's end the Allies gained a foot-hold in Continental Europe.

The war was becoming much more real to Jack than it had ever been up to this point.

Steve poked Jack in the back as their line shuffled toward the train. "How you feeling, Oakland?"

"I'm feeling lucky, Dropout," he replied. "How about you?"

"Lucky as the day is long, son."

Jack laughed. His father told him time and again that luck was what pulled him through the First World War. Luck was what landed him in the hospital where he met Edyta. And luck was the only thing a soldier could count on, because war was comprised of chaos.

Jack pulled himself up the train steps, moved down the aisle to the next available seats, and stowed his duffel bag in the shelf overhead. He dropped into the window seat and Steve took the aisle seat next to him.

"Back where we started," Steve observed quietly.

"And off to a new adventure," Jack countered. He turned toward his friend. "I'm glad to be serving with you, Knowlton."

Steve smiled. "I feel the same, Franklin."

June 23, 1944

Just as Jack feared, Camp Swift outside of Austin, Texas proved to be a hot, humid, dusty, snake and bug-infested hellhole without a single mountain for hundreds of miles.

At this point Jack thought his dad was getting the last laugh, and at his sorry expense. And judging by the snippets of grumbling conversation around him, he wasn't the only one who felt that way.

F Company arrived at Camp Swift in their standard woolen Army uniforms, which were fine for Camp Hale at over nine thousand feet, but completely wrong for a sweltering Texas summer, which hit them full force and without mercy as soon as they stepped off the train.

Steve elbowed Jack's arm and pointed to a group of German prisoners of war who were also disembarking at the Camp Swift train station. "Look at how those guys are dressed. They must be from the *Afrika Korps*."

Jack turned to where Steve pointed and evaluated the Germans' uniforms. Made of cotton twill and with open collars, the prisoners' jackets were much better suited to the Texas heat than the wool uniforms that the ski troops wore.

"They're wearing cotton shorts." Jack wondered if his envy was obvious.

When the Germans saw the heavily perspiring ski troops, they began to nudge each other, laugh, and make rude gestures in their direction.

"Damn Nazis," Steve growled. "But they do have a point."

A red-faced and sweating Captain Rideout lifted his arm. "This way, men."

Jack shouldered his duffel bag and followed the captain toward their new barracks. "Only two months ago we were freezing in the mountains."

Steve wiped his brow on the sleeve of his jacket. "Wish I was there now."

*****

Jack was happily surprised to be handed a letter from Beth while he was unpacking and settling into F Company's new barracks. Stripped down to a sleeveless undershirt and with his trousers rolled above his knees, he sat on his cot, leaned against the cool plastered wall at its head, and crossed his bare feet on the blanket he doubted he'd ever need.

"Please tell me something good, Beth," he whispered as he slid his thumb under the seal and opened the envelope.

My poor, dearest Jeff ~

I have never heard you speak so dejectedly in the two years we have known each other. I ache to be with you, to hold you close, and tell you that everything will be fine. Only we both know that nothing we do can change things as they are.

Even so, I have decided to travel to Austin to see you. There isn't a reason for me to come in my official capacity as an aide to John, unless he decides to make a visit to Camp Swift for some reason. Though I can't think of why he would, I will ask him before I make my plans.

No matter his answer, I will come. And I will come within a month.

Thank you for the large photograph of F Company. When it arrived, I told my mother it was to thank me for recruiting a bunch of the men in the picture. My parents are still ignorant of my special love, as I assume yours are as well.

One thing is true: you are the most handsome man in the entire group.

No, I haven't heard from the Red Cross. Hopefully I will have before I see you. Please send me a phone number where I can reach you and tell me when I can call. I'll do so when my plans are set.

All my love and admiration,

Beth

July 10, 1944

Instead of men falling out due to altitude sickness, the soldiers in the Tenth Light Division were now succumbing in droves to Texas's blistering summer heat and oppressive humidity. And heat exhaustion was just as dangerous as altitude sickness.

Frustrated by the Army's mishandling of their situation, and suffering from the depression brought on by cold-weather men living under inescapable and sweltering conditions, Tenth soldiers began applying for transfers to divisions already in combat.

Being shot at while hunkered in a muddy foxhole was apparently better than living at Camp Swift.

The Airborne Divisions that parachuted into Normandy, France on June sixth had sustained casualty rates in unprecedented numbers, and now they were scrambling for volunteers to replace those thousands of troops lost on the bloody beaches. They even offered an extra fifty dollars a month in incentive pay, and hundreds of the mountain troopers took advantage of that offer.

"You thinking about it?" Jack asked Steve over beers in the crowded enlisted men's club—one of three air-conditioned buildings at the camp.

Steve shook his head. "I'm an optimist. I think we'll get our chance."

Jack agreed. "I can see the guys who were new to skiing not sticking with it. They've trained for over two years and right now there's no guarantee they'll ever use that training in the war."

Steve chuckled. "I have to be honest. I'm a patriot through and through, but I have no desire to die by German ordnance."

"Japs for you, then," Jack teased and punched Steve's arm. "But seriously, for guys like you and me, and the Austrians and Norwegians, skiing is in our blood. We'll wait it out and hope for the best."

"Yep." Steve waived Pete Seibert over and changed the subject. "When's Betty coming?"

Jack smiled. "Two more weeks. Can't wait."

"Lucky." Steve slid his chair sideways to make room for Pete. "What's new?"

Pete set his beer on the table while he stuffed bills back into his wallet. "Hope you guys are happy here, because no more transfer requests will be accepted."

Nothing we do can change things as they are.

Jack flashed a rueful grin and raised his glass. "To the swamp troopers!"

Chapter
Twenty-Two

July 20, 1944

Jack knew he should write to his parents and let them know where he was, but he'd been putting it off since arriving at Camp Swift. Once he saw the conditions which he and the other ski troopers would be training under, he struggled with how to tell his father in a way that wouldn't give that man more anti-Army ammunition.

That was especially hard, since Jack was staunchly on his father's side at the moment.

In the light of the Army's continuing mishandling of the mountain troops, their contention that their training in Camp Hale was nothing special, and the three failed demonstrations of what the Tenth soldiers could actually do, Jack could not help but wonder if he had made a critical error by stubbornly insisting on joining the Army ski troops instead of the Marines.

Was he going to end up sitting in this barren God-forsaken heat while the war was brought to an end by brave men who made less selfish decisions?

Jack didn't think he could live with himself if that happened.

Or—with Pops and his future contention that Jack 'did nothing' after all.

He tried to push those gut-wrenching concerns and fears aside and settled on writing to his folks about the extra men and munitions that had been added to the Tenth since their arrival here almost a month ago.

He knew that was the sort of thing that interested his ex-military father anyway, and because they expected to deploy after being here, the letter would sound much more positive than Jack felt at the moment.

> *Here in Camp Swift the Army Ground Forces is reorganizing the 10th Light Division. They're adding 2600 enlisted men and officers to the Division, plus heavy weapons, including the 81mm Mortar and the .50 Caliber machine gun, to the fourth company in each battalion.*
>
> *We're getting ready for battle, Pops. It's been a long time coming, I know. But we're ready, we've been ready, and the Army finally agrees.*
>
> *With the addition of the new recruits to the Division, Captain Rideout put my name in for promotion to sergeant because, as he says, I'm a good leader. So I'm officially Sergeant John Franklin now.*

Jack paused. There was no reason to tell his father that Aston Hollinghurst had been promoted to first lieutenant. At least in the wake of his own promotion Hollinghurst went easier on Jack this time when he too stepped up another rank.

> *With my new stripes came the responsibility for training newly enlisted soldiers in infantry tactics. To be honest, all the time I spent as a ski instructor made me a darn good teacher. Now I have twelve men that I'm in charge of and they're all doing really well.*

Jack smiled a little. If he didn't brag on himself, no one else would do it for him. One more bit about how hard he was working and the letter would be pretty much done.

And he hadn't let his disappointment or frustration creep into any part of it.

> *Our training here includes hikes of varying length and duration. At first the hikes were easy, only six to ten miles*

*because of the new recruits and the Texas heat. Since then
we've built up to fifteen, twenty, now twenty-five miles with
full 90 pound rucksacks. Thankfully I didn't lose too much
endurance while the new guys caught up.*

Jack finished the letter with questions about how Harry was
doing, and a paragraph assuring his mother that he was eating well
and getting enough sleep. Then he folded it, sealed it, stamped it,
and headed outside to drop it in the camp mailbox.

With the sun below the horizon and a light breeze ruffling the
branches of the camp's sparse trees the temperature outside was
actually tolerable. A full moon, with its face streaked by thin and
useless clouds, was rising slowly through the eastern sky.

Was Beth looking at the moon tonight, he wondered. And if she
was, was her moon wearing a scarf of clouds, too?

His claim to be sleeping well was mostly true, but Jack was
pretty sure he'd have a hard time tonight. He dropped the letter in
the mailbox then turned back toward his barracks with a deep and
impatient sigh.

Safe travels, Beth.
I'll see you tomorrow.

July 21, 1944

Jack waited at the entrance to Camp Swift, staring down the
road in search of a taxi. Beth was flying into the Austin Airport and
her flight should have landed an hour ago.

Jack didn't have any experience with airplanes, only trains, so
he wasn't sure how long it would take her to get off the plane, get
her luggage, and find a taxi to bring her to the camp. So he paced
the entire length of the guard building and back again before settling
in the shade of its roof to continue his vigil.

He'd secured Beth a Visitor's Pass, which was easy since she
worked for the Army and was again traveling with John Jay on their
last recruiting trip across the country.

Jack planned to show her around—and to show her off, if he
was honest—until his weekend pass started at seven o'clock this
evening. After that, he was free until Monday morning at seven.

He had no idea how they'd spend their time and he didn't care. Whatever Beth wanted to do was what they'd do.

A flash of yellow appeared on the horizon. Jack stared it down, unrelenting, until it proved itself. Then his face broke into such a wide smile it actually hurt.

When the taxi stopped in front of the guard gate, the driver hopped out and opened the back door. The vision of loveliness that emerged from the vehicle stole Jack's ability to breathe.

Beth wore a green sleeveless blouse that matched her eyes, and snug navy blue pedal-pushers. Her dark brown hair was tied back in a ponytail with a gauzy scarf. A pair of dark glasses perched on the bridge of her nose.

Beaming, she scurried around the taxi and straight into Jack's embrace, kissing him without hesitation.

The taxi driver's throat-clearing at close proximity startled Jack into abruptly ending the kiss and stepping back, bumping against Beth's large two-toned suitcase.

Seemingly unfazed, Beth turned toward the man and flashed a blinding smile as she pulled some bills from her purse. "Here you are. Thank you."

The man's brows lifted appreciatively at the amount she gave him. "Thank you, miss. Do you still want me to return tonight at seven?"

"Yes, please." She giggled and tossed a thumb over her shoulder. "I sure can't sleep here on the base, can I?"

"No, miss." He touched the brim of his cap and glanced curiously at Jack. "I'll see you later then."

Beth faced Jack again and touched the insignia on his sleeve. "Why didn't you tell me you got promoted, Sergeant Franklin?"

Jack felt his cheeks warming even more than the weather warranted and he flashed a shy smile. "I wanted to surprise you."

"Well I'm not surprised, Jeff. It's very well deserved." She slipped her arm through his and kissed his cheek. "Shall we?"

After retrieving the Visitor's Pass, Jack stowed Beth's suitcase in his barracks for the rest of the afternoon while he gave her the ten-dollar tour of Camp Swift, from the Officers' Club to the Prisoner of War enclosure full of German soldiers.

"There was a POW enclosure at Camp Hale," she said casually. "Did you ever go over there?"

Jack stopped walking and stared at her. "Are you kidding?"

Beth faced him, confused and amused. "No. John told me where it was. He said there were two hundred prisoners there."

Jack frowned and tilted his head. "I had no idea. Where?"

"Beyond the motor pool and the hospital." She shrugged. "In the woods, I guess. So they couldn't see the sky, or be seen."

Jack wagged his head and started walking again. "Can't believe we didn't know."

Beth's gaze swept over the view of the camp from their vantage point. "And I can't believe this is even worse than you made it sound."

"Is it?" Jack squinted in the intense sun from behind his green-tinted glasses. "I thought I was pretty accurate."

"You can't mail heat in a letter. Or humidity." Beth fanned herself with a little notepad she dug out of her purse. "Is any place in the camp air-conditioned?"

"Yep." Jack turned her toward the enlisted men's club. "Let's get something cold to drink. What do you want to do for supper?"

*****

Jack and Beth opted to forego the mess hall food and wait to have supper at her hotel. The taxi was waiting by the entrance gate at seven as planned, and the drive into Austin was about twenty minutes.

Jack held Beth's hand in the back seat, but didn't talk much. The car's open windows sent hot wind blasting through the inside making conversation difficult.

"I'm going to need a minute to freshen up," Beth said while Jack held the hotel lobby door open. She retied her pony tail as she walked through. "I feel like I've just run through a blast furnace."

Jack followed, carrying her suitcase. "So do I."

He set the suitcase beside Beth while she signed the register and it was immediately picked up by a uniformed bellman who waited for Beth to finish.

The desk clerk handed the bellman her room key. "Suite six-oh-one."

"Is there someplace where my friend can wash up before dinner?" Beth asked the clerk.

"Yes. The men's room is right down that hall." He pointed to Jack's left.

Beth turned to face him. "I'll meet you in the restaurant. Would you order us a bottle of wine? I like your choices."

Jack smiled. "Happy to."

The men's room was nothing like he'd ever seen before. The marble floors and dark paneled walls with shiny brass fixtures probably cost about as much as his parents' modest little home in Oakland. He relieved himself before washing his face and hands, drying them on the fluffy white hand towels stacked by the marble sinks.

Jack walked back across the lobby toward the bar and restaurant. "Two, please," he answered the waiter's inquiry.

He was shown to a table by the window in the nearly full restaurant and asked for the wine list. By the time Beth appeared, the bottle of red wine was open and breathing on the table.

"I have news too, Jeff." Beth lifted her wine glass once the waiter backed away and smiled adorably. "Want to guess?"

Jack figured it could only be one thing. "The Red Cross?"

"Yes, sir! I got the acceptance letter three days ago!" She clinked her glass against Jack's, which emitted the distinctive ping of fine crystal. "I don't know where I'm going yet, but since the recruiting tours are finishing, the timing is perfect."

Jack snorted. "No sense in recruiting for the ski troopers anymore."

Beth made a face at him. "None of that tonight, Sergeant. We're here to celebrate your promotion and my new job."

"You're right, Beth." Jack smiled apologetically. "We can't waste our snippets of time together on anything but us."

"To us." Beth held out her glass again. "To Jeff and Beth and their secret love."

Jack clinked her glass again, though her awkwardly true words and their current situations demanded more of him.

Later.

"To Jeff and Beth. And whatever lies ahead."

*****

Two hours later Jack followed Beth up to her room. Correction, her suite. Up on the top floor of the hotel, she had a living room, bedroom, and large bathroom with a claw-footed tub and separate shower.

Jack whistled. "This is nice, Beth."

She blushed a little. "Sometimes I like to treat myself. The hotels on the recruitment tour are paid for by the Army…"

Jack laughed. "Understood. And I'm not going to ask how much this costs."

"Good. Don't." Beth kicked off her shoes and sat on the couch. "Will you pour the wine?"

Jack turned toward the large window and the marble-topped bar. He selected two glasses and poured from the newly-opened bottle they brought up from the restaurant. "Will you let me take *you* to dinner tomorrow?"

"Maybe." Beth reached for the glass he handed her. "We'll see."

That means no.

Jack sat on the couch next to Beth. Being with her always challenged his thoughts about men and women and who paid for what. Even though it made logical sense because he didn't make much in the Army, and she was a shipping company heiress with a trust fund, it still rankled.

After a moment of comfortable silence Jack ventured, "We do have something serious to talk about."

Beth gripped her wineglass with both hands. "What?"

"We," he emphasized the word, "are going to war."

Beth's shoulders slumped. "Yes. We are."

"At some point, hopefully soon, my regiment will be deployed into battle. Real, actual battle this time," he clarified.

Beth countered soberly, "And I hope to go to England and parts beyond with the Red Cross."

A thought jarred Jack. "Do your parents know you applied yet?"

She nodded slowly.

"Do they know you were accepted?"

Beth's cheeks flushed furiously. "No, not yet. I wanted to tell you first."

"Because you wanted the first reaction you got to be a happy one."

"Yes." Beth sipped from her glass without looking at him.

Jack set his glass on the polished table in front of the sofa. "I could die, Beth."

She gasped. "Don't say that!"

"It's true and you know it." He pulled a deep breath. "And you could die, too. I could survive, but lose you."

Jack's chest tightened at the thought. He cleared his throat and coughed behind his hand to loosen the constricting bands of fear before he could continue.

He met her wide-eyed gaze. "And if that happened, no one in either one of our families would know to tell us."

Beth's eyes filled with tears and one spilled down each cheek. "What do we do?" she whispered.

"We have to tell them. Before we leave the country, we have to let our families know that we are serious about each other." Jack gripped Beth's free hand. "Can you do that?"

She leaned forward and set her glass down next to his, then took both his hands in both of hers. "We don't have a choice, do we?"

"Not really. But remember this: we are both adults. We make our own decisions. If our parents object, then they don't understand either one of us."

Beth's smile trembled. "We're rebels, aren't we, Jeff?"

That was a perspective he hadn't thought of. But she was spot on. "You are rebelling against the empty socialite life."

"And you rebelled against joining the Marines in spite of your father."

Jack smiled and felt like another piece in their shared puzzle just fell solidly into place. "That's why, isn't it? Why we fit so well from the start."

Beth looped her arms around his neck and he pulled her against his chest. Their kiss was deep, passionate, and consuming.

Jack lost track of time. He didn't know how long they had been lying on the sofa kissing, touching, and holding each other tightly. He only knew he could not physically move from that spot.

Beth yawned and relaxed against him.

"I should go," he whispered.

"No," she answered in kind.

He brushed her hair back from her face. "I have to leave at some point."

"Why?" She propped her chin on the fist resting on his chest. "You don't have to be back at the camp until Monday morning. Stay here."

Jack's shock must have been evident because Beth looked horrified.

"On the couch!" she yelped. "I'm not suggesting anything else. Oh, Lord." She covered her eyes. "Gosh, that came out wrong."

Jack chuckled and pried her hands away so he could look at her. "Are you inviting me to sleep on your sofa tonight and tomorrow night while there is a solid door between us?"

Beth winced. "Yes. That. Only that."

"What about your reputation?"

"The *only* person who knows I'm in Austin is the friend who's been accepting your letters. My parents think I'm staying with her."

Jack was beginning to like this idea. A lot. The only glitch was, "Steve and Pete know you're here. If I disappear they might get suspicious."

"Then tell them we stayed in different rooms." She shrugged one shoulder. "We actually will be."

"Maybe this could work," Jack admitted.

Beth's eyes teared up again. "I don't know if I'll ever see you again, Jeff."

She sat up and wiped her eyes as she began to cry in earnest. "We don't know when you're leaving or how much notice you'll have. And the same goes for me and my situation," she managed between increasingly strong sobs. "And if something happens to either one of us—"

"It won't!"

"You don't know that!"

Jack pulled her close again. "Please don't cry, Beth. I'll stay."

She wrapped her arms around his waist, but didn't stop crying right away. Jeff fought back his own tears. Her words—true words—made the perils of war as clear as their crystal wine glasses at dinner.

Nothing was guaranteed.

Risks needed to be taken.

Love must not be ignored.

"I'm sorry for making a scene," she said finally.

Jack was so overwhelmed by emotion he couldn't speak right away. After a moment he managed, "I love you Elizabeth-Anne

Harkins."

"And I love you, John Edward Franklin."

Jack tipped her chin upward and his lips claimed hers once again."

July 24, 1944

Jack returned to Camp Swift briefly on Saturday to shower and pack a clean uniform, something to sleep in, and a toothbrush. After that, he and Beth were inseparable for the rest of the weekend. And while he slept on the couch on Friday and Saturday nights, they fell asleep fully clothed on her bed on Sunday. But there was a good reason.

Sunday evening over the dinner Beth had delivered to the suite, Jack got down on one knee and proposed.

He hadn't planned it. Hadn't thought about it. He just did it.

And it was the right thing to do.

And she said yes.

"I don't have an engagement ring for you," he apologized. "I didn't expect to ask you this soon."

"It's fine, Jeff. I can't wear anything but a plain band when I'm working with the Red Cross anyway." She laid her hand against his cheek. "But rings don't make promises to marry. People do. And we've just done that."

Jack huffed a laugh. "Now we *really* need to tell our families."

Between their shared declarations of love, and talk of their future together—if they were blessed enough to have one—Jack and Beth dozed off in each other's arms and didn't leave each other's side until the alarm woke them at six in the morning.

They said their goodbyes, repeatedly, until Jack really did need to get into the taxi and speed back to Camp Swift.

He made it with three minutes to spare.

Chapter
Twenty-Three

August, 1944

Jack buried himself in combat training for himself and his men. They spent days and nights working through different battle scenarios, which helped the newly formed squad to bond as a unit.

One advantage Camp Swift offered was the opportunity to learn weapons systems and procedures that had not been available at Camp Hale. In Colorado, the bulk of their training involved skiing, rock climbing, and cold weather survival.

Obviously none of that was continuing here.

In spite of that, Jack was fascinated with the different weapons. Recruits with the least skill started with the Browning Automatic Rifle, which weighed nearly twenty pounds and fired thirty caliber bullets. From there, the recruits moved to the M1 Garand, made by Winchester, which only weighed nine-and-a-half pounds.

Officers and senior non-commissioned officers like Jack were issued the M1 Carbine, only five-and-a-half pounds, and fired automatic cartridges.

The best part—and the part Jack wrote to his father about—was the chance to fire a German MG42 machine gun. That gun was heavy and powerful, and gave every man that had the chance to shoot it a hefty dose of respect for the enemy they expected to face someday soon.

Part of the training involved calling in artillery fire during battle. Jack's men spent the entire month identifying fire from the eighty-one-millimeter mortars and one-hundred-and-five-millimeter howitzers, both in daylight and at night under illumination flares.

They also practiced moving at night as a company and battalion while heavy machine guns from both sides fired live ammunition around them. The men learned to make use of supporting fire to run or crawl from one foxhole to another.

Relief from the unrelenting Texas heat came in the unexpected form of the Colorado River. Jack and his men repeatedly practiced how to tactically cross the river, and managed to get wet and stay cool in the process.

The one thing Jack had not managed to do that month was tell his parents about Beth. He knew he was avoiding it because, even though he thought his mother would be fine with the news, he expected his father wasn't going to be at all happy.

On the last day in August, after a couple beers for liquid courage, Jack sat down at a desk in the barracks and started writing. He decided to talk first about his training, and drop the revelation that he had a serious gal in later. Like that wasn't the main reason for writing.

> *Training at Camp Swift has its own unique challenges, Pops. Unlike Colorado, and especially the European theater where we expect to deploy, here in Texas poison oak and poison ivy curse us every time we're training in the field.*
>
> *Not only that, we also get to enjoy scorpion stings, ticks, chiggers, fire ants, and snakes. Our poor medics are practicing all sorts of remedies which, if they're lucky, they'll never need again for the rest of their lives.*
>
> *As long as they don't move to Texas, that is.*
>
> *It's so bad that the division doctors have to go along with us into the field, march with us in the heat, and sleep in our field bivouacs so they're close enough to treat us. But don't worry, Mom. I'm surviving. None of this is fatal, just annoying as all get-out.*

Jack reread his words, satisfied that his tone was casual enough. The time had come to mention Beth. Jack sucked a deep steadying breath and set his pen on the paper.

> *Do you remember that gal who was traveling around the country with the ski trooper's recruiting film a couple years ago? I took her out for drinks the next night.*
>
> *Anyway, we've been in touch ever since through letters and phone calls, and she came to Camp Hale twice when the film crews were there.*
>
> *I guess what I'm trying to say is, we began officially dating about a year ago or so, and it's going well. Her name is Elizabeth-Anne Harkins, but she goes by Betty.*

Jack paused, unsure of what else to say. To admit he proposed to her and she accepted was probably not wise at this point. But to talk her up and say he was serious about her seemed safe enough.

> *She's really a great gal, very down-to-earth. She was actually one of the first female ski instructors to get certified, so we have that interest in common. She's just finished the recruitment tours and has been accepted into the Red Cross, so now she's a soldier in her own way.*

Jack reread his words. They sounded pretty good. Time to move on and wrap this little bombshell in more Army stuff.

> *Speaking of soldiering, we've just received word that the Louisiana maneuvers, which was the <u>entire</u> reason we left our training in Colorado, have been cancelled.*
>
> *Can you believe it? We haven't been told why, but my buddy Steve thinks it's because the war effort is going well and the Army wants to bolster that momentum with more troops as soon as possible.*
>
> *We still don't know when or where we'll be sent, so for now we just keep training, because it doesn't make sense to increase the size of the division and invest so much time and effort to create a cohesive unit if they plan to ship us off individually. I'll let you know what's happening when I do.*
>
> *Love, Jack*

September 1944

Jack and the other soldiers from Camp Hale still wore their Tenth Division patch with the crossed bayonets on their uniforms. They hadn't been told that their name or mission would be changed, so Jack took that to mean that, thankfully, they were not going to be converted to an ordinary infantry division.

"We're still mountain troops," he said to Steve and Pete one Saturday night over beers in the enlisted men's club. "And mountain troops go into mountains."

"I agree," Pete said. "And the Germans still have a stronghold in the Italian Alps from what we know, so it only makes sense for us to be sent there."

Steve nodded. "No one else can go where there aren't roads and the terrain is so mountainous. Maybe the powers that be are finally getting that through their thick skulls."

"Either that..." Jack chuckled. "Or Minnie Dole is still pounding it in!"

The confirmation of their speculations arrived with a new herd of mules—proof that the Tenth would remain a Mountain Division. The Army's idea that the mules were capable of pulling heavy artillery up snowy slopes had been disproved to some extent with the D-Series test last spring, but the men at Army Ground Forces were apparently as stubborn as their animal of choice.

The mules arrived by boxcar, and the regular infantry guys—who've had no experience with these hard-headed creatures—were sent to collect them from the train.

Jack laughed hard at the situation and the mental image it prompted. He wiped tears of mirth from his eyes as he wrote to Beth about the encounter.

Unfortunately, most of the mules stampeded as soon as they got out of the boxcar, and they ran all over Travis County. The task of rounding up the stray mules fell to us Tenth soldiers, because we do have experience working with the dang animals. So our mule packing lessons at Camp Hale actually served a purpose here.

So... have you told your parents about me?

*****

Beth called Camp Swift a week later.

Jack ran to the servicemen's center at top speed, then grabbed the heavy black receiver and dropped, panting, into the chair in the phone cubicle.

"Hello? Beth?"

The voice he dreamt about answered. "Hi, Jeff! How are you?"

"Better now that I'm talking to you." Jack sighed and settled in his seat. "How are you?"

"Good. And I have news."

Jack closed his eyes. "Good news?"

"I think so. John just called me and said he's planning on going to Austin to see his Tenth Mountain guys before they leave on their assignment."

"When?"

"The last weekend in October."

Beth's voice held an impish tone, which prompted Jack to ask, "Are you coming with him?"

Her playful tone held. "Do you want me to?"

"Is the Pope Catholic?" he quipped. "Hell yes, I do!"

Beth laughed. "Such language, soldier."

"Get used to it, Miss Red Cross," Jack teased. "So you *are* coming?"

"Even if I have to stay in the Army's hotel room."

Jack smiled and twirled his finger in the phone cord, much like Beth always fidgeted with her hair. "I'm so glad to hear that."

Her voice softened. "I thought you would be."

"I can't believe I'll see you in just four weeks."

Beth cleared her voice. "So..."

"Yes?"

"What did you parents say when you told them about me?"

Jack winced. "Mom was happy."

"And your Pops?"

"He'll come around."

His father's assertion that Beth's only reason to be with Jack was because she hoped to marry him and collect his ten thousand dollar life insurance if he died, thereby leaving his parents high and dry in the process, prompted his furious response.

She's an heiress with a trust fund, Pops, he'd written in strong jagged letters. *A measly ten thousand dollars isn't worth her time.*

Pops didn't write back.

"Will he come around, Jeff?" Beth asked quietly. "Or will he resent me for being born into money?"

"Both," Jack answered truthfully. "But once he meets you, he's going to love you like I do. And when we start a family and continue the Franklin name, he'll forget all about the differences."

"They'll have to be boys."

Jack smiled. "There will be boys. I promise."

"I'll hold you to it."

Jack shifted in the wooden chair. "What about your folks?"

Beth was silent.

"Did you tell them?"

"I tried. I started to."

"And?" Jack prodded.

Her voice hardened. "He threatened to take me out of his will if I married anyone he didn't approve of."

"What?" Jack jumped to his feet, though the phone cord was too short for him to stand upright. "What did you say?"

"I said he *will* approve of you. He just has to meet you." Beth paused, then said, "I'm so sorry, Jeff."

"Sorry?" Jack sank back into the chair, pushed down by a bony hand of foreboding. Was she choosing to abide by her father's ultimatum?

"Sorry for what?"

"Sorry that my father is being an ass."

Her strong language shocked him, but he still didn't have an answer. "Do you love me, Beth?"

"Of course I do. You know that."

"Do you trust me?" Jack pressed.

"I said I'd marry you, didn't I?" She sounded angry now.

Jack nodded though she couldn't see it. "If you love me and you trust me, then you *have* to know that I will always take very good care of you."

Beth sniffed again. "So he can take his threat and..."

"Yes."

She sighed heavily. "I do love you, Jack. And that's one of the reasons why."

Relief flushed through Jack's frame. "I love you too, Beth. And in four weeks I'll show you how much."

October 27, 1944

Beth and Captain John Jay arrived on a stormy afternoon at the Austin railroad station. In spite of the thundering downpour, the platform was crowded with soldiers who served together in the Mountain Training Group, eager to reconnect with their recruiter, commander, and champion of the Tenth.

"We've arranged an MTG reunion supper tonight," Steve told Jay after he saluted the captain. "You're our guest of honor."

Pete saluted as well. "We wouldn't be part of the Tenth if it wasn't for you, sir."

Standing behind Captain Jay, Beth peeked out from under her umbrella. Her eyes moved over the crowd until she spied Jack, standing in the middle of the crowd and smiling at her.

She smiled back and Jack's heartbeat stuttered.

"Sounds great." Jay shook both their hands. "Now let's get out of the rain."

While Steve and Pete directed men to the waiting buses to take them all back to Camp Swift, Beth picked her way around puddles toward Jack. When she reached him, he ducked under her umbrella and she slipped her arm through his.

"You look beautiful, Beth," Jack murmured.

She scoffed. "I look like a drowned cat."

Jack shook his head, still grinning like a fool, and escorted her to the buses. "Just accept the compliment."

Beth squeezed his arm. "Fine. *Thank you.* And you are as handsome as ever. Maybe more so."

"It's only because I'm engaged to a wonderful woman." Jack reached into his pocket. "I was going to give you this later, but…"

He handed her a little black box.

Beth's eyes widened. "What did you do?"

"Open it."

Beth stopped walking, handed Jack the umbrella, and unwound her arm from his. She flipped open the lid.

Resting in a white satin nest was a delicate gold chain with a tiny pear-shaped diamond hanging from it.

"Oh, Jeff…"

"You can't wear a diamond engagement ring, but you can tuck this inside your uniform, close to your heart, and no one will be the wiser."

"I love it! Thank you!" Beth closed the box and hooked her arm through Jack's again. "I'll put it on when we get to the camp."

Jack leaned toward her ear. "I wish I could kiss you right now."

Beth's eyes sparkled happily. "We'll have time. We're here for three days."

*****

At the reunion dinner, Captain Jay was swamped by guys from the Mountain Training Group, and because of the casual camaraderie between officers and enlisted men in the MTG, conversations at the tables were boisterous and informal.

Half of the men wanted to talk to Jay about their times at Camp Hale, another half wanted to find out if Jay knew anything about their deployment—but everyone wanted to complain about sitting on the steaming plains of Texas for the last four months.

"I don't have much to tell you," the captain admitted. "But I do know that our training is finally being considered in the decision-making process."

"Only took three years," Pete grumbled.

Steve chuckled. "Three years of skiing and rock climbing and *not* being shot at. Things could have been worse."

From his prized seat across from Beth, Jack looked down the long table at Captain Jay.

"We haven't seen much of Major General Jones since we got here," Jack said. "Do you know how he's doing?"

Jay's expression sobered. "I do. The doctors originally thought he just had a chronic case of Pando Hack. But since leaving Hale they've figured out that he's actually suffering from a bronchial disorder."

Jack met Steve's eyes, wondering what that meant.

"Because he didn't get better," Pete posited.

"Not only did he not get better, he got worse." Jay sighed heavily. "Turns out the cold air was actually helping him, and the heat and humidity here in Texas have severely exacerbated his condition."

"That's why he never comes out to the field to observe the

training events." Jack looked at Steve again. "Can't imagine he'll deploy with the Division, then."

Jay wagged his head. "I wouldn't think so. Not in his condition. Apparently he's been hospitalized here for weeks at a time and that's why you haven't seen much of him."

That wasn't good news.

Especially for Jones.

The captain shrugged. "I expect the Major General will be medically discharged and the Tenth will get a new commander."

Jay paused then added, "Again."

"Hope the next one actually understands what we do," Pete said somberly. "I feel like the Army's been assigning leadership of the Tenth as a sort of banishment."

"It's true," Jay admitted. "Neither Rolfe or Jones moved up from this command."

Jack looked across the table at Beth. She was listening silently to the talk around her, and Jack happily noticed the diamond glittering from its chain in the V of her blouse.

Talk quieted as the soldiers dove into their roast beef and mashed potato suppers.

"Have you heard anything more from the Red Cross?" Jack asked Beth.

That caught the attention of their tablemates.

"Red Cross?" one soldier asked. "Are you signing up?"

Beth looked surprised to be the focus of the shift in conversation. She began to twirl a lock of her glossy brown hair.

"I already did, and I was accepted."

"So no more recruiting?" another said. "That makes sense since our mountain training is apparently finished…"

Beth turned her attention to Jack. "I'm going to New York on November sixth to fill out paperwork and get cleared to travel."

So soon?

Jack pressed down his disappointment and struggled to look happy for his secret fiancée. "That's great, Betty."

"Where are you headed?" the first man asked.

"England." Beth pulled her eyes away from Jack's and faced the man who asked. "I'm boarding an ocean liner a couple days after arriving in New York. We're expected to dock in London by Thanksgiving."

So damn soon.

"London's getting the royal shit bombed out of them." The soldier who blurted that gem blushed as soon as the words were out of his mouth. "Oops. Sorry, miss."

Beth gave him a forgiving moue. "That's fine, soldier. I've been talking with Army men for over two years now, and I've heard far worse language on a regular basis."

Jack needed to pull those green eyes back to his. "Do you know what you'll be doing there yet?"

Beth looked at him again and the twirling stopped. "I've been assigned as a Recreation Staff Assistant."

Anything with the word recreation in it didn't sound too dangerous.

"That's great." Even Jack heard the relief in his voice.

Beth's eyes twinkled like the diamond he gave her. "And I've been assigned the rank of Captain."

Chapter Twenty-Four

October 28, 1944

Jack had time to grab a quick kiss in the twilight before Captain Jay and *Captain* Beth took a taxi into Austin to check into their hotel. Jack had secured a three-day pass so he, Steve, and Pete shared a cab to the Broken Spoke, a dance hall popular with both the soldiers from Camp Swift and the coeds from the University of Texas campus in Austin.

When they arrived shortly after eight, the place was crowded. The haze of cigarette smoke and the yeasty scent of beer hung in the air, mixing with a heady variety of perfume and aftershave. If a guy wanted to find companionship on a Saturday night, this was the place to get it.

Jack only wanted one companion, but he didn't see her yet.

The three friends ordered their drinks and found a place to sit. A local band was playing standard dance tunes that were currently on the radio and couples were dancing closely in the center of the hall.

There she is.

Beth was dancing with a handsome young private, clearly holding him at arm's length in spite of the man's attempts to pull her closer.

Steve nudged Jack. "You going in for your girl?"

"Hell, yeah."

Jack took a big gulp of beer then snaked his way through the crowd. He tapped the private on the shoulder.

"I'm cutting in, Private."

"What? Hey. No!" he blustered. "Get your own—"

Beth disengaged herself from the soldier and turned to Jack. "I'm honored. *Sergeant.*"

Jack took Beth's hand, slid his arm around her waist, and swung her away from the fuming private.

"You look beautiful, Beth."

Her smile pinched the corners of her eyes. "You always say that."

"You always do." He leaned in and spoke in her ear. "I don't have to be back at camp until Monday evening."

Her brows pulled together. "I don't know, Jeff. Someone might notice."

"We'll cross that bridge later. Have you had dinner?"

"A light one. You?"

"Same." *Perfect.* "We can stay and dance for a couple hours, then grab a late night bite. What do you think?"

Her expression turned dreamy. "I love it. As long as you're the one dancing with me all night."

Jack pulled her closer. "That's my plan."

After three more songs, and fending off three attempts by clueless soldiers to cut in, the band took a break. Jack escorted Beth to his table and put Steve and Pete in charge of guarding her while he went to get her a chilled glass of white wine.

When he returned, Ralph Bromaghin had joined the group. All eyes were on Beth and she looked like she was holding court.

"What's going on?" Jack asked as he handed Beth her wine.

"Just wondering how a goof like you landed a looker like this," Ralph joked. "I asked for the next dance and she declined. What's your secret?"

Jack peered into Beth's eyes, his expression asking a significant question.

She gave a little half-smile and nod before stating, "It helps if you propose marriage."

Three soldiers turned identically shocked faces toward Jack.

He raised his eyebrows and smirked. "And then the job's done when she says yes."

*****

Now that their secret was out, Jack's buddies ran defense, dissuading anyone from trying to take a turn dancing with Beth. When the band played the opening bars of *Moonlight Serenade*, Jack decided that when the beautifully romantic song ended there wouldn't be a better moment for he and Beth to slip out to spend some time alone.

"Let's go." He took Beth's hand, walked past his friends and winked, then led Beth outside. The night was chilly and damp from the previous day's rainstorm, and scattered clouds still obscured the moon.

Jack helped Beth with her coat. "Any suggestions for where to eat?"

"There's a diner attached to the hotel," she offered. "We could see how crowded it is…"

Jack leaned in and spoke in her ear. "And then decide if it's safe for me to go to your room?"

Beth smiled over her shoulder. "That's what I was thinking."

Jack hailed one of the cabs waiting outside the Broken Spoke and paid for the five-minute drive to the little Austin Inn. It wasn't anywhere near as swanky as the last hotel Beth stayed at, but then the Army probably wasn't as rich as Mr. Harkins.

They settled into a booth and looked over the plastic-covered menu. Beth ordered soup and a salad, Jack ordered steak and eggs.

"So. London." Jack offered a resigned smile as he held the cup of black coffee in front of his mouth. "And you'll be gone in a week and a half."

"I know. It's so fast." Beth mixed sugar into her iced tea.

"Are you scared?"

Her eyes flicked to his. "Of the bombs? In London? I'd be a fool if I wasn't."

"We weren't certain the last time we were together," Jack said carefully. "But this really is the last time we're going to see each other."

Beth's reply was stern. "Until after the war."

"Right. Until *after* the war." Jack reached for her hand. "When we both have a wedding to get to."

Her expression eased. "What do you think the Tenth will do?"

"Well, winter is coming. And the Army has dragged us away from the Rockies." Jack sipped his coffee. "Honestly? If we don't get sent to Europe, I have no idea what else would happen."

"Too bad there aren't mountains in England."

Jack huffed a laugh. "Yeah."

The waitress set down their plates of food and refilled Jack's coffee. The diner was quiet for a Saturday night and the clerk at the hotel's check-in desk was reading a book.

"I noticed that all the rooms open to the outside here," Jack said softly. "No one inside could see who goes in or out."

Beth chewed her lower lip while her gaze moved around the diner, out the window, and to the lobby. "I think you're right."

"How about this." Jack leaned over the table and lowered his voice. "When we're done eating, we'll say goodbye. You leave. I'll have another cup of coffee then pay the bill."

Beth took a deep breath and nodded her assent as she fingered a lock of hair. "Room two-twelve."

October 29, 1944

Jack left Beth's hotel room before sunrise and walked around the block before approaching the hotel from the opposite direction of the rooms. He opened the front door and approached the yawning clerk at the front desk.

"I'm meeting a guest for breakfast and I caught an early bus. Would you mind if I waited in the lobby?"

The young man rubbed one bloodshot eye. "Nah. That's fine."

The smell of coffee wafted from the all-night diner and Jack considered going in and getting a table. He would have if that didn't feel ungentlemanly, and Jack was one hundred percent a gentleman where Beth was concerned.

Jack pointed at the desk. "Can I read some of your paper while I wait?"

"Take it all." The clerk lifted the limp stack of newsprint over the counter. "I'm off in twenty minutes anyway."

Clearly not a moment too soon.

Jack settled himself in one of the two stuffed chairs by the front window and angled it slightly so he could see the front door better. The sun was over the horizon now, if not over the buildings in town, and pink to orange to yellow light tinted the pages of the paper as he read.

Half an hour later the door opened and Beth walked in. She was dressed for another day at the camp in slacks and a sweater set.

Jack put the newspaper aside and prepared to stand when Captain John Jay walked in behind Beth.

What's he doing here?

Beth's eyes moved straight to Jack. "Oh, good—you're already here." She walked toward him, her expression pleading for understanding. "Captain Jay invited me to breakfast and I said I already had a date. I hope you don't mind if he joins us?"

Jack knew he had no choice if he wanted to maintain Beth's spotless reputation. "No, not at all."

He saluted Jay. "Morning, Captain."

Jay returned the salute looking a little perplexed. "Morning, Sergeant."

Jack swung his arm toward the diner. "Shall we?"

*****

Jay offered Jack a ride back to Camp Swift in the taxi with himself and Beth, and Jack accepted. Even though he had the day off, he would go wherever Beth went—and if that meant returning to camp while he was still on a pass, so be it.

Breakfast was not entirely unpleasant. The captain told stories about his and Beth's cross-country experiences, many of which were downright hilarious. Jack soaked up every word about Beth's life, enjoying the variety of scenarios she hadn't told him about.

Today was Sunday and life at Camp Swift was relatively calm. Jay was obviously puzzled when Jack didn't leave them as soon as they climbed out of the taxi, so to avoid any further awkwardness Jack excused himself, intending to go his barracks to shower and shave, and promised to meet Beth for lunch.

"I'm free this afternoon, Jack," Beth said, forestalling any other arrangements Jay might suggest. "So I'll see you later."

Jack smiled into her eyes. "I look forward to it."

Haloed by the morning sun on this cool autumn day, and framed by an impossibly blue sky, Beth never looked more radiant. Jack intently imprinted her face in his memory. He needed to be able to recall everything about her: her hair, her scent, her New

England accent, and the touch of her skin, because they didn't have much time left.

He intended to make the most of every minute.

October 30, 1944

Last night was perfect.

Dinner at a well-known Austin steak house, drinks at the top of the tallest hotel, and a night of intimacy spent kissing, touching, and sleeping in each other's arms.

Jack and Beth talked seriously about getting married at the courthouse this morning before she returned to Boston, but both of them knew that wasn't the best plan.

"When I take you as my wife, I want the world there to see it," Jack admitted. "And I know your parents wouldn't accept me any other way."

"It's true." Beth sighed. "But I wish we were parting as a couple."

"We *are* a couple, Beth. No one could ever take me away from you." Jack paused, hesitating to continue but knowing what he was about to say was true. "Besides, if something happens to one of us, and we weren't married yet, then when we eventually move on we'll have something new to give. Does that make sense?"

"I'll still be a virgin," Beth said plainly. "And you won't be a widower."

"Yep." Jack pulled her close to his chest. "So many people are getting married in a rush that they barely know each other."

Beth nodded a little against his heart. "If and when they reunite, they'll be strangers."

"That won't be us, Beth."

"No. We'll come back, set a date, and plan our wedding." Her breath heated his skin through his shirt.

"A big one." Jack kissed the top of her head. "I can't wait."

A knock on the hotel room door was followed by, "Betts? You in there?"

Beth clamped a startled hand over her mouth, her eyes wide.

Jay continued from the other side of the portal. "I'm heading to breakfast."

Jack put his finger to his mouth and stepped inside the closet, pulling the door shut. His heart pounded so hard he was afraid Jay would hear it. Thank God both he and Beth were dressed.

"Hold on," Beth answered.

Jack heard the sound of the bedclothes being straightened before the door opened. "Good morning, John."

"You ready for breakfast?"

"Almost. I just need to, um," Beth paused. "To put my shoes on."

"Can I come in while you do? I wanted to talk to you about something."

"Oh—of course."

Jack heard the creak of the bed. Beth must be sitting down to slip on her sensible flats.

"What's on your mind?" she asked.

"You and Franklin." A jolt of adrenaline zinged through Jack when he heard his name. "What's going on between you two?"

"We're dating, John. I thought that was obvious." Her tone was cautious.

"It *is* obvious, Betts," he stated. "What's *not* obvious is why."

Jack's jaw dropped.

What?

"I don't understand, John. What are you saying?"

"Don't get me wrong, he's a great skier and a good teacher. His students always excelled. He's earned his stripes and the guys in the division love him. But…"

"But what?" Jack heard a warning tone in Beth's voice that he was pretty sure Jay didn't notice.

"But he's not one of us, Betts."

Damn it.

Jack felt his cheeks heating and his temper simmering.

"One of *us*, John?" The bed creaked again and Jack guessed Beth stood to face the captain. "You're saying he's beneath us?"

"Not as a man, of course not. But socially, he comes from a very different class. You know that."

Beth didn't answer right away. A stab of concern shot through Jack's gut, afraid that John's words might have hit their target.

"Perhaps you'll recall that I did hope to date—and marry—one of *us*." Beth's voice was as cold as the Rocky Mountain blizzards at thirteen thousand feet. "Tell me how well that worked out."

"Marry? Betts, you can't be—"

"Shut up, John."

Jack's eyes widened in the dark and he clamped a hand over his mouth to keep from making any noise.

"You knew how I felt about you," she continued in the same tone. "And you strung me along until you up and married for your family's sake, or so you claimed. But then I met Jack Franklin and I began to realize what a *real* man is. He treats me like an equal, not an elbow decoration."

"I never—"

"Please don't speak anymore, John." Beth sighed heavily. "You've made your point."

"So you'll break it off before you go to England." Jay sounded confident.

Beth huffed a dry laugh. "Of course not."

"Why not? Are you going to string *him* along now?"

"I sure am." Now Beth sounded confident. "Through the rest of the war, and right through our wedding when the fighting's over."

"Be realistic. Is that marriage even going to happen?"

"Well, let's see. He proposed, I said yes, and he gave me a diamond." She chuckled again. "I'd say the chances are pretty good."

Jay was silent. Jack smothered a laugh.

"Go to breakfast, John. I'll catch up with you when it's time to leave."

Jack heard the door open, but it didn't close right away.

"If you want your dalliance with the sergeant to be private," Jay snarled. "Tell him not to leave his boots by the door."

Jack felt the door slam from inside the closet.

SHIT!

*****

Jack stepped out of the closet, wondering what storm he'd face.

Beth turned and stared angrily at him. "He'll tell my parents you spent the night as soon as we get back."

She's mad at Jay? Not me?

That wasn't what he expected. His soldier training kicked in.

"Then you take the offensive. You tell them first."

Beth's eyes narrowed. "Tell them what?"

"The truth. That you and I wanted to spend our last hours together, so we stayed up all night talking in your hotel room."

Without a word, Beth turned immediately around and walked to the telephone on the nightstand. She picked up the heavy black receiver and dialed the operator.

"Collect call to Mister Laurence Harkins in Boston, Massachusetts from Miss Betty Harkins."

Jack sat on the only chair in the room and watched in fascination while Beth recited the number and waited for the connection to go through.

"Hi, Daddy. No, everything's fine. John and I leave for home this afternoon. Yes. Of course." She drew a deep breath. "There is something I wanted to tell you and Mother about before we get there, though."

In plain and simple sentences, Beth told her parents that Jay came to her hotel room to say he was going to breakfast, and when he did, he discovered Jack was in her room.

"Jack Franklin. The sergeant I told you about, remember? No! Will you please be quiet and listen?"

Beth looked at Jack and rolled her eyes while she continued.

"It was our last chance to be together before I go to England and he is sent to—" She shrugged. "Italy. Anyway, we sat up all night talking. And with all of our clothes on."

Jack agreed with the little white lie. There was no need to go into exact detail when the outcome was the same.

Beth listened for a moment, her expression darkening.

"Daddy, I swear to you that nothing happened," she huffed. "Even though I *am* twenty-six years old, and a grown woman, and it's none of your business anyway."

Good for you, Beth.

"The only reason I'm telling you about this, is that this morning when John discovered that Jack was in my room, he made his own assumptions. Being the way he is, he'll probably come running to you and Mother with his inaccurate version the minute we reach Boston."

Beth listened for a minute, her expression grim, and then said, "Actually it's *not* any of his business either. He didn't marry me, so why should he care whom I date or fall in love with? That's my choice, and no one else's."

Beth listened again while she turned to face Jack with a soft smile.

"Yes, Daddy, I said in love with."

Jack heard her father speaking but Beth interrupted him. "Daddy, I have to go. Give Mother my love. I'll see you tomorrow."

She dropped the receiver in its cradle. "That's done. And I'm starving."

Jack rose to his feet. "I could not ever love you more than I do at this very moment."

Beth ran into his arms and kissed him soundly. "Put your boots on, soldier, and take me to breakfast. Anywhere but here."

*****

Half an hour before Beth expected John Jay to meet her at the train station Jack said his final goodbyes and took a cab back to Camp Swift. He hoped that he and the captain would pass like ships and not encounter each other until Jay had a chance to calm down.

It didn't happen that way.

Jack walked through the gate into the camp and Jay pounced like he was lying in wait. "Drop and give me twenty, Sergeant!"

Jack stared at Captain Jay like he'd grown an extra nose.

Is he serious?

"Now!"

Jack dropped to the push-up position and did twenty push-ups in rapid succession, counting them crisply out loud. When he finished he jumped to his feet and saluted the captain.

Jay closed the gap between them. "What the hell do you think you're doing?"

Jack's brows wrinkled. "Push-ups?"

"With Betts!" Jay barked. "You had better make an honest woman of her."

"She's already an honest woman." Jack's Polish genes riled. "What *exactly* are you suggesting about her?"

Jay scowled. "If you touched her…"

"Look Captain, *sir*, I might not be one of you—" To Jack's satisfaction, Jay flinched. "But I do know how to treat a woman. I know how to respect her for being smart and capable. To love her for who she is, not what she has. And *that's* why she's with *me*, and not one of you Massachusetts boys."

Jack wondered if he was about to be socked in the jaw and steeled himself for the blow.

Jay pointed a stiff finger in his face. "If you hurt her in any way, I'll shoot you myself and save the Nazis the trouble."

"She's already had her heart broken once," Jack hissed. "Be assured I won't let *that* happen again."

Captain Jay sniffed and stepped back. "You're dismissed."

Jack saluted, turned on his heel and walked away without looking back. His insides quivered with rage, but he wasn't about to let Jay see his fury.

He'd rounded the first corner when he heard, "Now drop and give *me* twenty, Sergeant Franklin."

Jack halted and spun toward the voice.

Hollinghurst.

"What?" Jack blurted at the lieutenant.

Hollinghurst clasped his hands behind his back as he sauntered toward Jack. "I said drop and give me twenty."

Damn it.

Jack complied, copying his actions of moments before. When he climbed to his feet he stood at attention, glaring silently at his nemesis.

"So." Hollinghurst folded his arms over his chest. "Tell me what you did to piss off Captain Jay."

None of your fucking business, asshole.

"Date his assistant."

"Betty Harkins?" Lieutenant Hollinghurst's head fell back and his loud, derisive laugh ground on Jack's last nerve. He looked at Jack again. "What in God's name were you thinking?"

Jack did not respond.

He shook his head in disbelief. "She's out of your league, boy."

Jack struggled to keep his cool and focused on not clenching his fists. "Is that all. Sir."

Hollinghurst rested his hands on his hips. "A word to the wise, Sergeant. You'll have better luck sniffing around the docks."

Jack glared at Hollinghurst from under his brows. "Better than asking for her hand in marriage, having her say yes, and giving her a diamond? Sir?"

The lieutenant blinked his disbelief. "What?"

"Miss Betty Harkins has agreed to be my wife." Jack smiled with his mouth but not his eyes. "But thank you for the advice."

When Aston Hollinghurst just stared at him, Jack risked asking, "Is there anything else, Lieutenant?"

Hollinghurst turned around and strode away, tossing a growled, "Dismissed" over his shoulder.

Chapter
Twenty-Five

November 6, 1944

On the same day that Beth left Boston for New York, Captain Rideout gathered the men of Second Battalion's F Company after lunch.

"Do you think we're finally getting deployment orders?" Jack asked Steve as they took their seats on Camp Swift's gymnasium bleachers.

"I sure hope so. We're the last remaining division of the Army and we're still sitting in Texas," Steve groused. "I'm beginning to wonder if we're ever going into combat."

Captain Rideout stepped up to the podium in the center of the gym and tapped the microphone to be sure it was on. Then he smiled at the gathered soldiers.

"Welcome, men. I have good news, and I know many of you will understand the significance of what I have to say." He put up one hand. "No, we don't have our marching orders just yet, but this news is just as important."

"Just as?" Jack grunted his frustration. "I highly doubt it."

Steve elbowed him.

"First of all, the Tenth has been officially reorganized as you all know, and since coming to Camp Swift two thousand men plus heavy guns and artillery have been added to the division. We've grown to nearly fourteen thousand five hundred members. Therefore, the designator 'Light' has been omitted from our title."

The soldiers responded with polite applause.

"He said first," Jack observed. "So what's next if it isn't deployment?"

Steve snorted. "Jeez, you're impatient, Oakland."

The captain waited for the men to grow quiet before he spoke again. The expression on his face showed gleeful anticipation.

"I'm very pleased to announce the additional change in our name." Rideout paused, his gaze moving over the assembled men. "Starting today, we'll be called the Tenth *Mountain* Division."

Jack sat up straight on the bench. "What?"

"The Army has finally recognized us as an elite unit with specific skills. They understand—and I do apologize to the men who joined us here in Texas—that those of us who trained at Camp Hale for over two years, and endured altitude sickness, frostbite, and Pando hack only to emerge stronger, are fully able to fight and survive in conditions which the regular foot soldier cannot. Congratulations, men!"

The soldiers went wild. Standing, cheering, clapping, and stomping their feet on the bleachers, the celebration lasted a full five minutes before Captain Rideout could regain control. He leaned into the microphone.

"To designate the difference, each of you will be given tabs on your way out that say 'Mountain' to be sewn onto your uniforms above the Tenth's barrel patch." Rideout laughed. "I don't know about you all, but mine will be sewn on before supper."

Jack and Steve waited in the line for their tabs, reminiscing with other ski troopers about the Homestake debacle, the failure at Kiska, and the D-Series test. They all agreed that this recognition from Army Ground Forces was long, long overdue.

Steve grinned. "I'm sewing these right now. It's great news."

"Okay, Dropout, I was wrong to be skeptical," Jack admitted. "This news was just as important as deployment."

"Can you write to Betty and tell her?"

Jack shook his head. "Not until she writes to me and gives me an overseas address." He smiled and lifted one brow. "But I sure can write to my Pops and tell *him*. I'm a sergeant in an elite division now, and that counts for something. Even a decorated Marine has to admit that!"

November 7, 1944

Orders for the Tenth Mountain Division arrived the day after their new name was bestowed. They were going to be deployed by regiment, to facilitate the movement of over fourteen thousand men.

"The Eighty-Sixth is going first," Jack read from the posted notice. "We're scheduled for November twenty-eighth."

"With the Eighty-Seventh leaving December tenth," Steve read over Jack's shoulder. "And the Eighty-Fifth on December fourteenth."

"Even better," Jack pointed at the posting. "A maximum leave policy is in effect for the rest of the month."

Steve gave Jack a significant look. "They wouldn't be giving us max leave unless we're going overseas."

"It's finally happening."

I can't wait to tell Pops.

November 10, 1944

The train ride from Austin to Oakland took a day and a half. Aston Hollinghurst was unfortunately on the same train as Jack, and Jack tried to avoid the lieutenant as much as he could. But when they were about an hour outside of Oakland, Hollinghurst walked into the car Jack was riding in and dropped into the seat next to him.

Jack pulled a deep breath, his jaw clenched.

What now?

"I have something to say to you, Franklin."

Jack cut his gaze to Hollinghurst's but didn't reply.

"I've been thinking since you told me you're engaged to Betty Harkins."

Jack waited, tensed against what might follow.

"You're a good soldier, I have to admit that." Hollinghurst pointed to the sergeant's stripes. "And you've been promoted twice. Maybe even make second lieutenant soon."

Jack's tone was non-committal. "Thanks."

"Anyway…" Hollinghurst looked uncomfortable. "If Betty and John Jay think you've got the stuff, I guess I should believe it, too."

Shocked, Jack wasn't about to correct any of that statement.

"Thank you, sir."

Hollinghurst shrugged. "If I'm honest, your skills are just as good as mine."

Nope. Better.

"And since we're about to ship out, and we'll be fighting side-by-side, what do ya say we put this feud to rest?"

The feud you started?

Jack still didn't like Aston one little bit, and the man certainly wasn't apologizing for making Jack's life hell whenever he could. But the fact that they would need to rely on each other in battle wasn't something Jack could ignore.

He held out his hand. "Done."

First Lieutenant Hollinghurst sagged with relief. He shook Jack's hand, stood, clapped Jack on the shoulder, and returned to wherever he'd come from.

Didn't expect that.

Jack turned back to the window. He never considered that his relationship with Beth would make others see him differently.

Wonder what else will change.

*****

Pops picked Jack up at the station at seven that evening. When Jack stepped down from the train car he looked around and met Hollinghurst's eyes down the length of the platform. Jack flashed half a smile.

Hollinghurst bounced a quick nod.

Jack returned his attention to his father.

"Your mother's at home, cooking of course," Pops said after they shook hands. "You need help with your duffel?"

"I've got it." Jack slung the bag over his shoulder.

His father frowned a little. "You look different."

Jack patted his midsection. "Gained a few pounds."

"It looks good on you."

A compliment from Pops?

"Thanks."

As they walked to the car, John pointed at the badge on Jack's arm. "That's the Mountain tab you told us about?"

"Yes, sir." Jack looked at his father, trying to assess the man's thoughts. "I'm a sergeant now, like you were, and in an elite division. And—we're shipping out at the end of the month."

John opened the driver's door of the familiar family sedan and looked at Jack over the roof of the car. "Where to?"

"Don't know for sure. They haven't told us." Jack opened the back door and tossed his duffel into the back. He closed that door and opened the passenger door. "What's Mom cooking?"

Both men dropped into their seats.

John chuckled and started the car. "What *isn't* she cooking?"

*****

When Jack walked into the house the comforting aromas of stuffed cabbage and floor wax washed over him. As she always did, Edyta ran into the hall from the kitchen when he opened the front door, and she wrapped sturdy arms around Jack as soon as she reached him.

"Hi, Mom," Jack managed, though his ribcage was severely restricted. "Whatever you're cooking smells great."

She loosened her grip and looked up at him. "Are you hungry? Come. Sit."

She grabbed Jack's hand and dragged him toward the kitchen while John reached for his duffel. "I'll put it in your room."

"Thanks, Pops," Jack said over his shoulder.

Jack sat at the kitchen table in his regular chair while Edyta spooned soup into a bowl. "How long can you stay?"

"I need to be back before Thanksgiving because I'm leaving Camp Swift the next week." Jack inhaled the scent of the creamy, peppery chowder. "That smells wonderful."

"Before Thanksgiving?" Edyta looked heartbroken. "Can't you stay a little longer?"

"Sorry, Mom. I need to get ready to go." Jack lifted a spoonful of heaven to his mouth. The soup tasted even better than it smelled if that was possible.

John walked into the kitchen. "Leave him be, Edyta. He has responsibilities. Just be glad he's here."

Jack stared at his Pops as he took the seat opposite Jack's. His father's attitude toward him had definitely changed.

"How's Harry?"

John glanced at his wife. "He's back at Camp Pendleton, I think."

Jack noticed something in the look, but he couldn't decipher it.

"What rank is he now?"

John kept his eyes on the bowl of chowder Edyta was setting in front of him. "Still a corporal."

Jack spooned more soup into his mouth while he digested that bit of information. The celebrated Marine brother was back in California, while the black sheep Army brother was promoted beyond him, his division was given the status of an elite branch, and he was finally deploying under the designation of Mountain Division—meaning his ski training was recognized as valuable.

Considering all of that, Pops was being more pleasant than Jack would have expected.

Might as well ride this wave.

"I have other news." Jack smiled at his dad then his mom. "Really big news."

Her brows shot upwards. "What n—"

"Anybody home?" Harry's voice boomed from the front door.

"Harry!" Edyta cried before running out of the kitchen.

Jack looked at John. "You didn't tell me he was coming home, too."

John looked stunned. "We didn't know!"

Harry and Edyta entered the kitchen with their arms around each other's waists, but the minute he clapped eyes on Jack he attacked his older brother.

"Look at you!" Harry bellowed, trapping Jack in an arm-pinning embrace from behind and shaking him. "How the hell are you?"

"Language!" John chastised without conviction. "What are you doing here?"

"I got a pass to come see the black sheep!" Harry teased, unwittingly using the same words that were in Jack's thoughts. He released Jack and dropped into the chair next to his.

He recoiled a little when he saw Jack's stripes. "You're a sergeant?"

Jack glanced at his parents. Obviously they weren't bragging about their eldest son's accomplishments to his younger brother.

"Yep. And see this?" Jack pointed at the new insignia. "Army Ground finally gave us the name we deserved: Tenth *Mountain* Division."

Harry blew a low whistle, but said nothing.

Edyta set a bowl of steaming chowder in front of Harry. "How long can you stay?"

"It's only a weekend pass." Harry lifted his spoon and blew on the liquid. "I have to be back for Monday morning formation."

Harry looked sharp in his Marine Corps uniform, Jack had to admit. "You look good, Harry."

Harry smiled. "You, too."

"Jack was just about to tell us some good news." Edyta took the fourth seat at the table and turned an expectant expression to Jack. "Go on now. What is it?"

Jack turned to Harry. "Remember that gal who gave us the ski trooper applications when we went to the recruiting movie with Hannes Schroll and Fred Klein?"

"The one you had drinks with the next night?" Harry shrugged. "Vaguely."

"That's her." Jack tried to decide whether to build the story or jump to the end and fill in the rest afterwards.

Build.

"She wrote to me a few months later, and then ended up coming to Camp Hale a couple times when there were movies being filmed there."

Harry slapped the table making the silverware dance and clank. "I saw the wink!" He laughed. "Was she there?"

"She was. And to shorten the story, we've been dating ever since."

Edyta stiffened and looked at John. His eyes narrowed dangerously.

Better speed this up.

"Anyway, she's been accepted into the Red Cross and is on her way to London right now. But before she left, she came to see me in Austin."

Three pairs of eyes were pinned on him. No one spoke.

Jack forced a smile that he hoped looked confident. "In short, I asked her to marry me and she said yes."

*****

Three hours later, Jack and Harry climbed the worn carpeted steps to their long-ago shared bedroom. His announcement of his engagement prompted a storm of questions which he was happy to answer, and in the end his parents were resigned if not necessarily thrilled.

"Trust me, Mom. You're going to love her," Jack insisted.

"But will they love you?" John challenged. "The parents of this trust fund girl for whom ten thousand dollars is nothing?"

Jack winced as his own words were thrown back at him. "All that matters is that she does," he countered.

John glanced at Edyta then. "How little you know, son."

Harry turned the light on in their old bedroom. "It looks so small."

Jack stepped past him. "Haven't you been back?"

"A couple of times before this, yeah." Harry dropped his duffel on his old bed. "But now that we're both in here it feels a lot more cramped."

"Because it *is* a lot more cramped." Jack hung his jacket in the closet and unbuttoned his shirt. "We've grown up, Harry."

The brothers changed clothes and washed up before climbing into their childhood beds.

"It's no longer than my barracks' bunk, but at least it's wider," Jack commented.

"You should try sleeping on a ship," Harry countered. "There are walls at the ends of the bunks—every six feet—so we don't even have the luxury of hanging our feet off the end."

Jack switched off the overhead light. A soft glow from the streetlights outside seeped around the curtains and into the room. Obviously there was no blackout order in effect at the moment.

After his eyes adjusted to the darkness Jack asked Harry, "How's it going for you?"

"Good. I really like being stationed at Camp Pendleton. The world doesn't get much nicer than southern California."

"Where have you sailed?"

"Hawaii mostly. Once up to Alaska. Recon patrols." Harry turned on his side. "What about you?"

Jack told his brother about the Mountain Training Group, and working with Bill Klein and the other European skiers who were instructors.

"Sounds like a cushy job to me." Harry rolled onto his back again. "No wonder Pops has been on your case."

Jack sighed, reluctant to admit the snafus he'd experienced, but unless he did Harry would think he'd been doing nothing but skiing and rock climbing for the last three years.

"Not exactly." Jack rolled over on his side and propped himself on one elbow. "Let me tell you about our deployment to Kiska, Alaska and the Division Series testing that followed."

November 21, 1944

Harry returned to Camp Pendleton that Monday morning but Jack stayed another week. He talked about Beth a lot with his mom and knew he had gained at least one ally by the time he said his goodbyes.

After another day-and-a-half train ride he reached Camp Swift the Tuesday night before Thanksgiving. When he got back to the barracks, a letter from Beth was waiting for him. As always, Jack showered and got ready for bed before opening the letter while stretched out in his bunk.

Dearest Jeff,

I board the ship bound for England today and I'm really excited. I've met the other gals who are going with me and they're a super group. As for writing to me, you can simply address the letter to Captain Elizabeth Harkins, American Red Cross, London, England. The central office there will forward the mail to wherever I'm stationed. I'll write to you again when I arrive.

That would be simple enough. Jack knew that the Red Cross acted like a sort of postal system for American soldiers overseas, so it also made sense. And it was easy for him to remember.

With his deployment next week he doubted her next letter would reach him in time, so he'd have to write to her before he left to let her know he was gone. If he found out to where, he'd add that, too.

I have more news, which I think you might be pleased to know after our last awkward day together.

John Jay has been transferred to the Army Air Corps to work in public affairs there, so now he's headed for the Pacific arena. You probably won't cross paths with him again, so whatever he might have thought about you and me that morning in Austin doesn't matter anymore.

Jack lowered the letter. He never told Beth about the captain's confrontation the day he and she left Camp Swift, but now Jack wondered if Jay ever did. Either that, or Beth was more intuitive than he realized.

That news really was a shame, though. John Jay was an original member of the Eighty-Seventh at Mount Rainer, and commander of the Mountain Training Group. He and his films were responsible for the recruitment of the majority of the ski troops.

That, and his beautiful assistant, of course.

Jack stared at Beth's neat, feminine handwriting and heaved a deep sigh.

She was on his mind all the time.

Not always part of conscious thought, but always in the background as a sort of scaffold holding up his life. He was always aware that he loved her and that she loved him back.

Stay lucky, my darling Beth.

Stay lucky.

Chapter
Twenty-Six

November 23, 1944
Thanksgiving

On Thanksgiving morning there was a meeting in the field house for all the Tenth Mountain Division soldiers who'd returned to Camp Swift. The officers—including non-commissioned officers like Jack—were specifically there to meet the new Commanding General for the Tenth, who was replacing Brigadier General Jones who was still hospitalized.

There was nothing but a microphone on the stage when the Division Adjutant called the soldiers in the hall to attention. The men stood straight and still, facing forward, while an unimpressive figure in uniform walked briskly through their ranks.

All Jack could see was the back of his graying head.

When Brigadier General George P. Hays reached the stage and turned around, Jack saw a middle-aged man with a leathery face and big jug ears.

He barked into the microphone which he didn't seem to need, "At ease. Seats."

Jack and the others sat.

Among the multiple service ribbons on Hays' chest, the visible resume of the officer class, one had white stars on a pale blue field and stood out like a neon sign.

The Congressional Medal of Honor from World War I.

The field house was silent.

Hays began with, "I wanted everybody to get a good look at their new Commanding General right at the start."

Then he launched into his speech. "I'm actually quite lucky to be assigned to the only Mountain Division that the US Army has ever had—because I'm actually an artilleryman—and I'm very honored to be able to lead such a fine body of men."

Hays spoke calmly, deliberately, and succinctly. There was no pretense, no pomposity, only authenticity. The boots he wore were scuffed, not polished to tar-colored mirrors. His language, stance, and demeanor indicated he was primarily a soldier, just like every one of them.

Jack was cautiously impressed.

"We're going to have good times as well as bad times in our combat overseas," Hays continued. "And as much as I can, it will be my policy to make everyone as comfortable as possible, and to have as good a time as possible, so long as we accomplish our mission. If you're going to risk your life, you might as well do it in good company."

An approving murmur wafted through the assemblage.

Jack looked at Steve and Pete sitting beside him and lifted his brows in question. They looked at each other and both shrugged.

"Too soon to know," Steve whispered. "We've been hopeful before."

"We are going into combat, men," General Hays continued. "That is a certainty. And as soon as I am allowed, I'll tell you where. But the skills you've honed over the last couple years will be put to good use, I promise you that. Your time is now."

Jack's pulse surged. The fear that he'd never get to a combat zone was just banished.

After the twenty-minute speech was finished the men filed out of the field house and headed for their mid-day Thanksgiving meals.

"What do you think?" Jack asked his two best friends.

"He talks a good game, I'll say that," Pete answered first.

"And he doesn't seem full of himself," Steve offered, "even though he's won a fucking Medal of Honor!"

"Yeah, that's impressive, no doubt about it!" Jack agreed. "Do you know for what?"

Pete did. "During the First World War when he was a lieutenant he had seven horses shot out from under him while he called in artillery fires on advancing Germans."

Jack stopped walking and stared at Pete. "No shit?"

"No shit."

"Wow." Jack started walking again.

After dinner Jack returned to the barracks to write a letter to his father about their new Commanding General and his Medal of Honor.

> *I'm glad a man like this is our Commanding General, Pops. Since I'm actually going into combat at this time, I'm glad to be going with somebody who knows what the hell they're doing!*

December 11, 1944

In preparing for the overseas movement of the Tenth Mountain Division the first priority was getting all of the vehicles, equipment, and men accounted for before they were loaded onto the cross-country trains. And because they were the first to ship out, the Eighty-Sixth Regiment was the first to go through the laborious process.

Once everything was officially declared to be in order, the trains carrying the Eighty-Sixth soldiers and all their battle-ready paraphernalia departed Camp Swift on November twenty-eighth, and headed toward Hampton Roads, Virginia.

"So now we know for sure that we're headed for Europe," Jack said to Steve as he watched the plains of Texas pass by the window for hopefully the last time in his life. "If we were going to the Pacific, the trains would obviously be heading west."

The journey took three days on the heavily laden trains, and the regiment arrived at Camp Patrick Henry in Virginia on December second for overseas processing. On December tenth, the regiment once again boarded trains and left for the sea port at Hampton Roads.

The Eighty-Sixth's three battalions each assigned a platoon to move equipment from the train to the ship, the *SS Argentina*. As the soldiers boarded the ship, a team of women from the Red Cross handed each man a canvas bag containing a toothbrush, toothpaste, razor blades, cigarettes, and playing cards.

Of course Jack's thoughts went immediately to Beth.

He pictured her wearing the Red Cross uniform with the little cloisonné pin on her lapel and wondered if she was performing a similar duty for American soldiers somewhere in Europe.

A month had passed since she sailed to London. A long month of no communication since neither of them knew where in the world the other one was.

"Stay lucky," he whispered.

Before the ship sailed, each company was shown to its berthing compartment. The men claimed their bunks and deposited their gear there before heading back up to watch the ship leave port.

At six-forty-five in the morning the *SS Argentina* set sail, heading east into the rising sun.

After they were well at sea their commanding officer, Colonel Clarence Tomlinson, came over the ship's intercom and announced, "We are heading for Italy, gentlemen. The Tenth Mountain Division will be part of the Fifth Army."

So it was a lucky guess, Beth, that day you called your father.

When the ship started to move, I really wanted to get up on deck to look at the water. This was a day I'd wondered about so many times over the last three years: how would I feel when I was actually going to war?

Scared. Excited. Relieved. Scared.

Determined.

And scared.

The months I spent training at Camp Hale and Camp Swift are all behind me now, but so many memories fill my mind. I can't stop thinking about Kiska and all of our practice and preparation to meet the Japanese who weren't there.

How will we fare against the Germans? Because they sure as <u>hell</u> *will be there. But I have to honestly say that I believe we're as ready as we could ever be.*

And this time we're being led by a General who's already fought the Germans once before ~ and won.

*****

Except for the troops that sailed to Kiska, most of the Eighty-Sixth Regiment soldiers had never been on an ocean liner before. Swaying bunks would be their home for the next two weeks. Packed tightly to accommodate the three thousand soldiers, there was barely enough room to pass between tiers of bunks that stood eight high.

Seasickness was rampant.

The ship's movement still made Jack queasy like it had before, but thankfully he wasn't as sick as some of the other men. He spent as much time as he could on deck, and that helped some.

On the upside, recreation on the *Argentina* included movies, boxing matches, and endless card and dice games. The men read and exchanged books with each other. They were even able to listen to the radio over the ship's intercom. Jack was as comfortable as was possible, considering their cramped circumstances.

December 24, 1944

The chilled and windy decks of the *Argentina* were crowded when the ship sailed through the Straits of Gibraltar, as soldiers strained for a first glimpse of the Rock—their first sight of land in eleven days.

Thirteen days after embarking, and two days before Christmas, the *Argentina* sailed into Naples harbor, but it wasn't until the next morning that the ship was tethered at the pier. Jack greatly appreciated the lack of waves in the protected space, but conversely had trouble falling asleep without being rocked.

He was laughing about that with Steve and Pete while they hefted their gear and joined the line waiting to walk down the ship's gang plank to solid land. The sky was thick with clouds on this breezy day, and the damp harbor air slid cold tendrils down the collar of Jack's coat.

Steve's gaze moved to the dock and his brows pulled together.

"You okay?" Jack asked.

His attention returned to Jack. "Not as good as you'll be in a minute."

"What are you talking about?"

Steve's cheeks spread in the widest grin Jack had ever seen. "The Red Cross is here."

"What—" Jack spun so fast that he lost his balance and might have ended up in the turquoise Mediterranean Sea if Pete hadn't grabbed him.

Just as they had when the *Argentina* left Hampton Roads, Red Cross tables lined the pier. Uniformed young women handed out freshly made doughnuts, cups of coffee emitting curls of steam in the chilly morning air, and packs of chewing gum and cigarettes.

Jack couldn't believe his eyes. Or his luck.

Beth.

She was actually here, in Naples, handing out doughnuts.

Jack decided to try and surprise her, so he hid himself behind Steve and Pete until they'd left the ship and reached the tables. Jack noticed the ladies handed a single hot donut to every soldier, so he waited until Beth's attention was pulled away before he stepped up.

"Two, please."

"I'm sorry, it's one—Jack!" Beth's cheeks blanched then flushed. Her eyes were wide as dinner plates and she looked like she might burst. "I can't believe you're *here!*"

"I can't believe *you're* here." Jack reached for the donut and grasped her hand in the process. "When can we talk?"

"We have to clean up once everyone gets off the ship. When we're done with that I'll have time." Her eyes were glowing.

"How long?"

She wiped her cheek with a shaking hand and gave him a trembling smile. "Another hour or so?"

Jack squeezed her hand and took the donut. "I'll be back."

*****

All of the heavy weapons, vehicles, radios, cooking gear, and ammunition from the ship had to be sorted and loaded onto trucks for transport to the Eighty-Sixth's bivouac area. Every company was supposed to provide a squad for working parties, so Jack told the first sergeant his squad would volunteer.

Besides helping to pass the time, he could stay close to Beth.

"All we have to do is unfasten the nets containing the boxes when they come down on the cranes," he told his men. "Then the forklifts will put the cargo on trucks."

Though the weather here was chilly, Jack worked up a sweat while he was unloading the ship in spite of the overcast day and the constant sea breeze. Based on his experience living in a coastal city, they didn't have to worry about those clouds dumping any snow on them tonight.

An hour and a quarter passed before Jack excused himself for a few minutes and headed back to the Red Cross tables. The four women were packing up the doughnut machine, coffee maker, and the boxes of gum and cigarettes when he approached. He stopped and cleared his throat, catching Beth's attention.

She looked at him and smiled happily.

"Would you give me a minute?" she asked the other ladies as she set a box down. "I won't be long."

One of them grinned at Jack. "Take your time, Betty."

Beth walked up to Jack and hugged him. He got the message—no kissing in public here. Then she took his hand and pulled him about ten yards down the dock and away from the crowds. When she turned to face him, her expression was beatific.

"Hi, Jeff."

"Hello, Beth. It's so great to see you." Jack touched her cheek. "How long have you been here? And why Italy?"

"Two days after I got to London they sent me on to Rome. They said the Mediterranean Theater needed Red Cross Canteens set up as quickly as possible because the Allies were moving north. So I was assigned to the Fourth Corps, based in Lucca." She paused and squeezed his hand. "What about you?"

"We got a new name—the Tenth *Mountain* Division—on November sixth, the day you left." Jack showed her the patch on his arm that he was so proud of. "And the next day we were told we were shipping out on the twenty-eighth. But we didn't know where we were going until after the ship set sail. I wrote you letters on the ship. I'll give them to you here."

"This is where I'm staying in Naples." Beth scribbled on a scrap of paper. "Now that you're in Italy, I'll ask to be assigned to the Tenth, because you'll be under the command of the Fourth Corps and Lieutenant General Crittenberger."

Jack had no idea who that was or what that assignment meant, but if it gave him more chances to see Beth then he was fully on board. "I have to get back to work. Can I see you tomorrow? It's Christmas, you know."

"Yes. Come to the address I gave you after breakfast if you can. I'll wait for you." She stood on her toes and planted a solid kiss on his lips, rules be damned. "I love you, Jeff. And I'm so happy to see you."

*****

It took four-and-a-half hours for the working parties to empty the *Argentina* of its contents and load everything into the trucks provided by Fifth Army. When they finished, the men climbed aboard those trucks and the convoy headed for their staging area in the Bagnoli section of Naples, about four miles west of the docks. Jack paid attention to the route, making a mental map of where he was.

When he arrived at the makeshift camp, Steve and Pete cornered him.

"What's Betty doing here?"

"Did you know she could end up in Italy?"

"Can she spend time with you?"

"Does she have any cute friends?"

Jack threw his hands in the air, laughing. "I surrender!"

Pete punched Steve's arm. "Give him a chance!"

Steve planted his feet and crossed his arms. "Okay, one at a time. Why is Betty in Italy?"

Jack repeated Beth's explanation, adding, "I'm going to see her tomorrow. Alone."

Steve made a face and turned to Pete. "Looks like we're on our own for Christmas."

December 25, 1944

Church bells rang out from a multitude of Catholic churches, but Jack headed straight toward Naples Cathedral, the main church of Naples, because Beth's apartment was two blocks south of that landmark according to the directions he got from a couple of Fifth Army guys.

He realized once he reached the medieval structure that he didn't know what church Beth attended—or if she attended at all. Today was the perfect day to ask her that question. Hopefully her answer would match his.

The four mile walk in the cool, hazy morning was nothing after their Texas training and it only took him about forty minutes to reach her. He entered an ancient little courtyard and climbed a stone staircase to the door numbered six and knocked.

When she opened the door Beth looked happier than he'd ever seen her. "Come in. Did you have trouble finding me?"

"Nope." Jack stepped into a neat little front room. "I just headed for the cathedral and turned right."

"Good." Beth giggled. "I'm not Catholic, but I have gone to a couple services there. I'm sure that would horrify my folks, but honestly the cathedral and all the ritual is very beautiful."

Jack took off his jacket. "Do you attend church normally?"

She nodded. "Lutheran. You?"

"Presbyterian." He smiled and shrugged. "Close enough."

A tall red-haired woman walked into the room and offered her hand to Jack. "You must be this Army sergeant I've heard so much about. I'm Shannon."

"Shannon's my roommate," Beth injected. "They won't allow us to live alone. For our own protection."

Jack shook Shannon's hand, understanding exactly what Beth's explanation actually meant. "Nice to meet you. I'm Jack."

Shannon turned to Beth. "I'm going to Mass and then I'll check in at the office. I'll probably be gone about three hours."

Beth glanced at Jack, her cheek pinkening. "Thanks Shan."

Shannon retrieved her coat from the rack by the door and put it on quickly before opening the apartment door.

"It was nice to meet you," Jack said again, at a loss for any other words.

Shannon wiggled her fingers over one shoulder and closed the door behind her. Jack pulled Beth into his kiss and his embrace, and kept her there a very long time.

Chapter Twenty-Seven

December 26, 1944

On the truck ride back to the docks early the next morning, Jack felt through the fabric of his shirt for the Red Cross pin that Beth had fastened to the ball chain from which his dog tags hung.

"It's not a diamond," she said as she manipulated the clasp. "But now I'll be close to your heart like you are close to mine."

Jack looked down at the red-white-and-blue enameled pin. "Will you get in trouble for this?"

"No. I'll just tell them it fell off when I was cleaning up yesterday but I didn't notice until today." She patted the chain hanging against his chest. "There. Done."

They'd spent the entire Christmas Day together, first in the cozy apartment, and then walking the streets of Naples hand in hand. They searched until they found a few places that were open on the holiday and ate lunch and supper together.

Over supper, Jack told Beth what Aston Hollinghurst said to him on the train to Oakland.

"He's been cordial ever since, so I guess I don't have to worry about him anymore."

Beth made a disgusted face. "See what I mean about the people in my life, Jack? They're all so superficial."

She flipped her wrist. "All it took to change you in his mind from a lowly dock worker, to someone he could socialize with as an equal, was your relationship with me."

Jack understood her point and it rankled him as well, though he was relieved that his platoon leader was backing off. "Whatever it takes so we don't go into battle mistrusting each other, I'm okay with."

Beth's lips quirked. "Are you going to invite his family to the wedding now?"

Jack laughed. "Hell, no. I do have my limits."

When the church bells rang out the ninth hour, Jack reluctantly kissed Beth goodbye and jogged back to the Bagnoli camp, hoping the physical activity would work out some of the deep sadness he felt at leaving his fiancée's side.

At least he was able to give her the letters he wrote, and she gave him the address for the Red Cross Headquarters in Lucca—about three-hundred-and-fifty miles north of Naples—where he could send future correspondence.

"Write me letters, even if you can't mail them to me," Jack insisted. "Someday I *will* get to read them."

"I will," she said, crossing her heart. "I promise."

Back at the Naples port the Second Battalion boarded an old Italian freighter called the *Sestriere.* Fortunately the trip up the west coast of Italy to Livorno was only about seven hours, so the lack of any semblance of luxury wasn't a problem.

They arrived late that afternoon. The sun was low and orange in the winter sky and the temperature here was significantly colder than Naples. Jack pulled the collar of his jacket closed against the damp sea breeze and joined Steve and Pete in line.

"It's cold, but not close to freezing." He pointed in the distance. "And those hills don't have snow on them."

Steve stared into the expanse. "Nope. Too close to the water." He turned to Jack for confirmation. "Right?"

"Yep."

No hope for skiing yet.

After off-loading the *Sestriere,* the Second Battalion climbed into personnel trucks and proceeded to their staging area near Pisa, about fifteen miles northeast of the dock.

"Hey!" Pete shouted as the line of trucks rumbled past the landmark on the way. "That's the Leaning Tower of Pisa! Wish I had a camera."

The Eighty-Sixth was billeted in what turned out to be the

palatial hunting grounds of King Victor Emmanuel III.

"I wonder how His Highness feels about having fourteen thousand or so soldiers tromping all over his land," Jack mused as he pitched the tent that he'd once again share with Steve.

"Well, he abandoned the Axis powers in September of forty-three and made an agreement with the Allies," Pete said as he pitched his tent next to Jack's. "So he doesn't have much to say about it, I don't think."

Jack straightened and stared at Pete. "How do you even know that?"

"My family's favorite restaurant in town is Italian." Pete shrugged. "When I was home, and I mentioned at dinner that going to Italy was a possibility, the owner ran over to our table and started talking about all kinds of stuff." Pete chuckled. "We didn't get out of there until nearly midnight."

"Don't feel too bad, Oakland, the Army's probably paying rent," Steve interjected. His gaze moved over the teeming crowd of uniformed soldiers making their rough homes on the ground. "At least I hope they are, because we're going to tear the shit out of this place."

January 6, 1945

Five days later, on New Year's Eve, the Eighty-Sixth Regiment trucked out of the hunting grounds heading for their next bivouac area near Quercianella, about ten miles south of Livorno on the coast. A winter rain had been falling for the last two days, and it didn't look like it was about to let up anytime soon.

"Reminds me of Kiska," Jack grumbled as he wiped rainwater from his face. "What a God-awful place that was."

When the trucks rumbled to a stop in the center of tiny Quercianella, a captain shouted their orders. "Word is we're going to be moving again soon, so stow any personal or nonessential gear in your duffel bags and stack them over there so the logistics guys can pick them up and put them in storage."

He pointed to a small building where the bags would be out of the rain. "After that, you can pitch your tents wherever you can find level ground."

"Or dry ground. That would be great," Pete grumbled.

"I wonder what 'soon' means." Steve looked at Jack. "Tomorrow?"

Jack shrugged. "Who knows?" He eyed the hills that rose from the coast. "Let's see what we can find in the meantime."

'Soon' proved to be five more days—the same amount of time they'd been camping on the king's hunting grounds. At least the rain had finally stopped. And in the hilly and heavily wooded terrain the mud situation wasn't anywhere near as bad as Kiska.

Jack smiled to himself as he packed up his gear.

Thank God for small favors.

The sound of a nearby explosion shattered the otherwise pristine day.

Jack jumped up and faced Steve, his fists clenched. "What was that?"

"I don't know. Let's go find out." Jack straightened his helmet and shouldered his rifle, and the two men ran toward the sound, along with a dozen other members of their company.

Five more explosions happened in rapid succession, all from the same approximate direction.

"Are we being attacked?" Jack shouted. His pulse accelerated and the tingle of adrenaline flushed his limbs. "Be ready, men!"

The soldiers came out of the forest and faced a gory scene. The ground by the railroad tracks was pocked with gaping holes. Eight soldiers' annihilated bodies sprawled on the ground, including the Catholic chaplain. Bright red blood contrasted with the drab green uniforms of the dead men, but no obvious danger was evident.

"What the hell happened?" Jack shouted to another sergeant nearby.

"Stay where you are!" he barked back. "Don't move!"

"Land mines!" a lieutenant warned. "Stay back!"

Jack watched the scene, horrified, until Lieutenant Hollinghurst popped up behind him.

"One of the men on guard duty went off his route along the track and stepped on a German mine," he said soberly. "When the men in his company heard the explosion, they rushed to his aid and unfortunately detonated the other mines."

"I thought we were in a secured area," Steve said to their platoon commander.

Hollinghurst took off his helmet and scuttled his fingers over his short hair. "In a war zone any misstep can kill you. Remind your men of that, Sergeants."

"Yes, sir," Jack and Steve said in tandem

Hollinghurst settled his helmet back on his head. "Five soldiers from Second Battalion Headquarters are coming to clear a path through the mine field and extract the bodies." Then he spit on the ground and walked away.

"Poor bastards," Jack muttered.

"Yeah."

This is getting real.

Colonel Tomlinson, the Eighty-Sixth regiment's commanding officer, returned from Lucca later that day with word that they were moving to the first line of defense facing the Germans. The Eighty-Sixth would be under the command of Brigadier General Duff and Task Force Forty-five.

The First Battalion would be stationed near Castelluccio, the Second close to San Marcello, and the Third in Bagni di Lucca.

Only two weeks in Italy and we're already at the front, Pops. Can you believe it?

It's pretty quiet out here right now, but the section of the line that we're assigned to has some of the most rugged terrain of the entire Italian front. There's snow here, too, and lots of it.

Our mountain training is finally starting to kick in.

January 21, 1945

Lieutenant Don Traynor, head of the Intelligence and Reconnaissance platoon under the Eighty-Sixth Regiment, was ordered to send a reconnaissance patrol to Mount Belvedere— currently under German control and their launching site for repeated attacks on the Allied-held valleys below.

"This patrol has two purposes." He held up one finger. "First, to observe movements in the Germans' forward areas, particularly on Mount Spigolino."

He held up a second finger. "And to determine if there is any way to mount an attack on Mount Belvedere from the flank or rear."

Traynor looked over the assembled Second Battalion. "I need four good skiers to penetrate German held territory," he clarified. "Expect snow conditions, rough weather, and the enemy for the twenty-mile trek."

Jack, Steve, and Pete stepped forward before Traynor said the word *trek*.

Jack saluted the lieutenant. "We've all done similar patrols at Camp Hale sir, so the terrain, snow, and distance won't be a problem."

Traynor looked pleased. "Great. I need one more."

"I'll go."

Jack looked sideways at Hollinghurst, surprised that the lieutenant was volunteering. Did he feel like he couldn't let Jack outshine him in spite of his conciliatory words?

At least he can ski.

"Very good." Traynor flashed a grim smile. "Come with me."

*****

To allow the patrol to move quickly and quietly, the equipment they carried was kept at a minimum: sleeping bag, a sweater, extra socks, three days of rations, water, rifle and ammunition. The first aid materials were split among them. The soldiers donned their camouflaging white anoraks over their uniforms and tied the white caps over their helmets.

To Jack's relief, Lieutenant Traynor carried the binoculars and compass.

As long as it's not Hollinghurst.

Before they departed the camp, Lieutenant Traynor reviewed Army procedures in the event that any of them was taken prisoner.

Shit.

Jack glanced at Steve and saw the same trepidation in his friends' expression that he was feeling.

As the afternoon sun began to wane and temperatures dropped, Traynor made a call to the battalion switchboard to tell them the patrol was departing. "I request that all units be notified that a friendly patrol will be operating tonight. We don't want to get shot by our own side."

The five men carried their gear to a Weasel waiting to take them from San Marcello up to the town of Spignana. When the sun disappeared behind dark, thickening clouds that shrouded the mountain peaks, the men mounted their skis and launched their mission. Steve took point position first and broke trail for the four who followed.

Traynor took third position and kept track of the map and compass as they skied easily up the first mile. When they reached the top of the first ridge, however, it was obvious the gathering storm would soon overtake them.

Traynor consulted the map. "The British have artillery observer outposts on most of the ridgelines. There should be one…" He lifted his eyes and squinted against the strengthening wind. Then he pointed. "That way."

The men found the outpost in a requisitioned cabin just below a ridge. The British soldiers there were very cordial and Lieutenant Traynor announced that with the Brits standing watch the men in the patrol could grab a little shut-eye until the storm blew over.

After a supper of thankfully not-frozen K-rations, Jack unrolled his sleeping bag in a corner of the cabin and tried to get some rest, but his mind was spinning. The prospect of encountering Germans, even though the objective was to remain undiscovered, haunted him. What would he do?

Shoot a man point blank?

Be shot in return?

Try to escape?

All of the above, most likely.

Oh, Beth. If there wasn't a war, we'd never have met.

Being grateful for a war was stupid. Jack knew that. So maybe God was simply rewarding them both for doing what needed to be done at the time.

Now they just had to survive until it ended.

*****

Pete shook Jack awake. "Storm's passed. We're heading out."

Jack sat up, groggy, and rubbed his eyes. "What time is it?"

"Zero-two."

Jack nodded and climbed out of his sleeping bag. The cold air outside would wake him up, he knew that for a fact.

Though the clouds were clearing the weather continued to bluster, as if offended to have soldiers at war on the ridge. Jack had no objection—the wind and cold temperatures probably meant the Germans wouldn't expect any trouble tonight. If that was the case, their lookouts might be hunkered down inside their stations and not paying close attention to the landscape.

Jack took a turn as point man. Breaking trail against the wind and constantly turning back to check with Traynor to make sure he was on the route was exhausting.

The frigid wind sapped their body heat, so in order to keep warm, they had to keep moving. They climbed the ridge and skied for five hours straight, stopping only to check the map and switch out the trail breakers.

There was no banter, no conversation. Partly because they didn't want to give themselves away, of course. But mostly because it required every gasp of breath to keep ski-marching briskly over the snow.

As the sun streaked the eastern sky, the patrol reached the far side of the ridge and saw their first sign of enemy activity.

Pete was in the trailbreaker position now and he stopped the line, pointing at the ground. "Fresh tracks in the snow," he whispered.

Traynor nodded and motioned for them to keep going.

They made their way silently along the side of the slope. Jack was glad to be on his skis at last, doing what he signed up for in the first place. Hard as it was, gliding over the snow in the cold and breathing in the crystalline air made him feel alive in a way nothing else did.

When the dawning sun rose high enough for the men to see both sides of the ridge, they could see both the German and Allied positions.

Steve pointed out a building across the valley that could be a German observation post. Lieutenant Traynor checked it out with the binoculars, gave Steve a thumbs up, and recorded the location in his notebook.

From their high position on the ridge, skiing down the slope was easy. The patrol stopped for a break halfway down the mountain while Lieutenant Traynor oriented the map and determined their exact location.

"This valley leads to the town of Vidiciatico." Traynor tucked the map back in its tube. "We should be able to see Mount Spigolino from there."

Hollinghurst took his turn as trail breaker. After another three hours they spotted a patrol similar to theirs in the valley below.

Traynor took to the binoculars again. "First Battalion. Damn."

"If we can spot them, then the Germans can spot them too," Jack stated.

"And if you can be seen, you can be hit," Steve observed. "And if you can be hit, you can be killed."

Lieutenant Traynor made a note of the First's position in his report.

The ski patrol grabbed the chance to rest in the tree line and snacked on K-rations before they made their way back up a ridge, still looking for possible routes around Mount Spigolino.

"Too bad we're here to fight," Steve said as he put away his rations. "I'd love to challenge you four hacks to a downhill run right about now."

"You're all talk, Dropout," Jack chided. "But I'll take you up on that someday."

Steve grinned at him. "You're on, Oakland."

Not long after they were on the move again, Hollinghurst spotted the First Battalion forward listening post. "Should I ski ahead to let them know we're friendly and approaching their position?"

Traynor nodded. "Good idea."

Jack watched Hollinghurst ski away. He refrained from calling out, "Don't get lost!"

Barely.

The four remaining skiers watched to see that Hollinghurst made the run safely and that the First Battalion guys let him in before they followed.

Once the five skiers in the patrol were at the post, Traynor told them how vulnerable their position was. "We spotted you from high on the ridge. You need a more sheltered location."

The lieutenant in charge thanked him. "We'll move after sunset. Now take a look at this…"

The lieutenant lifted his binoculars and pointed out a German patrol of three men who were also on skis. Traynor shared his binoculars with the other four men so that they could see what their enemy looked like under these conditions.

"They're pretty far away," Jack said, handing the binoculars to Pete. "Across the valley there. But now we know they're here, at least."

After comparing his maps to the one at the First Battalion listening post, and asking the soldiers what they knew about the terrain surrounding their station, Lieutenant Traynor concluded there was no accessible route around Mount Spigolino which could handle a large scale attack on Mount Belvedere.

"I have to admit that's disappointing," he confessed to the four men in the patrol. "I just wish our mission had a better outcome."

"We do have intelligence on the Germans, sir," Jack reminded him. "That was the other part."

Traynor peered pensively at Jack. "Yes, it was. You're right."

"And we didn't get caught," Steve added. "That makes it a successful mission in my book."

It was only mid-afternoon on the second day of the planned three-day patrol, but their job was as complete as it could be. In spite of the risk of being seen by the Germans, a ski run down the valley and back toward their camp tempted the men.

"Let's just outrun 'em, guys!" Steve adjusted his green-glassed goggles and gripped his ski poles. "Try to catch me!"

Steve was on his way down the mountain before anyone could stop him.

Jack sped after his friend with Hollinghurst and Traynor close on his tail. For the next several minutes, the war ceased to exist. He was just a man on a pair of skis flying down a mountain on fresh, unspoiled snow—and it was glorious.

You should have seen me, Beth.

I beat the pants off Hollinghurst.

Chapter Twenty-Eight

Late that afternoon the ski patrol arrived at the Eighty-Sixth Regimental Headquarters in San Marcello for a briefing session. Lieutenant Traynor spoke from his notes and his memory as the rest of the group filled in any blanks.

"Thank you, gentlemen." The captain running the briefing looked frustrated—and with good reason, Jack thought.

Enemy installations in the vicinity of Mount Spigolino had been observed, true, but the results of the route reconnaissance proved that an alternate plan was needed if the Americans wanted to take Mount Belvedere.

"What are your thoughts, Sergeant Franklin?"

The question startled Jack. He straightened in his chair. "I'm glad I was part of the patrol Sir, because now I know for sure that our preparation and training are more than adequate to meet the obstacle at hand."

The captain quirked a brow. "Is that so?"

"Yes, sir." Jack decided to go on. "All five of us knew what we were doing, and because of our experience we were able to complete the mission in half the time allotted."

The captain leaned back in his chair. "What would you suggest we do next?"

"Well…" Jack drew a deep breath and mentioned what had

been rumbling around in the back of his thoughts for the last few hours. "A reinforced company *could* be moved through the territory, but only if they were expert mountaineers and properly equipped."

Jack glanced at Lieutenant Traynor who watched him intently. He gave Jack a slight nod.

Encouraged, Jack continued. "But unfortunately, Captain, the Eighty-Sixth currently doesn't have all of its winter gear, so we can't pursue that idea at the present time."

"Hmm." The captain looked at Traynor. "Thank you all. You're dismissed."

January 31, 1945

The end of January meant that the remaining battalions of the Tenth Mountain Division were finally in Italy and the Eighty-Fifth and Eighty-Seventh Regiments were moving up to relieve the Eighty-Sixth's positions.

The Eighty-Sixth Regiment was sent to a training area in the vicinity of Lucca near Fourth Corps Headquarters. The Regimental Command Post there was set up inside a beautiful villa less than five miles from the center of Lucca.

And the location of Red Cross Headquarters.

As Second Battalion rested and re-supplied, their backed-up mail was delivered to the soldiers. A stack of Beth's letters arrived and Jack was thrilled to see the most recent were postmarked with the APO Box in Lucca.

She's here.

After he read through them, Jack stowed the letters deep in his pack to reread later and requested permission to go into town. "Just a couple hours, sir," he said to Captain Rideout. "I'll be back for chow."

Rideout nodded. "Ride in with me. I have to go anyway."

Jack stifled a ridiculously happy grin and saluted. "Thank you, sir."

Though the winter weather in Lucca was far milder than any January in Colorado—only a few nights had reached below freezing temperatures—the wind generated by riding in an open jeep on this cloudy day made Jack's eyes water and his cheeks sting. And because he had no idea where the Red Cross was headquartered he asked to be dropped in the center of town.

"I'll find my way back, sir" he said to Rideout. "Thanks again."

As the jeep rumbled off toward wherever the captain was headed, Jack did a slow turn, assessing the town.

"You need help, mister?"

A young boy stood at Jack's elbow. "I take you where you go?" he offered. "Very cheap."

Jack chuckled. "Sure." As he reached into his pocket for some loose coins he asked where the American Red Cross was housed.

"Very close." The urchin held out a palm. "I show you."

Jack dropped the coins into the boy's palm. "Let's go."

The walk to the medieval stone-and-plaster building was a whopping two blocks.

Jack halted about ten yards from the entrance to the building and turned to dismiss his young guide. "Thank you. *Grazie.*"

"I show you more?" the boy asked.

Jack shook his head. "Not today. Maybe next time."

"I wait for you?"

Jack wondered how hard the boy was going to stick to him. He certainly didn't need a chaperone this afternoon, and especially not a child. "No."

"I show you ladies, *sì?*"

Jack shook his head. He gripped the boy's shoulders and turned him in the opposite direction from the Red Cross. "No. Now go find another soldier to bother."

Jack doubted the boy had enough English to understand all the words, but he clearly understood he was being dismissed.

"I see you again," the boy stated. "You ask for Mateo."

"Mateo," Jack repeated and dragged his fingers in the sign of a cross over his heart. "No one else."

After an awkward and unmoving moment of silence, Mateo seemed to accept the fact that Jack really wasn't going to engage his services further. With slumped shoulders he trudged off around the corner, headed toward where they'd just come from.

Jack turned back in the direction of the Red Cross building just as the heavily carved wooden door swung outward. Jack tucked himself against the building out of military habit to avoid being noticed.

A tall and trim American Air Corps captain stepped out and

turned his back to Jack as he offered his hand to the person following him. The leather-gloved hand that was placed in his was definitely feminine.

Jack recoiled when her profile appeared.

Beth?

She smiled up into the man's eyes and Jack spun around the corner of the building that he stood in front of.

Beth? With another man?

Jack scowled and risked a look around the stone edge. Luckily the couple was strolling in the opposite direction so they didn't see him. Jack couldn't hear their conversation, but Beth had her arm looped tightly through the captain's and her delighted laughter blew back toward him on the chilling wind.

Jack's heart battered his ribs and adrenaline flooded his veins.

What the hell?

He stood, rooted, trying to decide whether to advance his position and face the enemy, or to retreat, regroup, and form a strategy for attack.

When Beth stood on her toes and kissed the captain's cheek Jack's decision was instantly made.

He whirled on his heel and launched his five-mile run back to camp.

February 3, 1945

For the last three days Jack tried to keep his mind off Beth by determinedly focusing his attention on training the men in his platoon. Every waking moment from dawn to dark was filled with attention to battle details, and the constant repetition of drills and procedures.

Jack worked hard to ensure that every man under his command knew what he needed to survive the war. He couldn't live with himself if any man in his platoon died because he wasn't adequately prepared. The constant activity should have kept Jack's mind off Beth. So close to battle, there was no time for anything—or anyone—to be a distraction or diversion from the task at hand.

Should have.

But didn't. When Jack's head hit his pillow at night, no matter how exhausted he was, how cold, how hard the ground beneath his sleeping bag was, or even how comically loud Steve Knowlton's snoring was could stop the image of Beth from playing over and over on the silver screen in his mind. His beloved Beth, endlessly walking arm-in-arm with the Air Corps captain down the ancient cobbled streets of Lucca. Every night for the past three nights she stood on her toes and kissed the man countless times.

Jack groaned and laid his arm across his eyes. Maybe she finally realized that life with the son of a dockworker wasn't for her after all.

Oh, Beth…

*****

While the regiment rested and trained in its rear area, there was still a palpable undercurrent of anticipation. The highway writhed under a constant stream of military vehicles carrying ammunition and artillery, gasoline, radio equipment, uniforms, and all types of gear.

Their entry into battle was obviously close.

After breakfast, Jack and Steve sought out Captain Rideout for a briefing on F Company's status and orders for the day. But when they approached the company tent Jack halted like he'd hit a brick wall. He felt the blood drain from his face.

"Hey—isn't that your girl?" Steve's elbow hit Jack's. "Did you know she was coming?"

Jack's jaw clenched. He hadn't told anyone about Beth being in Lucca or seeing her with the Air Corps captain. And now she stood in the middle of his camp, dressed in her Red Cross uniform, and chatting with Lieutenant Hollinghurst like they were old friends.

Jack shook his head, his gaze locked on Beth. "I—no—their headquarters is in Lucca," he stammered.

Before he could say anything else, or even begin to sort his roiling thoughts and emotions, Steve called out, "Betty Harkins! What are you doing here?"

Damn it.

Jack had no choice but to put on a brave face and approach his fiancée. Damn but she looked beautiful in her gray military uniform tailored to hug her feminine frame. Her red-lined blue cape hung open on this relatively mild day.

Beth spoke before he did, but the look in her eyes was odd and her smile puzzled. "Sergeant Franklin! It's wonderful to see you again."

Jack walked up to her and gave her a brief peck on the cheek. "Hi, Betty. When did you come to Lucca?"

"A couple weeks ago." Her brow wrinkled. "I wrote to you from here. Didn't you get my letters?"

"Um, yeah. But I didn't have a chance to read them all. We were on a mission." Jack looked at Hollinghurst. "Is this Army business, sir?"

"Routine, Franklin. Just the Red Cross checking in to see what we need." The lieutenant flashed a crooked grin. "Do *you* need anything?"

Jack didn't look at Beth. "Just a moment of her time when your business is done, if that's not a problem."

Hollinghurst glanced at Beth and shook his head. "Not a problem, Sergeant."

Jack faced Beth again. "I'll be in Company F's tent, Captain Harkins. Come see me when you've finished up."

"I will." Beth's tone reflected the concern in her expression.

Jack saluted Hollinghurst before he turned around and strode stiffly toward the company tent.

"Trouble in paradise?" Steve probed as he matched Jack's pace.

"Shut up, Dropout," Jack growled.

I guess I'll find out soon enough.

*****

Beth stepped into the F Company tent about twenty minutes later. Jack stood, took her arm, and silently led her to the outer edge of the camp.

"Jeff, what's wrong?" she asked once they stopped moving. "Why didn't you tell me you were here? Or come see me?"

Jack saw no reason to beat around the bush. "I did come."

"When?" Beth looked crushed. "I'm sorry I missed you."

Jack couldn't help himself. "You didn't look sorry."

Beth recoiled. "You saw me? But didn't say anything? Why would you do that?"

"I didn't want to interrupt." Jack narrowed his eyes. "You and the Air Corps captain were having a good enough time without me."

A flit of understanding crossed Beth's face before the storm rolled in. "How *dare* you!"

"Me?" Jack yelped.

"Yes, you!" Beth's gloved hands fisted and her tone grew increasingly thunderous. "For your information, *Sergeant Franklin*, that Air Corps captain happens to be my *cousin*—and I hadn't seen him for three years when he found me here!"

Her words punched a very large, jagged hole through Jack's indignation. "Your cousin?"

"Yes! His mother and my mother are sisters—we grew up together!" Beth loosed an impressive growl of frustration from her belly. Jack had never seen her so angry. "You could've met him if you weren't such an *ass*."

Jack knew he needed to apologize, but none of the words that came to his mind were strong enough. "I—I'm sorry, Beth."

"Sorry? For what?" Her eyes shot green grenades at him. "For making assumptions about me? For not trusting me? For thinking I'd *ever* cheat on you?"

"Yeah. All of that." Jack reached for her hand, but she jerked it away. "I'm really sorry."

Beth stepped back. "Well that's not good enough, Jeff."

"What do you want from me?" he asked. "Name it."

Tears breached Beth's eyelids and flooded her cheeks. "I need your trust. I thought I had it, but now I know that I don't."

"You do!" Jack insisted.

Beth continued as if he hadn't spoken, "And I can't marry someone who would ever doubt my character."

"I don't doubt your character, Beth," Jack tried to assure her. "I really don't. You're right, I'm a complete ass."

He stepped forward and reached for her hand again. And once again she pulled it away.

"That's not enough, Jeff." She pulled off her leather gloves and wiped her cheeks. "I'm sorry, but it's not."

Jack felt like crying himself. "What can I do to fix this?"

"I don't know." Beth's watery gaze pinned his. "But you better figure it out. And fast."

She pulled her cape around her, gloves still clutched in one hand. "I have to go."

She strode past him and through the camp.

Jack watched her go, devastated and at a complete loss.

February 7, 1945

Brigadier General Hays was promoted to Major General, so he held another of his 'all officer speeches' with the Tenth Mountain Division officers. Afterwards, Captain Rideout pulled F Company into formation under heavy clouds to tell them what he learned.

"The spring offensive will begin as soon as two things happen," he began as he pointed to the sky. "First the weather has to clear enough for Air Corps to gain—and maintain—air superiority over Northern Italy."

His hand moved to indicate the growing mounds of tarp-covered supplies. "And second, we're still waiting for sufficient supplies to sustain a lengthy campaign. And *that* is dependent on gaining control of Highways Sixty-Four and Sixty-Five, both defended by the Germans from high on the Mount Belvedere ridges."

The first thought that occurred to Jack was that if they waited until spring, then there was little chance of using their skis when they actually entered the fray. That was disappointing.

"The mission of the Tenth Mountain Division, gentlemen, is to take and hold the Mount Belvedere ridges."

Jack's pulse surged and he looked at Steve. Steve looked at Pete. Clearly the three friends were thinking the same thing: the Mount Belvedere Ridges were covered in snow.

"This mission has to be completed *before* the spring offensive can commence," Rideout continued. "Once Belvedere is Allied-occupied, Fifth Army can push the Germans out of Italy."

Jack raised a hand. "Permission to speak, sir?"

Rideout nodded. "Yes, Sergeant."

Jack chose his words carefully—the Army's three previous attempts to take Mount Belvedere had not been successful because the Germans' high position was strong, defensible, and unassailable.

"So we'll launch another uphill assault on Mount Belvedere?"

Rideout shook his head. "The key isn't Belvedere itself, but the adjacent ridgeline—and Riva Ridge specifically. That's where the Germans' forward observation post is. Firing their artillery from up there defeats and prevents any frontal assaults on Belvedere."

Rideout paused to give the men a moment to process what he was saying before he continued. "By removing their forward observation post, the Germans will no longer be able to defend Belvedere, or fire down on Highways Sixty-Four and Sixty-Five."

"How are we going to attack Riva Ridge, Sir?" Steve blurted.

Captain Rideout's lips twisted in a grim smile. "I'll let you know when I do, Sergeant. Company dismissed."

*****

Jack contemplated the information they'd just received as he hitched a ride into Lucca. After his argument with Beth, Jack wracked his brain to come up with a gesture that would let Beth know he was completely wrong to doubt her, and that he would never do such a thing again.

As he wandered the streets of Lucca two days after their fight, the perfect gift appeared in a shop window. Jack hurried inside and selected one of the thick-papered journals covered in beautifully tooled Italian leather—a red one for the Red Cross.

After writing out several versions of his apology, he decided that making promises was the most effective. Once he settled on the right words, he copied the text onto the first page of the journal. And now he was on the way to give it to her.

My dearest Beth ~

I love you more than any words can say, so I hope you'll take these promises as proof of my unending admiration of the woman that you are, and how grateful I am that you've chosen me to spend your life with:

I promise to love only you for the rest of my life.

I promise to trust you always and without question, no matter the situation.

I promise to uphold your character and defend you

against any attack.

I promise to protect you against anyone who tries to hurt you.

I promise to become the man you deserve, and will spend the rest of my life working toward that goal.

And I promise that nothing on this earth will stop me from keeping my word.

With all my love, now and forever, Jeff

Chapter
Twenty-Nine

February 10, 1945

Once again Captain Rideout pulled F Company into formation.

"Army consensus is that a single battalion will be able to attack, gain, and hold Riva Ridge," he told them. "First Battalion of the Eighty-Sixth is the one designated to attack."

Jack felt a stab of envy. He was itching to get into the fray now that he was so close to the front. He had to prove himself to Pops, and show him what an elite Army outfit could accomplish.

And the sooner the better.

"However, a reconnaissance patrol found at least eighteen positions and at least four observation posts." Rideout's gaze swept over his men. "Because of those numbers, First Battalion has asked for help."

Rideout allowed a small grin. "So F Company from Second Battalion will be attached for a night climb of Riva Ridge."

A night climb?

A jolt of adrenaline zinged through Jack's frame. "So we're sneaking up behind them?" he clarified.

"Yes, Sergeant, we are. Beginning immediately we'll shift our training from night infiltration to night climbing."

Their training turned out to be identical to that at Camp Hale, and because Jack and Steve were climbing instructors in Colorado they were pressed into that service once again, concentrating on the new and inexperienced men who joined their company at Camp

Swift.

The significant difference was that their mountain climbing in Colorado was done in the summer. Now they were climbing in February in cold and ice—and in the dark. Soldiers carried their packs, weapons, and supplies while they trained, to become re-accustomed to the conditions that they were once fully prepared for.

The face of Riva Ridge was divided into sectors by First Battalion and the companies were assigned to various routes up the ridge. Company F was assigned to ascend Riva Ridge on trail route number five.

Actual orders for the attack—called The Encore Plan because this was the *fourth* Army attack on the Mount Belvedere ridges—were issued today, seven days before they were scheduled to depart.

"The Germans consider the ridgeline impregnable because of those steep, icy cliffs. But this time, soldiers trained specifically for combat in mountainous terrain will take the lead," Jack told his squad. "I hope you're all ready. Because the Tenth Mountain Division is the *only* Army Division that's had to justify its existence. So we all have something to prove."

*****

Beth appeared at F Company's camp just before supper, pleasantly surprising Jack.

He kissed her cheek and asked, "What are you doing here?"

She flashed a self-conscious smile and her cheeks flushed adorably. "I'm shamelessly taking advantage of my Red Cross position to check in on F Company."

Jack grinned. Since he gave her the journal three days ago, causing her to break into great gulping sobs of forgiveness followed by innumerable kisses, this was her second visit to their staging location.

"You know I'm glad to see you," he murmured in her ear. "But I'd like to visit you in Lucca next time."

Beth looked up into his eyes. "When do you think you'll be able to come?"

"Tomorrow." *One way or another.* "I'll run a test of my men's skills then release them for the rest of the day." He chuckled.

"They'll love me for it."

"Not as much as I do." Beth squeezed his hand and didn't let go. "I found the most adorable little restaurant a couple blocks from Headquarters. We can sit in one of their alcoves and share a bottle of wine."

"That sounds swell." Jack stroked Beth's cheek with his free hand. "We're headed into battle a week from today, so I want to spend as much time as I can manage with you."

Beth's expression sobered. "And I with you."

Jack tucked his knuckle under her chin and tilted her face upward. He stared into her eyes. "I'm going to be fine."

Beth pressed her lips together in a tight resolute smile.

February 17, 1945

It's go time.

After the sun set, Jack joined his men in the back of a crowded Army transport vehicle as the soldiers from the Eighty-Sixth's First Battalion, plus F Company from the Eighty-Sixth's Second Battalion, trucked the twenty-five bumpy miles northeast from their training area in Lucca to the village of Vidiciatico.

Once there, the assembled soldiers quietly ski-marched eight miles in the dark to Madonna del Acero, one of five tiny villages at the base of the east wall of Riva Ridge.

From north to south along the eastern base of Riva Ridge, eight hundred American soldiers moved into farmhouses, barns, sheds, and any other place they could find to hide from German eyes during the coming daylight hours so their presence would not be detected by the enemy.

Jack and Steve, along with a dozen other men, found a barn and climbed into the hayloft, much to the disapproval of the milk cows below them.

"Moo all you want, Bessie," Steve said as he laid out his sleeping bag on a pile of hay. "I'm tired enough to sleep in spite of your racket."

Jack unrolled his bag and climbed inside, thankful for both the warm shelter and the comfort of hay beneath him instead of half-frozen ground. He felt for Beth's Red Cross pin hanging from the chain with his dog tags.

Stay lucky Beth, and I will too.

Tomorrow night his luck would be put to the test.

February 18, 1945

F Company assembled at the bottom of trail route number five the next night and, in addition to his rifle, every man carried ninety-six rounds of ammunition, two grenades, extra K-rations, water, and either a machine gun belt or mortar rounds. All of their personal gear was packed in rucksacks and left behind.

When the grenades were passed out, Jack hefted the iron-clad bomb in his palm. "This is the real thing, Dropout."

"More real than Kiska, that's for sure." Steve tucked the grenades inside his backpack. "I hope you can throw these things accurately, Oakland. If not, remind me to stay behind you."

Jack looked around F Company, who was assembled and waiting in the medieval Sanctuary of Madonna Dell'Acero church. Unlike Kiska, he now had the safety of the men in his squad to consider not just himself, and he felt the heavy weight of that responsibility.

Stay lucky, men.

Jack checked his watch, his impatience grabbing hold of him and making time drag. Ten-fifteen. Their time of departure was ten-thirty. Waiting was the worst part so far.

F Company's objective was the far southwest end of the ridge, Cingio del Bure. Their mission was to attack and defeat the Germans, then hold and defend the ridge. The plan was for all the companies to be in place on top of Riva Ridge and have control of it before dawn. It sounded so simple and clear-cut.

But there was a ferocious enemy waiting above them, and they would fight just as hard to hold on to what F Company would fight to take away from them. The ammunition was real. Men were going to die.

Though the evening was cold, it wasn't freezing yet. But as the sun set and the temperature dropped and a heavy fog shrouded the base of the ridge and clouds obscured the moon.

"Couldn't ask for better cover, huh guys?" Pete Seibert squatted next to Steve. "I'm feeling pretty good about this."

Jack dragged his thoughts from their morbid path and nodded his agreement. "Sure beats climbing Cooper Hill this time of year."

Steve fastened his pack. "True words."

At ten-thirty Captain Rideout stood. "Get up, men. Let's go."

The soldiers trundled to their feet and the march began.

The night air was cold and damp under the fog and heavy cloud cover. The soldiers' only light came from the reflection off the clouds above as German searchlights, shining over the top of the ridge, continued their nightly search for air attacks.

Captain Rideout led the march toward the wash at the base of the ridge, which was swollen with rain and melted snow.

"We'll use that crossing there," he said as he pointed in the dim light. "That crossing made from rocks. Do you see it?"

"Yes, sir," several men answered quietly. They headed toward the spot in single file.

Some of the men had trouble keeping their balance on the slippery rocks, especially with their heavy loads. One soldier in Jack's squad wind-milled his arms and fell into a swirling part of the wash. Without hesitating, Jack jumped into the icy waist-deep water to rescue him.

Private Johnson, soaked from head to toe, scrambled back to the south shore and refused to try to cross again no matter how strongly Jack ordered him to.

Shit.

Jack grabbed the soldier closest to him. "Tell Captain Rideout what happened, and tell him I'll catch up with the company after I get this guy straightened out."

"Yes, sir."

Jack was just as wet and cold as the shivering private. In spite of his numb and aching legs, Jack marched the private back to a farmhouse they had passed which was requisitioned by the Army as an aid station. When they got there, the medics got Johnson out of his wet clothes and into dry pants and shirt.

Jack also got a pair of dry trousers and dug a pair of dry socks out of his pack. "Johnson, come up the ridge with the first re-supply effort in the morning. Do you understand?"

"Y-yes, s-sir," he chattered.

Jack stood and pinned him with a hard gaze. "This is a direct order. Do not disobey me again or I'll have you court-martialed. "

Johnson nodded spastically but emphatically.

Jack ran back to the wash, taking the opportunity to flex his cramped legs and create enough body heat to warm himself after his freezing bath. He crossed the rock bridge quickly and hurried forward to find his men.

When he caught up to F Company, the soldiers who joined them in Texas were bent over and breathing heavily, laboring under their burdens of packs and ammo. The rest had already begun their silent climb up the steep trail.

"Be quiet. Don't let the Germans hear you," Jack whispered to the lagging men. "If they discover our presence they'll wipe us all out."

The men nodded their understanding, straightened, and followed the first half of the company. They walked in silent single file, taking careful steps in the dark, tracking after the man in front of them.

Jack took the rear position to assure that no one else in his squad fell behind. He regretted that he couldn't see the stars and orient himself, but the route seemed pretty obvious so far. As long as his inner compass didn't argue with the direction they were headed, he'd assume they were going the right way.

When F Company reached the halfway point in the hard uphill climb, word was passed by hands and whispers that they were taking a break. The soldiers sat where they were. Some men opened their jackets to cool themselves after the hours of exertion.

Jack rested and listened in complete amazement to… nothing.

Incredibly, eight hundred soldiers were currently preparing to ascend the back side of Riva Ridge along multiple paths, and so far not a single sound gave them away. All Jack heard was the splash of the tumbling wash nearly a thousand feet below.

Maybe that was covering the sound of the occasional boot-dislodged rock. After all, no German alarms had sounded.

The sweeping, searching lights above them shot ghostly crisscrossing shafts upward through the damp air until multiple circles danced in incongruent gaiety across the bottom of the low heavy clouds.

Their light reflected back to earth and illuminated the soldiers' path with just enough light that their dark-adjusted eyes could see their way. The soggy presence of fog and clouds helped muffle any sounds from below as the droplets of water absorbed the vibrations.

We couldn't have picked a better night, Beth.
So far, so good.

Their break over, Jack and his men rose to their feet to resume the unrelenting march upward when the silence was shattered by a clanging, banging, ringing of steel on rock as something bounced down the column, down into the night, and down into the wash below.

"What the—" the soldier in front of Jack blurted, then clapped a hand over his mouth.

Did the German sentries hear that?

The line of mountain troopers froze, silent and unmoving, waiting. Jack barely breathed as he strained to hear any reaction from the enemy above them.

Surely some alert sentry would challenge the unseen soldier approaching—wouldn't they? Captain Rideout had wisely placed two German-speaking soldiers at the front of F Company if anyone did.

Minutes passed like hours.

But they passed without a word, a reaction, or a change in the angle of the searchlights. Either the clouds above or the rushing water below must have masked the sound.

Or they're not paying any attention because they think this side of the ridge is impenetrable.

The men quietly checked their weapons. A wave passed down the line and restarted their stealthy advance. Steve dropped back to Jack's position.

"Word's coming down the line that one of the machine gunners up ahead took off his helmet during the break. It slipped out of his hand and he couldn't catch it."

"Warn the men," Jack said. "Another dumbass move like that can get us all killed."

Steve's whisper was stern. "Yep. I have been."

*****

Once F Company reached the bottom of the vertical face of Riva Ridge, Jack took a moment to catch his breath and watch the incredible view above him.

Scaling the vertical ridge, and lit only by the searchlights reflecting off the low-hanging clouds overhead, were hundreds of silent soldiers looking much like an invasion of giant ants at a huge nighttime picnic.

The first men up used picks to test cracks in the granite and pound steel pitons into them at scalable intervals, their blows muffled with wads of fabric. Snap links were attached to the pitons and ropes were run through the snap links. Soldiers used the ropes, plus their own scrambling skills, to climb the remaining one thousand feet to the top of the ridge.

The foggy haze hanging over the lower elevations of the ridge helped conceal the ascending mountaineers. Searchlights above them continued to scan, their reflection off the clouds unintentionally lighting the climbers' way.

And all Jack could hear was the faint metallic ping of the snap links and the occasional scrape of a boot against the rock.

He sent his squad up and once again took the rear position, so if any of them got stuck he could give the man a hand. With an odd sense of disbelief, he grabbed hold of the rope and began his own climb.

The physical exertion was daunting. Jack's arms burned as he held the rope, blindly searching for foot holds by sliding the toes of his boots along the granite wall. Foot by dearly won foot, he moved upward.

When he looked to his side he saw dozens of men—mountain trained men—climbing with quiet, singular determination. Below he saw dozens more soldiers emerging from the patchy fog below and following his ascending path. At that moment a strong sense of pride and camaraderie swelled in Jack's chest.

Not only were the mountain troops finally doing something they trained for, but they were doing a damned fine job of it.

I wish Pops could see this.

The wind had turned wet this high up and was now bitterly cold. As he climbed, Jack was constantly showered with ice crystals blown over the edge of the snow-covered ridge above them.

Climbing silently in the dark along with F Company were the men from the First Battalion. As planned no man spoke—only the occasional hand signal could be seen in the dim light. Each of the elite Army soldiers focused on their shared task: climb the ridge as quickly and quietly as possible.

As the last member of F Company on the climb, Jack reached their objective at the top of Riva Ridge just after four o'clock in the morning.

The soldiers immediately set about securing their section of the ridge. Gunners planted their machine guns to cover their assigned sectors below, while the rest of the soldiers dug foxholes into the snow and prepared to fire downhill at the Germans.

The combined upland positions of the various companies involved in the attack would make it possible to effectively eliminate all of the German observation posts on the sloping side of Riva Ridge.

As Jack and Steve settled into their shared foxhole to wait for the nearing sunrise, Jack smiled.

The arrival and military preparations of eight hundred American Army soldiers had gone completely undetected by their enemy.

Chapter Thirty

February 19, 1945

With the sun rose that morning the Germans realized that the American Army was positioned above them in force. They scrambled to realign their weaponry and launched an attack on F Company, with both mortar and machine gun fire aimed at Jack's platoon.

"I can't see where they're shooting from!" one of Jack's men shouted. "Their guns are hidden in the snow!"

Before Jack could respond their platoon sergeant was hit about twenty yards to his left. Clearly their whole end of the ridge was endangered.

"I'm moving a machine gun team to hold the end of our position!" Jack barked at his squad. "Cover us!"

Jack ran to the right with German bullets hitting the snow all around him. He grabbed the closest team of machine gunners and together they headed toward the downed sergeant.

When they reached the sergeant he was already dead. Jack and one of the gunners lifted the sergeant's body out of the snowy foxhole he'd dug and put the machine gun in his place.

"How quick can you be up and firing?" Jack asked, ignoring the surge of fear that gripped him when he lifted the suddenly dead platoon sergeant's body.

"Give us a couple minutes, Sarge," one answered as he worked. "We've got this."

They proved true to their word.

As Jack moved away from the gunners he thanked God that he wasn't the one hit. He shoved aside a brief twinge of guilt at the prayer, knowing that war wasn't a him-or-me situation. All of them were equally at risk—even the Germans. Bombs didn't discriminate.

I'll thank You every single day that You let me live.

In the momentary calm after Allied counter-artillery stopped an aggressive German attack, a group of Germans came forward carrying a white flag and with their hands up in surrender.

Jack frowned. "Be ready, men. I don't trust the bastards."

When the 'surrendering' soldiers dropped to their knees and started shooting, Jack's men responded with heavy artillery fire and launched their grenades. They drove the Germans back, killing half of the tricksters.

By noon F Company had advanced, taking one German prisoner as the intermittent firefight continued. Though the Germans came up and at them from all sides, the mountain troops held the far end of the ridge, successfully repelling the Germans' concerted attempt to retake their stronghold.

At battle's end, Jack's platoon confirmed twenty-six Germans killed, seven captured, and more Nazis bleeding all over the snow than Jack could tally.

*****

In the late afternoon, men from Service Company made their way up to the top of Riva Ridge, carrying a fresh supply of ammunition, rations, and water. Jack was admittedly surprised to see Private Johnson with them—he wasn't a hundred percent sure the soldier would actually return to the platoon.

"Dig in, men!" Captain Rideout ordered.

Jack did so gratefully. After his first day of actual warfare, following a night with no sleep, he was shaken and exhausted, but oddly energized at the same time. He knew both were after-effects of adrenaline and all he needed was a few hours to rest and recoup.

He honestly didn't know if he'd killed anyone. The uncertainty left him unsure of what to think about that. On the one hand, he hoped he'd upheld his end and taken out as many of the enemy as he could.

On the other hand, lifting the body of their dead sergeant from the hole was surreal. Seeing the dead Germans sprawled and abandoned in red-rimmed snow was also surreal. One minute they were living breathing humans and the next they were gone, just a flesh-and-bone shell with no spark.

Jack knew at that moment that war was going to change him. He knew it was inevitable. The question now was, how?

Time will tell, I guess.

After they distributed the supplies, Service Company lowered the American bodies and the wounded over the Ridge before escorting the German prisoners down. As F Company organized for the night defense, Captain Rideout summoned Jack.

"I'm making you acting platoon sergeant for your platoon," he said brusquely. "You're a good leader and you're quick to adjust and make decisions."

The ramifications of Rideout's decision to move Jack into their dead platoon sergeant's position sunk in quickly. Instead of being responsible for twelve men, he was now second in command of forty. "Thank you for your confidence, sir."

Rideout allowed a tired smile. "You've earned it, Franklin. Dismissed."

Jack left the captain's tent and went on the first task of his newly elevated position—checking each of the platoon's defensive positions in the event of another attack. He'd retrieved the dead platoon sergeant's helmet and now handed it off to the bare-headed machine gunner who had dropped his as they climbed the path up Riva.

Satisfied that F Company was well positioned for any coming attacks, Jack pitched his single-man tent, glad to be alone for now. He unrolled his sleeping bag, stretched out on top of it, and closed his eyes. But far from being restful, disturbing visions of the day's battles roiled repeatedly through his mind.

Please, God, let me keep my humanity.

Jack sighed and rubbed his forehead.

And please don't let me return to Beth so changed that she can no longer love me.

*****

From F Company's location they couldn't see the other companies, but they knew that the Division was scheduled to attack the Germans from their newly established position on Riva Ridge at eleven o'clock that night.

After a brief rest, Jack joined Steve and the other soldiers of F Company, ready and waiting in foxholes dug through the snow and into the ground.

Like the night before, the sky was dark and overcast.

And bitterly cold.

The Germans were close enough that Jack could hear them dropping mortar rounds into eighty-two millimeter launching tubes. Resultant volleys came their way with about twenty shells falling around them, but not on them.

"Thank God it's dark," Steve whispered as he crouched in the hole with Jack. "They're just guessing where we are."

Jack snorted. "Until the shooting starts."

As if the enemy heard him the German mountain battalion began firing in their direction. F Company's machine gunners opened up and fired back, aiming at the German rifle flashes. In retaliation the Germans fired at the flashes coming from the Army's machine guns.

After an hour of heated battle, however, they were unable to prevail over the Americans. Defeated for the moment, the Germans retreated down their side of the ridge. F Company advanced silently to establish a new position.

The night remained quiet for the next hour or so before the resituated German troops assaulted F Company's new position with mortar rounds and rifle fire.

And once again, F Company rebuffed the attack with heavy machine gun fire, grenades, and mortars of their own, fighting until the night fell silent once more.

February 20, 1945

At dawn, exhausted F Company soldiers moved down and

south to the next objective, securing the village of Cingio del Bure. Thankfully, the area was already free of German soldiers who had, according to the villagers, pulled out the night before sometime after their two assaults were beaten back by F Company.

Jack was startled by the news. "The Krauts are already retreating," he said to Steve incredulously. "After just twenty-four hours of battle."

Steve looked at him, his eyes bright. "The mountain troops are doing exactly what we trained to do. And it's fucking working!"

At Captain Rideout's order, the grateful soldiers spread out and found places to rest in the freed village while they waited for their next battle orders. Jack took time to scribble a quick note outlining what had happened while the last forty-eight hours were still fresh in his mind. Someday he could tell Beth—and Pops—all about it

> *Not a single man was lost during the climbs of the ridge, so that speaks to the excellent training we all had.*
> *During actual battle, only twenty-one Americans were killed, fifty-two wounded and three taken prisoner. Three more men were reported missing. Not bad considering over eight hundred troops were involved.*
> *And I was made Platoon Sergeant.*

Rideout received their orders in the early afternoon. F Company was going to rejoin and then remain with the Second Battalion at Vidiciatico.

"From Vidiciatico we should be able to see and hear the fighting to take Mount Belvedere," he told Jack. "It's just three-and-a-half miles across the valley from that mountaintop village."

"And we'll be handy if they want to call us back into action," Jack pointed out to Steve as they prepared to move. "I'm betting they won't wait long to do so."

Once F Company reached Vidiciatico, the soldiers were given a week to rest and recuperate. And somehow, Pete and Steve managed to find some skis.

"You up for it?" Pete asked.

"Hell yes!" Jack laughed. "You don't have to ask *me* twice!"

Armed with their mountain combat boots and the Army-issued skis that were over seven feet long, the trio headed to the slopes on the edge of the little town. The snow was perfectly softened by the morning sun, and the men took run after run.

"I'm out of practice," Jack moaned after a couple hours.

"We're out of *equipment*," Pete countered.

"Yeah—I wonder when we'll get the rest of our winter gear," Steve mused. "But I'm glad to be on the slopes again. Makes me feel alive—and that's a good thing in war."

Jack looked across the valley. "Speaking of war…"

The assault on Mount Belvedere by the Eighty-Fifth and Eighty-Seventh Regiments was in full swing. At such a close distance they could watch American planes bomb and strafe the topmost ridges of Belvedere where the Germans were deeply dug in. They could see grenades explode and the spitting fire from machine guns. The exchange of fire from fighter planes to the entrenched enemy and the enemy's response was loud enough to be heard over the roar of the planes' engines.

"They can't survive this assault," Jack observed. "I wonder if they'll give up or choose to die."

Pete snorted. "From what I've heard about Hitler, they'd be better off dead than surrendering."

*****

While F Company rested in Vidiciatico with the rest of the Second Battalion of the Eighty-Sixth Regiment, Jack kept his platoon busy with weapons cleaning and maintenance, regular inspections, and training the replacements who arrived sporadically.

On Riva Ridge the casualties had been fairly light but the Eighty-Fifth and Eighty-Seventh Regiments had not been so fortunate in the battle for Mount Belvedere. Two hundred and three men had been killed while Jack and his buddies skied and watched Americans and Germans battle fiercely for that key piece of terrain.

I can't let myself feel guilty, Beth. I just can't. The minute I believe that it should have been me, then I will get shot. Or blown up. Because I'll stop being careful enough.

I fully intend to survive this war, marry you, and raise a bunch of champion skier kids. Are you with me?

Beth wrote back straightaway.

> *I __am__ with you, Jeff, and I have the same dream. I hope we can talk about it soon, now that I have a new job.*
>
> *My roommate Shannon and I have our very own doughnut machine and jeep now, which we're driving to different outfits in the Fourth Corps area to deliver doughnuts, coffee, and cigarettes. And since I'm on the team supporting the Tenth Mountain Division, you should see me in the field sometime very soon.*

Coffee, hot doughnuts, and his beloved Beth. Jack couldn't think of three things he'd enjoy more at the moment.

Jack wrote a letter to his Pops and told him everything that he was allowed to about what Tenth Mountain Division was doing in the mountains of Italy. The Division had its own paper, *The Blizzard*, which was published to all the units. So if anything was printed in that paper, Jack figured it was safe to recount the same information to his parents.

He desperately wanted to tell Pops about climbing up Riva Ridge at night and fighting the Germans, but knew those statements would not get past the censors. At least he could say he was Platoon Sergeant now. He just didn't mention how that rise in his status came about.

No reason to upset Mom.

February 28, 1945

A mud-spattered jeep with two women and a little trailer drove through the camp. Each one of them wore a snug khaki-colored one-piece suit, a blue sweater and a helmet. They pulled to a stop in front of the mess tent and parked.

Jack turned away from the instructions he was giving a new recruit on how to tie a belay knot and his heartbeat stumbled when he saw who was climbing from the jeep.

"Here. Try again." He shoved the rope against the flummoxed private's chest and sprinted toward the vehicle. "Can I assist you, Captain?"

Beth whirled to face him, her happy grin crinkling her eyes. "Thank you, Sergeant. I would very much appreciate that."

Jack walked around to the back of the little trailer and loosened the stainless steel coffee urn from its secured spot. He slid it onto the edge of its dropped gate. He frowned a little.

"Boxed doughnuts?" He'd been dreaming of hot ones.

Beth gave him an apologetic moue. "We made them this afternoon, if that helps. We just weren't sure we'd have electricity to run the machine once we got here."

That was fair. At least *she* was here.

Shannon opened the first of three boxes of donuts and then opened a package of paper napkins. Beth got out cups, cream, and sugar.

"Have some coffee with your donut, Platoon Sergeant?" Beth pushed on the urn's lever and the dark, fragrant liquid flowed into a cup sending curls of steam into the chilled winter air.

Jack grinned. "Sure!"

Shannon handed him a donut wrapped in a napkin, and Beth handed him the coffee. Her eyes moved over his shoulder.

"Hello, soldier. Coffee and a donut?"

Jack knew he'd lost her attention for the next hour because she had a job to do. When the private came over to show Jack his knot, Jack motioned for him to get the snack.

"We'll sit on that bench over there," he pointed with the hand holding the coffee, "and we'll work on your knots after you've had a donut and coffee."

The private looked relieved. "Thanks, Sergeant Franklin."

Jack caught Beth's eye and smiled. She winked and nodded without stopping her offers to the gathering soldiers.

*****

"I only have about twenty minutes." Beth sat next to Jack at a table in the mess tent and handed him another cup of coffee. "But at least we have that."

Supper was cooking and it smelled like stew. Again. Thankfully it was warm, filling, and contained fresh meat.

"That's twenty minutes more than if you hadn't come at all,"

Jack countered as he blew on the hot liquid. "So what's happening in the world?"

"I like this new job, and Shannon is great to work with," Beth began. "But it's been… awkward."

Jack's brow twitched. "Awkward how?"

"Well, for some reason, General Hays left it up to the Regimental Commanders whether or not to allow Red Cross staff to come into their areas. Both the Eighty-Sixth's and Eighty-Seventh's commanding officers have welcomed us with open arms." Beth gave a little shrug. "But the commanding officer of the Eighty-Fifth doesn't want us around. At all. Ever."

Jack scoffed. "If that's the case, give us double visits. Makes sense, right?"

Beth laughed softly. "You're funny."

Jack leaned his arm against hers. "Not funny. I'm a man in love who wants to see his fiancée as often as possible."

Beth laid her palm on his thigh under the table. "I'll see what I can do. I promise."

Jack rested his hand over hers. "Have you been writing in your journal?"

"Most days. But I have a hard time deciding what to write about," she admitted.

Jack shrugged. "Just write what's on your mind, I guess."

Beth laughed softly. "Then every page would simply say *Jeff.*"

Jack's lips landed on hers and stayed there for a very long time.

Chapter
Thirty-One

That evening at supper the latest issue of the Army's newspaper *Stars and Stripes* was distributed to the men. The most notable thing about this issue was the photo on the front page showing six Marines raising the American flag on Iwo Jima, a tiny island south of Japan in the Pacific Ocean.

Jack's first thought was to wonder if one of the six men in the photo could possibly be his younger brother Harry. He hadn't heard from Harry at all since their visit home in November. Mom and Pops did their best to keep Jack updated, but they only had limited information from Harry as well.

Jack folded the paper to read later.

Probably not him.

On the way out of the mess hall a rush copy of *The Blizzard* was also handed to every man.

"What's this for?" Jack wondered aloud as he and Steve ambled out into the chilly Italian evening.

Steve was already reading the front-page article. "The Fifth Army issued a press release mentioning the presence of the 'Tenth Division Mountaineers' in the European theater."

"That's better than calling us mountain troops of the Fifth Army—again," Jack huffed. "But why mention us at all?"

"Apparently, our successful attack on Riva Ridge has garnered praise from the entire Mediterranean Theater's chain of command."

Steve grinned at Jack. "Every single General from Field Marshal Alexander to Major General Hays offered congratulatory quotes about us."

Jack carefully folded his copy, his voice thick with pride. "This goes straight to Pops with my next letter."

"Yep—it's official now." Steve folded his copy as well. "The Tenth Mountain Division has succeeded in one of the most difficult maneuvers in American military history."

Jack grinned. "The whole world will know about us now!"

March 2, 1945

After resting and recuperating in Vidiciatico, the Second Battalion marched six miles northeast to Gaggio Montano—only a mile as the crow flies from Mount Belvedere and just behind Mount Della Torraccia—where they were due to relieve Third Battalion.

Soon after F Company arrived an explosion shook the dirt beneath Jack's feet and set his ears to ringing. Without hesitating he grabbed his rifle and ran toward the resultant commotion.

"What happened?" he shouted into the gathering crowd.

"A mortar shell dropped out of nowhere," another sergeant answered him.

"Anyone hurt?" Jack already knew the answer. He saw the remnants of a uniform but honestly couldn't recognize the face on the corpse.

"Yeah." The sergeant who looked younger than Jack drew a shaky breath. "That's where Captain Bromaghin was just brewing his coffee."

Jack's heart sank. "Not Ralph Bromaghin?"

The sergeant nodded.

The ebullient, high-spirited man, an actual legend in the Tenth Mountain Division for writing their marching songs, was gone. Just like that. Not a blink of warning.

Jack stood rooted with shock and unable to move a muscle, while what remained of Ralph Bromaghin was placed inside a mattress cover and prepared for transport by mule out of the combat zone. It wasn't until he turned back toward F Company that he realized he'd been crying.

March 3, 1945

Jack's platoon was the lead for F Company as they advanced on the south side of German-held Mount Terminale the next day. The embattled slopes were already littered with unclaimed dead soldiers, both American and German.

A horribly wounded German soldier pleaded repeatedly with them as they marched past him, "*Bitte schieße mich. Töte mich. Ich bitte dich...*"

Jack didn't speak German, but he had a good idea what the man was asking.

Please kill me.

Jack couldn't do it. He had no qualms about killing the enemy during battle, but this was entirely different. He couldn't look a living man in the eyes and shoot him dead point blank. That was too much.

Feeling guilty, Jack trudged onward. A moment later there was a single sharp shot ringing in the air behind him. He never turned around to see who fired it, but silently thanked the man who found the courage to serve up that mercy.

As F Company approached a small Italian farm near a well defended point in the German line, Jack raised his fist to halt the column. "Scouts, move out. Determine the enemy's location."

The platoon crouched in a small grove of trees and grass near the farm's outer rock wall, and waited silently for the scouts to return. A swish of dead foliage made Jack put a warning finger to his lips. He pointed his rifle toward the approaching footsteps in the tall grass.

"Halt!" he warned as he stood. "Hands up!"

"Don't shoot!"

Jack blinked. He lowered his rifle. "What the hell are you doing here?"

"Franklin? Thank God." Aston Hollinghurst lowered his hands and resumed his approach. "I was on a reconnaissance mission from Colonel Tomlinson when I got separated from his team. I'm looking for Regimental Headquarters."

Of course Hollinghurst was the one to get lost. The man had zero sense of direction. "They're at the front." Jack pulled out a map. "Here. On the north slope of Della Torraccia."

The lieutenant stared at the map and pointed. "And we're here right now?"

"Close." Jack refused to show his disgust as he pointed to the correct spot. "We're here."

"Oh, yeah." Hollinghurst's gaze lifted from the map and moved across the landscape. "Got it. Thanks."

"Stay lucky," Jack offered the departing officer. He reluctantly meant it.

Jack's platoon was farther up the slope from the farm than the rest of F Company when the German artillery attack on them began. Mortar shells bombarded without mercy as soldiers scrambled for protection against the deadly bursts.

Obviously, they had been spotted.

Or Hollinghurst was.

Jack flattened himself on the ground against the side of the farm's rock wall, plugging his ears against the roaring barrage of explosions. He and his men were massively out-gunned at the moment and there was nothing they could shoot at that would make any difference. For now they just needed to stay alive.

The hot, acrid smell of gunpowder mixed incongruently with the cool and fertile scent of the dirt pressed to his face. Life and death in one inhalation.

A brief break in the attack gave Jack a chance to sit up and take account of his men. What he saw downhill turned his stomach.

Pete Seibert was hit.

Without a thought for his own safety, Jack launched himself over the low wall and stumbled down the hill. Pete sprawled against another rock wall under a small scrub oak tree and was bleeding badly from his mouth. His left arm and right leg were shattered. Blood from his chest stained the front of his shirt.

Pete's eyes rolled back in his head.

"It's Jack. I'm here." Jack shifted his leg under Pete's body and cradled his buddy. "You'll be okay, Pete."

Jack kept repeating the frantic words, willing them to be true. "Lie back. I've got you. You'll be okay."

Someone was shouting, "Medic! Medic!"

The medic sprinted to Pete, dropped to his knees, and tore open Pete's shirt. Multiple shrapnel punctures peppered his chest. Then he cut away Pete's pants and the rest of his shirt revealing the frightening extent of his injuries.

Grabbing a packet of sulfa powder from his bag, the medic

barked at Jack, "Keep him still. I'm going to try and stop the bleeding."

Jack held his friend tightly, praying silently that Pete would live, and that he wouldn't vomit on his friend. The medic treated Pete's chest, leg, and arm with the sulfa powder. Then he swabbed Pete's mouth and wrapped bandages around his jaw to sop up the blood.

"How's he doing?" Jack managed.

As if to answer, Pete began to moan.

"I'm giving him morphine," the medic answered, jabbing the little needle into Pete's neck.

He was leaning over Pete and Jack when another mortar shell landed behind him, showering the trio with dirt and rocks. When Jack opened his eyes he realized the medic had been hit.

Nothing could be done until the second round of shelling stopped. Jack held Pete, both of them protected by the unconscious body of the medic whose name he didn't even know.

When the first ambulance arrived from Second Battalion Headquarters they took the medic first.

Either he's worse off than Pete, Jack worried. *Or Pete doesn't stand a chance.*

A third bombardment began when the medics came for Pete. They put him on a stretcher, and as soon as the attack let up they carried Pete to their jeep.

Jack grabbed his unconscious friend's hand. "Come back to us. We need you."

The driver revved the engine and rumbled away down the hill.

March 6, 1945

In the three days after securing Mount Terminale, Captain Rideout and F Company took the town of Tamburini. And after that, Second Battalion moved into Sassomolare while First Battalion took Mount Grande.

Once their presence in those towns was solidified, the entire line of the Eighty-Sixth Mountain Regiment was firmly established. From east to west across northern Italy the Tenth Mountain Division was now linked together as all three mountain Regiments held solid defensible positions.

The Tenth Mountain soldiers were chasing the Germans out of Italy through the high, rough, and frigid terrain just as they had been trained to do.

Fifth Army declared the Fourth Corps sector—the areas up to Mount Della Spe, which overlooked the Po Valley—secured. All the objectives planned for Operation Encore had been achieved.

But as a result, Fifteenth Army Group Commander, General Mark Clark, ordered a stand down, incredibly stopping the Tenth Mountain Division in its place.

Infuriated by the stoppage, and the possible risk of his mountain troops losing momentum, Major General Hays announced that soldiers in each battalion would rotate through four days of furlough to nearby cities where the Red Cross and USO had service clubs.

While he waited his turn for furlough, Jack finally had the chance to write to his parents.

He was still dazed by what happened to Pete and couldn't shake either the sight of the blood running from so many holes in his friend's chest, or the smell of gunpowder, dirt, and smoke that choked the air. Their precarious situation was solidified by the injured medic whose body acted as an unintentional shield for Pete and prevented him from further injury.

And the two of them protected me.

Once again Jack struggled with the guilt that he knew in his head was ridiculous, but what his gut kept taunting him with even so. Why was he still fine and healthy when the two of them were not?

> *Mom, your prayers are working. Please don't stop! I'm in good shape aside from needing a bath with a fire hose and then burning my field clothes once I can finally peel them off my body. At least the other guys are as dirty as I am. And some of us are growing pretty impressive beards. There's an Armenian guy in E Company whose face no one has seen in weeks.*

Jack smiled. He knew that if he used humorous anecdotes that his mother's concern would be assuaged for the moment and she would understand that her oldest son was still okay.

At least for today.

Meanwhile the Eighty-Sixth Regiment has captured over four hundred German prisoners. In fact the Tenth Division's total is almost a thousand Krauts.

That number of prisoners (plus the German casualties we can count) lets us know how many German troops have been pulled from other fronts while they try to stop the advance of our Tenth Mountain Division.

The ski troopers are getting the job done, Pops. I'm sending an article from our Division newspaper so you can read it for yourself.

Anyway, we're all getting some furlough before the next round of battles. When I went to see our first sergeant to ask when we were scheduled for our furlough, I got a surprise.

First sergeant told me that after I became platoon sergeant I was doing a damn fine job. Because of that, I was promoted to Staff Sergeant!

He said Captain Rideout put me up for the promotion after Riva Ridge.

When Jack finished his letter, he folded the article from the *Blizzard* and slipped both inside the airmail envelope. He tucked the flap inside the envelope—the censors would seal it after they checked what he'd written—and addressed it.

Then he pulled out another sheet of paper and smiled.

My dearest Beth ~

I have great news! I have four days of furlough coming starting March sixteenth. Right now we're closest to Montecatini. Is there any way for you to join me? I was promoted to Staff Sergeant and we need to celebrate...

Chapter Thirty-Two

March 10, 1945

Jack waited in a long but fast-moving line for his mail. In addition to a letter from Beth, he was glad to see one from his parents. He did notice that the letter was addressed in his father's handwriting, not his mom's, and a sense of foreboding clutched his chest.

He tried to shake it off and sat on a boulder at the edge of camp to read Pops' letter. He carefully tore open the seal and unfolded the paper. The words accosted him as if they were actually screaming.

Harry's battalion ~ First Battalion, Twenty-Third Marines ~ was one of the lead units to hit the beach at Iwo Jima. Your brother was killed in action.

The pages blurred and Jack's hands began to shake.

No.

No no no.

Not Harry.

Visions of Harry on the slopes of Sugar Bowl flooded Jack's mind. Harry laughing. Harry flirting with the girls. Harry skiing down the mountain, flying like a bat out of hell.

Harry in the little twin bed the last time Jack saw him. Less than four months ago. How could he be dead?

"Harry! You weren't supposed to *die*." Jack croaked. "You were on a ship. What were you doing on land?"

The *Stars and Stripes* ran the story about the Marines raising the American flag on Iwo Jima. Jack had scanned the article when the papers were being passed around but didn't pay much attention to it.

If he'd known that was where his little brother died he would have memorized the account—and kept a copy for his parents to see.

Jack swiped his eyes and read the rest of the brief letter. Harry was awarded a Purple Heart and the medal was being mailed to his parents. His body would be interred in the Veteran's Cemetery. They should receive a death benefit soon but hadn't decided what to do with that money.

Pops ended with: *For God's sake and your mother's stay lucky Jack. Please. Stay lucky.*

Jack folded the letter and put it back in the envelope. Then he sat very still for longer than he knew, saying a silent prayer over and over again for Harry and Pops and Mom.

He knew his parents were now praying even more fervently for him, but all he could manage on his own behalf was *please don't let me die. It would kill my mom.*

The clang of the noon bell from the mess tent jerked Jack back into the present and the camp.

Jack had lost his appetite,

He stowed his father's letter in his pocket and opened Beth's.

I'm so sorry, Jeff. I can't get away to meet you that week. I'll be miles and miles away...

Jack stopped reading the letter. He stuffed it back in the envelope and tucked it in his pocket next to his father's.

March 15, 1945

For five days Jack refused to sit down and answer either letter. He spent his time working relentlessly with his platoon, both to keep the men in fighting condition and his mind occupied. They seemed eager to train and Jack figured it was because they had absolutely nothing else to do.

No one knew how long this halt in their advance would last, but when they finally got the go-ahead Jack wanted to be ready.

He tried not to think about Harry or the fact he'd need to tell Beth. Or that he wouldn't be able to tell Beth to her face because her Red Cross duties had her at odds with his furlough.

Which started tomorrow.

Jack hunched in his pup tent and stared at the blank paper. He needed to take care of this business before he left, or he wouldn't be able to focus on anything else.

At least he had some interesting news to begin with.

> *The 10th Mountain Division held its first memorial service at the American Cemetery at Tavarnuzze near Florence. Each of the three regiments was represented by a non-commissioned officer, and I was chosen to represent the Eighty-Sixth.*
>
> *So a couple days ago the Army drove us to the cemetery, which was almost a hundred miles from camp. The other guys and I expected a large group of soldiers to be there but there were only eight of us.*
>
> *Here was Major General Hays addressing only a few enlisted men and it was serious stuff. There was a US Army band and three chaplains. I guess Hays said there should only be a small group because the reason we're here is to fight a war, not stand in formation and listen to speeches.*
>
> *After the ceremony, Hays joined us in reviewing the graves of some of our comrades killed in action and he expressed his sorrow to each of us.*
>
> *Speaking of sorrow, I received a sad letter from my parents. My brother Harry was killed leading the attack on Iwo Jima...*

March 16, 1945

The soldiers heading out on furlough were shuttled back and forth from the front at Mount della Spe to Campo Tizzoro in the pretty little mountain village of Montecatini. Army Engineers had set up portable showers in a long tent on the main street of the town, and when his turn came Jack appreciated the hot water and soap more than he expected was possible. But then he hadn't showered or changed clothes in nearly four weeks.

He ditched his filthy field clothes before he showered and now picked up clean clothes at the far end of the makeshift shower room. He even had a chance to shave.

Finally presentable enough for civilian company, he slapped Steve on the shoulder. "Ready?"

Steve looked sideways at Jack. "Are you?"

Jack knew why he was asking. He hadn't told Steve about Harry until they were being trucked into town.

Steve handled the news perfectly. He swore quietly, shook his head, and stared out the window—not at Jack.

After a minute of silence, all he said was, "Let's take all the goddam bastards down."

God bless Steve.

Now he looked at Steve with a grim smile. "Might as well make the best of our few days. We'll drink to Harry and the others."

Steve nodded briskly. "Good plan."

*****

Montecatini turned out to have the perfect mix of pretty Italian girls, and a rowdy night club—Club Trianon—which boasted both a swing orchestra for dancing with those pretty Italian girls, and a bawdy burlesque show for the overflow of single men.

As they explored the town Jack saw soldiers lined up outside movie houses and streaming in and out of bars. Military Police strolled through the streets for the sake of the civilians' peace of mind, but they seemed pretty unconcerned about the soldiers' behavior.

"What's this?" Jack lifted the shot glass which held a mysterious red-tinged liquid.

"Local specialty. Cherry brandy." Steve clinked his glass against Jacks. "To Harry."

"To Harry," Jack repeated.

He gulped the drink, letting the sting of the alcohol running down his gullet burn a little of the pain away.

"I'll get us another round."

*****

At the end of the night, and while they could still walk, Jack and Steve staggered to the billeting area set up for the soldiers on furlough. They grabbed a couple unclaimed cots and undressed. Jack made an attempt to fold his uniform, but mostly he just wanted to lie down.

He climbed under the frayed white sheets and drab green wool blanket, resting his head on the worn feather pillow. He tried to stare at the ceiling, but it kept swirling, so he closed his eyes.

Steve told everyone they knew about Harry and the men toasted to his memory. Jack lost count of the shots of cherry brandy and he couldn't remember ever drinking so much in his life.

At the thought of brandy his stomach lurched.

Shit.

Jack rolled off the cot and made it to the latrine in time to empty his belly. When the spasms finally stopped, he stumbled to the sinks to wash his face and rinse his mouth.

"You good?" Steve mumbled from the next cot when Jack reclaimed his.

"Yeah." Jack grunted. "Better now."

"You honored Harry's memory well today, Oakland."

Jack's throat thickened for a different reason now. "Thanks."

As Steve started to snore, Jack ignored the tears slipping sideways from his eyes and prayed once again that God would let him survive the war.

March 22, 1945

Sleeping in a foxhole, living in the dirt, and eating lousy food from his mess kits again would have made Jack's furlough feel like a dream—if he could sleep. Rounds of German artillery continued to fall in sporadic bursts, and usually at dinner time.

Making his life even better, was the reappearance of Lieutenant

Aston Hollinghurst.

"I thought he was doing recon with Tomlinson. What's he doing here?" Jack grumbled to Steve. The two sergeants were at the edge of camp training replacement troops.

"Guess we'll find out." Steve tipped his head. "He and Rideout are headed this way."

Captain Rideout stopped in front of Jack. "Sergeant Franklin, I have an assignment for you."

"Yes, sir?"

"I want you to take a squad of ten replacements to get some experience in front of the lines." Rideout tipped his head toward Hollinghurst. "The lieutenant will lead the patrol."

Jack glanced at Hollinghurst keeping his reaction neutral. "Yes, sir. When are we leaving?"

"Tonight. Twenty-three-thirty." Captain Rideout stepped back. "I'll leave you men to it."

He turned and walked away and Hollinghurst addressed Jack. "Are they ready?"

"I'll pull ten men who I think will be. Then I'll run them through immediate action drills to be sure."

"Good." Hollinghurst nodded. "After lunch I'll inspect their progress. If they're ready, they can pack their gear."

If they're ready?

"They will be." Jack was glad that saluting officers in the open was forbidden at the front—they didn't want the men in charge targeted by snipers—so he didn't have to salute the lieutenant.

*****

Hollinghurst headed back to the command tent and Jack took his ten select replacements to another area to practice the drills. About a quarter hour in, a soldier he didn't know approached him.

"I heard you're going out on patrol tonight, sir?"

Jack nodded. "That's correct, Private."

"Can I go with you?"

Jack was taken back by the odd request. "What's your name, soldier?"

"Private Larry Kohler, sir."

That's a Jewish name. "Have you had experience in front of the line patrols?"

He nodded. "Yes, sir. I've had plenty."

Jack shrugged. "Well, if your platoon can spare you, I have no objection."

Private Kohler grinned. "I already cleared it with my platoon and company. I'll take any chance to kill Germans, sir."

Jack had no objection to that either. "All right. Join the others."

The newly formed squad drilled for the next hour. Kohler—who carried a forty-five caliber submachine gun with the words *Sempre Avanti* carved in the stock—turned out to be very helpful with the replacements' instruction. It was clear the private had plenty of experience.

Once Jack was satisfied that the squad knew enough to go out on patrol and come back safely, he released the men. "Go get lunch, pack your gear, and report back for inspection in an hour."

Kohler held back and approached Jack. "Can I be point man tonight, Sergeant?" he asked.

Again, Jack was surprised. No one ever volunteered to walk point because it was so dangerous. "Why, Private?"

"Because I know what I'm doing," he stated confidently. "And I'll get first shot at the Krauts that way."

That satisfied Jack. "Okay. You'll be point man."

"Thank you, sir!" Kohler spun and sprinted toward lunch.

*****

On the way to inspection after lunch Jack told Lieutenant Hollinghurst about Larry Kohler's unexpected request. "So I asked some of the other sergeants about him."

Hollinghurst shot him a sideways glance. "And?"

"They all agreed that Kohler's very good. In fact, he has a deadly reputation. His kill numbers are pretty high."

"Good." Hollinghurst faced the eleven soldiers gathered about ten yards away and barked, "Ten-*hut!*"

The men scrambled and straightened.

"I had them go ahead and pack up their gear," Jack told Hollinghurst.

The lieutenant shot him a sideways glance. "You're that confident they're ready?"

"Yes, sir."

As the two soldiers walked through the squad and inspected the packed-up gear the men would carry, Jack stopped in front of Kohler. "This is our new addition, sir. Private Larry Kohler of E Company."

Hollinghurst pointed at Kohler's tommy gun. "What's that?"

Kohler appeared confused. "That's my weapon, sir."

The lieutenant frowned. "I mean the *words*, Private."

"Oh. *Sempre Avanti*—that's Italian for always forward. Sir."

Jack chewed his amusement into submission. "Did you carve that yourself?"

Kohler looked pleased. "Yes, sir."

"I suppose there's no regulation against that," Hollinghurst grumbled. "As long as you put the weapon to good use."

"I always do, sir," Kohler replied. "You can count on it."

Chapter Thirty-Three

Hollinghurst dismissed the squad after another hour spent drilling. "Get food and rest, men. We'll meet back here at twenty-three-thirty."

Jack took the chance to wash out some underclothes and socks, hanging them to dry in the afternoon sun. Then he wrote letters to Beth and his parents and walked them to the post station. After supper he managed to grab a few hours of sleep, though he woke up a couple times.

The more battles he experienced, the harder it was for him to clear his head before leaving on a mission.

Thirty minutes before midnight the assembled squad walked to the line of departure at the forward observation post.

"Remember," Jack repeated the coordinating instructions. "If we meet a German patrol we peel back as rehearsed, using the running password of *trooper-trooper*. Got it?"

"Yes, sir," the squad answered in unison.

"All right. Let's go."

Private Kohler took the point with Lieutenant Hollinghurst and a private, who was new to the platoon and nicknamed Shooter by the other guys, walked behind them. The rest of the patrol followed three abreast as the squad left the relative safety of the Eighty-Sixth's front line of defense.

The Po Valley stretched fifteen miles in front of them with an unknown number of Krauts hiding out there. Headquarters assigned them to check out Pra del Bianco, a little bowl-shaped valley where Italian farmers claimed Germans were entrenched. If those reports were accurate, there was likely an advance observation post located there.

A partial moon gave the soldiers only a minimal amount of light so they advanced slowly. The single sound in the quiet night was their boots scuffing on the narrow dirt track through dark trees.

Jack halted the squad. "I need half of you to wait here and cover our backs. The rest come with us."

The soldiers divided themselves up and five of them, including Shooter, followed Jack, Hollinghurst, and Kohler.

The advancing group reached a curve in the path where the tree cover thinned to almost nothing and revealed a typical village house nearby. No light escaped its little windows. Kohler backtracked to Hollinghurst.

"How about me and Shooter advance to see if we can hear anything?"

"Agreed." The lieutenant looked at Jack for confirmation.

Jack nodded.

Kohler and Shooter carefully moved forward. Jack crouched next to Hollinghurst while the other four soldiers moved to either side of the trail behind them.

Rap-rap-rap! Rap-rap-rap!

The distinctive report from a German burp gun fired two three-round bursts shattering the silence. Jack and Hollinghurst flattened on the ground.

Kohler shouted from the dark in front of them, "Go back! Go Back! The village is strong!"

Because of the darkness Jack couldn't tell exactly where the shots came from—and he hadn't seen the fire from the guns' muzzle flashes. The men behind Jack and Hollinghurst jumped up and ran for it.

Alarmed, Jack grabbed Hollinghurst's arm. "They're not sounding the password!"

"Shit!"

Rifle shots ricocheted behind them.

"Damn it!" Jack swore. "Stay here, Lieutenant. I'm going to check on Kohler and Shooter."

Before Hollinghurst could stop him, Jack crawled forward on his belly, inching ahead until he could barely make out the two bodies lying motionless in the road.

Fuck.

He scooted back to Hollinghurst. "Both are down."

Hollinghurst growled wordlessly. "We have to rejoin the rear guard.

If there's anyone still alive there.

*****

Arms at the ready, Jack and Hollinghurst circled back to find the squad's rear guard.

When they got close Jack had two choices: call out the password and risk alerting any Germans of his presence, or approach his own guard and risk being mistaken as the enemy and shot at by them.

Jack made his choice. "Trooper-trooper!"

Hollinghurst echoed, "Trooper-trooper!"

"Come," came the grunted reply.

When he saw what was happening, Jack felt like he'd been kicked in the chest by a Camp Hale mule.

Four men were dragging two of their comrades off to the side of the trail. A quick count confirmed that two of the four retreating soldiers were killed by their own squad's rear guard.

"They didn't use the password." The soldier who spoke quietly was clearly in shock and his voice trembled. "Why didn't they use the password?"

"We'll have to come back for the bodies." Hollinghurst began piling brush on the two dead soldiers. "Give me a hand."

The soldiers did, and Jack heard more than one of the raw replacements sniffling.

When the bodies were sufficiently covered he said, "Let's head back."

The squad took a circular route back, going through the trees and avoiding the trail in case the Germans decided to pursue them. They got back into the perimeter of the Eighty-Sixth as dawn was changing the sky from gray to lavender.

March 23, 1945

Hollinghurst and Jack headed for Regimental Headquarters to make their report.

"We made contact at Pra del Bianco," the lieutenant recounted. "Four members of our patrol were killed in action. Two by German fire and two by…" Hollinghurst cleared his throat. "By, uh, friendly fire."

That caught their attention. A colonel growled, "How did that happen?"

"The men were instructed to use a password when returning to the rear guard," Jack explained. "Unfortunately when our point men were fired on and shouted for us to retreat, the new replacements panicked."

"They didn't use the password," Hollinghurst continued. "The rear guard thought they were under attack and responded with gunfire."

"Were you able to bring the bodies back?" the colonel pressed.

Jack shook his head. "No, sir. Not *yet*."

"Yet?"

Jack looked at Hollinghurst, willing him to pick up the challenge.

He did. "We'll go after them tonight. Two were exposed, but we were able to hide the other two."

Jack faced the colonel again. "We'll leave as soon as it's dark."

*****

Later that day one of the mortar team's forward observers, who's job was to keep watch across the Po Valley for any movement by the Germans, sent a message to Hollinghurst and he showed it to Jack.

It looks like the body of one of your soldiers is hanging from a beam in a partially damaged barn.

Jack went with the lieutenant to the forward mortar position to see for themselves.

Hollinghurst pressed the heavy black binoculars against his eyes. His lips were pressed together so hard they lost all color.

"To your left, sir."

Hollinghurst shifted his view. "Shit."

He handed Jack the binoculars and he looked in the same direction. The partially destroyed barn was easy to spot. And strung up from a crossbeam by a rope around the neck, Private Larry Kohler's corpse swayed in the brisk breeze

Jack lowered the binoculars. The sight of the desecrated body infuriated him. "That's Kohler."

"Thanks for telling us." Hollinghurst took the binoculars from Jack and handed them back to the sergeant who sent him the message. "We'll go get him tonight."

*****

For the second night in a row Hollinghurst led the patrol to Pra del Bianco. Jack offered men who were in the previous night's patrol the chance to come again as litter teams. He knew that facing the situation again on a mission to help would give them a way to handle the friendly-fire tragedy.

Flashbacks of the deaths on Kiska flooded him with anger.

How do you tell a mother her boy was shot by his own squad?

Jack shook himself mentally and focused on the dirt trail. He needed to remain clear-headed or he might become a casualty himself. At least there was a little more moonlight tonight since they had embarked on the mission earlier than last night.

Jack and Hollinghurst led the column of eight men who would carry out the four bodies. All four men in last night's rear guard chose to return.

"I'm glad they did," Hollinghurst admitted. "It will help us find the hidden bodies faster."

Jack bit his tongue and only grunted. He knew exactly where the two corpses were, but wasn't surprised that the lieutenant wasn't sure.

In addition to the eight litter volunteers, Hollinghurst procured two men with experience using captured German *panzerfausts*—which were similar to bazookas—to be part of the team. The plan was to surround the small house where they thought the Germans were sheltered and the two men with the *panzerfausts* would blast the building simultaneously. Chances of the Germans surviving the blasts were approximately zero, which suited Jack just fine.

"We're almost there, sir."

Hollinghurst stopped and turned around. "What?"

Jack answered for the private who spoke. "Where we hid Hughes and Dawson."

"Oh. Yes, of course," Hollinghurst covered. "Why don't you take the lead, Private."

When they reached the hiding place Jack helped the men from last night uncover the bodies while the rest stood guard. The four soldiers lashed their dead comrades to two of the litters.

"God speed," Jack murmured. "Be careful going back."

"Yes, sir. Thank you, sir."

Jack watched the four men head back for a moment before he said to Hollinghurst, "Let's go."

The remaining eight men walked single file, retracing the squad's steps from last night. Jack took the lead.

Hollinghurst didn't challenge him.

Once they reached the end of the trees, the patrol huddled together to confirm the plan.

"Cortez, you'll cut any and all communication wires. Make sure they can't call for help," Hollinghurst reiterated.

He pointed at the men with the two *panzerfausts*. "While he's doing that, you two get in position."

"Two of you, stick with the lieutenant. You'll cover the front of the house," Jack said. "The other one, come with me. We'll cover the back."

The patrol silently moved to their assignments. Jack whistled when everyone was set.

A moment later the *panzerfausts* went off with an ear-shattering roar, tearing two gaping holes in the walls. The men dropped their *panzerfausts* and rushed into the house with guns blazing.

Hollinghurst's group followed.

"Out the back!" Jack shouted and took aim. He and his partner quickly took the escaping Kraut down.

The attack was over quickly. Three Germans inside were dead.

One soldier tried to keep the senior enlisted man escaping out the rear alive long enough for Hollinghurst to interrogate him, but he bled to death before they could get anything from him.

Hollinghurst turned to Jack. "Take the litter teams to retrieve

Kohler and look for Shooter. We'll search the house and the bodies."

Jack nodded and turned toward the decrepit barn. The men stumbled across Shooter lying inside the partially destroyed barn, so one pair of soldiers tied him on their litter and covered his face with his shirt.

Jack found a ladder and climbed up to cut Kohler down while the other two lowered the body onto their litter. They secured him to the litter while Jack climbed back down.

Poor bastard.

When the two teams were ready, Jack led them back to the house. Hollinghurst met them outside the destroyed cottage.

He nodded somberly toward the bodies, then faced Jack. "We retrieved this satchel of maps and orders, but none of the grunts had anything on them. Except these."

The lieutenant held up four German watches. "Who wants one?"

While the limited spoils were claimed, one of the *panzerfaust* guys handed Jack Private Kohler's tommy gun with the carved stock. "We found this in there, too."

Jack slung Kohler's gun over his shoulder. "Good. Are we ready?"

On their slow way back the patrol kept a close watch to their rear to ensure no German patrol was in pursuit, but none appeared. They reached the safety of the Eighty-Sixth about two hours past midnight. They turned the bodies over to the morgue, where they were reassured that the first litters teams made it back safely as well.

Hollinghurst carried the satchel to Headquarters while Jack retreated to his foxhole and his sleeping bag.

He kept Kohler's gun for himself.

*****

Everything that transpired the previous two nights made Jack realize how easy it was to die under the conditions that he currently lived in. He felt like he understood for the first time what his Pops experienced in World War I.

Sleeping in a foxhole, going out on patrols, watching my men get killed and bringing back their bodies ~ while I thank God it wasn't me ~ isn't anything a person can understand unless they live through it. I'm sorry I didn't listen to you, Pops. But I hope I'm making you proud now.

April 6, 1945

The beginning of April brought a distinct warming in the weather.

And mules.

Captain Duncan's Transportation Platoon picked up a hundred and fifty of the stubborn animals in Montecatini and led them the sixty miles up to where Second Battalion was stationed on the front line. Once again the Eighty-Sixth Regiment consisted of men and what Jack thought of as *those damned mules*.

Captain Rideout had Jack training the replacements literally day and night. Though up to this point the Tenth had been fortunate and hadn't sustained large losses, there were still ongoing casualties. Men were lost to mortar shells, howitzers, or the ever-present land mines and booby traps.

And the stream of replacements had to become familiar with all weapons the battalion had in its arsenal. Every man had to know how to operate all the machine guns, the mortars, and of course his own rifle. Jack relentlessly pounded tactics, techniques and procedures into each soldier's head, using the friendly fire deaths at Pra del Bianco as a chilling example of why it all *mattered*.

Captain Rideout pulled F Company together to tell the men what was coming next.

"The formal name of the operation is Operation Craftsman, but the higher-ups are calling it the Big Push," the captain explained. "And the final objective of this all-out offensive is the complete destruction of the German army in this country, resulting in the liberation of Italy."

The soldiers burst into cheers, Jack and Steve among them.

"Kill the bastards!"

"Show Hitler how little he is!"

"Always forward," Jack shouted. "*Sempre avanti!*"

Several members of F Company picked up the chant and the rest chimed in as well. "*Sempre avanti! Sempre avanti! Sempre avanti!*"

Jack smiled.

That's for you, Kohler.

Chapter
Thirty-Four

April 14, 1945

The original date set for the Big Push was April twelfth, but it was postponed when heavy fog rolled in and forced all Air Corps bombers to be grounded.

On April thirteenth it was postponed again, partly for the continuing fog, and partly because of the announcement that President Roosevelt had died of a cerebral hemorrhage in Warm Springs, Georgia.

"He's been President for as long as I cared," Jack told Steve. "I wonder how that'll change the war."

"War's almost done," Steve countered. "At least it is here in Europe. We're about to kick some serious German ass."

This morning the fog began to lift around eight o'clock on the southern airfields, so the air attack started at nine. The Air Corps' B-24 bombers flew overhead to initiate the attack, followed by waves of Thunderbolt fighter bombers. Thousands of rounds of artillery hammered German positions for the next forty minutes before the Tenth Mountain Division entered the fray.

Jack pulled a deep breath.

Here we go.

F Company advanced toward the smoking landscape ravaged

by the devastating firepower.

Because elaborate underground German bunkers still provided the enemy protection, Army weapons companies fired heavy machine guns overhead to cover the advancing infantry as the three regiments moved abreast down the north slope of Mount della Spe.

But they couldn't protect the men from German land mines. Explosions all around Jack took a heavy toll on the Mountain Division.

Please God, don't let me step on one.

Once they reached the lowlands between ridges, Rideout's men moved quickly, covering the ground at a run until F Company reached Torre Iussi. The battle for Torre Iussi took all afternoon, but once the outcome was clear, F Company was assigned to stay and secure the hamlet. The rest of Second Battalion headed toward their main objective of Rocca di Roffeno.

Jack's platoon advanced cautiously through the rubble-filled streets looking for a defendable position from which to take out the remaining Germans. Captain Rideout and his radio man crouched behind a pile of bricks next to Jack's position and Rideout took out the radio handset.

Jack could hear the crackling orders from battalion command demanding that F Company move faster.

"The Krauts have a strong position here!" Rideout shouted into the handset. "Taking them out is slowing us down!"

After a pause the promise came. "We'll send help."

F Company soldiers continued to push and gradually surround the enemy as the Germans fell back. Jack lost count of how many of his bullets hit their target, realizing that it didn't matter—as long as he continued to take the Germans down.

Captain Rideout rose from his protected position and headed toward a damaged building to his right in spite of the barrage of bullets ricocheting off the buildings around them.

That was when Jack saw the front of the captain's head explode. Blood spurted from the sides of Rideout's face.

Horrified, Jack shouted, "Medic! *Medic!*"

The radio man dragged the captain into the damaged building. Jack crossed over to the captain as well, shooting above himself for cover. He was followed quickly by a medic running through the rubble.

Rideout was rapidly going into shock. The bullet had entered his left cheek and exited through the right cheek. The medic pressed bandages on both cheeks to try and staunch the blood loss.

Again, Jack tried not to vomit.

He knew they could get pinned if the Krauts saw soldiers gathering around a fallen officer, so he grabbed the radio man.

"Meet me in the building across the street. I'm going to help move the captain"

"Yes, Sarge."

Once Rideout was settled out of direct view of the German snipers, Jack made a run for the radioman across the exposed street. They called Battalion Headquarters.

"Captain Percy Rideout has been hit," Jack shouted into the handset. "He's not dead, but it's bad. The medics have him."

After a moment the reply came. "Take your men and head toward Rocca di Roffeno. When you get there report to Captain Jack Carpenter at E Company."

Jack nodded out of habit. "Roger that."

He searched out the other two platoons, still engaged in battle though replying enemy shots had sharply fallen off.

"Rideout's down," he told them. "We have orders to join E Company near Rocca di Roffeno when we finish here."

"I think we're about done," one lieutenant told him. "Should we start taking prisoners?"

"Yes. I think so."

*****

The mortar blast took Jack by surprise—he never heard it coming. But when the explosion happened his right leg crumpled under him and he fell hard to the cobblestone street.

His leg was on fire. Jack rolled to his back and looked at the wound. A jagged triangle of metal six or eight inches long had penetrated his thigh and it hurt like hell.

Shit.

I have to find cover.

Jack clambered to his feet, keeping weight off his right leg as best he could, and hobbled to a doorway. Tucked inside the deep jamb against the door he tried to see how badly he was hurt.

There wasn't much blood.

The metal was hot. It must have cauterized the wound.

Don't pull it out or you'll bleed to death.

Jack moaned a little, panting with adrenaline and pain.

Voices. Coming through the wooden door.

Speaking German.

Shit and shit.

Jack looked up and down the street. One of the lieutenants was down, most likely dead. He didn't see anyone from F Company, even though shots were sporadically fired from all directions.

What should I do?

Jack reached into his pack and pulled out a grenade, thinking he could toss it behind the door and bolt. But when he tried putting weight on his leg the pain made him woozy.

He couldn't call out for a medic without alerting the Krauts inside of his presence.

Think.

He heard movement behind the door and the latch rattled. There was nothing for Jack to do but take command of the situation. He had no choice. Jack shoved the door open and stood in the doorway, held out the grenade with his thumb securing the detonator, and pulled the pin.

Four startled Germans stared back at him. Dirty and emaciated and dressed in ill-fitting uniforms, these guys couldn't be more that seventeen or eighteen years old.

One lifted his gun but Jack shouted, "*Kapitulation! Oder Tod!*"

When he heard Jack shout surrender or death, he lowered his weapon.

Jack was out numbered and wounded, and somehow he had to disarm four German soldiers and take them to the prisoner transport. But he couldn't even walk. His right leg quivered and was losing feeling.

Shit shit shit.

"Need a hand, Oakland?" Steve spoke quietly from behind him.

Thank God.

Jack didn't turn around and was light-headed enough that he couldn't risk nodding. "Disarm these men."

Steve carefully eased past Jack and took the rifles from the four boys. He dumped the ammunition on the floor before demanding their knives and anything else they had.

Jack's arm trembled with the strain of holding the detonator and heavy grenade, but he wouldn't replace the pin until their enemy was completely disarmed.

Steve used the soldiers' belts to tie their hands behind their backs. All the while the boys' wide eyes remained fixed on the grenade in Jack's hand

It wasn't until Steve finished the task and turned around that he saw the impressive piece of shrapnel sticking out of Jack's thigh. His eyes jumped to Jack's.

"You're hurt."

Jack lowered the grenade. With shaking hands he managed to replace the pin while five men watched. "Flesh wound. I'll be fine."

"You're in shock," Steve stated. "Let's get these guys taken care of and call the medics."

Jack backed out of the doorway and sank to the doorstep.

Steve walked the four prisoners out of the building, shouting, "Medic!"

Jack was aware of a couple of Army guys running in his direction. One dropped to his knees beside him. The other helped Steve remove the Germans.

Jack felt his body dissolving and his world went black.

April 15, 1945

Jack sat up on his cot in the field hospital and demanded to know when he could return to F Company.

"You're smart and lucky," the doctor told him. "Smart because you didn't yank that shrapnel out. It nicked your femoral artery. You would have bled to death on the spot."

"But the heat of the metal cauterized it?" Jack wanted to confirm his assumption.

"It did—that's why you're lucky."

"So when can I go back?" Jack asked again.

The doctor looked at Jack over the rim of his glasses. "When you can walk, and I know you don't have an infection."

"How long is that?"

"Five more days." The doctor pointed a finger at Jack. "And you stay put in that cot for the next three."

Jack growled a little and laid back down. "Did Captain Rideout come through here?"

"He did. We sent him on to better facilities." The doctor moved to the next cot before Jack could ask any more questions.

Jack sighed and closed his eyes.

At least the captain was still alive.

*****

Later that afternoon Steve Knowlton appeared at Jack's bedside. "I hear you've been giving the medics hell."

"They're making me stay five more days," Jack grumbled. "Did you hook up with E Company?"

"I sent the others ahead while I came to check on you."

Jack drew a deep breath. "How bad was it?"

"We took a beating, there's no doubt about it." Steve glanced away before he answered. "Forty-six killed or wounded."

Jack blew a low whistle. "That's bad, Dropout."

"Yeah." Steve fiddled with his helmet. "But F Company did capture eighteen German prisoners."

At least there was that. "So we're joining E Company. Do you know what the orders are?"

"I assume we'll keep driving the Germans off the high ground. We're making a slow but steady advance." Steve kept fiddling with his helmet. "The men have been in continuous motion for four days, though, so whenever they drop their rucksacks they fall asleep."

Jack felt guilty for his cot and hot meals. "I feel so useless right now."

"You captured four prisoners, Jack," Steve countered. "And you helped get Rideout out of danger when he was hit. Enjoy this little bit of R and R. You earned it."

Jack straightened his blanket, not wanting to admit how much he wanted the rest and food. "Well... tell the men I'll catch up in five days."

He looked into Steve's eyes. "And don't you get hurt."

Steve didn't flash his usual grin and his tone was somber. "I'll try my best."

April 20, 1945

Jack returned to F Company after six days in the field hospital, and what he found was horrific.

After six days of continuous combat, carnage was everywhere. German losses in men and equipment were heavy. The numbers of killed and wounded who were left on the field testified to their decimation.

Dead horses, mules, cows, and even bloated human bodies covered with flies joined the abandoned and destroyed machinery that blocked the roads.

Steve wrinkled his nose. "Nobody told us about the smell."

Jack nodded in silent agreement.

When men died their bodies voided waste, so battlefields reeked of shit and urine, not only blood. Then there was the stench of unclaimed bodies beginning to rot. And the flies they attracted. Always flies.

I won't write to Beth about that part.

Jack was afraid these gruesome sights would haunt him so he forced himself not to stare out of morbid curiosity.

The day Jack arrived a group of eight Germans were captured without any exchange of fire.

"They know their war's lost," Steve said while he and another soldier disarmed the young men. But we don't have anyplace to put them and no food to feed them."

"So we just disarm them and tell them to walk south until they get picked up?" Jack asked.

"Pretty much."

Jack watched the bemused Germans walk away. "What are our orders?"

"Tenth Mountain is descending into the Po Valley tomorrow." Steve's impish grin made a welcomed but brief appearance. "We're way ahead of Fifth Army, Oakland."

*****

About an hour before sunset, Lieutenant Frank Foster returned from a briefing and gathered F Company to report what was happening.

"General Clark told Hays to stop our advance at the edge of the

Po Valley to let the flatland divisions catch up and move through."

An indignant, "What?" burst from the assembly.

"Why?" Jack asked the question he was pretty sure they all shared.

"He said the Tenth's done its job and flatland infantry will continue to attack and pursue."

"And Hays is going along with it?" Jack pressed.

That didn't sound like the general he knew. And he sure didn't fight to return to his company to just sit idly by while other soldiers advanced past them.

"He's livid. To be honest, the Tenth has spearheaded the push and taken all the hills and towns back from the Germans. And now Clark wants us to stop?" Foster shook his head. "Hays has no intention of letting other troops pass us by."

"So we keep going?" Steve clarified.

"Yes." The lieutenant rested his hands on his hips. "Hays says the Germans are heading north so fast that their command is in chaos. To stop and reorganize would be a grave tactical error."

Jack agreed, but, "To knowingly disobey the orders of the commander puts Hays' career at risk."

Foster looked pleased. "I guess he's more concerned about stopping the Germans before they have a chance to blow the bridges across the Po River than he is about possibly losing rank."

Chapter Thirty-Five

April 21, 1945

Major General Hays decided to leave his cannons in the mountains, while the trucks used to pull those cannons would instead ferry the Tenth soldiers into the Po Valley. So the Mountain troops rode north on anything that could roll.

Jeeps, tanks, self-propelled artillery, and six-by-six trucks were all pressed into that service. They even used vehicles, ambulances, and bicycles abandoned by the retreating German Army.

Jack was grateful for the ride. His leg still throbbed if he walked too much, and he was concerned with ripping out the stitches. If he did, the wound could easily become infected.

That could be life-threatening out in the field if the medics couldn't control it. Gangrene was a very real casualty of war.

As the regiment moved into the valley en masse, the road was choked with vehicles and marching soldiers, raising a fog of thick dust in the dry spring weather.

General Hays also created a Task Force under the leadership of Brigadier General Duff, which was comprised of mobile units who'd race ahead of the Division. Their assignment was to seize and hold the bridges over the Po River. Second Battalion of the Eighty-Sixth was chosen for the job.

Again, Jack was happy to be riding and not walking.

Someone's looking out for me.

The Task Force headed for Bomporto and the bridge over the Panaro River. Their approach must have shooed the Germans away because, though the job was started, the enemy hadn't *finished* placing explosive charges on the bridge.

"Hays was right," Jack said to Steve. "They're going to try to blow all the bridges.

April 22, 1945

In the morning the Task Force convoy continued northward toward their next objective, San Benedetto Po. They arrived in the early afternoon, and Second Battalion entered on foot to check for Germans waiting in ambush.

"They're gone," Jack reported to Lieutenant Foster. "They must know we're right behind them because they took everything with them."

Brigadier General Duff instructed his aide to guide the lead tank commander through the town to the river bank.

"He wants to keep moving toward the Po River," Jack opined.

"I don't see a reason to stop—do you?" Steve responded. "Might as well not waste our time."

Jack rubbed his aching thigh. "Agreed."

Halfway through the little town the lead tank ran over a German land mine. Metal fragments from the explosion hit Duff in the abdomen.

Jack felt as if he was thrown sideways when he saw that Duff was injured in the blast. A sense of panic surged in his chest—painful memories of his own injury made him tremble.

"You okay?" Steve asked.

"Yeah." Jack sucked a breath. "Leg's sore is all."

Duff ordered the tanks to keep moving and would not allow himself to be evacuated for medical treatment until all of the tanks reached the banks of the River Po.

While Brigadier General David Ruffner assumed Duff's duties and sent out reconnaissance patrols to assure they would not be attacked during the night, General Hays sent his engineers off to find boats to carry his division across the river.

When Hays' engineers returned, they reported passing twisted and burnt out German vehicles and blackened, charred forms—almost unrecognizable as human beings—lining the south bank of the river, grim reminders of the Allied bombing and strafing of the fleeing Germans.

The two engineers also found boats.

"We persuaded the truck drivers to follow us back here to deliver their cargo to the troops waiting to cross," one of the officers told Jack when they returned at dusk. "They were happy to deliver the boats since their mission *was* to get the boats to the infantry so they could cross the river."

Jack laughed out loud. "How many did you snag?"

"There are five flatbed trucks and each carries ten small row boats." The engineer looked around and leaned closer. "They were supposed to be sent to the Eighty-Fifth Army Division."

Jack crossed his heart. "My lips are sealed."

That evening First and Third Battalions arrived. By defying General Clark's orders, the entire Tenth Mountain Division had reached the Po River ahead of any other divisions in the Fifth Army sector.

The next day the river crossings began. The Po was treacherous at the moment: two hundred yards across and running swiftly from the spring thaw. The Eighty-Seventh Regiment went first, followed by the Eighty-Sixth, then the Eighty-Fifth.

F Company waited in a staging area behind a dike until it was their turn to go. An engineer handed every man a paddle.

"From here you run over the top of the embankment to the river's edge, find an empty boat, and put your rifles into the row boat," he instructed them. "With four men on each side of the boat, lift the boat and walk into the water. Once the boat's in deep enough, jump in and paddle across. Got it?"

Jack knew that was simple enough, except, "How do you get the boat back?"

"Two of us ride over with you, then row the boat back."

The plan worked well.

After fighting the rushing water for a good quarter of an hour, Jack, Steve, and six other men waded onto the north shore of the Po. They dropped the paddles back in the rowboat, collected their rifles, and followed a guide to the bridgehead they were to secure.

With the entire regiment on the north side of the Po River, Second Battalion was charged with taking the town of Verona as quickly as possible in order to block the Germans' retreat toward the Brenner Pass. After securing Verona they moved through Bussolengo, then along the east edge of Lake Garda to Trento—ninety miles northwest of where they started a week ago.

This morning, Jack and F Company were headed toward the first of six two-lane-wide tunnels that ran along the east side of Lake Garda and were bored out of solid rock.

And the Germans were waiting for them.

F Company exchanged machine gun and rifle fire with their enemy as they approached the first tunnel, but they clearly had more firepower than the Krauts did. Even though the Germans tried to blow up each tunnel as they retreated, F Company miraculously pressed forward without any casualties.

Finally the Krauts just gave up and ran.

Second Battalion followed, taking the town of Riva del Garda at the far end of Lake Garda. By nightfall the Eighty-Sixth Regiment also held Torbole and Nago. These three towns were the crux of the Germans' defense line. The Nazi soldiers had no choice now but to surrender or continue to run.

Second Battalion soldiers were exhausted by the long charge, but once the German presence was pushed out of these three key towns they stopped to celebrate their hard-won victory.

And because of their undeniable success, Hays was being called a hero and not facing court marshal for defying orders.

"Conqueror of the Po!" Steve shouted as he lifted his glass of abandoned German stout. "Long may he reign!"

Jack clinked his glass against Steve's. "Finally I have something good to write to Beth about. And Pops."

Hollinghurst pressed his way through the tavern crowd to Jack's table and pulled up a chair. He had obviously been celebrating with purpose.

"What are you toasting?" he asked, lifting his shot glass.

"Hays," Steve said. "He's conqueror of the Po."

"Well I've got much better news than that…" Hollinghurst left the statement hanging in the air.

Jack went ahead and bit. "What news is that?"

"Just heard it on the radio. It's official."

Jack wanted to punch the smug lieutenant. "For the love of—just say it."

Hollinghurst grinned. "Adolf Hitler shot himself in the head. Today. In his *Führerbunker* in Berlin."

Jack's jaw fell slack.

"No shit?" Steve yelped.

"God's honest truth," Hollinghurst crossed his heart with his free hand. "Eva Braun also committed suicide, but with cyanide."

Jack stared at the lieutenant. "Is the war over?"

"Nah. Not yet. But it can't last long without a leader." He wagged the shot glass. "You ladies gonna toast with me, or what?"

May 2, 1945

The death of their *Führer* had to change things for the German soldiers—assuming they knew about it. General Hays ordered the Eighty-Sixth Regiment to take a few days of rest while he sent out patrols to determine whether the enemy had established any defensive lines on the way to Brenner Pass, or if they'd given up.

That night after chow, Captain Carpenter abruptly assembled F Company. Jack noticed he wasn't armed, which was odd.

Once the men were in formation, Carpenter smiled and announced, "It's official, men. German forces in Italy and Austria have surrendered. We did it!"

Jack was stunned.

It's over.

Steve whooped and cheered, as did most of the men, and Jack enthusiastically joined in. One man pointed his rifle at the high mountains surrounding them and fired off the clip.

"No!" Captain Carpenter barked. "Absolutely *no* celebratory firing is permitted."

Those orders did not apply to the Italians however, and if a partisan had a gun he was shooting it. Bells rang without stopping, lights were turned on in every building, and horns sounded from every direction.

They sang heartily, danced in the streets, and kissed each other happily while the American soldiers looked on.

And of course, wine flowed like water. Special bottles were brought out of hiding for the first time since the German occupation. The bars stayed open and drinks for the American soldiers who liberated them were on the house.

Relieved Tenth Mountain soldiers told each other, "We made it."

Or, "Our luck held out."

It was true. Jack and Steve made it until they assured that the Germans were soundly defeated in Italy and surrendered.

Their Führer was dead.

The Third Reich was dying.

But there was still plenty of work to do. The American soldiers would remain in Italy doing clean-up.

Jack wagged his head at their sudden shift in status. "And as the winners, we're now responsible for the *safety* of all those Krauts we were trying to kill just twenty-four hours ago."

The next day, Major General Hays addressed the Tenth Division, expressing his thanks for their fine performance in the 'spectacular but grueling drive' across the Po Valley.

And five days after that, on May seventh, the last nail was pounded into the Third Reich's coffin when the Germans gave up completely. They unconditionally surrendered all of their European forces to the Allies in a meeting at General Eisenhower's headquarters in France.

"And we had a lot to do with their defeat," Jack said as he offered multiple toasts to his platoon-mates. "To the Tenth Mountain Division and elite Army ski troops!"

May 21, 1945
Riva del Garda

Three months had passed since Jack saw Beth, and during the Big Push he didn't have a spare minute to write a letter. That was just as well—he couldn't tell her where he was or what was doing anyway. And he would never tell her about the horrors of battle or the desecration of Larry Kohler's body.

Those horrors had caused a shift in Jack, one that was uncomfortable and inexplicable. On the one hand he no longer recoiled at firing Kohler's gun at another human. He'd grown accustomed to dead and mangled bodies—the sight of a field of them was normal.

On the other hand, when he laid down at night the reality of taking human lives by the dozens made him break out in a cold sweat. Thankfully, once the Germans surrendered the killing stopped immediately. Jack hoped he would eventually be able to distance himself from the sights and sounds of war and find his internal balance again.

He did send Beth and his parents a quick postcard letting them know he was physically okay, but didn't mention the mortar attack and his leg injury. He promised to write more when he had a chance.

That was two weeks ago.

And in those two weeks Jack's responsibilities took an entirely different direction. The Tenth soldiers were now disarming Italy, scouring the countryside for weapons and confiscating them. Italian partisans weren't allowed to keep their arms any more than the occasional German they flushed out of hiding.

Reveille and retreat formations were still held daily, and between patrols Jack held minimal training sessions with his men. In the event they were sent on to the Pacific, they needed to remember how to shoot and clean their rifles at the least.

But to be honest, he had a lot of time on his hands in these beautiful and now peaceful surroundings. Jack's favorite thing to do was find a courtyard away from camp, sit in the sun, and soak up the sounds of life returning to normal.

Today he brought along paper and pen, determined to get enough words written so that Beth wouldn't worry about him. The note she sent immediately after she got his postcard expressed her deep relief that he was safe, and begged him to write more as soon as he could.

Jack stared at the blank paper. He'd made it through. He was alive. He was *lucky*.

Dearest Beth ~

I'm sorry I haven't written, but we've been surprisingly busy since the surrender with collecting weapons and making sure any stray Germans are rounded up.

What's the Red Cross up to?

Jack stopped. The words in his heart were pushing aside the ones in his head.

> *Oh, Beth. I miss you so much. I think about you every single day. At night I picture your face before I go asleep, and when I wake up in the morning you're the first thing I think of. I need to see you again. To look in your eyes, see your smile and hear you laugh. I want to hold you close to my chest and never let you go.*

A shadow darkening the paper made Jack look up. For a split second he wondered if his emotional outpouring might have somehow conjured Beth's presence.

"Hey, Steve." He tried not to look disappointed.

Steve sat down next to him. "Writing to Betty?"

"Yeah." Jack folded the paper so the words were hidden. "I owe her a letter. Finally getting to it."

Steve nodded and his gaze moved to the hills. "What do you think they're going to do with us?"

Jack wondered the same thing. "To be honest, the Tenth came into the war so late I wouldn't be surprised if they end up sending us to fight the Japs."

Steve nodded slowly. "And because we were the last to come to Italy, we'll probably be the last to leave."

Jack chuckled. "I'm okay with that. There's still snow up there and we have a lot less work to do."

Steve turned and grinned at him. "And nobody's shooting at us."

"We are Mountain troops," Jack said slowly. "Don't you think we should scout for suitable training areas for climbing and skiing?"

"Before the snow melts?" Steve slapped his thigh. "You're a certified genius, Oakland. Let's do it!"

The welcome idea of getting back on skis lifted Jack's spirits enormously, and he was eager to test his right leg's recovery "Let me finish my letter, and then we'll go to battalion headquarters and make the arrangements."

"Great!" Steve stood and ambled in the direction of camp, hands in his pockets and whistling.

Jack unfolded his letter.

Steve and I are asking permission to scout out training areas in the mountains, so hopefully we'll get back on skis soon. Where are you?

June 1, 1945

Part of Beth's Red Cross job was to set up servicemen's clubs to be run by the USO. She wrote to Jack immediately after he said he was heading north, saying she got permission from Tenth Mountain Headquarters to visit Italy's northern border area and look for locations to set up Officer and Enlisted USO clubs.

There's a ski resort in Solda, she wrote. *I'll have time off there. Can you meet up with me?*

The drive was three hours north from Riva del Garda. Jack and Steve took a day-and-a-half to get there, seriously scouting for usable training areas along the way.

Jack spied Beth waiting for him on a restaurant's sundeck overlooking the ski runs, and he thought his heart would burst with joy. When she saw him walking toward her she jumped to her feet with a blazing smile and ran into his arms.

"It's so great to see you," he mumbled into her hair. "God, I've missed you."

"Me too, Jeff," she effused against his shoulder. "I'm so glad you're safe."

"I'm Margaret." The feminine voice startled Jack.

"I'm Steve," his buddy replied. "Nice to meet you."

Jack unwound his arms from their grip on his fiancée. "Hi. I'm Jack."

Margaret's lips quirked. "Well, I certainly hope so."

Beth coughed an embarrassed laugh and wiped her eyes. "Margaret and I are traveling together."

Jack saw Steve's evaluative gaze sweep over Margaret's raven hair and sturdy frame. When her blue eyes turned back to his, Steve smiled happily.

"Looks like it's you and me." He offered his elbow. "Can I buy you lunch?"

*****

Jack and Beth sat at a table alone and ordered a bottle of red Italian wine. He'd thank Steve later for entertaining Margaret, but from what he could see the two were getting along well and her company wasn't anything close to a hardship for his buddy.

"So," Beth said after she took her first sip of wine. "How was it? Really."

Jack felt a rush of emotions choke his throat. He swallowed a gulp of wine to clear his voice.

"I—I can't tell you everything…"

Beth laid her hand over his. "You don't have to. Just what matters."

Jack drew a steadying breath. "Twenty-two guys from F Company are dead. A bunch more were wounded. But there was one incident that really shook me."

Beth squeezed his hand and waited silently while Jack told her about what happened to Larry Kohler.

"I shouldn't have let him come with us," he confessed.

"Don't do that, Jeff." Beth's tone was stern and it forced him to meet her eyes. "It's not your fault. Not one tiny little bit. He knew what the risks were and he faced them willingly."

She was right. He knew it in his head.

Just not in his gut.

"I kept his gun, the one where he carved *sempre avanti* into the stock." Jack took another gulp of wine before he continued. "And I used that Thompson to take revenge on those bastard Krauts."

"Good for you," Beth whispered.

Jack pulled his hand from hers and rubbed his face with calloused palms. "I killed so many Germans, Beth. With grenades, mortars, machine guns… it's a miracle that I wasn't killed."

Beth nodded. "I agree. And I thank God every day for sparing you."

"It's shocking, really. All those refined east-coast college boys turned into vicious warriors." Jack refilled his wine glass. "I don't know how we'll ever go back to who we were."

"You won't." Beth's gaze was reassuring in spite of her words. "You all entered the Mountain Troopers as inexperienced boys. You'll all leave the Tenth Mountain Division as stronger and wiser men."

She was right. Again.

Jack decided to flip the conversation. "How was it for you? Really."

Now Beth took a sip of wine before she spoke. "We only saw the severely wounded when they came through the Red Cross stations on their way to hospitals. But at our locations near the front we could see the bombers and fighters, and we could hear the artillery."

"Did any bombs go off near you?"

"No. But…" Beth looked chagrined. "There was one time when we were passing out doughnuts and coffee when the Germans started firing shells. All the soldiers dove for cover but we just stood there."

Jack found that alarming. "Was anyone hit?"

Beth shook her head. "The shells fell short and the soldiers came back out. One of them commented on how brave we were. Then I said we weren't brave. We just didn't know where to go."

Jack figured they'd laugh about that someday down the road. Way down the road.

Really, really far down the road.

"But I will say this." She pointed a stiff finger at him. "If the tables were turned, no woman worth her salt would *ever* have left a pair of men so exposed to danger while they scurried like cowards!"

Jack had to admit that was probably true.

"Do you know when you'll be released for home?" he asked.

Beth sighed and shook her head. "Right now I don't, but I suppose I'll be here as long as American soldiers are."

"We expect the Tenth to be the last to leave because we were the last to arrive," Jack said. "So maybe we'll ship out about the same time."

"That would be nice." Her brow wrinkled. "Will you be sent to the Pacific?"

"We don't know."

"Maybe the Japs will surrender, too," she said hopefully. "And then we can start planning a wedding."

Chapter
Thirty-Six

When Jack and Steve returned to Riva del Garda the next night after their combination scouting and skiing excursion, they heard that while they were gone the Eighty-Sixth received orders for a new assignment.

"Guarding German prisoners at the abandoned airport at Ghedi," Steve grumbled. The German-built airport was about fifty miles south and west on flat land. "So much for our mountain training plan."

Jack pointed to the map. "But it's closer to the port at Livorno. Looks like the Army's positioning us to leave."

That wasn't the only surprise posted.

Jack's jaw dropped. "I've been selected for promotion to Sergeant First Class?"

Steve slapped Jack's shoulder. "Congrats, Oakland."

Jack skimmed the list to see who else was moving up. "First Sergeant Uriel's been promoted to Battalion Sergeant Major." He glanced at Steve. "That means I'd move into his job as F Company First Sergeant."

"True." Steve turned to face him. "Are you planning to stay in the Army?"

Jack shook his head while he considered his options. "No. Not after the war."

"If you accept the promotion, you'll have to stay in at least two more years." Steve shrugged. "But the extra money would be nice. And your dad would be proud."

"But as it stands now, it looks like F Company might be fighting the Japs soon." Jack made his decision at that moment. "I'm not pressing my luck any farther. I'm going to turn the promotion down."

June 1945

The Second Annual Military Ski Championships was held on Mount Mangart in the Carnic Alps—before the last of the mountain's remaining snow thawed. The race was a memorial for the late Captain Ralph Bromaghin, who initiated the competition just one year ago at Camp Hale.

It seems like so much longer...

This was the first time Jack was on skis since he was hit by the mortar's shrapnel, and he didn't do well. His right leg was still significantly weaker than his left and that threw his balance off. Jack was frustrated and angry when he finished the race, his thigh burning as bad as the day it was hit.

The race was won First Sergeant Walter Prager, a former Dartmouth ski coach. Steve Knowlton placed second, just six seconds behind him.

"I'll have to get back to training as soon as I can," Jack grumbled to Steve after congratulating him. "I just don't have the opportunity here."

"It's been what, eight weeks since you were hit?" Steve made a face. "Cut yourself some slack, Oakland."

After a brief stay at Ghedi, the Eighty-Sixth was moved to Udine in the northeast corner of Italy. Yugoslavia's Marshal Tito was refusing to evacuate the area because he wanted territory back that he lost to Italy in the First World War armistice.

But no peace agreement in Italy included returning any territory to Yugoslavia, so the Eighty-Sixth's presence was both a reminder of that fact, and a strong encouragement for Tito to leave the country.

While Jack was there he got a letter from Beth saying the Red

Cross was pulling major operations back to Rome since the Army's divisions were preparing to return to the United States.

Be sure to let me know as soon as you do when you're heading home, she wrote. *And where you'll be stationed.*

At the end of June, the Eighty-Sixth Regiment boarded rail cars that carried them back to Livorno, where all Army personnel and their gear were definitively accounted for. Jack made sure his *Sempre Avanti* tommy gun was carefully logged and stowed in the armory along with the rest of their Regimental weapons and gear.

July 14, 1945

Uninvited, Lieutenant Hollinghurst joined Jack and Steve's table in a little Italian tavern. "We got orders today. Have you heard?"

Jack straightened and his grip on his beer tightened, assuming they going straight to the Pacific. "No. What have we got?"

"We're sailing on July twenty-sixth on the *SS Westbrook Victory.* After a thirty-day furlough, we report to Camp Carson, Colorado."

"Carson?" Jack was both relieved and surprised. "Why not Hale?"

Hollinghurst waved one unconcerned hand. "I heard Hale's being dismantled. Anyway, after we get there we're going to prep for an invasion of Japan."

Jack raised a brow at Steve. He and Steve had expected as much for weeks now. What did surprise the trio was who pulled a fourth chair up to their little table and dropped onto the seat.

"Bill Klein?" Jack yelped. "You son of a gun! Where'd you come from?"

"Hello, boys." Bill grinned broadly. "Buy me a beer and I'll tell you."

Jack bought a pitcher—it was more efficient. While they drank, Bill told them he'd been working at the Tenth Mountain Division Headquarters since they got to Italy last January.

"I'm an interpreter, of course," he said in a German accent that had become more pronounced, obviously because of his job. "I interrogate Germans and transcribe their documents."

"You headed home, too?" Jack asked.

"Not just yet, but when I do I have big plans for Sugar Bowl. Hollywood celebrities are staying closer to home to ski so…" He let the sentence dangle and took a long draught of the rich, dark beer.

"How's Fred?" Jack risked, steeling himself for bad news.

Bill set his half-empty glass on the table. "He's good. He and Hannes are set to go back to Sugar Bowl and gear up for the coming season."

Jack blew a sigh of relief. "That's great, Bill."

"What about you, Jack? And your brother, Harry?" Bill leaned on the table. "You guys want to come work with us again?"

Jack felt the jagged shard of grief that was nowhere close to softening. "Harry died during the invasion of Iwo Jima, Bill."

Bill straightened. "I didn't know. I'm sorry, Jack."

Steve lifted his beer. "To Harry Franklin."

"To Harry," Hollinghurst and Bill chorused.

Jack took a long pull on his beer to wash the lump from his throat.

"Any other news?" Bill asked, his expression hopeful.

Jack smiled into his beer glass. "Yeah. There is."

"What?"

Jack looked into Bill's eyes. "Betty Harkins and I are getting married as soon as we're finished with all this war stuff."

"No shit! Really?" Bill whooped with glee. "Now that deserves another toast."

When the men lifted their glasses, he said, "God bless Minnie Dole and his determination, Captain Jay and his films, and Staff Sergeant Jack Franklin for winning the best prize of all!"

"Hear, hear!" Jack shouted.

The sooner the better.

August 7, 1945

Steve and Jack stood on the bow of the *Westbrook Victory*, leaned on the railing, and watched the blessed American coastline rise slowly from the sea. Neither one had said anything for several minutes when Steve broke their silence.

"So, Oakland. Want to do some traveling with me when we

reach land?"

Jack turned to his friend, intrigued. "What kind of traveling?"

"Turns out Pete Seibert's in the Army hospital in Martinsburg, West Virginia. Can't be too far from Newport News where we're docking."

Jack sagged with relief to hear that their friend was alive. He had serious doubts if that was even possible when Pete was carried down the mountain torn, bleeding, and unconscious.

"That'd be great! Sure. I'm in."

"And then..." Steve turned around and rested his elbows on the ship's rails behind him. "We could go see Percy Rideout at Fort Devens in Massachusetts."

Jack mentally adjusted his own plans to make room for the change. "I'd love to see how he's doing."

"The best part is that my mom lives in Boston." Steve gave Jack a knowing look. "Come home with me for a few days before you head to California."

"That'd be great, Dropout." Jack pulled a deep breath and flashed a wry smile. "Maybe I can visit Betty's folks and introduce myself while I'm there."

"My thoughts exactly."

Headlines on the newspapers in the ships' terminal said a new and deadly bomb was dropped on Japan yesterday—August sixth. Jack grabbed the paper and read the details out loud to Steve.

"An American B-29 bomber dropped the world's first deployed atomic bomb over the Japanese city of Hiroshima yesterday."

Jack set the paper back in the stand. "I wonder if that'll change our situation."

Fingers crossed.

"I guess we'll find out at some point." Steve pointed to a line of buses. "That bus will take us to the train station."

August 8, 1945

The next day Jack followed Steve into the Army hospital in Martinsburg, West Virginia. When they entered Pete's room, Steve was his usual tactful self.

"What the hell happened to you?"

Pete broke into a broad smile. "If you goons are back, then all the Germans better be dead."

"We did our part," Jack said. "How are you doing?"

"Coming along." He lifted a bandaged arm. "Fragments from the shell almost severed my left arm at the elbow, but the docs got it put back."

"And your leg?" Jack remembered how bad it looked.

"Fragments smashed my kneecap and broke the end off my femur. So they tell me, anyway." He shook his head. "I have no memory of how I got to the hospital in Livorno. I just woke up in a bed with clean sheets. My head was bandaged and I could only see out of one eye."

Steve sat in a chair near the bed. "How long were you in Livorno?"

"Month and a half. I was on penicillin for most of that time."

"And then they sent you here?"

"Got here in June. They specialize in orthopedic medicine."

"I'm just glad you're alive," Jack admitted. "I wasn't sure you'd make it."

"Yeah, well. The hospital voyage nearly killed all of us." Pete reached for a glass of water and Jack handed it to him.

After taking a drink, he handed the glass back to Jack. "We were seasick, with no way to bathe, no way to get out of bunks, no way to get to the outside decks. Stank like a son of a bitch down there."

Jack felt bile creep up the back of his throat at the thought. "That's over with now."

Steve smiled. "And you're alive and recuperating."

Jack quickly changed the subject. "We ran into Bill Klein before we left. He's going back to run Sugar Bowl. When you're better, you should come west and ski with me."

"He's not going to Japan, then." Pete's brows pulled together. "Are you?"

"That's what they tell us," Steve said. "But we have a thirty-day furlough to enjoy before we head for Camp Carson."

Pete was obviously as surprised as Jack and Steve were when they heard the news. "Carson? Why not Hale?"

"Seems they're tearing it apart."

Pete fell silent for a moment. "I guess nothing lasts forever."

"Just friendship."

Pete looked at Jack. "Yes. Comrades in arms. Members of the very first American Mountain Division."

Jack grabbed Pete's right hand and shook it. "No one can ever take that away from us."

August 10, 1945

Just before Jack and Steve boarded the first in a series of trains that would take them from Martinsburg, West Virginia to Fort Devens in Massachusetts, a news announcement replaced the usual litany of arriving and departing trains.

"The United States Army Air Corps has just released information that earlier today a second atomic bomb was dropped on Nagasaki, Japan, completely destroying the city."

Jack felt a terrible mix of horror for the hundreds of thousands killed, and the relief that such drastic action was sure to bring Japan to her knees long before the Tenth Mountain Division could invade.

Steve must have read his mind. "Maybe we won't have to go."

Jack snorted. "As my mother often said: your mouth to God's ears, my friend."

Today they were visiting Percy Rideout, their former captain. The gruesome image of Rideout getting shot through the face was probably going to stick with Jack for the rest of his life.

"Felt like Babe Ruth hit me in the mouth with a baseball bat," Percy managed to mumble clearly enough for Jack and Steve to understand. "They operated on me four times. Put skin grafts over the holes."

Once again Jack—who never thought of himself as queasy when he wasn't on a ship—found himself on the verge of getting sick.

And once again, he changed the subject. "You coming back to us?"

Percy nodded. "S'posed to after dentist fixes everything. Lost some teeth."

"We'll look for you at Camp Carson," Jack promised. "I hope we can serve under you again, sir."

Jack thought the captain would have smiled if he could. "I'd be honored to have you in my company. Both of you."

*****

The bus from Fort Devens to Boston only took an hour, so that same afternoon Jack followed Steve into his mom's modest two-story house on the northern outskirts of Boston proper. After greeting her son the way every soldier's mother did, with an avalanche of hugs and tears, Mom Knowlton turned her attention to Jack.

"Welcome, Jack. And thank you for watching out for Steve." When Steve opened his mouth to object, she silenced him with a look. "I know my son well, Jack. He tends toward mischief."

Jack had no idea whether Steve's mom knew about the Brown Palace rappelling incident, but guessed it would not come as a surprise to her if she did.

"Thank you, Mrs. Knowlton." Jack smiled. "But I have to say Steve watched out for me in return."

"Good to hear it. Now go on and get settled in." She shooed them toward the stairs. "Dinner's at six."

Jack called his parents that night—reversing the charges, of course—and told them he was back on American soil and would be heading their way in a few days.

"Why are you in Boston?" Pops asked.

"Steve Knowlton and I wanted to visit a couple guys from our company that were pretty badly wounded. Pete's in West Virginia, not too far from where we docked, and Percy is an hour from Boston, so Steve invited me to stay with him and his mom for a couple days."

"A couple more days?" His mom's voice cracked. "Can't you leave sooner than that?"

"I can't leave until I introduce myself to Mr. and Mrs. Harkins—Betty's parents. They live just outside of Boston."

"Do they know you're, um, engaged?" Obviously Pops still had a problem with Jack's choice of a bride.

Jack wasn't certain the Harkinses did, so he answered with, "I'm going to ask her father for his blessing."

"What if he says no?"

"Pops, I am going to marry Elizabeth-Anne Harkins as soon as I possibly can, and no one is going to stop me." Jack drew a resolute breath. "No one."

Chapter Thirty-Seven

August 11, 1945

Jack dismissed the taxi and stood in the growing darkness outside the grand, gated, two-story, and beautifully landscaped house that Beth grew up in. He straightened his cleaned-and-pressed uniform and pushed the intercom's buzzer next to the gate. He was confident he was doing the right thing, and he really hoped Beth had told her parents that they were engaged.

"May I help you?" a tinny and disembodied female voice asked.

"Staff Sergeant John Edward Franklin to see Mister Laurence Harkins."

"Do you have an appointment?"

Jack hesitated. The idea that he might need an appointment hadn't even occurred to him.

"No, I'm afraid I don't. I just returned from Italy and am only in Boston for a couple days. I was hoping to catch him in…"

"One moment."

Jack rocked on his heels, hands clasped behind him, while the minutes dragged by. He was about to give up and leave when the heavy gate unlocked with a loud click.

He pushed the tall and wide wrought-iron gate open, swinging it wide and then pushing it shut again. He turned to face the house.

Across the perfect lawn and at the apex of the curved drive he watched the front door open slowly. A woman appeared in the opening, lit from behind by a glittering crystal chandelier.

Jack strode up the driveway and stopped at the foot of the steps leading to the wide columned porch. "Mrs. Harkins?"

"Yes." She wasn't smiling. "Please come in, Sergeant."

She turned around and walked into the house.

Jack hurried up the steps.

Mr. Harkins sat in a large leather chair in a room that smelled pleasantly of tobacco. When Jack followed Mrs. Harkins into the room through the pair of carved oak doors, Mr. Harkins set aside his newspaper, rose to his feet, and removed a pair of reading glasses. He wasn't smiling either.

Jack charged right into it. He'd faced far more formidable foes recently, and this man wasn't even aiming a rifle at him.

"Hello, sir." He offered his hand. "I'm Staff Sergeant John Edward Franklin the Second. Most people call me Jack."

"I know who you are." Laurence Harkins shook Jack's hand briefly. "This is a surprise, soldier."

"Yes, sir. And I apologize about barging in without an *appointment*." Jack hesitated briefly hoping the word would startle the man. "But I didn't know I would be visiting Boston until I docked in Newport News four days ago. I was in Italy, you see, and your daughter was assigned to my division."

"You were with Betty?" Victoria Harkins' eyes widened. "How is she? Is she safe?"

Jack turned to face her and smiled reassuringly. "Yes. She was perfectly fine when I left, and all fighting stopped three months ago so she's safe."

He shifted his attention to Laurence. "May I sit?"

The subtle suggestion that he was being rude apparently did startle Laurence.

"Of course. Forgive me," he blustered. "Victoria, dear, why don't you ask Helen to bring coffee."

As Victoria walked to the door she admonished Jack, "Not one word about Betty until I get back!"

Jack crossed his heart. "I promise."

He made a quick assessment of which chair Victoria probably preferred and sat on the small couch facing both that one and Laurence's seat.

Laurence sank back onto his leather throne. "So you saw action?"

"Yes, sir. I'm in the Tenth Mountain Division, which was formed at Camp Hale."

"Ah, yes. You're a skier. I remember Betty mentioning that."

"That's right. I was an instructor in both skiing and mountain climbing." Jack cleared his throat. "Anyway, when we were deployed to Italy our job was to push the Germans out of the country through the Alps."

"I see." Laurence stroked his chin. His gaze was evaluative. Clearly he was sizing Jack up. "And did you?"

"Pardon my language, sir, but we sure as hell did." Jack grinned and kept talking so Laurence couldn't chastise him. "I know that a lot of what happened there hasn't been in the papers, but we started that push with eight hundred men climbing to the top of a two-thousand-foot ridge. In the dark. In silence."

Jack chuckled at Laurence's astonished expression. "The Krauts were pretty surprised at dawn the next morning to see the American Army'd snuck up behind them."

Victoria hurried back into the room. "What are you talking about?"

"War stuff," Laurence said shortly.

Victoria settled in the chair that Jack thought she would and leaned forward. "Tell us about Betty."

*****

For the next half hour over coffee and cookies Jack answered every question he could about Beth, the Red Cross, the fighting, the weather, the terrain, the enemy, and his two Purple Hearts. He was careful not to be too graphic while still impressing on the Harkins' the severity of war.

He thought he was winning them over but he didn't want to overstay his welcome. Jack set his empty cup down. "I should be going. But there is one thing I want to ask you first."

Laurence peered at him. "And that is?"

"I would like your—" He stopped himself from saying permission and instead said, "Your blessing. Betty and I are planning to marry."

It was obvious Laurence wasn't surprised. "She mentioned that in a letter."

"I love your daughter, sir. With my whole heart. And she loves me." Jack shifted his gaze to Victoria. "You raised a strong, intelligent woman who knows her own mind. I commend you for that. And I can't wait to make her my wife."

Laurence snorted. "What if we don't give our blessing?"

Jack expected this might happen. "I'm twenty-five and Betty is twenty-seven. We *will* get married, but it's important to both of us that you agree. Makes it easier for everyone."

"What do your parents think?"

Jack couldn't reveal Pops' initial reaction. "They haven't met Betty yet, but they love what I've told them. And of course my mom's biggest concern is whether she'll make me happy. Which she does."

"How will you support her?" Laurence pressed.

Jack answered truthfully. "I'm not sure yet. I have job offers in the ski industry out west—"

Victoria gasped softly and covered her mouth.

"But I'm probably going to take advantage of the GI Bill and try college." He shrugged. "I'm a hard worker, sir. You can trust me to take care of your daughter. Though…"

Jack waved an appreciative hand at his surroundings. "It might take me a few years to reach this level," he joked.

"When do you plan to get married?" Victoria asked.

"As soon as we're free from our commitments, me to the Army and Betty to the Red Cross."

"When will that be?" she prodded.

Jack didn't have a definitive answer. "I'll be in the Army until the war with Japan ends. But I turned down a promotion that would have kept me in longer."

Laurence leaned forward. "You did? Why?"

"When my furlough is over, I report to Camp Carson in Colorado to prepare to invade Japan." Jack ran his hand over his short-cropped hair. "To be honest, I've made it this far and I really hope the Japs surrender before I have to go over there. A man can't stay lucky forever."

Laurence leaned back again. "That's a very good answer."

Jack smiled a little. "Thank you."

"What about Betty?" Victoria's tone was plaintive. "When do you think she'll be free?"

Jack shrugged. "She could answer that better than me. But I do know the Red Cross is pulling back. That said, the ships are allocated to bring soldiers home first and auxiliary personnel after that."

"Where will you get married?"

Jack was on safe ground with this question. "I believe that is customarily up to the bride and her family. Whatever Betty and you two decide on is fine with me."

August 17, 1945

On August thirteenth, having secured a less-than-enthusiastic but definite blessing from Mr. and Mrs. Harkins, Jack got on the train which carried him west to Chicago, Denver, Salt Lake, and finally to Oakland. He'd secured a sleeping bunk for the four-day journey, deciding that the money was well worth the ability to lie down at night.

And on August fourteenth he bought a special edition newspaper at Union Station in Chicago whose headline shouted in capital letters WAR OVER! JAPAN SURRENDERS!

He nearly dropped to his knees with relief. He wasn't going to have to invade Japan. His war was over. And Beth should be heading home soon.

Pops picked Jack up at the train station at dusk. He stuck out his hand to shake Jack's and then pulled him close and wrapped his free arm around Jack's shoulders. "I'm so glad your luck held, son. I really am."

Jack was pretty sure they were both thinking about Harry and his eyes filled with tears. "Me too, Pops. It was close. Too close."

When mom saw Jack in his uniform she started crying.

She hugged him, hard. "I prayed for you every day."

"I know you did, Mom. And it worked."

"Come on," she said when she released him. "Are you hungry?"

As was usual, Jack and Pops followed her to the kitchen. Jack sat at the familiar kitchen table while his dad got two cold bottles of beer from the fridge. He set them on the table along with the bottle opener. Neither one of them mentioned the fourth chair, the one which Harry sat on the last time the brothers were here, and would now remain empty.

"So." Pops opened his beer after Jack. "What's next?"

Jack gave the same answer. He'd be in the Army until the war ended, but no longer than that.

"Then what?"

Jack sipped the beer before he answered. "Then I'll marry Betty."

"How do you plan to support her?"

Once again, Jack talked about skiing and college.

His father was not impressed. "How will you support a wife and go to school at the same time? And what would you even study? You could be working with me tomorrow."

Jack's temper flared. Clearly his father had forgotten that his son had been at war and war changes a man.

Pops should know better

"But I don't *want* to work with you. I want to do something that I like. With people I like."

Pops wagged his head. "You're still dreaming. I thought you'd have grown up by now."

"I *have* grown up. I've been to war, too, Pops. Just like you."

Pops made a face and took a gulp of beer.

"And now that the Japs have surrendered, I don't have to invade Japan."

His mom spun away from the sandwiches she was making, her expression stricken. "Is that where you were going?"

Jack softened his tone. "Yes. It was. But I can start planning a future instead. One that I want. With Betty."

Mom relaxed a little. "I can't wait to meet her."

"You're going to love her."

"You getting married in Boston?" Pops asked and took another swig from his beer.

"I told her parents that's usually up to the bride and her family." Jack lifted one shoulder. "But my guess would be yes."

*****

During his time at home in Oakland, Jack wrote to Beth every single day. Soon he started getting her replies every day as well, and some days even more than one.

I'm so tired of this life here in Italy now that the war is over. The soldiers get drunk every night at the USO clubs and Army discipline is slipping. I felt safer when the bombs were dropping.

Jack ached to be able to do something to ease her situation, but he was powerless. All he could write to her was:

Now that the war is over I should be discharged soon. Hopefully you will be, too. Now that I have your father's blessing there won't be anything else standing in the way of our marriage.

September 12, 1945

Once again Jack was taking the long train ride from Oakland to an Army camp in Colorado, but now with an entirely different sort of excitement.

Having fulfilled his dream—and his nightmare, as it turned out—of fighting the war as a Mountain Trooper, he looked forward to returning to civilian life and finding his place in the world.

He'd gotten a brief letter from Steve yesterday that said only six thousand men were left in the Tenth Mountain Division, and that the Army was processing them out as fast as they could.

"I could be home in a month," Jack told his parents when they *both* dropped him at the train station this time. "Before Thanksgiving for sure."

When he reached Camp Carson, Jack settled into F Company's barracks, glad to see his comrades again. All of them agreed that it was odd to be back in their parents' homes on furlough, now that they'd traveled across the world and fought a bloody war.

"Did you get the 'what now' questions?" Jack asked.

"Oh boy, did I," nearly every man replied.

And they seemed just as angry about that as Jack was.

Rather than ask about what they'd achieved in their three years of training and their four fraught months of freezing, high-altitude battles against vicious Germans—battles that no American soldier had ever fought before, *thank you very much*—they were met with questions about a future that none of them had any time to think about yet.

"I just want everyone to acknowledge what we accomplished!" Jack complained loudly. "We—the Tenth Mountain Division—did something absolutely *amazing* and that needs to be *talked* about. Not pushed aside like it never happened."

Chapter Thirty-Eight

October 15, 1945

Jack's days at Camp Carson started with formation in the morning for roll call and continued with short classes about the educational and medical benefits which the men would receive once they were discharged. As the numbers at Camp Carson dwindled and Jack's time to leave approached, he decided to try and find Kohler's machine gun and remove the carved stock to keep.

That was the only Army souvenir he cared about.

Jack went to the regimental armory where the Tenth Mountain Division's weapons were stored. When he got there, the armory was staffed by one lonely corporal.

"I need to check the guns from my platoon to make sure they're properly accounted for," he told the corporal. "There's some confusion with a guy that's mustering out."

"Sure, Sergeant. Sign in here." He handed Jack a clipboard. "Would you do me a favor?"

Jack looked up from the sign-in sheet. "What do you need?"

"I have to deliver some paperwork to E Company's office. Could you stay here until I get back?"

Jack nodded. "Not a problem. I'm not sure I'll even be finished that fast."

"Thanks." The corporal grabbed a stack of forms and hurried out the door.

Jack walked quickly down the rows of logged and labeled weaponry searching for Eighty-Sixth Regiment, Second Battalion, F Company. When he located the spot, he opened the wooden crates until he found Kohler's Thompson machine gun with *Sempre Avanti* carved into the stock.

"There you are," he whispered, feeling like he'd found a long-lost friend.

Jack knew he couldn't take the gun, but he could remove the wooden stock and take that. The stock could be replaced, but the memories of his life with that weapon and what it meant to him never could.

Jack trotted over to the weapons repair bench and grabbed a screwdriver. He went back to the crate, lifted the gun out, and set about removing the stock from the metal gun. When he got it off, he tucked it down the back of his pants and covered the part that stuck up with his shirt.

Then he replaced the top of the crate and shoved it back in place on the shelf. Next he ran over to the workbench and dropped the screwdriver back in its slot.

He was walking toward the front of the armory when the corporal walked in the door.

"Any luck?" he asked Jack.

"Yep. Turns out the guy's weapon *is* back there. Somebody left part of the serial number off his forms." Jack turned so he kept his front toward the corporal and his back out of sight. "No one else came by while I was here, by the way."

"Yeah, it gets quieter every day." He handed Jack the clipboard. "Don't forget to sign out. And thanks again."

*****

Jack walked back to his platoon's barracks in the cool autumn breeze feeling the chilled wooden stock grow warm with his body heat. When he went inside, he waited until Steve was the only man around before he risked removing the souvenir.

"I can't believe you found it," Steve said reverently. "Hide it well."

Jack removed everything from his duffle, wrapped the stock in a t-shirt, and put it back in the bottom before packing everything else on top of it. "That should do it."

A soldier appeared at the barracks door. "Sergeant Franklin, you have a visitor in F Company's office."

Jack looked at Steve. "Wonder who that could be?"

"Maybe Percy Rideout finally made it back," Steve suggested. "But we don't know because he's been reassigned to another company."

Jack walked to the door. "Maybe it's Bill Klein coming to repeat his offer of a job."

"Would you take it?"

That was the question of the season. "Maybe. I guess it depends on when Betty gets back and when we can get married."

Steve stepped up to F Company's door and looked through the windowed top half. He grinned back at Jack as he pulled the door open. "One of your questions is answered."

"Which one—Beth!" Jack stopped like he'd hit a wall.

Beth's smile lit up the office on this gray Colorado day like a dozen suns. "Hi, soldier."

Jack rushed forward. "When did you get back?"

"I docked in Newport News two days ago. The next day I bought a plane ticket to Denver. And here I am." She reached for his hands. "I didn't go to Boston. Jeff. I came to see you first."

That was great but, "Why didn't you tell me you were on the way?"

"I didn't have time. We got word that there was room on a transport ship for four of us, but we had to board within the hour." Beth giggled. "I just threw what I could in my duffle and ran to the dock."

Steve leaned close. "Would you kiss her already? I have other things to do than wait here."

Jack obliged. With gusto.

*****

Procuring a two-day pass was easy since there wasn't anything for the few thousand remaining Tenth soldiers to do at Camp Carson but wait their turn to leave. Jack and Beth spent those two days—and nights—together. Jack was still a gentleman and didn't overstep any intimate boundaries, but being together made him eager to tie the knot.

"Let's get married in six weeks—the first Saturday in December," he suggested.

"That soon?" Beth pressed her lips together for a moment before she nodded. "Yes, let's do that. The only reason to wait is make bigger plans, and I want a simple ceremony."

Jack was glad to hear that. Less for Pops to complain about afterwards. "Where do you want to get married?"

"My home church in Boston. For my parents' sake." She tilted her head. "Will your parents come?"

Jack smiled. "In a heartbeat."

"Where will we live?"

Jack thought long and hard about this, and came to a decision he hoped Beth would understand and see the wisdom of.

"I think we should go to California," he said slowly. "The GI Bill will pay for college and I could work part time with Pops."

Beth grew quiet. "I know my parents want me in Boston, but the truth is I'm afraid that if I'm so close to home they'll interfere in our lives."

Jack didn't expect her to agree, but curiosity pushed him to ask, "Interfere how?"

"They'll want me to move into their social circles, and they'll probably try to 'fix' you and push you into them as well." Beth shook her head. "No, I started this whole journey to get away from that. So California it is."

Jack pulled her close and kissed her well. When he pulled away, he leaned his forehead against hers.

"My mom's gonna love you," he murmured.

"And your dad?" she whispered.

"You'll win him over."

Beth leaned back and looked into his eyes. "I love you John Edward Franklin the Second."

"And I love you Elizabeth-Anne Jane Harkins. For the rest of my life."

December 8, 1945

The final ceremonies for the Tenth Mountain Division were held on October twenty-seventh at Camp Carson, Colorado, and the division was officially inactivated on November thirtieth—almost exactly four years after the first mountain battalion was created at Fort Lewis Washington. Jack's discharge date was logged as November thirtieth, even though all the remaining soldiers actually departed from Camp Carson by the fifteenth.

Jack was glad for the extra time, since his East Coast wedding preparations were in full swing. He and his parents booked a sleeping car and spent six days traveling by train from Oakland to Boston.

After a three-night honeymoon at the Waldorf Astoria in New York City—courtesy of Beth's folks—Jack and Beth would fly back to San Francisco.

Jack laughingly referred to the plans as his first and last big splurge. Thanks to the GI Bill he was enrolled in the School of Business Administration at the University of California at Berkeley.

"Starting in January, you'll be the wife of a part-time laborer and college student," he reminded Beth last night.

She kissed his cheek and snuggled under his arm. "I can't wait."

Jack waited at the front the little First Lutheran Church in Malden, Massachusetts while wedding guests assembled inside. He was pleased to see several of his buddies from the Tenth sitting in the pews. Even Pete Seibert made it.

Steve Knowlton, his Best Man, leaned over and spoke in his ear. "You ready, Oakland?"

"Ready and eager, Dropout. Let's get this show on the road," Jack replied.

As if she heard him, the organist began to play the processional, *Ode to Joy*. The doors to the narthex opened and Beth's Maid of Honor and best friend—the one who helped her and Jack in the early part of their relationship—walked down the aisle. She took her place opposite Steve and turned around to face the back.

When the first chords of Mendelssohn's *Wedding March* echoed through the sanctuary, Beth stepped into view holding her father's arm. Jack thought his heart was going to burst.

She was stunning in the white silk-and-lace gown that floated over her body highlighting her athletic curves. The hem flowed backward in a train that was nearly as long as Beth was tall. She wore a little hat like a turban, and white netting covered her face.

Most of the ceremony was a blur to Jack, who focused mainly on not messing anything up. The last thing he wanted to do was look like a West Coast bumpkin to the Harkinses and their society friends.

But when the pastor said that the bride brought her own vows to the altar, Jack looked at her in confusion.

"Was I supposed to write vows, too?" he asked, terrified that he'd screwed up their wedding after all.

Beth smiled up at him, her eyes glittering through the netting with unshed tears. "You already did."

Then her Maid of Honor pulled Beth's journal from behind the enormous bouquet she held on Beth's behalf, and handed it to her. The same beautifully tooled red one that Jack bought her after their big fight in Lucca.

Worlds away from this little church.

Jack's heart pounded so hard he was afraid the entire congregation could hear it.

Beth opened the cover and slowly read back the words he'd written on the first page before he gifted her with her the blank book.

"I promise to love only you for the rest of my life. I promise to trust you always and without question, no matter the situation. I promise to uphold your character and defend you against any attack."

Beth's voice cracked and her friend handed her a little linen handkerchief. She dabbed her eyes and sniffed. After a moment she continued.

"I promise to protect you against anyone who tries to hurt you. I promise to become the *woman* you deserve, and will spend the rest of my life working toward that goal. And I promise that nothing on this earth will stop me from keeping my word."

Beth lowered the journal and looked up into his eyes. "I promise this with all my love, Jeff. Now and forever, I'll always be your Beth."

.

*****

San Antonio, Texas
March 2017

Jack looked up at his great-grandson. He'd spent four days telling seventeen-year-old Taylor his story while Taylor's dad handled the video camera. He was tired.

"You know the rest. Pete was born in nineteen-forty-eight, and Linda here in nineteen-fifty-two."

"Did you graduate, Papa Jack?" Taylor prompted.

Jack nodded. "School of Business. With honors. Nineteen-forty-nine."

"Did you ski?"

"Sugar Bowl on winter weekends. Bill Klein was teaching there for years."

Taylor closed his notebook. "How long were you and Mama Beth married?"

Jack felt the stab of sorrow that even now, a decade after his beloved wife slipped from this life, hadn't eased noticeably. "Almost sixty-two years."

Taylor looked surprised. "I didn't realize it was that long."

"You were seven when she passed. What did you know?" Jack reached for his bottle of water and took a sip. "We're done here."

"Can I ask you one last question? Please?"

Jack looked a Taylor. "One."

Taylor slid off his off-camera stool and squatted next to Jack. "What advice would you give me, Papa Jack? One thing."

Jack's mind flooded with so many memories that he almost forgot where he was. Yet in the myriad of images and actions, one thing did stand out.

He reached for Taylor's hand and squeezed it.

"Love the right woman, boy. Everything else is just gravy on top."

ARMY ORGANIZATION:

10th Mountain Division
    85th Regiment
        1st - 2nd - 3rd Battalions (as below)
    86th Regiment
        1st - 2nd - 3rd Battalions (as Below)
    87th Regiment
        1st Battalion
            A Company
            B Company
            C Company
            D Company

        2nd Battalion
            E Company
            F Company
            G Company
            H Company

        3rd Battalion
            I Company
            K Company
            L Company
            M Company
                3 Infantry Platoons of 40 Soldiers, and
                1 Weapons Platoon of 73 Soldiers
                    per Company

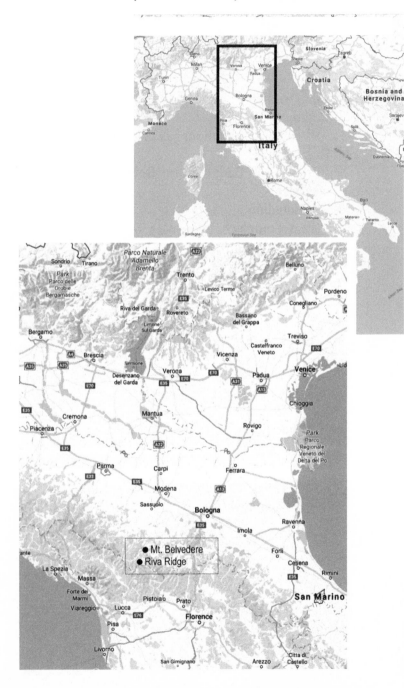

Camp Hale Colorado 1942-1945

Army jeep facing Riva Ridge - 1945

Epilogue:

The US Army's Tenth Mountain Division was deactivated on November 30, 1945. Camp Hale was subsequently dismantled.

Nearly forty years later on February 13, 1985 the Tenth Mountain Division (Light Infantry) was reactivated at Fort Drum in upstate New York.

In accordance with the "Reorganization Objective Army Divisions" plan, the Tenth no longer consisted of three regiments. Two brigades were activated in the Division instead.

The Camp Hale Series:

Sempre Avanti:
ALWAYS FORWARD
The 10th Mountain Division
in World War II

Ice and Granite:
The Snow Soldiers of Riva Ridge

Viking Spy:
The 99th Battalion and the OSS

Ice and Granite

Chapter One

"Geez, it's freezing!"

Lucas Hansen tugged his Army-issued wool coat tighter around his neck as he stepped out of the overheated train along with hundreds of other new recruits. Hit by a glacial Arctic blast on the crowded wooden platform at tiny Pando Station, high in the Rocky Mountains, he wondered if he'd made a terrible mistake.

But whatever he was, he wasn't a quitter.

And it's time to get back in the game.

Lucas hefted his tightly packed duffel bag onto his shoulder and trudged after the line of men who got off the train before him. Their heavy-soled Army boots thudded loud and hollow against the platform's boards in the otherwise quiet morning. He assumed someone in front of the line knew where they were supposed to go.

When the group came to a halt, he pulled a deep, frigid lungful of the thin mountain air and lifted his eyes to the surrounding snow-covered peaks, pink-topped in the sunrise.

For a guy who grew up his whole life in the flatlands of rural Kansas, the Rocky Mountains of Colorado were astonishing. It took all night for their train from Denver to climb the Tennessee Pass and ease down the other side into the high valley where Camp Hale was situated.

Now here he stood, utterly amazed by all that he saw.

"Over here, privates!" A sergeant in a line of sergeants waved a clipboard. "Check in with one of us."

Lucas stepped forward.

A red-cheeked sergeant squinted up at him and blew a frosty breath. "Name?"

"Lucas Thor Hansen."

The man awkwardly flipped a couple pages with glove-clad hands before he spoke. "Eighty-Seventh Regiment, Second Battalion, E Company." He tipped his head to the right. "That way. Your platoon sergeant is holding a sign."

Lucas nodded.

87th, 2nd, E.

Should be easy enough to remember.

He joined a small group of men, counting them out of habit. Eleven plus himself.

An extra man on the field.

Lucas grimaced. Six years after walking off the football field at the end of his final state championship game he still felt the sting of the touchdown called back for having an extra player on the field. At least they won the title, thanks to a two-point safety in the fourth quarter.

"Welcome, privates. I'm Sergeant John Simpson, your platoon sergeant." A muscular man with brown eyes and thick black hair grinned at them without joy. "Welcome to Camp Hell."

Lucas glanced at the men standing with him trying to discern if the sergeant was making a joke. They looked as confused as he was.

"We are standing at nine-thousand and four-hundred feet of elevation. The air here is thin. Altitude sickness is real," Sergeant Simpson continued. He gave each one of them a stern look. "Your first goal is to become accustomed to the conditions here at camp, because they only get worse from here on out. Got it?"

The men nodded.

"The correct response is *yes, sir!* Got it?"

"Yes, sir!" Lucas barked.

Simpson shot him an evaluative glance. "Good. Follow me."

The sergeant led his silent platoon of strangers through the huge, flat-bottomed valley filled with hundreds of two-story, whitewashed wooden barracks hunkered in straight rows along paved and plowed roads.

The air above the camp was hazy and stunk from the coal smoke belching from both the train and the smoke stacks on the camp's perimeter. Everything they walked past was covered with soot, even the snow.

Maybe hell was an accurate description after all.

Sergeant Simpson led them to one of the barracks and opened the wide front door. "Welcome home, boys."

Lucas climbed the steps and entered the heated building. His chilled cheeks stung from the sudden change in temperature.

"Take any bunk you want that's empty," Sergeant Simpson instructed. "Breakfast's at eight in the mess hall. Don't be late."

Lucas hurried forward to grab a bottom bunk.

"Mind if I take the top?"

Lucas turned to face a lanky private with shockingly red hair. "No. Go ahead."

"Thanks." The private threw his duffel on the top bunk and then extended his right hand. "David Fraser."

Lucas shook his hand. "Lucas Hansen. Pleased to meet you."

"Hansen? That's Norwegian, right?"

Lucas grinned. "Yeah."

Fraser smirked. "Explains the blond hair and blue eyes. You speak Norwegian?"

"Nah." Lucas waved a dismissive hand. "My father's ancestor settled in Boston not long before the Revolutionary War, so it's been a few generations. Why?"

Fraser stuffed his cold-reddened hands into his pockets. "I heard a group of guys who speak the language are training here at Hale. The Ninety-ninth. They call themselves the Viking Battalion."

"Yeah, I heard about them. That's what got me thinking about joining up in the first place." Lucas shrugged. "But like I said, I don't qualify."

Fraser looked confused. "So what drew you here?"

Lucas pulled a breath while he thought about how to put his feelings into words. "I wanted to be part of something... special. Not just another regular soldier, you know?"

"So you're a skier, then."

Lucas chuckled and wagged his head. "No. I'm from Kansas, near the Nebraska border. Never been on skis a day in my life. You?"

"Yeah. The Smoky Mountains in North Carolina." Fraser frowned a little. "How'd you get into the Ski Troops?"

Lucas shrugged. "I went to the recruiting station and signed up. Why?"

"Because..." Fraser glanced around the room of recruits settling in. "The guy who started this whole program, Minnie Dole, insisted on personally vetting every man who was assigned here."

That was news to Lucas. "Really?"

"Yep. He asked for three letters of recommendation and an application from everyone wanting to join the Ski Troops."

Lucas sank slowly onto the bottom bunk. "The recruiters didn't mention anything like that. They just assigned me here when I asked for it."

Several of the other men gathered around Lucas and David Fraser, obviously drawn by their conversation.

"I don't ski, either," one of them said. "And nobody at the recruitment office said anything to me about it being required."

"Same here." The stocky brunette who spoke looked around the group. "But the office in San Diego was really crowded and they were trying to process guys through as quick as they could."

Lucas returned his attention to Fraser. "I guess we all had the same idea. Once the Japs bombed Pearl Harbor we knew it was just a matter of time until we joined up. And when the Ski Troops came around it sounded like a great opportunity."

Fraser looked resigned. "I guess they'll have to teach you all, now that you're here."

"Guess so." Lucas grinned again. "But I'm sure I'll catch on. I'm really good at physical things."

Fraser, who was a couple inches shorter than Lucas, swept him with an evaluative gaze. "I believe you."

Lucas looked at his watch and stood. "It's almost eight. Let's go find the mess hall."

The men left the heated barracks and once again faced icy winds and soot-filled air as they headed across camp toward the mess hall. Conversations floated back to Lucas on the thin breeze as the soldiers began the process of getting to know their new brothers in arms.

In spite of the obvious challenges ahead, Lucas felt a surge of belonging that had been missing from his life for the last six years. This was where he should be, where he would thrive.

This is my team now.

Thank you for reading this book! I hope you enjoyed the characters and their stories.

Please consider leaving a review on Amazon.

And follow me on Amazon for an email notice about the next Hansen story release:

1. Go to any of my book pages on Amazon and click on "Kris Tualla" by the title. This will take you to my Author Page.

2. One there, click **+Follow** under my photo. It's that easy!

Thank you for your support!

Kris Tualla is a dynamic, award-winning, and internationally published author of historical romance and suspense. She started in 2006 with nothing but a nugget of a character in mind, and has created a dynasty with The Hansen Series.

In 2019, Kris was inducted into the **Colorado Authors Hall of Fame** for her *Camp Hale Series* of World War II novels. Two of those novels, *Sempre Avanti: Always Forward* and *Ice and Granite* have been optioned for a screen project.

This book is Kris Tualla's twenty-fourth novel. To find out about her family-saga trilogies spanning two continents and nine centuries, go to:

www.KrisTualla.com

Or search for "Kris Tualla" on Amazon Books. All of her novels are available both in print and on Kindle.

*****

Colorado resident Colonel Thomas Duhs, USMC Retired, brought his passion for the largely unknown story of the founding of the Army's Tenth Mountain Division and their triumphant battles in Italy to this project—along with three-hundred pages of research and information.

During his decorated career, Tom served as a Mountain Warfare instructor in California and Alaska, and he deployed to Norway in the winter for a total of five NATO exercises. His actual on-the-ground experience gave him the in-depth knowledge of the training the Tenth soldiers experienced at Camp Hale, Camp Swift, and the Apennine Mountains of Italy.

While Jack and Betty are composites of real people, most of the other characters that Jack interacts with at Sugar Bowl, Camp Hale, and in Italy are real people.

Aston Hollinghurst, however, is completely fictional.

Made in the USA
Las Vegas, NV
30 September 2021

31404688R00215